MATERNITY LEAVE

Trish Felice Cohen

Bella
BOOKS
2013

Bella Books, Inc.
P.O. Box 10543
Tallahassee, FL 32302

Printed in the United States of America on acid-free paper
First published 2013

Editor: Katherine V. Forrest
Cover Designer: Linda Callaghan

ISBN 13: 978-1-59493-340-0

Acknowledgment

First I'd like to give a special thanks to Peter Zheutlin, your substantive suggestions and editing were invaluable. Thank you also to Ellis Weiner, the Simon Cowell of literary critics. I'd also like to thank Karin Kallmaker of Bella Books for believing in me, and Katherine V. Forrest for fixing what Peter and I missed.

Thank you also to Baron Karl von Drais, the inventor of the bicycle (per Wikipedia), and everyone who has improved it since 1817.

To all the professional racers out there. Sorry about the inaccuracies. I am aware of the vast divide between local, state, national and world caliber athletes even if it does not seem so from this story. It is purely a work of fiction and if it makes you feel any better, *Law & Order* is very frustrating to me.

To Scotty—you're the best friend two girls could ever ask for.

To my parents and TJ—I love you and thank you for always supporting me.

To Suzy—You make me so happy and I love you.

Dedication

To my would-be bride. I love you Suzy.

About the Author

Trish Cohen and her partner Suzanne live in Florida, where they enjoy biking and boating with their two dogs. They're both in the process of making babies.

CHAPTER ONE

I am a lawyer, an occupation I fell into by default. Like every other smart-ass child who does well in school but sucks at math and science, I enrolled in law school upon the realization that my dual degree in history and political science qualified me to live in my parents' basement and wait tables.

While law school was interesting, lawyering removed my will to live. I first realized my error in career choice during the summer after my second year in law school when I was employed as an intern at a large law firm. I sent an email to all of the associates in the firm, advising them that I was available to assist them as needed. Though I did not specify, my intent was to assist with legal matters, such as drafting motions or researching legal issues. The only response I received was from a third-year associate. His email reply stated, "Please sneak up behind me with a gun and blow my brains out." I have become that third-year associate and I fully understand the desire to die rather than endure twenty-seven additional years of sitting at a desk for ten hours every day.

Part of the problem is that my chosen practice area, subrogation law, is unsatisfying and lends itself to extreme boredom. I stay where I am because the more interesting areas of law, as portrayed on *Law & Order*, come at a price. Namely, associating with criminals and participating in intensive trial preparation. While a *My Cousin Vinny*-like trial may be fun, it would not compensate for the previous five weeks of living in the office with an alleged murderer while subsisting on Cheetos and coffee.

My passion in life is racing bicycles, an activity not as well suited to paying a mortgage as suing the crap out of people. To the contrary, cycling actually costs money, in addition to being a tremendous time suck. As a lawyer, I have the money to ride, but not the time. If I quit my job, as I ponder doing every six minutes when I bill my time for the previous six minutes, I would have the time to ride, but not the money. Thus, instead of excelling at law, I bill the minimum amount of hours to avoid being fired, and put forth the minimum amount of skill to avoid a disciplinary meeting with the Florida Bar grievance committee.

Needless to say, I am not and never have been, on the partnership track. By lawyer standards, I am lazy. I work the firm minimum of 2,000 billable hours a year, often to the minute. I have never worked a weekend or past 5:00 p.m. and utilize every second of my fifteen vacation days and two personal days. At least once or twice a month, I take a half day, where I work for a few hours, then take the rest of the day off. So far, HR has not noticed that I'm not taking vacation time for these days.

Even while I'm at the office, I tend to procrastinate; not starting my work until I check the cycling news from four different websites, the local and national news on seven different websites, my bank statement and home email. I also take extended lunch breaks and often hold in my morning shit so that I can do it on the clock rather than my free time. Even with all this, I feel that I am wasting my life at a desk eight to ten hours a day.

I work as an associate attorney at the law firm of Johnson Smith Jones Greene Taylor LLP. Most people call the firm Johnson Smith. However, I work directly under David Greene. As a result, I must refer to the entire firm name to prevent David from crying himself to sleep, and more importantly, to avoid being fired. Several times a month, David reminds me that, technically, his name should be ahead of "Jones," though he is okay with the reversal due to the fact that he's not petty. He reminds me of the anorexic people with body dysmorphia. Essentially, the twig looks in the mirror and sees a fat person instead of a sixty-five-pound skeleton. David has personality dysmorphia. As a result, he fails to realize that his perception of David Greene and the rest of the world's perception of David Greene are day and night. A perfect example is that David actually called one of our coworkers a nerd on one occasion. It took all of my will power not to discuss black pots and kettles.

David is not my only complaint at Johnson Smith. Johnson Smith has a software program that severely limits my internet surfing options. When I try to view a friend's photo album, access Facebook, watch YouTube, search for a new job, buy something on eBay or watch porn, WEBSENSE pops up in big letters on my screen to inform me that I am on an unauthorized webpage. It scared the shit out of me the first time it happened. I expected an alarm to go off at Johnson Smith headquarters, followed by a stern talking to about surfing the Internet during work hours. Fortunately this does not happen, as I receive a WEBSENSE warning at least three to four times a day and I'm pretty sure I would no longer be employed if this were monitored.

WEBSENSE adds new restricted webpages every day and I'm sure it won't be long before Westlaw, a legal research website, becomes the only site I have access to. Each time WEBSENSE pops up, it gives you a categorical explanation of why access is being denied. Thus far, I've been rejected in the categories of "Blogs and Forums," "Streaming Video," "Tasteless Content," "Entertainment Gossip," "Online Auction," and "Adult Content." One day, I spent my morning typing in various porn sites to see if they fell under "Tasteless Content" or "Adult Content." I instigated this experiment after viewing two email-forwards, both of which were tasteless and adult-oriented, and noticing the differing classifications. The first email-forward was a link to a twenty second clip of a naked woman kneeling on a pool table, crotch facing the camera. All of the sudden, a cue ball pops out of her vagina and knocks the eight ball into the corner pocket. WEBSENSE deemed this site to be "Tasteless Content." The other email-forward was a photograph of a woman's labia, hopefully PhotoShopped, which stretched down below her knees. WEBSENSE classified this site as "Adult Content." Though WEBSENSE is well intended, it's much more inconvenient than it is restrictive since I have an iPhone with a full data plan. Even if I didn't, my office cannot block websites as fast as I can create new methods of procrastination.

Another indignity of my profession is the billing requirements. Billing breaks my day into six-minute increments. Six minutes is equal to a 0.1. I bill at least a 0.2 (twelve minutes) for every task I complete. If I make a phone call and leave a message, I record a 0.3 even though it only takes me thirty seconds. This breaks down into 0.1 for preparation to call John Doe; 0.1 for telephone call to John Doe; and 0.1 to document the file to reflect the detailed message left for John Doe. This is clearly taking advantage of the system. However, the system is quite flawed and the "taking advantage of" is a three-way street between the law firm, its employees and the clients.

Johnson Smith Jones Greene Taylor's only clients are insurance companies. Insurance companies give Johnson Smith all of their business in the southeastern region. In exchange, Johnson Smith is the insurance company's bitch. Most large law firms charge at least $250 an hour for an associate's work and $500 an hour for a partner. My office bills the insurance companies $125 an hour for an associate and $250 an hour for a partner. Johnson Smith can't increase its rates because it would cause its four insurance company clients to remove each of their 6,000 cases to a different firm.

Billing for an insurance company is particularly difficult because insurance companies restrict the type of work for which an attorney can submit a bill. Insurance companies don't like to pay for research, reviewing a file or any other preliminaries which are required in order to provide competent legal services. On the plus side, the insurance companies never fail to send Johnson Smith caramel-covered popcorn at Christmas time.

I specialize in subrogation law. My brother, Jason, once told the African American wife of a friend of mine that I practice "segregation" law. This is not the proper pronunciation. I told Jason that in the future, if he's going to misrepresent what I do, I would appreciate it if he would tell people I practice desegregation.

help you 'stay afloat' like your 'parents' did for you. Essentially, I'm your 'parent' here."

My focus during this kindergarten tutorial was on whether I was more annoyed by David's clichéd sports analogy, or his insistence on using air quotes inappropriately every third word.

"…Then you're on your own with 'water wings.' Eventually, you take off your 'water wings' but you can only swim 'doggy style.'" David started cracking up at his hilarious double entendre, which was inappropriate both situationally and substantively.

"Actually David, I think the appropriate term is doggy 'paddle,'" I said while flashing exaggerated air quotes back at David.

"Either term is appropriate, Jennifer. Next, you start swimming 'for real' and can even do 'flip turns.'"

Even though I'd heard this analogy before, I was stunned to be back at square one after twenty years of schooling and three years of practicing law, not to mention David's four previous recitations of the same exact speech.

David mistook my expression of disbelief for confusion because he said, "Oh, I just remembered, you're a 'biker' or is it 'bicyclist?' I'll put this in terms you can understand. First, you sit in a seat in the back of your 'parents' bike…then you get a 'tricycle'…finally, a 'two-wheeled bike' and 'training wheels'…then, you get your first 'big girl bike'…"

As David air quoted big girl bike, I snapped and explained that in spite of the subtleness of his first analogy, no further explanation was necessary. I felt compelled to nip this conversation in the bud before it morphed into something more difficult, like learning the alphabet or subtraction.

* * *

My dissatisfaction at work was forgotten when I clipped into my pedals to warm up for the Ocala criterium. A criterium course is generally a loop around a few city blocks. The blocks add up to approximately one mile and each race covers the course repeatedly for a set amount of time. For women, this generally equates to between twenty and forty laps. This sounds extremely boring but in reality, criteriums, commonly called crits, are fast paced and exciting, with cheering crowds on every lap. In contrast, cows are the only spectators during cycling races that take place on the open road. To add excitement to the crit, the announcer puts up cash or prizes called *primes* every few laps. The announcer yells, "Prime, five dollars, next lap," and the racers initiate a race within the race to claim the coveted five dollar *prime*. In a field of competitive cyclists, the *prime* prize, pronounced "preem," could be a stapler and each woman would turn herself inside out to nab the Swingline. It is not until later, when claiming your two dollars and a pencil, that you think, why did I sprint for that crap?

The Ocala women's criterium was to be an hour, plus five laps over the 0.8 mile course. Based on the average speed of the women's field in past races, we would probably complete about thirty laps of the rectangular shaped course that offered a scenic view of downtown Ocala: turn one had a general store called the Old Time Shoppe; turn two, a diner which may have doubled as the studio set for the 1950's scenes of the movie *Back to the Future*; turn three had a misplaced-looking McDonald's and Starbucks; and turn four was a horse feed store. Your typical downtown metropolis.

After the crit, I used the drive time back to Tampa to bitch about the race to my friend Danny since he was my captive audience in the car for at least an hour. I am relatively new to cycling, which is the least welcoming sport in the world. Once you're "in," cyclists will do anything for one another. However, when a newbie shows up for a ride, they're on their own. There is an unwritten rule in cycling which prohibits racing cyclists from initiating unknown newcomers into the sport. To compound the situation, you're often in the middle of nowhere when you realize you suck at cycling. This is because group training rides often start on the outskirts of civilization at a leisurely warm-up speed. This pace, which an electric wheelchair could maintain, remains steady for approximately five to ten miles of winding back roads, lulling newcomers into a false sense of security. Then, once the warm-up officially reaches the middle of nowhere, the real ride begins and weaker riders are spit out the back of the fast-paced pack and left to find their way back to their cars without the benefit of a map or a draft. This welcoming attitude is only magnified in the field of women's racing, where cattiness merges with the golden rule of cycling: "Do unto others as you have had done unto you." I began cycling at group rides around Tampa less than a year ago and was quickly able to mix it up with the strongest men, who encouraged me to race. However, with only half of a racing season under my belt, I am still "the new girl" at Florida women's races.

"She's a bitch and a cheater," I said to Danny. I knew it wasn't exactly true, but I was so pissed about being beaten by Brenda again that I didn't care.

"I'll grant you the bitch thing, but having experience and teammates is not cheating."

"She has a monopoly over all of the talent in Florida and uses it to fuck me over at every opportunity."

"You have two teammates."

"I have a fifty-five-year-old woman and an eleven-year-old junior, both of whom are teammates by virtue of the fact that the same bike shop sponsors us. Neither of them has ever lasted longer than two laps, let alone offer me any sort of assistance. Brenda has six teammates, each of whom take turns attacking me, then sit up and refuse to work with me once I catch them."

"You're a bad-ass, you don't need teammates in a little Florida race."

"Today's results beg to differ."

"What are you talking about? You did well and won a few *primes*."

"Objectively, they were the worst *primes* ever," I pointed out. I won two T-shirts that were free to begin with. Someone had re-gifted their drawer of XXL blood donor T-shirts. The shirts fall below my knees, and say, "Be a Donorsaurus" and "Donate for a Porpoise."

"You still won the *primes*, it was a good race. Brenda is the queen of Florida racing and has been for twenty years. She's not going to pass the torch to you willingly in your first few months of racing."

"She's forty years old and I hope to be in her shape when I'm forty, but I kick her ass on every group ride and during some races, she has to realize that the end is near."

"No, you beat her on every group ride with a hill. She smokes you in the sprints each and every time. Plus, she's still really strong. As long as she can sprint and has teammates to get her there, she's not relinquishing her designation as top dog, especially to a new rider like you."

I turned on Danny who sat casually in the driver's seat, arm out the window, trim and tanned in his shorts and white T-shirt. "What does that mean?"

"You're already stronger than her and you've not even been racing a year *and* you're doing it in your spare time when you're not doing your little gig as a lawyer. It took her five years of sucking before she got to the top and she didn't have a full-time job. You're making it look too easy. She's going to go ape shit when you learn how to sprint."

"I was a runner before becoming a cyclist. She was a chain smoker. Besides, if I'm so worthy of jealousy, why does every other girl in Florida want to be on her team? I swear Brenda is slipping those girls some sort of tainted Gatorade because there is no other reason for them to adore her."

"She's the only professional female racer Florida has ever produced. Every single one of them thinks they're racing for Lancette Armstrong and wants to impress their team captain. Besides, she's mercurial. Her teammates have only seen her good side and you've only seen her bad side. Her teammates are actually nice, they're just being aloof with you because they're intimidated by you and don't want to piss Brenda off."

"No one is intimidated by me. Did you see her henchman ram me into the curb?"

"Sammy is a former track rider, that's how they ride. Scary, but legal. Tomorrow is a hilly road race. It's more suited to you and less suited to Brenda and her teammates. You'll be fine. Sammy's fat ass won't even make it over the first hill."

"That's a relief."

"Relax, everyone's fighting to be the big fish in the little sea here. Things will be better when you go pro and the women are more supportive and less threatened by you."

"Yeah," I agreed. "They seem respectful and professional when I read interviews and post-race comments on the Internet. I want to race at the level when that happens."

"You will." Danny said this matter-of-factly.

"I'll never be able to turn pro unless I quit my job and sell my house. A drastic move to chase a dream where even the most seasoned professional woman rarely earns a five figure-salary."

"You're smart, you'll figure something out."

When I got home from the race, I napped for four hours then went out for drinks with some of my friends. I am single, as I have been for most of my life, save for a few disastrous relationships and horrendous first dates. I bear a lot of the fault for this, because I want to be swept off my feet by somebody tall, dark and handsome, who is athletic, brilliant, funny, nice, rich, and lives to please me. This results in being alone for long stretches of time. In reality, I like being alone and am not interested in any of the men I meet. However, I have made a concerted effort to date more often recently because I am nearing thirty and it is clear to me that, at this rate, I will surely be alone for the rest of my life. Consequently, I have forced myself to lower my standards and agree to dates that my gut urges me to avoid. If a guy is off-the-wall brilliant, he can be slack in all other areas and becomes dateable as long as he isn't bland, hideous, on welfare, fat, and so forth. The same theory applies if a guy is an Olympic-caliber athlete, obscenely handsome, filthy rich or ridiculously funny. As a result, I have not dated the most well-balanced men.

Even when I think I meet "the one," there's always a problem. Jason preferred *Friends* to *Seinfeld*; Alex sent emails confusing *to, two* and *too* (keeping *their, there* and *they're* straight is also very important to me); Peter kept Kosher; Dan went to church; Aiden disliked beer; Mike knew too much about wine; Matt designated Bennigan's as a favorite restaurant; Martin went to a hair salon instead of a six dollar barber; John saved a movie stub as a souvenir because "it will be cool to show our kids someday if we get married;" Jarred had a "*W*" bumper sticker; Aaron went to tanning beds; Scott believed in horoscopes; Ed designated half of his refrigerator to be a reptarium for snakes; Brian preferred cats to dogs; Alex had a vanity license plate; Dave sent emails with winking smiley faces or LOL; Seth wore a bracelet and necklace; Joel shaved his chest and arm hair; Tyler used the phrase "this guac is delish,"; Brett walked only on his tiptoes; Sean drove exactly the speed limit in the left lane on the highway; Vinny used a Band-Aid for a paper cut; Jeff parked diagonally so that no one could park near his precious car. I feel like I'm forgetting a lot. The only guy to ever dump me was James and he did so because I suck at Trivial Pursuit. Good riddance, I'm better off without that judgmental asshole.

My friends and I went to the Dubliner, an Irish pub that sells beer by the liter. I generally drink two beers at the Dubliner, a reasonable number, but a bit excessive when you look at the size of a two-liter bottle of soda. While I was at the bar ordering my second liter, I overheard a guy quoting *Tommy Boy*. It was like hearing a Shakespearian sonnet. I turned around. He was tall, no ring on the left hand, two days beard growth. A little on the hairy side, but attractive enough. I finished the *Tommy Boy* quote for him. "Try association. Like uh…let's say the average person uses ten percent of their brain. How much do you use? One and a half percent. The rest is clogged with malted hops and bong resin."

"Hi, I'm Paul."

"Jenna, nice to meet you. I also do *Happy Gilmore, Groundhog Day,* and *Super Troopers.*"

"Wow, I've always wanted to date the female equivalent of Rainman."

"You found her," I said. "I was about to buy a drink, but it would be so much more meaningful if you bought it for me."

Paul put my beer on his tab and we walked outside. From the conversation, I garnered that he recently moved from Minnesota to Tampa to take a job as an engineer. At some point during the night, I mentioned cycling. Paul told me that he was a cyclist too, though he stopped riding in college to play varsity rugby, the only sport more marginalized in the U.S. than cycling. At the end of the night, we exchanged numbers and gave each other an awkward hug and kiss on the cheek goodbye. We planned to go for a ride at some point the next week. It was the first time in years that I wasn't dreading a date.

I was a bit hung-over at the start of the road race the next morning. Fortunately, I had raced like this before and knew what to expect. The important thing is to sweat out the booze while hydrating. Once the fluids are exchanged, the carbohydrates from the beer kick in and the end of the race is smooth sailing.

Brenda lined up next to me and spoke her first words ever directed at me.

"You smell like a brewery."

She looked even shorter standing next to me than on the bike, where she is by far the worst draft of the *peloton*, as riding behind her is not much different than riding directly in the wind. I'm five-two and not used to looking down on anyone. Brenda couldn't be more than four-eleven, though more filled out and muscular than me, especially in her upper body. The reason I climb so well is that my quads and hamstrings are as big as tree trunks, but the rest of me is a rail. It's disproportionate, but perfect for having enough muscle strength to push my slight body against gravity. Brenda is built like a sprinter, but on a smaller scale. Her tiny but powerful stature is how she is able to muscle through bikes that are inches apart, and accelerate for the win.

I had hoped her first words to me would be something pleasant like, "Hello," but given her hostile introduction, I responded in kind.

"Thanks, it's my new perfume. Want some?" I said with my most charming smile as I offered her some sweat from my arm.

"You're fucking nasty!" she squealed.

The maneuver wasn't really that gross, as I didn't actually touch her, and even if I did, she was already sweaty from her warm-up and it was only going to get worse. Florida is so hot and humid that for at least six months of the year, sweat from the rider in front of you drips onto you as you draft behind them. Three months of the year, it's so hot that this sweat is actually refreshing.

After the gun went off, I sat comfortably in the pack, not expending any energy. Sammy went off in the front of the pack and I let her go. The first half of the course was flat. I didn't plan on making a move until the hills kicked in.

When we hit the first hill, I exploded out of the pack. Not surprisingly, Brenda was glued to my wheel, getting the best possible draft. As we crested the first hill, she and I had a sizable gap on the rest of the main field, except for Sammy who was still ahead. After the descent, Brenda sat in my draft without pulling through as I pedaled into the wind through the next flat section of the course at about eighty percent effort. I had to go hard enough to distance myself from the pack of chasing girls, but not so hard that I was too tired to catch Brenda if she stopped drafting off me and tried to get away. Technically, Brenda was under no obligation to help me work by sharing the time in the wind. Her team strategy was quite straightforward and customary: helping her teammate by sitting in my draft and staying fresh. If I slowed down in order to stop giving Brenda a free ride, then the pack would catch Brenda and me as Sammy continued to put time into all of us. By continuing to chase Sammy, I was forced to do all the work while Brenda stayed fresh in my draft. The bitch of it was that once we caught Sammy, Brenda's move would be to accelerate on her rested legs and leave me in the dust.

While Brenda's strategy was technically correct, it was ridiculous for her to act like a team player. First, everyone knew that Brenda would not hesitate to chase down a teammate at crunch time. Second, Brenda knew that it was only a matter of time before we caught her 150-pound teammate. When sprinting, extra weight helps, to an extent, by cranking out more wattage. However, when going up an incline, extra weight keeps you down. Sammy, weighing in at forty pounds more than Brenda and me, would never win a solo breakaway on a hilly course. Therefore, it would behoove Brenda to help me distance us from the rest of the pack, as it was a matter of time and gravity before we caught Sammy.

By the end of the first sixteen-mile loop, I had Sammy in my sights. We scooped her up just as we passed the start/finish line for the first lap. Brenda accelerated away from me just as I expected. I was able to close the gap without much effort and within seconds, we had put fifty yards into Sammy. When Brenda finally turned around and saw me on her wheel she stopped pedaling, thereby ending my free ride and giving Sammy an opportunity to catch back up. I rode in front of Brenda and Sammy and took a long pull into the wind, then moved out of the way to give them an opportunity to contribute to keeping the pace high. Neither of them moved forward. If they just worked with me, the three of us were guaranteed to fill out the podium. However, Brenda obviously felt more comfortable letting the field catch us and winning the field sprint. I moved back in front of Brenda and Sammy and set a hard tempo pedaling into the wind. My plan was to stay ahead of the main field, but not kill myself, until the last lap. Sammy and Brenda's other teammates were "blocking" for them in the main field, that is, setting a tempo hard enough to discourage attacks, but easy enough so they wouldn't catch Brenda and Sammy. Thus, as long as I had Brenda and Sammy with me, their teammates were, by proxy, helping me out as well. As a result, I opted to keep my pace until the last lap, where I planned to attack Brenda and Sammy by accelerating on the first of four hills located a mile before the finish line. Essentially, I was gambling that a tired Jenna could beat a fresh Brenda on a tough course. If not, at least I'd be in second place because there was no way Sammy would make it over the steep hill at the finish with us. The alternative was to engage in a field sprint with sixty women.

Technically, I am a fantastic sprinter in that I can accelerate quickly and hold my speed longer than most cyclists. Unfortunately, I'm terrified of field sprints. This fear is about as rational as a quarterback who is afraid of getting clobbered on every play. That is to say, completely rational, but not very practical. My phobia of field sprints originated during my first race. I had positioned myself perfectly for the sprint.

At one kilometer to go I was in the draft behind two rows of cyclists. There was a hole opening on the left that I planned to charge through once I reached 500 meters to go. Unfortunately, at 800 meters to go, the girl in front of me fell, taking me down with her. The only parts of me that hit the asphalt were my nose and mouth. My helmet would have been really hurt if my face weren't there to protect it. I broke my nose, lost six teeth and developed a severe bout of "Bike Tourette Syndrome;" an ailment whereby a cyclist freaks the fuck out and shouts obscenities every time they think they're going to crash due to a scary noise or sight, such as the rustle of leaves or another cyclist's slight deviation from a straight path. I've trained myself to stop freaking out, but still fear mixing it up in bunch sprints.

But now my gamble worked, just barely. I charged the first of the four hills just before the finish line at ninety-five percent effort and relaxed during the descents. On the fourth hill, which was the steepest, I stood up and sprinted as hard as possible. I looked behind me as I went over the hill and noticed a gap between Brenda and me. I rode down the hill and to the finish line as fast as I could, pumping my legs and also moving the bike back and forth beneath me with my arms for extra power. Brenda used all of her strength to get back onto my wheel, but she ran out of road before she could swing around me for the win. She punched her arm in the air in frustration, which is as big a temper tantrum as one can throw while sitting on a bike traveling at over forty miles an hour.

Immediately after my race ended, I started racing Danny's thirty-plus master's age group race. It was the last race of the season, so there was no need for me to tack on extra miles, but it was a nice day and I was on a high from my race. I'm not thirty years old yet, but the race organizers allow women to race the men's age-group categories up to ten years beyond their age. Since turning thirty last year, Danny alternates between racing with the local pros or racing with the age groupers, depending on which race is more convenient for his schedule. Calling thirty-plus racers "Masters" is absurd, as they are in their prime and nearly as fast as the pros.

Danny is six-three, which is above average among the general population but downright huge for a cyclist. He's thin, but with muscular legs, which he shaves as all competitive cyclists do. His straight hair is brown, not gelled and usually in need of a trim, so the ends of it poke out of the holes in his helmet and blow in the wind. This, along with his height, makes him easy to locate in a pack of sixty to one hundred cyclists and I usually seek out his wheel for a safe, full draft. I pulled out of his race after completing two of the sixteen-mile loops because I had to drive home, shower, and grab my dog before going to my parents' house for dinner. Between my race and Danny's race, I had pedaled nearly ninety miles before heading home.

* * *

Sunday night is family dinner night at the Rosen residence. My parents, Michael and Geri, live in North Tampa in the house where I grew up. I live twenty minutes away in South Tampa, as do my older brother John and his wife Julie. The remainder of the family consists of my younger brother Jason, and John and Julie's four dogs.

The *Sopranos*-like family dinner night is part of my dad's grand scheme to convert from Jewish to Italian. Unfortunately for him, he's one of the few Jews who can't pass for Italian, as he is very tall and Aryan-looking, even as his blond hair fades whiter and whiter. He lives his life by the Godfather mantra that the family is everything and you don't go against it. As he ages, he's started to take the Godfather thing a little far. I'm pretty sure he's the only accountant who insists on facing all doors and windows in an Italian restaurant and having his children kiss his ring as a greeting. Still, I enjoy the Sunday night dinners whenever I'm in town and had missed the previous three weeks of dinners because of race conflicts.

When I got there, dinner was ready but Jason wasn't there yet. I grabbed a drink and sat in the kitchen to shoot the shit with my parents. They asked me what I did for the weekend and I told them two races, one of which I won. With that, my dad stormed out of the room. My mom, who at the moment preferred to be Switzerland, said nothing. I took my drink and went to my parents' backyard to play with the dogs.

Ever since my face-plant, my dad has become staunchly anti-cycling. He refuses to contribute in any way toward my "death-wish" of a hobby. My mom, who is still pissed that I lost the teeth that she and my dad paid a fortune to straighten, takes his side on the issue. In addition to giving me the silent treatment every time I mention the word "race," my parents have started cutting out newspaper articles citing cycling deaths to convince me to give up the bike. I know cycling is dangerous, but the statistics are very inflated. The census has a loose definition of "cyclist." It bothers me when my parents find a newspaper article that says that a "cyclist" was killed on Martin Luther King Boulevard at three in the morning. My definition of "cyclist" is very narrow and sure as shit does not include bums on forty dollar bikes at three in the morning without helmets or lights. If I were to keep a "cycling" death tally, it would also exclude people who think ten miles is far. At a minimum, a "cyclist" should own clipless pedals, spandex and detach the spoke protector from behind their cassette. A twelve-year-old riding a bike to his friend's house is not a cyclist, but rather, a kid with a bike. Likewise, the following people are not cyclists: someone on a bike delivering a pizza, someone who rides because their driving privileges are revoked, or someone who watches television at the gym on a recumbent stationary bike.

After giving my parents ten minutes to cool down, I walked back into the house just as Jason was walking in the door. Jason is a senior in high school, whereas John and I are twenty-nine and twenty-eight, respectively. John and I believe that the age gap is a strong indicator that Jason was an accident. As my mother was giving Jason a hard time for being late and ruining dinner, my dad walked in and started in on him. "For Christ's sake Jason."

It's safe to say my dad does not get Jason. John and I quickly took bets on whether he was going to start in on Jason's baggy jeans and backwards baseball cap, or the fact that he reeked of cigarettes. I bet on the cigarettes and won.

My parents, especially my dad, are very anti-cigarette. By comparison, even marijuana is somewhat acceptable. Every time my brother walks into a room, he reeks of smoke, no matter how much he tries to cover it up with mints and cologne. I only swing by my parents' house a few times a month, but I'd memorized the ritual that was about to begin. First, my dad will accuse Jason of smoking and Jason will deny it. Jason's defense is always unique: that he was in a car or house where someone, but not him, was smoking. After the arguing comes the test, which involves my dad smelling Jason's left hand. Jason is notoriously anti-hygiene. He never washes his hands, brushes his teeth or wears deodorant. As a result, he never washes away the cigarette smell from his hands, which seems like the obvious solution to me. Another escape for Jason would be for him to smoke with his right hand, as my dad only smells his left hand. Jason has never tried either of these options. He is a smart kid, so I attribute this to the fact that he doesn't give a shit. Every time my dad smells Jason's left hand, it inevitably reeks of cigarettes. This causes my dad to become doubly pissed at Jason, for lying on top of smoking.

This initial conversation typically lasts five minutes, with the argument spilling over into the first ten minutes or so of dinner. I took a seat to watch the show yet again.

"Jason, did you smoke?" My dad asked.

"No, I was in a room with smokers."

"Don't lie to me."

"I swear to God, Dad. I did not smoke."

"Left hand?" Dad said, holding out his arm to grab Jason's left hand for a sniff.

"Why don't you trust me?"

"Because you're a liar. Now turn that goddamn hat around and get over here. Why the hell do you wear that hat backwards? When I was a kid, you didn't wear your hat backwards unless you were a fucking baseball catcher. Your dungarees are eight sizes too big so be careful not to trip on your way over here." Jason walked over to my dad and gave him his left hand. My dad sniffed it, looked up, smiled, and said, "PUSSY!"

Dad, Jason and John started cracking up and patting Jason on the back. I threw up in my mouth a little, as Jason said with a smile, "Wanna smell my breath for smoke?" In addition to grossing me out, this shocked me. It's not that I think Jason doesn't like women, but simply that he has a rather limited palate so cunnilingus was surprising. Jason's taste buds had stopped evolving when he turned three years old. His diet consists of cookies, peanut butter and jelly with the crusts cut off, and cheese pizza. He will literally not try any new foods, claiming that everything else is gross and of a bad consistency. So it surprised me to find Jason ventured out and actually tasted pussy.

Jason's pussy fingers really lightened the mood after the cycling and smoking snafus, and dinner became fun. That is, until Jason fucked up the mood by punching my dad in the arm and telling him to "stop crunching." My dad looked stunned even though he should have known it was coming, as Jason wasn't wearing his headphones.

Jason has a very severe case of Attention Deficit Disorder. His ADD manifests itself in all the normal ways in that he watches a lot of television, gets easily bored with activities, and can't sit still. When Jason arrives somewhere, the first thing he wants to know is how long he's going to be stuck there. Yet, he can watch television like it's his job and often sits in front of it for hours at a time, foregoing food and sleep. Though these ADD quirks are bound to interfere with Jason's ability to find a job and wife, I'm quite entertained by them, save one aspect of ADD that is quite obnoxious for friends and family alike.

Jason doesn't like the sound of breathing, crunching, chewing gum, sucking a lollipop, a spoon hitting the bottom of a bowl, clocks ticking or any other repetitive noise. I know a lot of people who say, "Oh, I'm like that too," but that's just when they're trying to concentrate. Jason's condition is constant. I can always tell when Jason has been to my house when I'm not there because he puts my clock in the refrigerator. Evidently, the refrigerator's seal muffles the ticking. This was his solution after I told him I was sick of resetting my clock each time he stopped by my house and removed the batteries.

I have learned a lot about ADD eating etiquette from Jason. For instance, the proper way to eat a chip, next to not eating one at all, is to put the entire chip in your mouth before biting down. This way, the initial crunch is muffled. Chewing gum or sucking a lollipop around an ADD person is also taboo, especially in close proximity, such as in a car. These rules are the Constitution of ADD. Amendments can be added and quite frequently are. When I was in high school, I had some friends over for dinner. Jason picked this occasion as the perfect time to inform me that I should blow my nose because he could tell by the squeaking of my breathing pattern that I had a dry booger in the back of my nostril. I took that embarrassment better than my dad did the punch now from Jason.

"Are you fucking crazy, I'm eating a taco. It crunches," my dad said.

"Can I go get my headphones?"

"No, it's a family dinner, you can't plug your ears."

"It hurts my ears," Jason responded.

And here we go again, another conversation I know by heart. I don't know why my parents get so bent out of shape when I go to a race and miss a Sunday dinner—they're all reruns.

After dinner, my mom asked me if I'd met anyone lately. I debated telling her about Paul. On the one hand, it would make her happy. Since my graduation from college, my mother has longed for me to rush into the house to tell her that I've found a keeper. This anticipation has become more pronounced lately, as I near my thirties single and not dating while all of her friends' children are married and having kids. With this in mind, I decided to tell my mom about Paul in spite of the fact that I barely knew him and that doing so would expose me to ninety questions I either didn't know the answer to or didn't want to answer.

I said, "Maybe, we'll see."

With that, my mom filled my wine glass to capacity and started in: What's his name? What does he do? How old is he? What does he look like? How did you meet? Are you going to see him again? When are you going to see him again? Oh, he's a cyclist, can you beat him? Where does he live? Where is he from? Do you think it could be serious? What were you wearing when you met him? How did you wear your hair? Tell me you had makeup on? You didn't drink too much did you? You should invite him over next week.

"Yeah, that's not going to happen," I said. "If he winds up being special I'll invite him over and you can grill him."

My mom is a guidance counselor for seventh graders and it just occurred to me how much she must love the daily drama that transpires at a middle school. I wonder if she tries to get them drunk before digging into their innermost thoughts.

CHAPTER TWO

The next morning at work, my morning procrastination ritual was extended because next season's NRC schedule was released online. NRC stands for National Race Calendar and it is the United States' professional schedule for the cycling season, which takes place annually between the months of February and September. While I have never participated in a professional race, I planned to hit next season's race schedule with as much of a vengeance as my fifteen vacation days permitted. Over the past five years, the NRC schedule had been quite predictable because the same race promoters from the same cities put on the same races year after year. However, this morning, women's racing got the boost of a lifetime.

Tour de West

The first ever all-women Grand Tour stage race will take place August 30 through September 23. The route will be from San Diego, California north to Seattle, Washington. The 24 day, 1,855 mile scenic race will zigzag up the west coast, hitting most big cities, as well as the wine country and the Redwood National Forest. There will be two rest days, a prologue and twenty-one stages, including two time trials and a near even distribution of flat stages and mountain stages. The Tour de West, which is being sponsored Lydia Jackson, a popular fashion designer, avid cyclist, and outspoken feminist, is likely to attract the interest of all of the big European and American women's professional teams. Thirteen teams, with nine women to a team, will take to the start on August 30th.

I sat stunned and then read the article again. By definition, grand tours are cycling races that last three weeks and are between 1,800 to 2,400 miles in length. While professional men have raced grand tours in Italy, France and Spain every year for over one hundred years, women's tours of these same countries generally last one week, and never more than two weeks. The distances covered in the women's version of the Tours of Italy, Spain and France, are always significantly less than the men's races, in terms of both overall distance and distance per day. Further, just as women's cycling has always lagged behind men's cycling, American cycling has always lagged behind European cycling. The longest cycling race in America, for men or women, is two weeks. Most U.S. stage races last only four to eight days. American race promoters have never bothered creating a three-week stage race for men because they know such a race cannot compete with the prestige of the three European grand tours. The Tour de West would be huge for both American and women's cycling. Figuring out a way to attend the inaugural Tour de West became my project for the day in lieu of both legal work and my other methods of procrastination.

There were a number of obstacles to my entering the Tour de West. First, assuming I was even talented enough to turn pro, I would have to be discovered by a professional team. Only professional teams, not individuals, would be welcome to race the Tour de West. There were no scouts at the Florida women's races where I competed on the weekends. As a result, I could only be discovered if I traveled to other professional women's races on the NRC schedule and did well. I needed to find a way to attend the five- or six-stage races leading up to the Tour de West so that I could try to get some results and increase my visibility to professional teams.

The second major challenge was my job, or more specifically, avoiding my job. My three weeks of vacation time for the entire work year began on July 1 of each year. Even if the firm allowed me to take my entire three-week break at one time, which was unheard of, I would only be able to attend the actual Tour de West. I couldn't even squeeze in travel days to and from the Tour, let alone other races in the months leading up to the event. It was a catch-22. I could use my vacation time to try and qualify for the Tour, but that wouldn't leave any vacation time to actually race the Tour. If I saved my vacation days for the Tour, I would not be able to qualify for it. Ideally, I would need time off from work in July, August and September, which was nine months from now.

The only way to do this was to quit my job, which would solve the time problem but create a money problem. I didn't have savings to support a week of racing let alone three months of racing. I could sell my house, but the market was in the shitter and I hear buying high and selling low is not the best financial move. Besides, I couldn't even imagine the hassle of moving all of my stuff into storage for three months, then moving it to an apartment during the off-season.

David walked by my office as I was pondering my dilemma.

"Hi Jennifer. Can you come by my office? I have a conference call on the Zimmerman file. I know it's not yours, but I need someone on it for about three months until Sandra comes back from maternity leave."

"Sure, be right there," I said as the most obvious idea in the world dawned on me.

I would pretend to be pregnant starting today, and in nine months I'd take a three month maternity leave. This would allow me to keep my job and salary, while I raced before and during the big event. Pregnancy is the ultimate perk if you can do it and avoid the inconvenience of gaining fifty pounds, stretching your vagina and raising a kid for eighteen years. I'd say I was a genius, except for the fact that I'd worked at my office for three years now and had not created three fake kids already. I walked toward David's office and clicked my heels together for the first time in my life because it just seemed like the right thing to do under the circumstances. The heel clicking did nothing for me.

I sat down in David's office and he said, "Jennifer, before I place this phone call, are you familiar with this case?"

"You mean the case you just assigned to me forty-five seconds ago?"

"Yes, did you have a chance to go over it?"

By virtue of the case arising in the subrogation department, I gathered that it was a subrogation case. Other than that, I was at a loss. "Yeah David, I've gone over it pretty thoroughly."

"Great, let's call Ralph."

"Ralph?" I said hesitantly.

"Yeah, Ralph Walker, the personal attorney of our client's insured. What's funny is that Ralph has been pursuing this case for over a year. But now that Ralph's client's insurance company completed its adjustment of the claim, it hired us to pursue payment. So now Ralph will be our co-counsel. I have to schmooze him so he's not upset that we're taking over."

David spent the first fifteen minutes of the conversation introducing himself and explaining why Ralph's firm and our firm should join forces. Then, David really turned on the charm and said, "Of course, Johnson Smith Jones Greene Taylor should be lead counsel. You know, the reason the defendant hasn't settled already is because he doesn't respect your firm. Now that Johnson Smith Jones Greene Taylor is involved, the defendants will get scared and settle immediately."

I sat in my chair turning darker and darker shades of red as David continued to insult Ralph and beat his own chest. I stared at his familiar features, hating him. He is middle-age with a receding hairline and average in every way, including height, weight and appearance. However, his face irks me because he has skin tags of some sort all over his right eyelid and below his right eye. His thick glasses magnify the tiny bumps so that they're the only things I can see on his face. I literally cannot avoid them and often sit in his office distracted, ignoring his babbling, wondering how many millions he has to earn before he pays a twenty-five dollar deductible to have them removed.

David told Ralph, "The defendants don't realize it yet, but they have awakened a sleeping giant. You've heard of MY firm right? We are a big player. When I call the defendants, they'll hear us roar. You know what I mean? ROOOAAARRRRR!"

Seriously, he roared to Ralph over the phone. I made a note to myself to call Ralph later in the day to apologize and distinguish myself as sane. David has a knack for making me cringe in front of other attorneys. One time, at a mediation, David and I were reviewing a release drafted by opposing counsel. Instead of just reviewing the release for content, David started adding commas and semi-colons to the release, which was drafted by a Harvard-educated adverse attorney. David's corrections were questionable at best. He insists that adding a comma before the word "and," is the only acceptable way to draft a list of items. For instance, "apples, oranges, and grapes." It was clear the opposing counsel did not appreciate the grammar tips, but the other attorney did not engage in a discussion about the point as I had hoped. Not that it would have helped. One time, I sent David the Wikipedia link about the "serial comma."

The serial comma, (also known as the Oxford comma or Harvard comma), is the comma used immediately before a grammatical conjunction that precedes the last item in a list of three or more items. The phrase "Portugal, Spain, and France", for example, is written with the serial comma, while "Portugal, Spain and France", identical in meaning, is written without it. There is no global consensus among writers or editors on the use of the serial comma.

David's response to this link was, "See, I'm right."

After a half hour, David finally let Ralph get his first words in. David used this opportunity to mute our end of the speaker phone conversation and explain to me his brilliance over the past thirty minutes. He said, "Do you see what I did there, see what I'm doing, I'm laying the groundwork and schmoozing him. Seriously Jennifer, do you know what I did? He sure doesn't. I'm getting him to agree with me, but making him think it's his idea, he has no idea what I just did to his mind." David's summary of his legal prowess was always very helpful, especially in lieu of listening to the other half of a conference call.

I zoned out for the rest of the conversation. It frustrated me that David was asking to be lead counsel because the lead was actually going to go to me since I'd be handling the file rather than him. Subrogation cases are handled on a contingency basis, so I always prefer to do as little as possible on my cases when there's another attorney to share the load.

I zoned back in and heard David saying "…just recently I settled a nine million dollar case. It actually went to trial, but after my opening statement, opposing counsel called a recess and just offered the money because he could tell that I was making a strong connection to the judge and jury."

David continued beating his chest, oblivious to the fact that I was more antsy than usual. Not only was I bored, but I was in a hurry to tell David that I was knocked up. I wanted to do it before I thought too hard about it and lost my nerve.

David finally turned off the speaker phone and looked very pleased with himself. Technically, mission accomplished. However, considering that the interests of our client and Ralph's client were the same, the task could have been accomplished with a one-line email which would have taken me four seconds to draft but for which I would have billed: "0.6—Draft correspondence to attorney Walker regarding litigation strategy."

"See how I did that?" David said.

"Yes. Impressive," I responded.

"Great, how's your load? Can you take on more cases?"

David asked this question a lot and his creepy emphasis on the word "load" never failed to make my skin crawl. "Actually, I may have to slow down. I just found out that I'm pregnant."

Mr. Socially Savvy responded by looking at me in disgust and asking, "Are you going to keep it?"

I responded with my own look of disgust and said, "Of course!" as though I were appalled by the suggestion that I would abort my fake fetus.

"Who is the father?"

Hmm. Probably should have anticipated this question. Somehow, the name "Ben Weinstein" came out of my mouth. David is a super-Jew and to him, the greater sin between an out-of-wedlock pregnancy and an interfaith coupling is the latter. As a result, I just blurted out an invented Jewish name for the father.

"Are you and Benjamin getting married?"

I almost said, "Who?" but caught myself, realizing that David had already converted Ben into the more formal, Benjamin.

I said, "Marriage isn't in the cards right now. He doesn't live in Florida anymore."

"Where does he live?"

I should have expected this peppering of questions. David was an obscene over-sharer and as a result, he expected his employees to be as well. "New York City."

"What does he do?"

"Marine biologist." I do not know a New York City marine biologist named Ben or Benjamin, but the occupation was a nice tribute to George Costanza.

"Where did you meet him?"

I decided to nip this in the bud before I had to tell David what imaginary position Benjamin and I were in while conceiving our imaginary child. I put on a somber face and told David that I was still processing the information myself and was just not ready to talk about it yet.

David shrugged and said we'd talk about it later. Then he switched into law mode. This was a talent of David's. Whether it be a party, funeral or six o'clock in the morning, David was in full lawyering mode. Therefore, not surprisingly, David set my impending bundle of doom on the back burner and spent the next forty-five minutes going over my case list so he could see how many of Sandra's maternity cases to shift to me.

As an afterthought, on my way out the door, I told David not to say anything to my parents. It's not that David and my parents hang out, but they coincidently live two houses away from each other and David might go out of his way to socialize with them to get the dirt on my pregnancy. Not only would this blow my cover, it would expose my parents to unnecessary David-time. Nobody should have to deal with David unless they're receiving a substantial paycheck to do so.

David assured me that he would keep my secret in the strictest confidence. His expression changed and he plastered a goofy smile on his face. I could tell he was very pleased that I told my deepest, darkest secret to him instead of my own parents. Inherent in his promise to keep quiet was the understanding that, other than my parents, he would tell everyone else the news immediately.

After being dismissed from Principal Greene's office, I went to the kitchen to grab a cup of coffee. As I rounded the corner into the kitchen I glimpsed Sarah Smith out of the corner of my eye and stepped back. Sarah has been David's paralegal for the past twenty years. He always introduces her as, "She's a paralegal, but she's like an attorney." He pauses for dramatic effect during this phrase. Even after twenty years, Sarah never fails to blush when David says this about her.

I turned the other way because Sarah has a reputation for trapping people in the kitchen for hours at a time to issue updates about her life.

She is sixty years old, which she works into every conversation just to hear you say, "Really? Sixty? You don't even look thirty." Sarah also likes to say, "I'm getting so fat," in every conversation, so that you correct her and tell her how thin she looks. This is when she tells you with a frown, "I'm a size two now, that's huge! I used to be a zero. That's when I was younger though. I'm sixty now…" (insert pregnant pause)

In actuality, Sarah looks fifty and is a size six. Not bad, but not as described. Her appearance would actually go unnoticed if she weren't constantly telling me and everyone else how hot she is, enticing us to observe her every flaw. While she has the potential to look very nice for her age, she's not helping herself by lying in the sun every weekend, dressing in tight shirts and short skirts, and updating her boob job biannually to maintain her freakishly flotation-device-looking-rack.

Talking to Sarah is excruciating, especially on a Monday, because she gives a blow by blow of her wild and crazy weekend, including detailed descriptions of every hot guy that hit on her at every bar in Ybor City and on Howard Avenue; the hangouts of eighteen-year-olds and twenty-five-year-olds, respectively.

As I was sprinting the other way to my office I heard, "Jenna! Hey Jenna!"

Shit! "Yes, Sarah." I said.

She responded, "I knew it! I could tell you were gaining weight."

I'd told David about the pregnancy three minutes ago and Sarah had already heard the news. This meant that the rest of the office knew or would know within minutes. I was a little pissed about the accelerated rumor mill, but mostly I was just pissed that she called me fat. Couldn't she have told me my boobs looked bigger or that I was glowing?

I replied, "I'm only two weeks pregnant, I'm pretty sure I haven't gained weight."

"No," Sarah said, "you've gained at least four pounds, I can tell. Do you know that I only gained fourteen pounds during my entire pregnancy? You'll be that big in six weeks."

"Weren't you eleven when you were pregnant?" I said as I grabbed my coffee.

"No, I was sixteen. What are you doing? You can't have coffee."

Damn it! I forgot about the nine months without coffee aspect of pregnancy. I grabbed the decaf and added a ton of sugar and cream to it. I'd get real coffee later when no one was looking.

Sarah started telling me the details of her weekend: the free martinis she received from hot guys, the people who mistook her for being her daughter's sister, getting carded at several bars, finally giving into temptation and getting a belly button ring…She was in the middle of asking me whether I thought she should get a "Truth" or "Honesty" tattoo in Chinese lettering above her right boob, when a secretary walked into the kitchen. I decided that the secretary could take my place as a captive audience and walked away without answering her tattoo question.

I shut my office door and Googled pregnancy. I figured that the ban on caffeine was not the only thing I should know about as an expectant mother. I found a website with a week-by-week description of pregnancy and bookmarked the page. This would come in handy. I looked at week two:

This may sound strange, but you're still not pregnant! Fertilization of your egg by the sperm will only take place near the end of this week.

What? I read on and discovered that pregnancy, which is forty weeks long in its entirety, is measured from the date of the knocked-up individual's last period, even though ovulation and fertilization doesn't take place until two weeks later and it's another two weeks before you miss a period and test positive for pregnancy. This means that by the time a woman pees on a stick, she's already a month pregnant. What a deal, first month is free.

In my imaginary world, I tested pregnant before I even ovulated. Oops. Thank God no one seemed to notice. I found it impressive that while I was not pregnant, in actuality or by the medical definition, Sarah could tell I was pregnant. She really does have a sixth sense. I skipped ahead to week three. Nothing much happens there either, though I should apparently experience spotting.

After work, I met Danny in the garage below my office. As per the usual schedule, Danny started playing bike bitch, pumping my bike tires and filling my water bottles while I changed into cycling clothes. After this ritual, we generally rode to Davis Island or St. Petersburg to meet up with other cyclist friends of ours.

Bike bitch is actually a narrow definition for Danny's role. In addition to being my bike mechanic, Danny acts as my unofficial teammate at unofficial group rides several times a week. We also usually travel together to each race in Florida and Georgia. Danny tends to be my regular bitch as well. In the two years I've known him, Danny has acted as pest control (removing roaches, rats, raccoons, opossums, dead squirrels and other vermin from my house and yard); driver (to the airport and races, occasionally driving through the night to races while I sleep in the back seat); and handyman (snake my sink, build me a deck, fix my air conditioner, build me a fence).

Danny's actual occupation is massage therapist and cycling coach. As a result, he works odd hours and often has downtime during the day while I'm at work. Thus, in addition to the aforementioned duties, Danny tends to be on-call for me unless he's working. Danny refers to my assignments as JRAs or Jenna Related Activities. I should clarify that Danny is my best friend, and when I call him from work to ask him to crawl through my doggy door and get the dead rat out of my attic, I am very nice about it. Still, I can't help but think on occasion that I owe Danny a blowjob.

I fully subscribe to the *When Harry Met Sally* premise that men and women can't be friends because one of them always wants to have sex with the other. My relationship with Danny works because I know he wants to have sex with me and he knows it's not going to happen. Though he's tall, smart, attractive, funny and all the other positive attributes of a man, he is solidly in the friend category. I thought about dating him when we first met, but I knew the result would be the same as when I dated my best male friends from high school, college and law school: As soon as I slept with him, I'd confirm my gut feeling that I wasn't sexually attracted to him. Then I'd spend the next few months trying to push him back into the friend category without breaking his heart. Simultaneously, Danny's infatuation with me would turn into full-blown obsessive love and he'd be proposing to me right around the time that I finally built up the balls to dump him.

To be clear, Danny has never formally asked me out and thus he has never formally been rejected. In fact, he scoffed at my arrogance the one and only time I accused him of having a crush on me and advised him that it was not reciprocal. I did not do this to be an ass, but merely to give him the opportunity to opt out of painting my house if he was only doing so in the hopes of getting laid. I suppose it's possible that Danny is not sexually interested in me and that he just likes hanging out with me and doing all of my chores, but I have my suspicions.

This dynamic sounds crazy, but somehow, it's not actually that rare in cycling. Brenda is married, but her husband rarely attends cycling events. Instead, Jeremy, a divorced doctor and competitive cyclist, travels with her to nearly every race, stays with her even if their races are hours apart, and helps her by tuning her bike and feeding her water and food in the feed zone on the course. To my knowledge, they've never slept together either, though I have no doubt that Jeremy, like Danny, is interested.

Once we got out of the parking garage, which I was paranoid had been bugged by an overly nosy secretary, I announced to Danny, "I'm racing the Tour de West."

"That three week women's race? How? Are you finally quitting your job? Do you have enough money?"

"Nope, taking a maternity leave." I knew it wasn't a great idea to advertise my fraud, but I had to tell someone about my ingenious plan and Danny was the most logical choice since he's one of the few people who knows that I measure my self-worth by my cycling ability. Even if I wanted to confide that information to other people, it would be difficult to convey my point since no one in America cares about cycling. Of the seven Americans who have heard of the Tour de France, five think it is a competition sandwiched between a swimming and running leg. It irritates me that people cannot distinguish between triathlons, which are two-thirds crazy, and cycling, the most beautiful and challenging sport in the world.

"Maternity leave? Don't you need a kid to do that?" Danny asked.

"Nope, just a pregnancy," I responded.

"You're knocked up?" Danny asked as his face went white and he nearly struck a curb.

"No," I said, as though it were the dumbest question in the world. "I'm faking a pregnancy so that I can take a maternity leave."

The color returned to his face and he grinned. "That's actually pretty funny."

"I know. I'm hilarious," I said in my most serious voice.

"Seriously, what's your plan?"

"I'm seriously faking a pregnancy," I said as we rode over the bridge onto Davis Island, one of the richest neighborhoods in Tampa.

"I swear you have testicles. Big, brass testicles," Danny said.

"The better to have a baby with."

"When's the due date?"

"I'm thinking July is a good time. Women get three months vacation for procreating, so I figure I'll race in July and August to prepare for the Tour de West, then race it in September."

"July? That means you just became pregnant today. No one tells people they're pregnant the day they pee on the stick. You're not supposed to tell anyone until after the first trimester."

"Why?" I asked, surprised that Danny knew any of this.

"Superstition. It's bad luck to announce a pregnancy before the fetus makes it to three months. Plus, it saves public heartache in case you miscarry."

"I'm pretty sure I'm not going to miscarry. Besides, I'm a pathetic single mom. People will probably think I spread the news early in order to jinx my baby's life."

"Don't you need to provide hospital records or something?" Danny asked.

"Home birth, dude. What am I, a pussy? Home birth makes me sound tough and takes care of the hospital record issue."

"Now you're talking crazy."

"I know. I'd like an epidural for my gyno's speculum, there's no way I'd have a baby without drugs. But no one has to know that. People have home births all the time. That's my story."

"Can you name it after me?" Danny asked.

"There's not going to be a baby."

"Right. Speaking of that, what are you going to tell people when there is no baby after your maternity leave?"

"That it didn't get along with my dog and I put it up for adoption."

"Seriously?" Danny asked.

"I am serious. People give their dogs away all the time when a new baby comes, I'll do the opposite."

"That's perfect. Name the kid after me in the meantime?"

"No way, I'll name it after me, regardless of its gender."

"You can't name your dog and your first born Jenna. It's too self-centered, even for you."

"The dog is Jenna II, the baby will be Jenna III. Both names are totally different than Jenna."

"I see your point."

As we reached the private airport at the end of the island, we saw some other cycling friends of ours in the distance. Davis Island is a very popular place to ride on rest days or in the off-season. It's thirteen miles long if you ride along its outer edge, and in addition to a private airport, it has its own hospital, Little League, Olympic-size pool, tennis courts, restaurants, yacht club and dog park. Since social hour was about to commence, I told Danny not to say anything to the other cyclists, or anyone for that matter, about the fake pregnancy and he agreed.

We spent the rest of the ride doing interval training. Danny said I should take a rest day, but there were a lot of people on the Island and I couldn't help myself and had to ride hard. I felt bad ignoring Danny because he's a very knowledgeable coach and wants to help. I'd actually hire him for coaching, in addition to massage, if I thought for a second I would listen to him instead of doing my own thing. Ironically, it's commonly assumed that Danny coaches me since we both ride together so much. Neither of us has corrected this misconception because it has resulted in Danny raking in a lot of clientele, particularly women, who think that Danny is responsible for my meteoric improvement in cycling.

When I got home after the ride, Jenna II went ape-shit as usual; howling, jumping around and licking my face. He keeps this up until he gets distracted, usually by the need to lick his ass. During his ass-licking, he forgets about his excitement and returns to normal temperament until I leave the house again. He does this every time I walk in the door. If I go out and get the newspaper and walk back in the house, he acts like I've been gone for months. This is the sort of attention on which I thrive and I think more people should feel this way about me.

Jenna II generally goes by his nicknames, Santino or Sonny, which he acquired within six months of my owning him. First, because Jenna II is a male dog and I felt bad about his overly feminine name. Second, the double Jennas was confusing to my friends and acquaintances, who, until the name change, believed that I had an annoying habit of referring to myself in the third person whenever I wanted to eat, take a walk or go to the bathroom. Finally, Jenna II got his nickname because, while he's a sweetheart, he has a bit of a short temper around animals such as cats, birds, squirrels and other vermin. He does not chase other animals in a playful sense. The hair on his back stands straight up, he bares his teeth and goes for the kill. I have no doubt that Sonny ensures natural selection is accelerated in my backyard. Sonny is biracial. When people ask what kind of dog he is, I reply "Brown." It's easier than explaining that he has the howl of a beagle, size of a Lab, tongue of a chow, hair of a terrier, temperament of a pitbull and intelligence of a shoe.

I had a hard time sleeping. My nerves finally got to me and I spent the night alternating between feeling giddy at the prospect of becoming a pro cyclist and anxious with the dread of winding up in jail for fraud.

At 5:00 a.m., I finally gave up on sleep. I arrived in the office at six-thirty a.m., so my first order of business was to send an email to David so that he could see, by the time stamp on my email, my extreme dedication to the firm. David walks past my office every morning at exactly eight-fifteen am. As a result, I make it a point to get in by eighten am so that I am at my desk "working" when he walks by my office. On days when I'm in my office on or before seven a.m., I'm always sure to send David an unnecessary email. My hope is that he assumes I get to my desk around seven a.m. each and every day that I'm in my office before him, as my early arrival is how I justify my four-thirty p.m. departure to ride my bike.

After an hour of procrastination, I started working on the assignments that I had billed for the day before. At 10:30 a.m., David came by to check on me. "How are you doing?"

"Good," I said.

"What's that?" David asked, pointing to the jar on my desk labeled "tip jar."

"A tip jar," I said, making a point to read right from the jar.

"Why do you have it?" he asked.

"It's mostly a joke," I said, "but some people feel obligated to tip every time they see a jar, so it's a joke with an opportunity for profit."

"That's very unprofessional," David said.

"I agree, but clients rarely come to our office, let alone this floor, and never my office, so it's pretty low-risk," I said.

David threw it in my garbage can. Some people can't take a joke. I took it out and waited for his head to get beet red with anger before I said, "Relax, I'm just recycling it." I set it down next to my purse, smiled charmingly and said, "What can I do for you David?"

"Nothing, I'm just checking on how you're doing with your pregnancy."

"So far so good," I said.

"You know," David said conspiratorially, "I find the female naked pregnant body to be one of the most erotic sights. My wife and I had an obscene amount of sex during her two pregnancies."

Goddammit, I was going to vomit. Did thinking about baseball help you avoid vomiting? I stood up and made it three steps before projectile vomiting.

David said, "Are you okay? My wife was really lucky when she was pregnant, she never got sick."

The mere thought of his wife being "lucky" during a time she was having an "obscene amount of sex" with David Greene nearly set me off again. I excused myself by pushing David out of the way and hauling ass to the bathroom.

For a brief second, I was actually happy about the vomiting, as it validated my story, which I was paranoid someone would see through. I was in first grade the last time I threw up due to non-alcohol related causes. Granted, David's story was nauseating, but my stomach had held up under worse conditions. My body had impeccable timing.

CHAPTER THREE

Pregnancy transformed me from a half-assed lawyer to a one-eighth-assed lawyer. Within three days of my announcement, I was way behind on my work and not showing any signs of motivation. Since I work for insurance companies, I've always remained guilt-free in my slackery. However, in my new condition I felt comfortable lowering the bar a few more notches. Instead of only performing the minimal amount of work to avoid being fired, I now performed the minimal amount of work to avoid being pregnant and fired. As I understood it, it was pretty risky to fire a pregnant woman. I decided to do a little more pregnancy research to determine when I should start rubbing my stomach at all hours of the day and eating ice cream with chunks of pickles.

Week Four:

Mom: You are probably beginning to feel tired, urinate more frequently, experience mood swings, and possibly have tender or swollen breasts.

I actually have three out of four of those symptoms everyday anyway. It's nice to finally have a reason to be tired, bitchy and in the bathroom every fifteen minutes.

Baby: The chorionic villi are fully formed by the end of this week. In one study, 100% of the transvaginal ultrasounds showed a gestational sac. The yolk sac that helps feed your baby until the placenta is fully functional is appearing as well.

Chorionic Villi? Transvaginal? Yolk sac? This all sounds icky.

Week Six:

Mom: Your breasts may tingle, feel heavy, the areola may become darker. Avoid changing cat litter for there is a risk of toxoplasmosis.

Yet another reason to be a dog person.

Baby: Upper and lower limb buds will appear this week. And the primordia of the liver, pancreas, lungs, and stomach are evident.

Limb buds actually sound adorable.

Week Eight:

Mom: You have probably scheduled your first office visit right now.
Sounds like someone is about to get a vacation day.

Baby: This week the baby's gonads will become either testes or ovaries.

Tough call. I guess I'm ambivalent as long as there's some guarantee that I don't have to take the girl to ballet or cheerleading practice.

Week Ten:

Mom: You are still tired, and nauseated. Your abdomen may begin to pooch out, but it will be more from bowel distension than the uterus.

Tired, nauseated and getting fat, from bowel distension no less. I can't believe people procreate.

Baby: The baby weighs in at 4 grams, or 4 paper clips. Tiny toes have formed. External genitalia are beginning to differentiate. External ears are completely formed, as well as the upper lip. The biggest accomplishment this week is the disappearance of the tail!

That's a shame. The tail sounds even cuter than limb buds.

Amid my pregnancy research, David walked into my office. I quickly minimized the pregnancy screen. Under the pregnancy screen was a Cyclingnews article; minimize. Under Cyclingnews was my bank statement; minimize. Personal email; minimize. Motion to Compel; I'll leave that one up.

"Hi David."

"We have a problem."

Oh shit, he knows. How the hell could he have figured it out? "Yes."

"You're not documenting your files thoroughly. I know you're doing the work, but you need to make notes in the file. Right now, if you were to die, no one would be able to pick up where you left off."

What a jackass. Couldn't he have just said, "maternity leave"? Does he really need to kill me in this hypothetical? "Sure David, I'll document the file."

"You understand right? I mean if a bus hits you while you're on your bike tonight, it would be very hard for us to manage your case load."

"Got it," I said, starting to worry that David had a hit out on me.

"Also," David said, "I presume you drafted the complaint in the Akers case."

David has a tendency to intentionally presume incorrectly. We have a system at the office whereby every employee can see the status of any case in all of the Johnson Smith offices. David checks the status of all of my cases on the computer; then, instead of telling me to complete an assignment, or better yet, just waiting until I have a chance to do it, given my "load" of fifty files, he says, "I presume you've done X."

I lied and replied, "Yes, I drafted the complaint." This response put David in an uncomfortable position because in order to accuse me of lying, he must admit that he was acting like a jackass and asked a question to which he knew the answer. On the other hand, if he says nothing, then I "get away" with lying. It would never occur to David that I'm just fucking with him.

Not surprisingly, David did not like being backed into a corner. "Can I see it?"

"Sure," I said nonchalantly. "I'll throw it in your inbox as soon as I finish up this motion to compel."

David stared at me, clearly trying to come up with a creative way to pursue the point. During his pause, I faced my computer screen and pasted a contemplative expression on my face, a look I imagined I would wear if I ever put my mind to my job. David, who could not come up with a sane way to pursue the matter, gave up and left. As soon as he was out of view, I hurriedly began drafting the complaint, which I would backdate and put in his inbox within the hour. Then, I'd bill two hours for it; on yesterday's billing of course. It would kill David not to call me out on the lie.

* * *

On Wednesday, I met up with Paul, the guy from the Dubliner who could quote *Tommy Boy*. We met up to ride around the Island. Paul's bike was an eight-speed steel Peugeot that was at least ten years old. I had been concerned that he would show up wearing an imitation Tour de France Yellow Jersey riding on a hybrid bike with goofy clip-on aerobars, so I was relieved when he showed up looking like a more seasoned cyclist than I. Paul was very comfortable on the bike and had no problem holding a conversation over the two-hour easy ride. In fact, he kept the pace a little higher than I would have on an easy off-season spin.

The goal during the off-season is to put in a shitload of base miles every day. Base miles are easy miles, usually at a high cadence and low intensity; a conversational pace using mostly easy gearing. Most professional cyclists ride a minimum of four hours and up to eight hours each day of the off-season. I do this on the weekends, but during the week, because of my awesome job, I can only ride two hours per day given the restricted daylight during this time of year. In addition to these two-hour rides, I run and lift weights during the off-season, but only with my legs. In cycling, the upper body is strictly for breathing and there is no need to bulk up.

During the ride, Paul and I talked about cycling, work and family. He was not particularly funny in that he didn't make me laugh, but he seemed to have a decent sense of humor nonetheless. Paul rode with me back to my house, then rode his bike home to his apartment. I thought about inviting him in and ending my increasingly lengthy sexual drought. I had a bike light I could have loaned Paul so that he could ride home in the dark. However, I aborted those plans when Paul leaned in for a kiss, then veered to my cheek. I guess the rumor about wholesome Minnesota boys was true.

The next day, Paul called me and invited me to go out Friday night for dinner at eight. I planned to do a double-century ride in Gainesville the next morning, so I preferred to slam beers at happy hour, then go to bed at nine, but I figured I had to eat anyway, so I accepted.

Over dinner, I told Paul about my weekend plans. A "century" is a 100 mile ride. A double-century is back-to-back centuries, usually on a Saturday and Sunday. While it was not uncommon for me to ride 100 miles each Saturday and Sunday during the off-season, it was uncommon for me to pay to do it with a bunch of inexperienced cyclists who had trained all year for the event. However, I always enjoyed riding in Gainesville, and was overdue to visit my old roommate Jackie, who was still in school finishing her nineteen-year Ph.D. program. I told Paul he was welcome to come along and ride with me, and he accepted immediately. While I wasn't crazy about Paul, I felt good about the possibility that he might grow on me. After all, he was a tall, handsome, well-employed guy who didn't balk at my desire to drive two hundred and fifty miles in order to bike two hundred miles.

After dinner, Paul dropped me off and kissed me on the lips and left. It was open mouth, but no tongue. What the fuck was this guy's deal? It worked out though, since I had to pack and get up early the next day.

The next day was perfect. The weather for the Saturday Gainesville ride was seventy degrees and sunny with only a slight wind. The campus at the University of Florida was beautiful and pristinely maintained. As always, the brick buildings and manicured landscaping appeared to be autoclaved daily. The funding for this upkeep flowed from alumni who paid $100,000 a year to the school for fifty-yard-line football tickets and great game day parking. The state of Florida often matched these generous donations, provided that the University showed that it was needed for a project. Consequently, it was not uncommon for the school to spend millions of dollars tearing down an old brick building and constructing an old-looking brick building in its place.

In stark contrast to the campus, the outskirts of Gainesville are mostly undeveloped with the exception of the thousands of acres of horse farms and citrus groves. The gated mansions on these properties are blocks away from the trailers and shacks of the people who work the properties. The smooth black asphalt beside the mansions changes abruptly in front of the trailers and shacks to white dusty roads comprised of crushed shells and sugar sand. As a seasoned Gainesville cyclist, I barely noticed the jarring transformation in the road surface. It was only when I rode with someone new, such as Paul, that it occurred to me how obnoxious it is that the county didn't just pave the entire road.

In between these residences are lakes and parks owned by either the state or the University. My favorite park is Devils Millhopper, a 120-foot limestone sinkhole that has transformed into a mini-rainforest. Devils Millhopper remains cool during the hot and humid Florida summer and wet during Florida's spring droughts. Since Paul and I were not in any particular hurry, we took a detour and rode down into the sinkhole. We also stopped at a "sag" station every twenty miles and filled up on Oreos, Fig Newtons and water. It crossed my mind a few times during the day that every bike ride of mine could be this relaxing if I didn't have a psychotic desire to turn every delightful task into a cutthroat competition, or even better, if I channeled my competitive nature in another direction. My life would be much easier if I were competitive at my office and relaxed on the bike.

After the ride, we had just enough time to shower before meeting my old roommate Jackie and her boyfriend for dinner. This was the third time I'd stayed with Jackie for a cycling-related event and I always took her out for dinner. Jackie didn't expect it, but she was still a student without a real job, so I felt obligated to treat her. Besides, if I didn't stay with Jackie, I would have to pay for a hotel, so I usually wound up ahead of the game. However, this time, we were a party of four at a nice restaurant instead of just Jackie and me at a bar. There seemed to be no tactful way for me to pick up Jackie's check and leave her boyfriend and Paul to pay, so, I resigned myself to spending two hundred plus on dinner instead of half of a one-hundred-dollar hotel.

Fortunately, by the time the check arrived I was filled with sangria, which tended to make me overly generous. I reached out to grab the bill, but Paul took it and put his card down without looking at it. I grabbed my wallet and made the courtesy offer to split the check with him, secretly hoping he'd decline. He obliged. Paul's picking up the check not only saved me money, but was a pretty good sign that he was trying to get laid.

When we got to Jackie's, Paul and I retired to the room that was my bedroom four years ago when Jackie and I were roommates. We lay on the dog-hair-covered futon and started making out. Paul seemed to be very involved and passionate even though five minutes or so had already passed and he had yet to put his hands anywhere but my face. I wanted to be into the prolonged romantic kissing, but it wasn't doing it for me and I really wanted him to move things along.

Ten minutes later, we were still making out like teenagers, minus the passion and dry humping. My mission to get laid and thereby feel normal was not going well. I didn't know what to do. I had never had to initiate sex before. I was beginning to think I was dating a gay guy. I knocked my leg into his crotch for research. He was hard, but he recoiled away from my leg. I was truly puzzled. He was picking up checks and getting hard-ons, then stopping at first base. I was so bored that I abruptly called it a night.

The next day, we drove back to Tampa. After dropping Paul off, I headed over to Sunday night dinner at my parents' house. I was tired and didn't feel like going, but they were watching Sonny and I had to pick him up. As I was getting out of my car, David jogged past their house in his nut-hugging jogging shorts. It was like seeing a teacher out of school and I was not happy, though I gave a very excited, "Hi David, I didn't know you jog."

"I run every day at four a.m."

Technically, he was not even jogging let alone running. He was putzing around at a ten-minute-mile pace. Still, I decided only to react to the 4:00 a.m. bullshit. I looked at my watch. "It's seven p.m."

"I mean during the week. I might have to choose a new exercise temporarily, I'm having neck surgery."

"Why? Are you okay?" Please be out of work a long time. Please be out of work a long time. Please be out of work a long time.

"When I was a child, my mom dropped me and damaged my neck. I've been able to push through the pain my entire life."

Everything was starting to make sense. I decided to fuck with him. "Why are you getting the surgery now then? You can't take the pain anymore?"

"I'm a partner now, I can afford to take time off. You on the other hand, this pregnancy will really set you back. You'll never make partner now."

I could not believe a lawyer could know so little about the law. I could sue him just for saying that. Too bad I wasn't actually pregnant.

I decided to switch gears. "Why don't you try riding a bike? That's low impact and shouldn't hurt your neck."

"I can't ride a bike, it hurts my balls."

I did not need to know that. I debated whether to engage and opted to do so. "You could get a more comfortable saddle and wear padded bike shorts."

"Nothing can help me. My balls are really sensitive, my wife will back me up on this."

I officially had way too much information about David's nut sac. "Good to know. I'm late for dinner, I have to go."

But David replied, "So do your parents know yet?"

"Know what?" I asked.

"About the baby."

How the hell did I forget about that whopper? "Not yet. I'm only a month pregnant and I'd like to enjoy a few more months of peace before I tell them."

"Well, if you need someone, you know I'm always here."

"Thanks," I said, pondering ways to confide in David and freak him out.

I was barely in the door before my mom started quizzing me about Paul. I told her we went to Gainesville, rode bikes and had a good time, but there was no need to start designing her mother-of-the-bride gown.

A few minutes later, John and Julie arrived. John is a funeral director and embalmer. In spite of their thirty-year age gap, John and my dad are clones. Both of them are workaholics who pride themselves on long hours and lack of sleep. Thank God I didn't get that gene. To make matters worse, they both practice in areas in which I would rather drink acid than work: accounting and funeral directing. While they are both very fun and personable, you couldn't help thinking about the inevitability of death and taxes whenever the two of them are together.

Dinner was fairly uneventful. John started telling us about his work week. The highlights were picking up a dead bum who wasn't found for three weeks and was decayed and covered in maggots; embalming an 800-pound woman whose arteries were so blocked that John had to run embalming fluid through her from six different points to get the fluid completely circulated, only to find out later that she was too big for her pre-ordered casket and had to be cremated; working on a kid whose forehead had to removed from a dashboard and re-formed prior to a viewing; and a guy with a Nazi tattoo that John got to cremate. Typical day at the office.

* * *

A week later, I went into David's office after he returned from his surgery. He had been out for the week and it seemed like I had been on vacation for two. This meeting was going to suck. I would have to hear about his neck surgery, then give him a detailed update of every single one of my cases. When David was in the office, I often went for months without dissecting each case with him. But every time he missed a day of work he insisted on discussing each case ad nauseam.

"How did the neck surgery go?" I asked, thankful he was wearing a neck brace which reminded me to offer sympathy.

"Excellent. The doctor said he's never seen anyone recover as well as me. It's because I'm so fit. It was funny actually, one of the tests the doctor gave me to make sure the strength returned to my arms was that he asked me to push against his chest. So I did it, and accidentally shoved the doctor across the room. I couldn't help it, I'm just so strong that he flew in the other direction when I touched him."

I involuntarily rolled my eyes and hoped David didn't see it.

He continued, saying, "I told the doctor he was lucky that I just underwent surgery because I was likely to kill him if he asked me to do that before I endured surgery. I told him I bench two hundred and twenty pounds and he couldn't believe it. Can you?"

"I have no frame of reference, I'm not a gym rat."

"It's a lot. Sometimes I see your dad at the gym and he only benches one hundred and fifty. Then again, he's not big like me."

I had no doubt that David actually checked out how much my dad benches, so I just gave the answer that every first grader gives and said, "My dad is bigger than you."

"No he's not."

"Well I don't know about chest and biceps measurements, but he's taller than you."

"No he's not, I'm six feet."

"He's six-two."

"No he's not."

I almost said, "Really, did you measure him while checking out how much he benches?" but refrained. I was not surprised that David had an irrational self-body image; just surprised I had never realized it. He's forty-four years old and in average shape; not skinny or muscular, just medium. My dad is sixty-one years old, also average, but apparently he benches less than David. Still, my money would be on my dad if the two of them fought since he was from South Philly instead of South Tampa. I suddenly had the urge to set up a fight between my dad and my boss. *Dad vs. Boss* could be a new reality TV series.

"So you agree, he's not six-two?"

"I haven't measured him lately, but the mark on the wall when we were kids said six-two."

"I think he shrunk, he's at least four inches shorter than me."

"You think he's five-nine? There's no way." How did I get involved in this conversation? I was defending my dad's height.

"I'll check it out next time I see him at the gym, but I don't want to measure until I'm completely healed."

"You should measure now, that brace has to be making you look taller," I said, smiling uncontrollably as I pictured David and my dad standing back to back for an official measurement.

David thought about that for a second, then said, "Let's go over your case list."

I never thought I'd be so happy to talk about subrogation.

After I left David's office, I told my co-worker Kimberly about David's insane height comparison to my father. She told me that when she was in his office hearing the story about his amazing strength and recovery from neck surgery, David had compared himself to Warren Sapp, once a multiple all-pro defensive tackle for the Bucs and retired for several years, but David wasn't exactly up to date in the realm of sports. Apparently, "pound for pound" David was stronger than that "fat ass" Sapp. What the hell else had David's mother done to him to make him so delusional? Dropping him as an infant could not have done all of the damage.

Later in the day, I met my dad for lunch. His office is a few miles away from mine, so we meet once a week. Dad picked up sandwiches and salads and met me at my house to eat them. We sat on the back deck, which was started by Jason during his last summer vacation. Jason is big on starting projects, but not finishing them. He built me a deck that fit one chair on it, then quit. Fortunately, Danny finished the deck and accepted payment in the form of a steady supply of cold beer.

The weather was a little hot, even in the shade, but it was nice to sit outside. Dad was finishing up a Tootsie Pop when I arrived.

I said, "Let me guess, cherry."

Ten years ago, Tootsie Pops began to celebrate Valentine's Day by selling bags of special Valentine's Tootsie Pops, all of which were cherry flavored. This has drastically improved the quality of my father's life. He calculates that there is an average of fourteen Tootsie Pops per bag. Ideally, he likes to have two per day. Therefore, he buys fifty-two bags of cherry Tootsie Pops every February and squirrels them away in the house, eating a bag a week. It is not uncommon to find him in the big corner office of his CPA firm eating cherry Tootsie Pops like a five-year-old while planning the financial future of large corporations.

"It is cherry as a matter of fact. How are you, Jenna?"

"Doing good. How tall are you?"

"Six-two."

"David said you're five-nine and that he benches eighty more pounds than you, I think you should beat him up."

"Excuse me?" Dad said.

"You going to beat him up?" I asked.

"I'll probably let it slide."

I give my dad a lot of credit for developing my personality, which may or may not be a good thing. Obviously, there's the genetics; but mostly he tormented me into having a sense of humor. Looking back, I can fully appreciate how much fun this must have been for my dad, but at the time I cried myself to sleep.

As a kid, I did not understand that the wailing of the fire alarm did not necessarily mean there was an actual fire. My dad realized this when Mom baked grouper with the oven door ajar. As soon as the smoke alarm went off, I ran out of the house. After this discovery, the fire alarm game became dad's favorite party trick. Whenever my parents had company, he showed off his little daughter's intellect by lighting a match next to the fire alarm and laughing his ass off as I ran out of the house screaming. When I finally came back into the house, he said he had to fight the fire all by himself and didn't appreciate me leaving the rest of the family to burn to death. The next time he did this, I tried to convince him to leave with me but he wouldn't do it, he had to stay and protect the family. I thought about helping out, but ultimately, I ran out of the house leaving them to die a fiery death without me. The guilt kept me up nights.

At my first grade birthday party, dad held my cake up to the fire alarm and all of my friends made fun of me when I ran out of the house screaming. My birthday parties were always a time for dad to humiliate me. In second grade I had a sleep-over party with fourteen friends. When we finally went to sleep, Dad played my mom's Halloween audio cassette of wolves howling and "ghost" noises. Once we were all awake and scared shitless, he and John jumped out from behind the couch dressed up like ghosts, and screamed. My mom really appreciated all of the piss and shit stains on her carpet courtesy of my terrified friends.

The third grade party wasn't much better. Dad told me to sniff the flower on my cake. I had seen this trick before and wisely declined. In response, Dad told me I was a smart girl, then lifted the cake to my face and smashed it. It was an ice cream cake and gave me an externally induced ice cream headache which I found surprising, even as I began crying. I kept crying during the thirty-minute shower that I had to take during my birthday party in order to get the icing out of my hair. From fourth grade on I abstained from birthday parties in the presence of Michael Rosen.

My pregnancy plan was surely an extension of my dad's old pranks. Granted, his pranks were just jokes, whereas mine served my self-interest. I thought about telling Dad about the invented pregnancy. Even though he hated competitive cycling, he should understand my obsession with competition because I inherited it directly from him.

He played competitive sports every spare minute of the day from the time he was born until he entered his mid-forties, at which time he still exercised religiously, but his competitive nature was forced to find other outlets. For instance, when Dad got contact lenses for the first time at the age of fifty, he spent an hour perfecting his technique, then asked me to time his performance. His latest competition is as a highly skilled omelet flipper. Each Sunday morning, after my dad's bike ride, swim and trip to the gym, he makes omelets while my mom reads the paper. Dad lets her read in peace for a time, then calls her name frantically, at which time she must look up from her article and applaud the velocity and precision of "the flip."

If anyone would understand the urge to get the fuck out of an office and enjoy the outdoors six hours a day racing strangers all over the country, it was dear old dad. In the end, I decided not to tell him because there was a good chance that, in addition to understanding, he would become a raving lunatic and disown me.

* * *

By the end of November, Paul and I had been dating nearly a month. A record for me I had never even come close to approaching. I wasn't sure what base we were on, but it wasn't home. I wasn't even remotely into him anymore, but I was determined to make it work because I hadn't found anything wrong with him, and I really needed to date someone longer than a month and get laid, because that streak was extending beyond the two year mark. Accomplishing these two goals before my thirtieth birthday would go a long way toward helping me feel like a normal woman. If ugly people, psychopaths and even Sarah Smith, the wonder paralegal, could handle that, surely I could.

On a Thursday night, I invited Paul over to cook for me. I wanted it to be romantic, but I don't cook, so this seemed the best option. Paul brought ingredients to make his family's recipe for Cincinnati Chili. I was prepared for the evening. I looked great, had clean bed sheets and plenty of empty peanut butter jars. In essence, empty peanut butter jars are my sex toys because my dog licks the peanut butter remnants while I have sex. Without them, or something equally yummy and time consuming, Sonny tends to howl and try to eat his way through my bedroom door, creating quite a ruckus. I had over two years worth of peanut butter jars that I stockpiled just in case I met someone. Unfortunately, they tended to serve less as a distraction for my dog and more as a reminder to me that I'd been celibate for an inordinately long stretch of time.

Paul cooked his chili, which tasted remarkably similar to spaghetti with cinnamon. We ate on the deck and played fetch with Sonny, who became excited and started humping Paul. It was frustrating that my neutered dog was getting more action than me from Paul. Sonny never humps me when it's just the two of us. But the second company comes over, Sonny gets really excited and starts humping anything in sight.

Initially, I tried solving this problem by having my friends tell Sonny that they had a headache. When that didn't work, I bought Sonny a girlfriend, a stuffed elephant that was slightly larger than him. Whenever Sonny started humping my friends' legs, I substituted their leg with his elephant. Sonny is not a gentle lover. He grabs his elephant by the trunk, thrashes it around, then humps it. My friends found this hugely amusing and it has become such a famous party trick that the elephant has become extremely tattered and worn out. Now, whenever Sonny shakes the elephant, its stuffing falls out of the holes where Sonny ripped out its eyeballs, and I have to clean every time a guest leaves the house.

Paul was familiar with Sonny's humping problem from past experience. So, when the humping started, Paul walked into the house dragging Sonny on his leg, and got the elephant. We watched the animal porn for a while, then went into the house. Paul brought a movie over, put it into the DVD player, and sat on the couch. I sat down next to him and initiated a make-out session. We were both fully clothed and on top of each other when I finally called a time out and invited Paul into my bedroom. I littered the floor with peanut butter jars, and shut my bedroom door.

Ten minutes later, we were still fully clothed. I was bored and absent-mindedly cracked my knuckles while he was kissing me. Then I said, "I have condoms."

He said, "That's not it. You're going to think this is weird, but I'm saving myself for marriage."

"Get the fuck outta here." I said laughing. Paul wasn't laughing, so I asked, "Seriously?"

"Yes."

"I didn't know you were religious."

"I'm not, but I went to twelve years of Catholic school and I think it's important to wait until marriage before having sex."

"That rule was invented when people got married at the age of twelve and lived until they were twenty-five. It's inapplicable today."

"Sorry, I know it sounds weird, but it doesn't mean we can't still have fun."

"What do you mean?"

"Well, you know."

"No, I don't. I have no idea what you're talking about. You're a twenty-five-year-old virgin by choice. What is the other way you have fun?"

"Oral and, well, anal if you want."

"You're kidding right?" I asked.

"No," he said. "It's not sex."

"You mean to tell me that, for God, you only engage in oral and anal sex?

Paul turned red and mumbled, "I've never had anal, but I'm okay with it if you want."

"Did the Jesuits teach you that? No wonder they're okay with molestation, they don't think its sex."

"No they didn't teach us that," Paul said, getting visibly angry. "It just makes sense."

"Actually, it's completely illogical. It's amazing that you blend into society like a normal person. I'm stunned," I said.

"This isn't funny."

"I'm not laughing," I pointed out.

Paul paused, looked at me earnestly, and said, "You know, I don't care that you're not a virgin if that's what this is about."

"That thought actually never crossed my mind. As an aside, you're not a virgin either if you've come in a girl's mouth while the two of you were bare-ass naked."

"Of course I am," Paul insisted. Then he said, "Stop making fun of my religion."

"I don't care what religion you are so long as you're not religious," I replied, just as earnestly.

"It's not just religion. You're treating me like a freak when this is just a decision I've made."

"I'm sorry, it's just that personally, I think you're crazy. Honestly, I would respect you more if you told me that this isn't really your belief system and it's just your ploy to create an all-oral sex relationship."

"I wouldn't do that," Paul insisted.

I opened the bedroom door, grabbed the untouched peanut butter jars off the floor and got dressed. Paul followed me out the door and went home.

* * *

The next day on the Island, Paul rode up to me and asked how I was doing.

I said, "Still in shock. You?"

"Still a little humiliated. Why don't we grab dinner tonight?"

Wow, he still thinks we're together. "Paul, I don't think this is going to work out."

"Why?" he asked in all seriousness.

"Didn't we already cover this last night?"

"That's it? You can't make a sacrifice for a while and see how it goes?"

That thought actually did cross my mind for one fleeting second. I thought, I can deal with this for a bit, during which time I'll convince Paul that his views on sex are warped and irrational. However, the real issue was that the relationship was going nowhere and now I had the perfect excuse to end it. While I was sure I could change him into a well-adjusted atheist, I was far from gaga. So, I decided it was best not to spoil him for his future wife.

I looked at Paul and said, "Sorry, your warped stance on sex is kind of a deal breaker for me."

"You're really breaking up with me over this?"

"Yes, and it's not me, it's you."

Paul sprinted off with a pissed look on his face and I let him go. A few minutes later, I met up with Danny. He immediately asked me why I wasn't riding with Paul. I swore him to secrecy, then told him the story. He laughed his ass off for a good three miles.

That Sunday night at dinner, I told my family about Paul. I hadn't planned to tell them. But after a half hour of listening to how picky I was and how I broke guys' hearts for no reason, I was forced to defend myself. I was glad I had such a good reason to dump him. Dumping him for improper earwax levels would have set my mom over the edge.

I said, "Paul's a virgin."

"So deflower him," my mom said, a bit too eagerly for a mom talking to her daughter.

"By choice, Mom. He is a virgin by choice. He's saving himself for marriage."

I told them the whole story. My dad said, "Well that's one I haven't heard before." Mom laughed. Jason said that from here on out, he was dating exclusively within the Catholic faith. Julie's comments were restricted to a "that's so fucked up" every few minutes or so, and John didn't believe me. On the plus side, they were all off my back for dumping Paul the Wonderful.

* * *

In December, I started wearing baggy clothes to work. According to my research, it didn't seem like maternity clothes were necessary just yet, but I figured I should begin the transition. Because it was the off-season for cycling, there were almost no cycling-related articles for me to read as a method of procrastination. I decided this was a good time for me to read up on my second trimester, which was just around the corner.

Week Thirteen:
Mom: *This is usually the time when mothers feel their best. They are also beginning to feel pregnant.*
These two sentences seemed at odds with each other.
Baby: *There are a lot of things going on this week! All twenty teeth have formed and are waiting (Teething is yet to come!). Your baby weighs in at approximately 1 ounce.*
I thought babies were born without teeth. One ounce? My cycling pedals weigh 5.7 ounces. I think I have a ways to go.

Week Fourteen:
Mom: *The hormonal changes in your body are becoming apparent. You may have also developed a dark line down the middle of your abdomen to your pubic bone called a linea negra. The areola may have darkened and gotten larger as well.*
Nice to know David finds linea negra and dark areola to be insanely sexy.
Baby: *Your baby is now producing urine and actually urinating into the amniotic fluid.*
That's fucking nasty.

Week Fifteen:

Mom: *Your belly starts to show.*

I marked my calendar to start wearing maternity clothes around the end of January.

Baby: *Your baby may have developed the habit of sucking his or her thumb.*

Stop it fake baby, because I'm not getting you braces.

It seemed as though there was nothing for me to do until I needed to look bigger after the holidays. Something that inadvertently happened anyway to us all. I shut the screen and continued my research project for the day: learning the in-depth historical significance to every lyric of *We Didn't Start the Fire*. As I was doing this, I received an email from "junk mail."

We have an interoffice email system whereby employees can email other employees by typing in their name, rather than their email address. This system also allows you to send emails to categories, like "Everyone", "Attorneys," "Paralegals," "Secretaries" etc.

There is also a category called "Junk Mail" to which any member of the office can opt in or out. Junk Mail is where employees try to sell or buy stuff from other employees, ask for feedback on restaurants and complain. I get about fifteen emails a day where people ask "Does anyone have a stamp I can buy?" This gets annoying, even if I'm just surfing the web and not working. However, I would never opt out of Junk Mail because it is a constant source of entertainment. I have a folder filled with Junk Mail highlights that I can't bear to throw out. The one I just received was focused on selling an algae-eating fish. I added it to my "Buy, Sell, Giveaway, Trade" Junk Mail folder. The fish was the fifth Junk Mail advertisement that made it to the folder this week. The other four items entered into the free market of Junk Mail were a used Halloween costume, a car, two cats, and a McDonald's sandwich. These items had very thorough descriptions. The costume was "Tina the Target" from "Psycho Circus Sideshow," including dress and accessories, for fifteen dollars. According to my colleague, it was a costume you "have to see, because it's hard to describe." The car was a fourteen-year-old Buick with 140,000 miles on it in need of "a little TLC" for only four grand. The cats, Andy and Cody, were described as "large and strong and let you pet them if you sneak up behind them while they're asleep." Both were free to a good home. A Filet O' Fish combo meal (without the drink) was available for two dollars and fifty cents because the meal was "buy one, get one free," and the person decided to sell the free sandwich, a picture of which was included in the Junk Mail advertisement. God I will miss Junk Mail during maternity leave.

CHAPTER FOUR

The week before Christmas, David sent an email to the entire subrogation department to inform us, "I do not want a holiday present. But if you insist, please make a charitable donation to the Tampa Jewish Community Center."

There are a lot of common sense notions that become workplace rules because people don't use logic. I'm quite sure that Johnson Smith will soon have a rule stating, "Do not ask people to donate money to your religious organization as a holiday present." There was no way I was going to give money to the JCC in David's name. First, because the JCC, like my alma mater, was doing quite well. I couldn't believe either institution had the gall to hit me up for money. Additionally, not to be insensitive, but I liked to give to charities that could someday benefit me. For example, I'm more likely to get breast cancer or have a head injury from a bike accident than to starve in Africa, so my funds go to brain and breast medical research. My final pet peeve about charities are the fundraisers. If anyone actually asked me to my face, rather than on email, to give them fifty dollars to walk three miles I'd punch them in the stomach. I donate to this shit all the time because it's for a good cause and it does some good, but I can't stand it. If someone wants fifty dollars for cancer research, I'll be happy to write a check. If someone wants to walk three miles or do a triathlon, register and do it. It's absurd for me to donate money to someone I barely know so that three months later they get off their ass and exercise one morning. It's even more ridiculous that a significant portion of the money raised by these do-gooders goes toward shutting down streets, providing refreshments and making crappy T-shirts instead of their worthy cause.

My gift from David was a fifty dollar gift certificate for the mall. David was incredibly cheap, so this impressed me until Kimberly told me that he gave her a $150 gift certificate for the mall. For some reason, it never occurred to me that my dislike for David was a two-way street.

The holidays came and went and it was still not yet time to start training or looking pregnant in earnest. On the biking front, I continued to crank out base miles even though I had become antsy to start riding balls-to-the-wall. The season was technically from February to October, but it was impossible to be in top form the entire time. Since my goal was to be competitive in September, there was no need for me to start intensity rides until at least February.

In mid-January, I took off for another of my five-to-seven-hour rides. I generally rode from my house to meet up with some friends in North Tampa. From there, a small group of us took off on a different route every Saturday and Sunday: to San Antonio, St. Petersburg, Lakeland, Tarpon, Plant City, Dunedin, Safety Harbor, West Chase, a loop around Tampa Bay, Zephyrhills, Palm Harbor, or Thonotosassa. This Saturday, we had a large group and rode to San Antonio via the Suncoast Trail. When we arrived, we ate Cuban sandwiches from the local market, rode around Dade City, then headed home through the well-fields, which required us to hop a fence. I'd ridden 104 miles by the time I arrived back at my house.

As usual, I wasn't hungry immediately when I got home, but I was starving ten minutes later when I got out of the shower. I ran out on my bike and picked up Thai food three blocks away. Make that 105 miles total for the day. I ate half of it, along with four glasses of water, then fell asleep outside on my hammock.

On Sunday, it was more of the same. A new face showed up on the Sunday ride, though he seemed to know everyone. I had been riding long enough to have had met nearly every serious cyclist in the Tampa Bay area, and even throughout Florida, so this surprised me that everyone knew this guy except me. During the ride, I learned that his name was Quinton and as it turned out, he rode and raced for several years, though this was his first ride in four years.

Quinton's reemergence on the cycling scene made me nervous because while I loved the social aspect of base miles, the main goal was to get the miles in. I didn't have patience for taking breaks for the guy who'd decided to take a four year hiatus. Fortunately, Quinton rode well and didn't bitch. We rode two abreast and there were seven of us. We rotated pulling at the front, each pedaling into the wind for a few miles, then peeling off and moving to the back until we wound up at the front again. We tended to pile up each time we approached a stop sign, disrupting our order and giving each of us a chance to talk to a new partner.

My goal on any ride with an uneven number of riders was to avoid being stuck without a partner. I like to talk a lot and feel better when someone is next to me either listening, or pretending to do so. The more someone laughs at my hilarious stories, the better. By the end of the ride, I had ridden with everyone, including Quinton.

The best way I can describe Quinton's appearance is average. Not tall but not short, maybe about five-ten with a medium build. He had decent leg muscles, but not the huge cycling thighs I've come to know and love. Average weight, but for a cyclist, he was on the heavy side in that he had more than four percent body fat. Quinton wore a helmet, so while I could tell his hair was blond, I couldn't decipher whether he had a receding hair line or bald spot. Either way, if he had a personality, he seemed datable.

I rode next to Quinton briefly and learned that he stopped cycling when his dad died, and never seemed to pick it up again until now. He was my age and grew up in Tampa as well. We talked about basic stuff like jobs and cycling. I gave him the short description of my job which was, "It's okay." He told me he was in the finance industry. Finance bores the shit out of me, so I didn't ask for any details.

Five years ago, before his father died, Quinton raced all over the country and lived out of his car. This intrigued me. I would never date a guy who, through some stroke of misfortune, lived in his car. However, if an intelligent person chose to live in his car rather than conform, I found that irresistible. I couldn't tell whether Quinton was intelligent, but he was quiet and worked in finance, so I was guessing that he was.

Even though Quinton wasn't very talkative, he asked for my number almost immediately. There is no better male quality than appreciation for Jenna Rosen. Clearly Quinton was gifted, as he picked up on my charm and beauty in spite of my goofy helmet and prolific shooting of snot rockets out of my nose to the ground.

Later in the ride, I told Danny that Quinton asked for my number.

Danny said, "I hope you gave him 867-5309 like you do with all of the other freaks who ask you out."

"Why?"

Danny got quiet and said, "Never mind, just be careful." I asked why but all I could get out of Danny was that Quinton was once very wild.

Danny tried not to act jealous when I had a date. That was the only explanation I had for the fact that, unlike everyone else we knew and gossiped about, Danny never had anything to say, good or bad, about any of my dating prospects, until they left the picture. He just sat back and waited for my bad date stories, which were always forthcoming, before he gave his opinions. But this was the first time Danny was acquainted with a potential suitor.

"Just tell me what you know," I said, annoyed by Danny's silence.

"I don't want to be an asshole and talk shit about the guy, especially since I haven't seen him in four years. Just be careful."

Danny's warning intrigued me. My impression of Quinton was of a quiet, smart guy with a wild streak that was presumably tamed by his father's death. Even though I only talked to Quinton for about twenty minutes, I was hoping he'd call me.

I learned my lesson after the virgin disaster and opted not to tell my parents about Quinton, or any other dates, until the relationship was firm. So Sunday dinner after the ride was pretty uneventful other than the fact that Julie showed up with a new set of boobs. I hugged her hello and complimented her rack, which was spilling unnaturally out of her top and looked ridiculous with her size zero waist.

My dad's response was much more classic. He said, "Holy shit, I think those are bigger than Jenna's."

"Thanks Dad, those are the words every daughter longs to hear," I said, rolling my eyes and turning bright red.

"Seriously, they're huge."

"They're a full C," Julie said.

"I'm calling bullshit on that," I replied. "They're a D. I'm a C and as Dad so eloquently pointed out, yours are bigger." In truth, I was a C when I used to run, but they shrunk to a B as I became leaner with competitive cycling. However, I did not want to point this out because it would weaken the boob inflation argument in which I was about to partake.

"I special ordered these. I assure you, they're a C."

"This is the problem with fake boobs," I explained. "Every woman wants huge knockers but no one wants to act greedy and ask for a size D. So C has become D and now I have to try on a bra before buying it because I never know what size the bra company is using for a C. It's boob inflation."

"They're inflated all right." John said. "I bought the left one."

"You're such a romantic."

"Thanks, Jenna."

"They don't even look real," Mom said. "No one's boobs are that big if they're as skinny as you."

"Mine are," Julie said, "and they look hot!"

Julie looked to me for approval, so I put my feminist thoughts aside and said, "Nice titties, Julie."

My mom play-slapped my face and said, "Jenna."

"Sorry. I always forget what words you hate other than cunt. Julie, I meant to say, nice breasts."

My Mom smacked me again for saying "cunt," then turned to Julie and said, "You're going to have to get a whole new wardrobe. Do you want to shop this weekend?"

"Sure."

"Jenna?"

"No, I'm still allergic. But feel free to pick out nice stuff for me."

My mom is my savior. I like to wear nice clothes, shoes and accessories, but hate shopping. Besides, I spend all of my money and time cycling. Fortunately, my mom loves shopping and spending money and has great taste. She started shopping for me when I was born and never managed to break the habit. Every time someone compliments my clothes or jewelry and asks where I got it, I shrug and say, "Not sure, my mommy bought it for me." I know my mom loves me, but somewhere in the deep recesses of her mind, I'm pretty sure she thinks that I was switched with her real daughter at birth.

Quinton emailed me on Monday at work, which I appreciated. I'm not a patient person and I hate the game where a guy waits the obligatory three days before contacting me so he doesn't appear to be desperate. Unfortunately, Quinton's writing was atrocious. He couldn't spell, didn't know grammar or punctuation, and wrote as if he were an eight-year-old girl.

He asked me, "What muzic u like"

I replied, "Anything but country," which is technically true, though in actuality, I barely own any CDs and mostly listen to easy listening stations or Pandora. I love Neil Diamond Radio and Air Supply Radio. The downside to these stations is that the advertisers are under the mistaken impression that I'm either a hopeless romantic or a baby boomer. Can't I just listen to *Making Love Out of Nothing at All* without anyone jumping to conclusion that I want to see the latest sappy romantic comedy or buy Viagra and anal suppositories?

Quinton typed, "Bluegrass 2nite"

Hmm. I typed, "What exactly is the difference between Bluegrass and Country?"

Quinton responded, "pic u up at 7"

I was officially nervous. I guess it was possible that he was emailing me from a Blackberry or iPhone and omitting letters out of laziness, even though the bottom of the message didn't say, "Sent from my iPhone." Or, he could be dyslexic, in a good way, like Einstein. I decided to withhold judgment and go with the flow.

Quinton picked me up exactly on time, bearing flowers. So far so good. He pet Sonny, and was a good sport when Sonny started humping his leg. We left my house and he opened my car door for me. What a gentleman.

Once we got into the car, Quinton put in an awful CD, played twelve seconds of a song, took it out, put in a new CD and said, "You have to hear this one, too." They were both techno songs, so I couldn't discern the difference, but I said I liked them both because I didn't want to instigate a conversation about my closet addiction to *Delilah After Dark*. Twelve seconds later, Quinton put in a new CD. More techno. This continued. It seemed very important to Quinton that I listen to his entire CD collection during our ten-minute drive. A little odd, but I focused on reserving judgment.

The concert was at the Tampa Theater, a beautiful building in downtown and a Tampa institution. We were early, so we went to the bar next door called The HUB. Downtown Tampa does not exactly thrive after the workday ends, so The HUB was strictly a drinking bar. The drink special was incredibly strong well liquor, two-for-one. I assumed Quinton had picked me up over an hour before the concert so that we could go to dinner, so I hadn't eaten anything. To make matters worse, I had just finished riding sixty miles, so I was especially hungry and dehydrated. I took my first sip of gin and tonic and felt it in my legs immediately. It tasted awful. I hadn't had such a strong well drink since I was able to imbibe legally. I nursed it and by the time I finished that first drink, I was already a little drunk, but mostly just nauseous. Quinton, on the other hand, finished two drinks. I prided myself on my ability to pound liquor with the boys, so I tried to step it up, but it was just too nasty. Plus, my stomach, which had been spoiled by a lifetime of square meals and top-shelf liquor, was in knots. Quinton downed my second drink for me, and got us another round. I like a guy who can hold his liquor, and was duly impressed.

The next gin and tonic seemed to be even stronger than the last. By now, other bluegrass concertgoers were entering the bar. Because I didn't own any thrift shop clothes, I didn't blend in with this crowd any better than the drinking crowd already gathered in the bar when we entered.

We hung out, talking very little. Then, Quinton announced it was time to get going. I looked down and his two drinks were gone. He downed my second drink, his sixth, and I'd put just enough of a dent in mine that I could leave it on the table without quite finishing it and feel I'd done my duty.

We walked next door to the Tampa Theater. Quinton bought three large beers; one for us to drink immediately, and one each for us during the concert. I took a sip of the communal beer and handed it to Quinton. He downed it and we were on our way. This was the moment when it occurred to me that rather than being embarrassed by my low tolerance, I should determine whether Quinton was an alcoholic. He was my driver after all. As we walked to our seats, Quinton ran into some friends and became animated. A good sign. Obviously he was very sociable once you got to know him. His friends passed us a joint. I'm no angel, but "Local Lawyer Disbarred for Smoking Marijuana in Public" was not a headline I aspired to read. Plus, I'd hate to get disbarred before my maternity leave. I passed the joint on like I was playing a game of hot potato. The concert began. The seats were good and I enjoyed the first two songs though I'd never listened to bluegrass before. Unfortunately, I didn't have a very long attention span for concerts. Music was something I listened to while I was driving, cleaning or riding my bike. It wasn't a visual medium and standing in one spot listening to music without multi-tasking was not my thing.

I told Quinton I had to go to the bathroom. I did have to go, but not that bad. I just wanted a break in the action. He said he had to go too, so we walked downstairs. I got in the long line for the ladies' room and he walked into the men's room. When he came out, I was still in line. Quinton told me to just go in the men's room because there was a stall I could use. I wasn't in a hurry to get back to the concert, but any method of avoiding a line sounded good to me. I went to the men's room, walked past the line of urinals and went into a stall. When I emerged from the stall, Quinton was still standing there. I walked over to wash my hands and he moved in with a kiss.

I was caught a little off-guard. After my last dating fiasco, I was relieved by his aggression. However, I was not expecting a first date make-out session to present itself until I was being dropped off at the end of the night, and certainly not in a men's room. The mid-date kiss was unique, particularly since I could see a line of men peeing in my peripheral vision. I ended the awkward kiss as quickly as I could and we went back to the concert, which seemed to go on forever. Just when I thought I couldn't stand there any longer, it ended. I said, "Great, I'm starving." It was then that Quinton informed me it was only intermission. Shit.

"Do you want to leave?" he asked.

"No, I'm enjoying myself," I replied. As the words came out of my mouth, I had misgivings. "Unless you want to leave."

"Whatever you want," Quinton said.

I was tired, hungry and bored. It was 9:30 on a Monday night and I hadn't even had dinner yet. "Yeah, let's get something to eat."

We left the concert and walked toward Quinton's car. He seemed to be walking a straight line, so I got in. Quinton immediately started swapping his CDs in and out again. It occurred to me that he had very severe ADD. Quinton took a few unfamiliar turns, then pulled into a bar called Tiny Tap, which was off the beaten path. I had heard of it through word of mouth, but had never been there.

The descriptions of Tiny Tap were not an exaggeration. It was a dive bar for serious drinkers, with six bar stools and Pabst Blue Ribbon on tap. It was super tiny, dark, smoky and depressing. However, it perked up when Quinton entered. Quinton was to the Tiny Tap as Norm was to Cheers. He said hi to all of his buddies, introduced me around and asked if I wanted a drink. My stomach felt like it was eating itself. I told Quinton that I didn't want a drink, but he ordered two Budweisers anyway. I don't even like Budweiser. Fortunately, and unfortunately, both beers were for Quinton. He downed one during the introductions and took the other one to go. Bold move. I had never been on a first date where the guy ordered a roader. I was now convinced that Quinton was an alcoholic.

I told Quinton I was tired and ready to go home. He said he would drop me off after dinner. I really wanted dinner and I knew I would have to get it myself if I declined Quinton's offer, as my refrigerator was only stocked with beer, wine and Yoo-hoo. Besides, I felt I had earned a free dinner after the night I'd had. I sat back and let him drive to a restaurant. Two seconds later, I sat back up and decided to stay alert in case I needed to grab the wheel.

Quinton pulled into an IHOP. At first, I thought an International House of Pancakes was an interesting choice, considering it wasn't three a.m. Then I remembered that Quinton was high and it all made sense. I felt like I was watching a movie of a bad date, instead of being in it myself. Quinton was unfocused and not making any sense. When the waitress came, he said, "The lady will have pancakes, bacon, sausage, scrambled eggs, toast and waffles." After placing his own order, Quinton got up, went to the bathroom, and didn't come back until after the food was delivered. I was beyond stunned.

He sat down and pulled my plate toward him. He placed a piece of bacon in a pancake, slapped a pad of butter in the middle without spreading it, poured syrup over it, wrapped it up and handed it to me. "You have to eat it this way." I obliged, as I was way beyond questioning Quinton. He took one bite, dropped cash on the table and asked if I was ready to go. I had barely eaten, but was more than ready to go. On the way out, Quinton stopped by the pie counter.

"Want some pie?" asked Quinton, his face hopeful like a puppy's.

"I'm good," I said.

"Not even an apple pie?" he implored.

"Especially apple pie." I hate any dessert involving baked fruit, especially when it's still in chunks.

"Okay," said Quinton with a small shrug. Then he ordered an apple pie and said, "You'll love it."

I was only a mile from my house and considered walking, but it was night and my parents raised me to believe every stranger on earth was planning to rape and kill me, so I got back in the car, even though, at this point, I wouldn't have been surprised if Quinton had raping and killing me on his agenda tonight. Three blocks later, Quinton pulled into the CVS on the corner near my house. Evidently we needed to get vanilla ice cream for my apple pie. The night seemed endless. I told Quinton ice cream wasn't necessary, as I wouldn't be eating the pie. He ignored me, pulled into the parking lot and went into the store.

As I sat in the car, debating whether to get out and walk the four remaining blocks to my house, a cop pulled into the parking lot. He had pulled over a car and was beginning to administer a DUI test. I figured Quinton would never walk out of the store for fear of walking by the cop while he was Charlie Sheen-wasted, so I decided to make a run for it.

I opened the passenger door just as Quinton strolled out of the store. He walked past the cop and waved. Then he opened the car door and presented me with a half-gallon of Häagen Dazs vanilla bean ice cream, a Chipwich ice cream sandwich and a Fudgsicle.

He drove me home and opened the car door for me. I got out, my ice cream and apple pie piled in my arms, and said thank you and good night. Not so fast. Quinton insisted on walking me to my door and then brushed past me into the house. Sonny started going ape shit, so I petted him and ignored Quinton other than to say goodnight again, this time with a little more conviction. Quinton agreed it was indeed a good night, grabbed a Corona out of my fridge and went, uninvited, into the bedroom.

Sonny, of course, jumped all over him, and began humping him and lining chew toys and tennis balls at his feet. This was one occasion where I would not be shutting my door and giving Sonny peanut butter jars. Quinton asked me if Sonny could be excused so we could have "alone time."

"It's late and I have work tomorrow, so alone time will have to wait," I said. "Until hell freezes over," I added under my breath.

Quinton could not focus on calming Sonny and romancing me at the same time, so he gave up and lay down on my bed. He poured the beer all over my sheets and the floor as he did so. Sonny started licking it up. Quinton said, "Wow, he likes it."

"No kidding. He'd eat cat shit for dinner and a used tampon for dessert if I let him. Of course he likes beer, it's delicious."

Quinton didn't hear any of this because he'd passed out. I should have expected that when an alcoholic actually spills his beer, passing out is imminent. Rather than try to wake him, I dragged him outside. I kept his car keys as a favor to society, and locked my door. The cool air roused him and he began banging on my door. I considered telling him about the hammock in the backyard, but I fell sound asleep on my beer-stained bed sheets before I had the chance.

My alarm went off early the next morning. Danny and I had planned to meet at my house to spin around Davis Island. I opened the door to get my newspaper and nearly tripped over Quinton, who was asleep on my doorstep. I stepped over him and walked down my driveway to get the newspaper. Quinton's car, which was parked askew, blocked my car in the driveway. On my way back inside, I dropped his keys next to him and shut my door, hoping the noise would wake him up and he would drive home in shame while I rode my bike. I went into the kitchen for breakfast and came upon melted ice cream all over my counter, along with an entire apple pie. Until that moment I had actually forgotten about that aspect of the night.

Danny knocked on my door at five forty-five a.m., stepped over Quinton and started petting Sonny, who barked madly and jumped all over Danny.

"What's with the bum on your doorstep?" asked Danny without so much as a faint look of surprise.

"Not sure I have time to tell you about the entire night on the two hour ride, but I'll try to get it in."

"That bad?" Danny asked.

"Worse."

We left the house and Quinton and went on a ride. Danny stared in disbelief as I told him the story. Danny admitted a bit sheepishly, "I knew he was crazy, but even I didn't expect that."

"If you knew he was crazy why did you let me go out with him?"

"Thought he might have changed. Plus, I didn't think you'd want to go out with him."

"Why?" I said. "He's my age, okay looking, works in finance, tamed his wild side with the death of his father. He sounded—"

Danny interrupted me with a roaring laugh and said, "He's at least thirty-nine."

"What? He said he was twenty-eight."

"He's not. Four years ago he raced in the thirty-five-plus age category."

"Damn, being honest was one of the only things he had going for him."

"He's not in finance either, unless you have a really broad definition of finance."

"What does he do?"

"He's a loan shark or something. I think he repossesses cars."

"I thought you had to be tough for that job."

"He got the job through his sister-in-law."

"Do you know if his father is actually dead?" I asked.

"It's possible, who knows?"

After the morning ride, hours later, Quinton was still on my doorstep. I started getting ready for work, which consisted of taking a shower then blow-drying my hair while I read the newspaper. I can be ready to go anywhere in twenty minutes. On my way out, Quinton was still there. His car was blocking mine in, so I couldn't move my car unless I woke him. But waking him inevitably meant talking to him, so I opted to ride my bike to work. I put on fresh cycling clothes and packed a bag of work clothes.

When I got to work, I realized that while I remembered to pack a matching necklace and shoes, I forgot to bring a bra and underwear. The air conditioning at my office tends to vacillate between ten and fifteen degrees below freezing, so this was a problem. I would have to avoid David more than usual throughout the day.

Around 2:00 p.m., Quinton texted me, "gr8 time-plans 2nite?"

The mail man probably woke him up. I ignored the text. An hour later, Quinton called. I answered the phone, apologized for not returning his text, and told him I couldn't meet tonight. He told me that he had an amazing time and couldn't wait to see me again. Clearly I needed to be more assertive.

"Quinton, how old are you?"

"Forty-one."

"You told me you were twenty-eight."

"No I didn't."

"Yes you did. I said I was twenty-eight and you said, 'me too.'"

"Oh, I was kidding. I thought you knew that. Are you mad about that?"

"No, but the six gin and tonics, five beers, two joints and sixteen hours sleeping on my doorstep freaked me out a bit."

"I didn't do that."

"Yes you did. Trust me, my memory is working better than yours today."

"So, is that it? You don't want to see me anymore?"

"No, I don't. Sorry. I'm sure I'll see you around on the bike though."

"I can't believe this," he said, and I think he was serious.

"I have another call, I'll talk to you later," I said. A white, but necessary, lie.

The next day, Quinton called me again. Stupidly, I answered.

"Hey, what are you doing Friday night?"

"What do you mean?"

"I have tickets to a monster truck rally." Excitement and optimism were palpable in his voice.

"Quinton, you're a nice guy, but I told you yesterday, it won't work out between us. As an aside, I have no interest in monster truck rallies."

"I thought about what you said, and I really appreciate it," said Quinton, suddenly serious. "I know it must have been hard for you to admit to me that you think I have a problem. It's great that you care about me enough to share that with me. Anyway, I took your advice, and decided to get help. I feel better already and I'm sure that by Friday, the problem will be gone."

"Your problem cannot be fixed in four days. It's great that you're working on it, but I wasn't telling you to get help so we could date."

"Why did you tell me then?" he asked.

"Just my helpful nature I guess."

"I think it's because you care about me. Can't you just give me another chance?"

"No. I'm really not interested," I said.

"Will you think about it?"

"No."

"Will you reconsider?" This was becoming worse than a telemarketing call.

"Reconsidering it is a lot like thinking about it or giving you another chance, Quinton. My answer is still no."

"I can't believe this. We had such a good time."

"I'm going to the gym now. Bye, Quinton."

Holy shit he was dense! Even I didn't think I was worth the level of humiliation he'd just put himself through.

* * *

I wore everything I owned for the ride with Danny the next morning. Even though we were well into January, it was the first real Florida cold spell of the season. In Florida, this means the temperature drops below thirty degrees in the morning and only goes up to sixty-five during the day. When this happens, the weather channel takes a break from predicting next year's hurricane season in order to provide minute-by-minute details on the chance of survival for each Florida orange against the deep freeze. I have bad circulation in my hands and feet, so if it dips below forty-five degrees, I wear three sets of gloves, wool socks, toe warmers and two sets of shoe covers called "booties." I also wore a thermal snow cap instead of a helmet. When given the choice between dying and being cold, I'd chose being cold every time. However, my winter wardrobe never reflected this choice."

Danny looked me up and down and said, "You're going to lose your mime hands if you wear gloves and long sleeves."

One of the negatives about cycling in Florida is the sun. It is inevitable that Florida cyclists will have horrible tan lines. When I ride, I wear a cycling uniform, referred to as a "kit," which is essentially a short-sleeve jersey and spandex shorts with a padded chamois covering the crotch. The rest of my get-up consists of ankle socks, gloves, a helmet and glasses. I look ridiculous naked. My legs from mid-thigh to ankles, as well as my arms from biceps to wrists, are practically black, while my ass, stomach and back are white as snow. I have a tan line midway across my forehead and around my eyes, where my helmet and glasses rest. The best part about the tan is the hands. I wear gloves when I ride so that I can grip the gears and brakes while sweating my ass off. My hands are white up to my wrist, where I have a sharp line. It really does look like I'm wearing white mime gloves at all times.

"Winter's almost over, the tan lines will be back with a vengeance soon enough."

"Is that all you're wearing?" Danny asked with a hint of sarcasm.

In addition to the gloves and booties, I wore three long-sleeve shirts, a vest and leg warmers. Danny wore shorts and a long-sleeve cycling jersey. After making fun of me, he froze the entire ride. I laughed at him, so he got in front of me and shot a snot rocket right into my face. It was cold, so he had a lot of snot saved up.

"Asshole!" I screamed.

"Sorry," he said, as he swished water in his mouth then spit it into my face. "That should clean off the snot."

"Do you have to be such a gentleman all the time?" I asked, wiping the snot and spit off my face.

The morning ride on Davis Island was always beautiful and today was no exception. We saw the sunrise as we pedaled past the yacht club like clockwork on our first of five loops around the east side of the Island. On the second, we passed crew boats training in the channel between Davis Island and Harbour Island. On the third, we saw dolphins playing near the yacht club. The fourth lap also took my breath away. A little boy kissed his mother goodbye, hopped on his bike without a care in the world and pedaled directly into a curb. This sent him sailing four feet into the air until he collided with the post of a stop sign. We paused for a moment, feeling both sympathy and regret that we didn't capture it for YouTube. Then, we started pedaling again because there wasn't any blood and his mom seemed to have it under control. Our luck broke on the fifth trip around the Island. Instead of sunrises, boats, dolphins and clumsy kids, we were treated to a crap-load of dirt in our eyes and mouths.

I moved my glasses to rub my eyes and said, "The person who invented the leaf-blower should be shot."

"No shit," Danny said. "It is literally designed to transport debris from your yard onto your neighbor's property."

"Fuck their property, my eyes are burning and I'm crunching on dirt."

Danny sprayed his water bottle into my face.

"Jackass. It's freezing out here."

"My bad, I was just trying to fix your eyes. You have snot, spit, dirt and leaves in there; I thought you couldn't possibly see without me spraying stuff into your face."

"Of course you were," I said, as I unscrewed the bottle top of mine and splashed my entire water bottle, which was now freezing cold, over Danny's head.

"I guess I had that coming," he stated nonchalantly. "Hey, how's the pregnancy thing going?" Danny asked, hopefully calling it even and ending the water fight.

"Great," I said. "I plan to go from plump to fat soon and start wearing real maternity clothes."

"Do you have any?"

"My friend Jessica just had a baby. I'm going to ask to borrow hers."

"What are you going to tell her?"

"The truth. I've known her since sixth grade, she won't turn me in."

"You'll never make it the full nine months, too many people know. You're going to get busted."

"I'll be fine," I said, with a confidence I didn't have.

"What if Jessica gets mad that you're abusing the system and turns you in?"

"Why would she do that? It's not like I'm faking being handicapped. She had maternity leave and got a little cherub of a baby boy out of it. She's as happy as a pig in shit. I'm not taking anything away from that."

* * *

I met up with Jessica at the Westshore Mall, halfway between her house and my office. She was already at the restaurant when I got there and was easy to spot because she had a stroller obstructing all of the foot traffic in the restaurant. I eyed Jessica to see how close we were in size since I'd be wearing her clothes for the next four months. Not surprisingly, nothing had changed since middle school. She was still six inches taller than me. Wearing her clothes, I'd be pulling up my pants and walking on them for the next four months. Jessica looked tired. Poor sucker was using her maternity leave to care for an infant at all hours of the day.

She spent the lunch squeezing her son's chubby legs and arms like a stress ball with one hand and picking at her salad with the other. She found my pregnancy scheme funny, but crazy.

"So, basically you're faking a pregnancy for vacation?"

"No. I'll enjoy the break, but I'm doing it so that I can qualify and compete in this three-week race."

"Why do you like cycling so much? It seems so boring."

"Says the girl who has the attention span for yoga."

Jessica said, "I love yoga, you should try it. You'd probably like it."

"Can you win at yoga?"

"No."

"Then why would I do it?" I asked.

"Forget yoga. Why cycling? Do you get a runner's high, or cyclists' high or something when you win?"

"Sometimes. I sometimes even get it when I just go out to ride for fun. But it's not that. It's hard to describe. Sometimes, I just ride my bike, enjoying the weather and socializing. When I run errands on my bike or ride to work, I feel like a kid with a mission instead of a cyclist. In the summer, I play meteorologist while I ride during the afternoon thundershowers. I look at the sky and try to ride around the massive afternoon storm that's going to hit the entire Tampa Bay area at some point. Sometimes it works and the storm clouds never catch me, though they're nipping at my back wheel the entire ride. Other times, I get hit right in the thick of it and I'm riding for my life trying to avoid lightning by crouching as low on my bike as possible. I love racing too, and group rides. Any competition really. But I also love training and just spinning around easy."

"Hello!" Jessica said as she waved her hands in my face.

"Sorry. John and Jason always tell me not to talk about cycling because it bores the shit out of people, but you asked."

"First, it was kind of a sarcastic or rhetorical question. I didn't know whether the runner's high was real or that cyclists got one too. Second, John and Jason are right. Third, who are you and what have you done with Jenna Rosen?"

"What?" I said, now embarrassed.

"Sorry, I'm just not used to you talking passionately and spewing rainbows out of your ass," she said, cupping her infant's ears even though he was six months away from talking.

"I wouldn't go that far."

"Well it was definitely out of character. Don't take this the wrong way, but it almost seems like you give a shit," said Jessica earnestly.

"I do. In fact, I not only give a shit, I care, as I do about everything that affects me."

"I know that deep down, you care about things, but I much prefer to hang out with your dark shallow side. I get my fair share of sentimentality at home with the kid. Quick, say something cynical."

"Sorry, other than faking the miracle of birth to get vacation time, I'm out."

"Don't be ridiculous. What did you do last night?"

"Grabbed a drink in Ybor City."

"Great, you must have pissed someone off there, so you have to have a story."

"Oh yeah. A bum asked me for some money and I said, 'Sure, can you break a hundred dollar bill?'"

"Did you really?"

"No, bums in Ybor scare me, but I thought about doing it," I said.

"So, have you slept with that tall drink of water who worships you yet?" Jessica asked.

I blushed. My life would be so much simpler if I wanted to sleep with and marry Danny. "No, I'm not sleeping with Danny. We're just friends."

"Why?" Jessica asked incredulously. "He's totally into you."

"No shit," I responded.

"So," Jessica said, then paused for me to think about and accept this brilliant matchmaking thought of hers.

"He's my friend. I don't know why I'm not into him. But I'm pretty sure I'm not and don't want to ruin the friendship." I changed the subject. "Did you bring the maternity clothes?"

"Yes, they're in my car."

We walked over to Jessica's car, which screamed "baby on board" even though she did not have the actual bumper sticker. Each window on the station wagon had a sun shield. Beside the large bag of clothes in the back seat was a car seat with spit-up stains surrounded by a sea of discarded Cheerios. I grabbed a pair of maternity pants out of the bag. They looked a bit like cycling bibs in that there was a wide elastic band above where the waistline should be. They actually looked pretty comfortable. How delightful it would be to not have to deal with buttons and zippers for a few months. It would be like living in yoga pants.

CHAPTER FIVE

In February, I started wearing Jessica's maternity clothes and putting a small pillow under my shirt. I also bought an "Empathy Belly," a tool that sex education teachers use to teach kids the perils of teen pregnancy. It looked very realistic, but it was too early for me to be that big. Instead, I strapped a pillow onto my stomach and wore an undershirt over the pillow to be sure no one would see it. Then I put my maternity top over my undershirt. To complete the ensemble, I added a big jacket because I was paranoid that my stomach didn't look real enough.

After the morning coffee rush, I went into the kitchen for my secret caffeine fix and almost ran straight into Sarah. Fortunately, I stuck my arms out. Otherwise, she would have been treated to a handful of fluffy belly. Sarah said, "Hey!" and reached forward toward my stomach. I grabbed her hands just in time.

"I want to feel your belly."

"Are you kidding?" I asked.

"No, I want to feel him kick."

"It's not a 'him,'" I said, switching topics.

"It's a girl?"

"I don't know. I don't want to find out. There's so few real surprises in life."

"But what will we get you for the baby shower?"

Oh yeah, I forgot about the obligatory office baby shower. "Cash?"

"Yeah right. You should register at Babies 'R' Us," Sarah said, ever helpful.

"Actually, I was thinking of registering at the bike shop and PetSmart."

"Ha ha," Sarah said, not laughing. "Target also has good stuff," she said.

"Target sounds good," I said, remembering that Target sells beer. I could exchange my baby gifts for about $500 in beer. I pondered whether $500 in beer was excessive as Sarah moved in again. I grabbed her arm.

"Come on, can't I feel the baby kick?" she said, physically grappling with me to touch my stomach.

"No, it doesn't kick yet. I think I have a lazy kid," I said, pushing her hands away with my left arm and blocking my belly with my right.

"Can I feel your stomach?" she asked.

"Do you have a pregnancy fetish or something Sarah?"

"No," Sarah said, "Everyone likes to feel a pregnant belly."

"Seriously?" This is going to be a problem.

"Yes, you'll see. Complete strangers in the mall will come up to you and rub your belly."

"They better not," I said.

"Why?"

Did I really need a reason? Probably not, but just in case I responded, "I don't want anyone touching my belly, I'm ticklish."

Sarah walked out, so I started to make myself some coffee. David walked in.

"Are you drinking coffee?" David asked.

"Decaf."

"I think even decaf has a little caffeine in it. You should be careful."

"I actually think the low birth weight sounds like a more comfortable delivery. I'm also snorting lines of coke to keep the kid really small." I often say stuff like this to David when he acts concerned, because his concern is always forced and insincere. He states his concern, then tunes me out.

David confirmed his disinterest in my health, and that of my baby's, by saying, "Well that's nice Jennifer, did you finish drafting the *punies*?"

"Punies" is David's super-cool slang for punitive damages. Punitive damages are only appropriate where a defendant acts with such wanton disregard that he should be punished in addition to paying compensatory damages to a plaintiff. The defendant in our case, which was one of my only non-subrogation files, was, at most, inadvertently negligent. We would be lucky to win our case, let alone obtain punitive damages. Consequently, I was not very enthusiastic about drafting a twenty page brief on the issue. Nevertheless, I think I could do it with a smile if David could just stop calling them punies. Every single day it's, "How's the motion for punies going?" Or, "Paragraph four on page seven of the puny motion is great, huh?" It really makes my skin crawl.

"The motion for PUNITIVE damages is almost complete, David. I'll get it to you before the end of the day." I said.

"Great, opposing counsel is going to cry when she sees our motion for punies."

"Right," I said.

"Hey Jennifer, are you still riding your bike?"

"Yes."

"Your stomach doesn't get in the way?"

"No David, I sit on my ass."

"Don't you lean down?"

"Only when I'm trying to get aero, I'm just spinning around now and not racing."

"Hey Jenna, what's with all those drug-addicted cyclists?"

I hate when people ask me this. "The sport is actually pretty clean now," I said.

"What about Armstrong and that Mormon with the tainted beef?"

"I think Lance should come clean about not really drinking Michelob Ultra and that Landis is a Mennonite and he was busted for testosterone. Contador had the tainted beef." While I hated the topic, I loved correcting David.

"Have you ever taken testosterone or steroids?" David asked me, and he seemed serious.

"No, do you want me to pee in a cup for you?" I asked, grabbing a water cup.

David was no longer listening to me. His question was merely a segue to tell me about his steroid use. He said, "I took steroids after my neck surgery. I don't know if I was stronger, but I was horny as hell. After I wore my wife out, I was ready to bend over the ninety-year-old nurse."

I was about to throw up again, but fought it back since I was now past the morning sickness trimester. "That's hot David. Thanks for sharing."

When I got back to my desk, I had about twenty emails. I was only out for ten minutes, which means that an interoffice chain was being exchanged. Not surprisingly, it was a food-related chain. Every day, someone's Cracklin' Oat Bran or chocolate pudding gets stolen, setting off a chain of emails about how ridiculous it is that grown adults in a professional environment resort to stealing food. This particular email chain was a discussion about some unsuspecting new employee who placed a box of Fruit Roll-Ups in the kitchen cabinet, and found them all gone the next day. My file of food-related office emails was so extensive that I'd separated "stolen food" emails from other "theft related" emails. Some of my favorites are:

-*To whomever has eaten my half ham & cheese on a croissant sandwich, pretzels, fun size Snickers and Capri Sun, please replace it!*

-*Dear person who took my lunch marked "Lauren" for the second time this month, I hope you enjoyed it!* (What's the saying? Fool me once...)

-*Whomever took my ravioli from the kitchen, I would of shared it if you asked.* Would of? Is the contraction for that would'f?

-*Please do not drink my Propel Fitness Water. It is mine. YOU didn't buy it. I did. MINE!*

-*To the person who took my Kashi Frozen Southwestern Chicken with Potatoes and Peas from the third shelf of the 5th floor kitchen. Not nice!!!!!!!!!!!!!!!* (I think a 15th exclamation mark and more detail on the food would have got the point across better).

…and the best food email ever:

-To the person who destroyed my pumpkin cheesecake pie (you know who you are): If you really wanted to try the pie you could have asked instead of acting like an animal and digging into something that's not yours to dig into that other people worked hard at. You have made a lot of people angry. This is absurd. For those of you who didn't see the pie, here is a picture. (Seriously, she attached a picture.)

Now that I was starting to look pregnant, I decided to check out what was in store for mommy and baby in March and April.

Week Seventeen:

Mom: *Your secretions all over your body may increase, due to the increased blood volume. So if you are sweating more, have nasal congestion, or are suffering from increased vaginal discharge this is nothing to worry about and will go away after the birth of the baby.*

Sexy!

Baby: *Your baby is forming brown fat deposits under his or her skin.*

Fat is brown? I always pictured it being clear.

Week Twenty:

Mom: *You are halfway through your pregnancy! Sleep may be increasingly difficult now, as your belly grows. Try doing pelvic tilts and urinate before going to bed. Your belly button may pop out and stay that way as your uterus presses upwards. Some people will have trouble breathing as their lungs become cramped.*

Is a pelvic tilt a sit-up?

Baby: *Your baby is up to ten ounces. Lanugo appears all over the baby's body. This fine hair will remain until birth draws nearer. Some women get an ultrasound at twenty weeks and get their first peek at baby.*

I'll borrow Jessica's ultrasound and show it around the office towards the end of January. I'm pretty sure no one will be able to tell that the creepy three dimensional fetus isn't mine.

Week Twenty-Two:

Mom: *In the second trimester libido is usually increased. With the increase in blood flow and secretions in the vagina and clitoris, some women become orgasmic or multi-orgasmic for the first time.*

No wonder David likes pregnancy sex, it was probably the first time he got a reaction from his wife.

Baby: *Develops eyebrows this week.*

Baby raises eyebrows at parents to tell them to stop doing it so often.

Week Twenty-Five:

Mom: *Soon you will begin to see your practitioner more often.*

Looks like I get to start missing work a little more often.

Baby: *Veins are visible through your baby's skin, although it is quickly changing from transparent to opaque.*

To recap, baby is transparent, veiny, hairy, and has brown fat deposits.

Toward the end of February, I replaced my stomach pillow with the Empathy Belly. The Empathy Belly was enough to scare any teenager into combining condom use with the pill and a diaphragm, if not complete abstinence. Of its many features, it added thirty to thirty-three pounds of weight in the stomach and boobs; put continual pressure on the abdomen and internal organs; changed the posture of your back by an increase in "lordosis" or "pelvic tilt;" shifted one's center of gravity instigating a lower backache; simulated mild "fetal" kicking movements every ten minutes; created awkwardness, shortness of breath, increased body temperature and pressed on the bladder, causing frequent urination. The Empathy Belly simulated these effects through the use of a rib belt and strategic positioning of various weighted components. Here's the kicker, it cost $500. Exorbitantly expensive for a test run at pregnancy, but a reasonable investment towards a twelve-week vacation. I bought it without hesitation, confident that I could recoup some of the belly's costs on eBay after my pregnancy. Or, I could have a second and third kid with it.

* * *

Last weekend was the first Florida race of the season. Cycling didn't start in earnest until at least March, but in sunny Florida, we got a head start. I was very excited to be racing after the long off-season even though I wasn't in great form. My body seemed to be excited too, because I had to stop for two McShits on the way to the race. McDonald's is my public restroom of choice because they're everywhere, generally clean, and you don't need a key attached to a cinder block to get into them. Once you get to the race, port-o-johns are the only option. You only need to get blue splash on your ass once to make the McShit a ritual.

The race was just outside of Tampa in San Antonio, Florida. San Antonio, Clermont and Ocala are virtually the only towns in Florida, south of Gainesville, with hills. Cyclists from Tampa, Orlando and even South Florida flock to them each weekend. Brenda, who lives midway between Tampa and Orlando, used to train in San Antonio religiously when I started riding, but she switched her loyalties to Clermont once I started beating her up the hills in San Antonio. I had been looking forward to racing against Brenda in San Antonio for the entire off-season, but when I lined up at the start, I noticed she was a no-show. My pre-race jitters immediately subsided, but I was disappointed, because San Antonio's hilly race course heavily favors me over Brenda.

The road race course was a twelve-mile loop we were to complete five times. The organizers combined the women's field with the Category 3 men, which made the race faster and more dangerous. Both men's and women's races are divided into categories; CAT 5, being the least experienced category for men, is often referred to as SPLAT 5 due to the prevalence of crashes by novices full of testosterone. Because there are fewer women cyclists, their novice category starts at a CAT 4 level. As cyclists race and accumulate results, they collect points which can be used to upgrade to CAT 3, CAT 2 and with enough points coupled with approval from USA Cycling's regional czar, to CAT 1. The cycling rule book actually contains a chart that dictates the number of points available for each placement in a road race, time trial and criterium race. It did not take long after returning from my face-plant to CAT up to a 1 last season. A cyclist's category level is printed on their annual cycling license. My goal for this season is to trade-in my CAT 1 license for a professional license.

Racing with the CAT 3 men put the field at over 100 riders. While this would make the race more dangerous than an all-women's race, I preferred it because my chicken-shit sprinting style did not come into play. When racing with the boys, I often win merely by staying within the draft of the *peloton* when all the other women get dropped.

A *peloton* is a pack of riders that looks magnetized together because they're all drafting off of each other. When the pace is relaxed, there are several rows and columns of riders that look like a big colorful moving blob from an aerial view. However, as the pace picks up, everyone tries to avoid being in the wind by "sitting" on the wheel (in the draft) of the rider in front of them. This stretches the *peloton* to one long line of riders, with less than an inch in between the front and rear wheel separating the riders. When this happens, it's important not only to stay on the wheel in front of you, but to make sure that the bike in front of you is on the wheel in front of it. If the bike in front of you gaps off the wheel in front of it, you, too, become gapped from the draft of the *peloton*. Cyclists do not appreciate closing a gap created by another cyclist and non-cyclists would be surprised at the hatred and cursing that can accompany the words, "Close that Gap!" If the gapper does not close the gap, the detached riders behind the gapper must do it; the sooner the better because a bigger gap translates into a more time in the wind to close it.

Because of my competitive nature, I treat every cycling ride with two or more people like it's the Olympics, so I am accustomed to riding fast with the guys without getting dropped from the pack. Sometimes, because I'm not as aggressive at holding my place within the pack, I drift to the back too much, but I'm strong enough to close the gaps if the guys I'm drafting off of can't hang in there. Because I've become skilled at hanging with the boys, it plays to my favor when race organizers combine the men's and women's races in an effort to save money.

The race did not go exactly as planned. Two miles into the course, I got a flat tire. I flagged down the wheel truck and changed my wheel quickly, then positioned myself within the draft of the wheel truck, hoping it would shield me from the wind and motor-pace me back up to the group. This is generally allowed as long as a rider is dropped because of mechanical difficulty rather than because the rider couldn't hang in the race. Unfortunately, the ninety-year-old woman driving the wheel truck didn't seem to know that her car could be of service to me by blocking the wind. To add insult to injury, she turned out to be the only ninety-year-old in Florida who drove faster than thirty miles an hour. She accelerated quickly up to fifty miles per hour, making it impossible for me to use the truck to catch the fast-moving *peloton*. I never caught up to the race. Not exactly the plan for my first race of the season.

After the race, I learned there were two professional female riders in the race and that they placed first and second. It was not uncommon for professional riders to travel to Florida and California in February to take advantage of early-season racing in the beautiful weather. I was enraged that I missed the opportunity to race with the pros on my home course.

The next day I fared a bit better. Sunday's race was a fast, technical criterium course with eight turns. The course started out downhill, with a right turn after two blocks. Still full of unused energy after flatting out of the previous day's race, I led into what I thought was the first corner. As it turned out, I turned a block early. I quickly made a U-turn, but the pack had already seen my error and hit the gas. Brenda, who showed up for this race, led the charge. When I finally caught up a few laps later, Brenda slowed down to call me a dumbass.

"I'm book smart," I sneered back and then attacked. Two girls came with me, the two professional riders. Forty-five minutes into the race, the three of us lapped the field. When this happens, the entire field is put on the same lap, meaning the other riders would ride one lap less. Even though we were all together with the same number of laps remaining, the main *peloton* was now racing for fourth place and above, whereas the two pros and I were racing for first through third. I was happy to be guaranteed a podium spot, but disappointed that after being in a breakaway for the entire race, I had to compete in a field sprint with sixty women rather than a much safer three-up sprint. In true Jenna Rosen fashion, I shied away from the aggressive sprinting pack of women and placed last in the field sprint. Brenda "brass balls" Bowers won the field sprint after expertly maneuvering through the field, then sprinting up the middle with her elbows pointed outward at anyone who dared to get near her. Even though Brenda is a fast sprinter, it is her willingness to risk life and limb through a crowded *peloton* that generally nets her wins. Technically, I beat her since I was guaranteed a podium spot by virtue of lapping the field but, it was hard to get excited after coming in last place in a field sprint and third out of three on the race within the race.

I'm not a bad sport in that I won't throw a temper tantrum and always congratulate the winner, but I HATE losing. I was not in a social mood after the race. Additionally, I had to get to the Rosen family dinner, so I took off in my car and asked Danny to grab my prize money for me. Once I left, I took out my frustration by racing everyone on the highway. Granted, none of the cars around me knew we were racing, but I needed a victory.

I don't drive like a maniac because I have road rage, but because I'm bored and impatient unless I'm speeding and weaving in and out of traffic. Because this is my normal driving pattern, I feel safe running red lights and ignoring traffic signs. I figure that if I don't get pulled over for driving seventy in a thirty-five-mile-per-hour zone, there probably aren't any cops around to catch me running a red light. When there is too much traffic to run a red light, I get out of my car and press the cross walk button rather than wait for the light to change on its own. Patience is not my forte.

After exiting the highway, I sped along a two-lane street that was merging into one lane. My modus operandi for this scenario was to drive in the lane that was about to end until the last possible second, then merge over in front of all the drivers who merged early and were now sitting in traffic. Yes, I know I'm a dick. I passed at least thirty cars before the big orange water-filled road blocks began gradually closing down the right lane. At the last second, I started to merge towards the SUV next to me. The blonde driving it was on her cell phone, so I proceeded slowly, waiting for her to brake slightly so that I could jump in front of her.

I completely underestimated my adversary. Blonde SUV girl saw me, but didn't budge. I had three choices: hit blonde SUV girl, hit the road blocks, or stop. Unfortunately, I had already hit my fourth road block before option "C" occurred to me. I slammed on my brakes; losing my third race of the weekend. While I was waiting for traffic to pass so I could merge safely, I tried to evaluate the damage to my car. This turned out to be impossible because my passenger side-view mirror was dangling from the side of the car. I planned to use the next red light to check out the dents that would no doubt complement my dangling mirror. However, I was afraid to get out of my car because blonde SUV girl, who was right next to me, spent the entire light-cycle laying on her horn and cursing me out. She had a point, I was driving like an ass.

Given the raging bitch in the SUV behind me and my pulverized car, I decided to drive conservatively the rest of the way home. It was only six miles and I drove it well except for cutting off a Hummer with a Gorrie Elementary School bumper sticker. I'm a Carrollwood Elementary Owl. Gorrie Cougars can suck it. Besides, I'm a bit put off by people who purchase a military tank in order to carry a kid and a soccer ball.

Once I pulled into my parents' driveway, I got out to inspect the damage to my car. Besides the dangling rearview mirror, there were three identical dents spaced evenly apart. As I looked at the dents, I heard a voice shout, "Hi, Jennifer!"

Shit, it was David in his nut-hugging jogging shorts headed right for me. I tried to open the passenger-side door to hop inside and get my Empathy Belly, but the door wouldn't open. I had dented the car in the perfect spot so that the "clamshell" doors on the passenger side of my Honda Element would never open again. With my back to David, I ran around to the other side of the car and grabbed the belly.

I was wearing short shorts and a tight top that bared a trace of my midriff. It was clear that I would have an extreme muffin top hanging out between my shirt and shorts once I added the Empathy Belly. Sure enough, there was a five inch gap of exposed fake stomach after I added the belly. I pulled my shirt down and my shorts up as high as they would go. The shorts were digging into my crotch and I am pretty sure I had some serious camel toe going. Unfortunately, I had to turn around and greet my boss.

"Hi, David."

"Were you in an accident?"

Yes, Captain Obvious. "Just a little fender bender," I replied.

"That's not your fender."

"You're right. I mean just a little broadside collision."

David said, "I think I saw you riding your bike the other day. I didn't want to honk because I didn't want you to fall. Then I realized it couldn't be you, because the girl wasn't pregnant."

My heart started beating fast. I said, "Then it definitely wasn't me. You can honk if you see me though. The chances of me falling as a result of you tooting your horn are less than zero."

Just then my mom came out. "Oh. Hi, David."

"Hi, Geri."

I kept my back to my mom so that she couldn't see my belly. Fortunately, my mom had heard enough about David to keep her distance and she just said, "Dinner's ready."

"I'll be right in."

David watched my mother a bit too closely as she went and said, "I don't know if I ever told you, but your mother is a very sexy lady."

"Yes, you've mentioned that before. Thanks, I guess."

David said bye and drove off. I came in just behind my mother.

"Jenna," Mom said, "Is your side-view mirror dangling?"

I looked at the dangling side-view mirror through the window and said, "No."

"Okay." My mom said, and went inside. My mom believes everything my brothers or I say, regardless of evidence to the contrary. She believes my brothers because that's what Jewish moms do. She believes me because I was an honest and literal child and she has not yet realized that I have outgrown that stage of my life.

When I was a child, my parents, like everyone's parents, told me not to drive in a car without a seatbelt. One time, my mom and dad had to take John from school to the hospital because John head-butted a soccer goal post. They sent our neighbor, Mrs. Thompson, to pick me up from school. Mrs. Thompson's car was at least thirty years old and didn't have seatbelts. When I noticed this, I opened the door and got out. Mrs. Thompson asked where I was going and I told her that I wasn't allowed to ride in a car without seatbelts. Mrs. Thompson told me that my parents would make an exception this time, but I wouldn't budge. This was in the days before cell phones. After a one hour stand-off, Mrs. Thompson had enough and went home without me.

Three hours later, my mom picked me up and drove me the three miles to our house. Instead of using this occasion to educate me about logic, deductive reasoning, and the relative safety concerns of a three mile car trip without a seatbelt versus being alone at night on the campus of a pedophile-magnet elementary school, my mom focused on my obedience and honesty. Thus, when I said my rearview mirror was fine, she believed me and walked back towards the house. Disaster averted.

* * *

In March, I finally remembered to bring Sonny's chocolates into my office for a food experiment. Julie had bought some doggy chocolates for Sonny for Chanukah. Sonny has a weak stomach and gets gastrointestinal distress anytime he eats anything other than Eukanuba dog food. This distress manifests itself in a bad case of the middle-of-the-night farts. Sonny's routine is that he farts, sniffs his ass, then runs all over the house crying, before clawing at his doggy door. What's great is that he acts this way even when I fart. This is funny during the day, but at night, it interferes with my sleep. As a result, I keep him on a very strict diet that does not include gourmet doggy chocolate.

The doggy chocolates came in a gold box with a ribbon, just like expensive human chocolate and looked like real chocolates. I placed them in the kitchen and walked back to my desk, eagerly awaiting the interoffice emails criticizing the person who put doggy chocolates in the kitchen. The emails never came. A few hours later, I walked back to the kitchen, a criminal returning to the scene of the crime. The chocolates were gone. I checked the trash. The box was in there, but there were no half-chewed then spit-out chocolates to be found. People ate them without complaint. So much for creating controversy. I walked back to my desk and realized that it was now official that I work with animals. My only hope was that David ate one.

Speak of the devil. "Jenna, do you have a minute?"

"Sure thing, David."

"Great. Have you spoken with Bob in our Alabama office about the Champions Bar case?"

"No."

"It's set for trial in a few months."

"It will settle," I said confidently.

"You still need to be prepared, and since it's an Alabama case, Bob needs to be prepared, too. I'm not licensed to practice there."

"We have the least amount of damages of the six co-plaintiffs, we can just tag along."

"No, we need to be ready. Let's go back to my office and get Bob on speaker phone now."

David dialed Bob's extension using speaker phone. When you call another extension at Johnson Smith, you only have to dial the extension and your initials show up on the other person's caller ID instead of a phone number. This works between the Tampa and Alabama office as well.

The receptionist answered the phone and said, "Hello."

I presume the receptionist answered the phone with "hello" instead of "Johnson Smith," because she could tell, by David Greene's initials, that another Johnson Smith employee was on the other line. David was not impressed by this greeting and asked her who she was.

"I'm the receptionist," she replied.

"I know that," he said, contempt oozing from his voice. "What is your name?"

The receptionist told David her name.

"Is that how you usually answer the phone?" asked David.

The receptionist was honestly confused and politely responded, "May I ask who's calling?"

"David Green."

She apparently did not hear him and said, "Who?"

David got angry and said, "Look at your wall!"

"Excuse me?"

"What does your wall say?" He said at a normal volume, but with an angry tone.

She replied "Johnson Smith," very quietly, obviously confused by the conversation.

I put on my best poker face because I was about to lose it. As he often does when he becomes upset, David began unconsciously and uncontrollably rocking forward and backwards. He was obviously pissed that the wall did not include "Jones Green and Taylor."

Instead of shouting when he gets angry, David begins whispering in a serious tone. He said, "Okay ma'am," took a deep breath, then barely audibly said, "Could you please advise Bob Jinkins that David Greene wishes to speak with him."

The receptionist did not even respond, opting instead to just connect David and Bob.

Bob picked up the phone. "Hello?"

David's rocking stopped and his voice returned to normal. "Hi, Bob, it's David and Jenna from the Tampa office. We're calling about the Champions Bar case. It's set for trial in a few months."

"Isn't that the one that's going to settle?" Bob asked.

"Probably, but we want to be prepared just in case." David said.

"There's fifty other plaintiffs on that case, we'll just sit back and collect the money."

"That's a good idea, Bob. We'll call you if anything needs to be done."

After we hung up, David said, "So do you get what you need to do?"

"Nothing," I said.

"Right, but pay attention." David said.

"No problem," I replied, wondering how you pay attention to nothing.

I went back to my desk and was greeted by an email to trump all emails. An attorney from our office had sent an office-wide email advising all of us that the airport line was long and to leave early if we needed to travel. In response, a secretary at our office (accidentally I presume) hit "reply all" and sent our entire office photos of her boobs and crotch. The message attached to the photos read "This is what you get when you get back." Two seconds later, we received another email from the secretary telling us to disregard the first message. In my opinion, the retraction email serves only to draw attention to the first email, which people may have overlooked otherwise. I put this email chain in the file labeled "miscellaneous," even though it easily trumped the other miscellaneous emails which were:

–*I need Scrabble tiles. Any letters are fine, just leave them at my door.*

–*I need a sheep skin rug and a wooden comb tonight.* (I question the word need on this email and the one prior.)

–*Today is Customer Appreciation Day at McDonald's. If you order one Big Mac, you get something, but I didn't hear the end of the commercial. I think there's a Quarter Pounder deal too.* (In case you're avoiding McDonald's because it's cost prohibitive.)

–*To the person who opened my desk, removed my bag of chips and poured apple juice in it, I WILL FIND YOU.* (Are you sure it's apple juice?)

–*What does an L on a report card mean?* (Your kid is stupid.)

* * *

I went to a St. Patrick's Day party at the beach at my friend Amanda's parents' condominium. The condo is beautiful and overlooks the water. Amanda regularly entertains there when her parents weren't in town.

Amanda invited a guy named Max, a lawyer from her office who she had been trying to set me up with for the past few months. I avoid blind dates because, like all of my dates, they inevitably fail. The difference is that when they fail, I not only have to reject the guy, I have to find a creative way to placate the friend that went out of her way to set me up with the guy. I usually have no concrete reason I'm not interested in a guy and I hate having to articulate a reason to the friend. That being said, I agreed to meet Max at the party: first, because it wasn't an actual date, and second, because I was now over the two year mark for not being laid, which seemed abnormal.

Max was taller than me, but shorter than I prefer. He was also a little too metrosexual for my liking, in that he had a salon haircut that almost reached his eyebrows and wore $300 designer jeans with holes in them. Nevertheless, I wound up hanging out with Max for most of the night, trying to give him a chance. As it turned out, in addition to being a lawyer, Max was a triathlete. Another black mark against Max.

While triathlons involve cycling, all but a few professional triathletes look absolutely ridiculous on a bike. A common triathlete mistake is to position the aerobars on the bike as an elbow rest at a chest high level. This tends to take the "aero" out of the aerobars. To make matters worse, triathletes use all the extra space between the two aerobars by inserting a long narrow water bottle with a straw so that they never have to move off their faux-aero position, even to drink water. My problem with triathletes is not just aesthetic however. Triathletes also generally suck at cycling since they view drafting as cheating rather than a strategic necessity. And they only ride triathlon bikes, which are not nearly as maneuverable as road bikes, making them dangerous during group rides. Fortunately, most triathletes get spit out the back of the *peloton* very early in a group ride so you don't have to gaze at their goofiness for very long.

Max said nothing to change my opinion about amateur triathletes. It turned out that he regularly went to the same group rides as me, but usually got dropped during the warm-up. I could hear my mom in my head: *"Jenna, he's good-looking, rides a bike, has a good job...Triathlon? Cycling? What's the difference? You're going to be single the rest of your life."*

I decided to put aside my prejudice against metrosexual triathletes, and spent the evening imparting to Max the absolute absurdity of draft-legal triathlons, which essentially turn a triathlon into a running race.

It's like having a draft legal time trial, even though by definition, a time trial is the rider against the clock with no drafting. Max was not nearly as impassioned as I on this topic. At the end of the night, Max and I exchanged numbers.

The following weekend, he picked me up to go to "Italian Fest." Italian Fest is an outdoor event in Ybor City where Italian restaurants give out samples of food and wine to anyone who purchases a wristband. I rode my bike from 6:00 a.m. to 11:00 a.m. in order to be ready when Max came by my house at noon. While March in Florida is typically delightful, this particular day was 92 degrees with 100% humidity. Walking around the Festival was comparable to strolling along the surface of the sun. To combat the heat, I hydrated on wine throughout the afternoon. I was drunk, hot and ready for a nap by 3:00 p.m. As I was debating whether it was rude to cut the date short, I saw Ryan Smith, the Smith of Johnson Smith, in line for Pastamore Italian sausage. Because I was in an un-pregnant state, I quickly turned the other direction into the crowd and told Max we had to go home.

Ever the wine snob, Max wasn't ready to leave until he thoroughly impressed me with his superior wine knowledge. "Let's go to the Italian Wines of Summer table," he said. The table was in the opposite direction of Ryan Smith, so I obliged. There were eight summer wines to sample. As he had all afternoon, Max made quite a production of twirling the wine in the glass and commenting to the vendor on the "legs." After taking an exaggerated smell of the wine, he finally took a sip and assigned an absurd adjective to each taste, such as, "buttery," "crisp," or "vegetal."

On glass number two, Ryan Smith walked towards the table so I began to walk away.

"Where are you going?" asked Max. "We have six wines left to taste."

"I'm going to get some of that Italian water ice," I replied.

"The slurpee stuff? Are you crazy? You'll destroy your palate."

I did not share his alarm as I walked towards the delicious water ice, my heart racing because of the close call.

Ryan and I work on different floors at the office and had actually only met once, on the elevator. The conversation was memorable because I stuck my hand out and said, "Hi, I'm Jenna and I work in the subrogation department. Nice to meet you," and Ryan responded by keeping his hands at his side and said, "No it isn't." That was that.

Ryan is well known for his eccentricities. His suits are all pastel pinstripes, usually baby-blue or yellow. Naturally, he wears these suits with a matching top hat and snake-skin loafers. His beard and hair have the yellowish tint of a smoker and he rarely cuts or grooms either so that they sprout from his face and head like a lion's mane. The only other bit of information I have about Ryan Smith is that he occasionally sends cryptic office-wide emails such as, "Bring a bag lunch next Tuesday to the conference room to discuss King Henry II," or "Please see me if you have any information on Vitamin E."

My days of socializing in public were, I realized, over until July. I couldn't risk being caught by work people in a normal state or by my regular friends in a pregnant state. From the water ice table, I could no longer see the summer wine table where Max and Ryan were tasting wine. I relaxed and tried each of the water ice flavors, marveling at the simplicity. The mango tasted like mango, cherry like cherry and lemon like lemon. If only it were infused with alcohol. As I was tasting the grape, Max walked over, Ryan in tow. Fuck, mother-fucking fucker.

"This is my girlfriend Jenna. Jenna, this is Ryan. I just met him over by the summer wines and he is an expert."

I was so stunned that Max introduced me as his girlfriend that I actually said, "Nice to meet you," once again setting myself up for, "No it's not." I cringed, waiting for the response, but instead, Ryan replied, "Nice to meet you." It was clear that Ryan had no clue who I was even though I had worked in his firm for nearly four years. I relaxed slightly, praying the conversation stayed on the exciting topic of aftertastes and fruit pairings and didn't venture into the equally exciting topic of lawyering. Over the next hour, I tasted fourteen different wines with Ryan and Max. The alcohol helped calm me and divert my attention from the fear of seeing Ryan on Monday, suddenly six months pregnant.

Ryan finished his last wine and walked away without saying goodbye. I wasn't surprised or disappointed by this behavior, though Max was clearly stung by his abruptness. Max drove me home and asked if he could come up and watch some of my *Family Guy* DVDs, which he had admired when he picked me up. I told him that I had a big fat nap in my future and there was no way I could watch *Family Guy*.

"You can sleep while I watch it," he offered.

I thought about just loaning him the DVD, but I was quite sure I wouldn't be having a second date with Max. It's often hard to reclaim your property after rejecting a suitor's advances, so I decided against a loaner. Instead, I invited him inside and made a beeline for my bed and shut the door behind me. I didn't assist him in fending off Sonny's humping, nor did I help him set up the DVD player.

I was in a deep sleep when I became aware of a weird sensation. I roused briefly but kept sleeping. I felt it again. I opened my eyes and realized that Max had come into my bedroom, lifted my skirt, and was going down on me while I slept. Oddly, my gut reaction was to be paranoid about the appearance and odor of my vagina, since I was walking around sweating in the sun all day and using public port-o-johns with no toilet paper. I immediately wished I had taken a European shower prior to my nap.

My next reaction, which was more sane, was that I was being violated. I very calmly said, "I'm pretty sure this is rape."

Max immediately stopped, pushed my skirt down, and said, "I didn't force you to do anything."

"You're a gentle rapist, but a rapist nonetheless," I replied.

"You're crazy. You invited me in."

"That's a novel defense to rape, 'Your Honor, she was asking for it, she let me in to watch *Family Guy.*'"

"Stop saying the word 'rape.' It's very dramatic. I think I better just go home."

"That's a great idea."

I locked the door behind him, then slept until the next morning.

CHAPTER SIX

On Monday, I was insanely jittery. I walked the halls like a secret agent; not turning any corners until I poked my head around to ensure that Ryan Smith wasn't walking toward me. Though I had run into Ryan only twice in the past four years, I became obsessed with how to avoid him. Every trip to the bathroom, kitchen or parking garage became a stealth mission. To do this, I had to start taking the direct route out of my office, even though it forced me to go by Valerie Bell's cubicle. Valerie's daughter is about six years old and into cheerleading, dance and gymnastics. Valerie's screensaver is a picture of her daughter in one of those midriff-baring cheerleading outfits, doing a split in the air. The kid is beauty-queen tan, with a full face of makeup, body glitter and her bloomers staring you in the face. The three pictures on

Valerie's desk are equally creepy and inappropriate: the kid in a string bikini sunning herself at the beach; posing seductively in a sequined leotard; and playing dress-up in a skin-tight cocktail dress. Because of the gentle rapist, I'd have to take the pedophilia route to the bathroom for the next three months.

Of course, now that I was intent on avoiding the halls, David seemed to call me to his office more frequently. Today, he called me in to see if I had updated my files yet, again reminding me of the difficult position the firm would be in if I suddenly dropped dead. This hypothetical was starting to freak me out. As I was leaving, David asked how my parents had taken the news. Since, in his mind, I ate dinner with them looking six months pregnant, I thought it best to come up with a story.

"They're excited. They want me to move back in so that they can be with their grandbaby at all times."

"Really? I'd kill my daughter."

"Your daughter is nineteen, I'm twenty-eight. I'm pretty sure my parents put plecebos in my birth control in order to cause this very result."

"I don't care how old my daughter is, I'd still kill her."

"I'm sure you won't have to worry, she's a good girl and she'll probably be married off by her twenty-first birthday."

"I hope so, she's not very smart. She needs to find a rich man."

I found it interesting that David spent forty grand a year for his daughter to attend a small, private liberal-arts college, when he thought her calling in life was to marry wealthy. I also couldn't believe that David would throw his daughter under the bus like that. I could have an I.Q. of eleven and my delusional parents would still tell me that I could be CEO of MENSA if I put my mind to it. Proof of this is Jason. He maintains a straight C average and watches television nine hours a day, but my parents are looking forward to touring the University of Florida with him next year, just like they did with John and me. I'd love to see his personal statement to get into a college. Jason uses "fuck'n" as a prefix and "n'shit" as a suffix for nearly all of his sentences. For example, "Fuck'n, let's go get coffee n'shit." I should set Jason up with David's daughter.

After the powwow, I went back to my desk and started updating my files so the business of insurance companies suing insurance companies could go on in the event of my untimely passing, or more realistically, my maternity leave. As I was doing this, David sent out an email congratulating one of my coworkers for settling his first case. I hate these emails because they're always entitled "Congratz." Few things are more annoying to me than intentionally misspelling something to be "kool."

After work and my bike ride, I went over to John and Julie's with Sonny for dinner and to watch a movie with Julie. We turned on the DVD player and television and heard grunting. I immediately averted my eyes in order to avoid the possibility of watching a home movie starring my brother. I hit "eject" and removed what turned out to be *Hardcore Fucking #9*.

I turned to Julie and said, "Don't you have the Internet? Where do you want me to put this? I don't see the box."

"Oops, sorry, I'll take that."

Julie opened a cabinet stuffed with sex toys. Real ones, not peanut butter jars. Sonny poked his nose in and grabbed a dildo and ran outside.

"He can have that now," said Julie with a tone that suggested it was one of her favorites.

"That's not necessary," I replied, "his elephant keeps him satisfied."

A few seconds later, Sonny ran back in with the dildo and dropped it at my feet. Julie picked it up and threw it. She continued to play dildo fetch with Sonny throughout the two-hour movie. When it was time to leave, Sonny grabbed the dildo. I told him to drop it, but he wouldn't. My other alternative was to pry it out of his mouth, but that involved touching my brother and sister-in-law's dildo. I told Julie to grab it, but she just laughed and said, "No way, he gets to keep it."

Finally, I gave up and let him take his pre-owned nine-inch cock with him to my house. I figured I'd pick it up with a plastic bag, like I do with his poop, while he slept.

* * *

In April, things were still going smoothly. I had a meeting with Human Resources in a few weeks. Our HR woman was a mother of six, so I decided a little preparation was in order. I Googled the Family Medical Leave Act and came up with a bunch of articles about laws concerning pregnancy in the workplace. Unfortunately, they all dealt with the rights of pregnant women and none focused on the necessary paperwork to prove pregnancy. The related searches at the bottom of the site were titled, "Pregnancy Do's and Don'ts," "The Pregnancy Diet," and my personal favorite, "How to Make a Belly Cast."

According to my search, hair dye was a "don't," but nail polish a "do." Hot tubs and saunas were "don'ts" because they raised the body's temperature, increasing the risk of a miscarriage. Lying in the sun was a "don't" for pregnant women as well, but the reasoning was different. Evidently, if a pregnant woman tans in the sun, it could cause skin cancer; not a unique side effect. Alcohol, cigarettes and fish were "don'ts" for pregnant women, in that order, but tap water was a "do."

I clicked on a few belly cast photos. The process seemed time consuming and messy, not to mention unnecessary considering that the new kid would be enough of a souvenir at the end of the pregnancy. The only useful purpose I could think of for one was for me to wear it for the next three months instead of the cumbersome Empathy Belly that had been created solely to scare teenagers into safe sex.

While researching FMLA, I got an email from David. My secretary had sent him an email with "The Martin Case," in the subject line. In the body of the email, she wrote, "Mediation on Tuesday, June 9th at 9:00 a.m." David's email to me said, "What case is this?"

Someone was not focusing today. I replied, "The Martin Case."

David responded, "What is it? What's going on?"

I toyed with writing "see supra," but opted to be cordial. "There's a mediation."

"When?"

Was he fucking kidding? "Tuesday, June 9th at 9:00."

"Will you still be here?"

"Yes, I'm due in July."

When I was certain David was out of stupid questions, I printed out our email correspondence and put it in my "An Attorney Actually Said That," category along with the following:

—Please join us in congratulating Jason Voss in his hard fought summary judgment award he received today in favor of his client, a night club that served alcohol to an underage individual who later drove his car home in an intoxicated state and killed a husband and father of four young children. Our client inspected his identification, which was fake and made him 32 instead of 16. This is a tremendous result and Jason should be congratulated. (Brought to you by Johnson Smith's patron saint, Satan).

–Will the person who took my newspaper please give me the classifieds back. I'd like to do my daily crossword. (At least I'm discreet about my time wasting.)

–Confidential High Priority Email: A couple of employees have been diagnosed with the contagious eye disease, "pink eye." Please wash your hands frequently and avoid excessive rubbing of your eyes. If you contract this, get the proper medicine to contain it prior to coming back to work. (Um, can I work from home until this blows over?)

–If Capital One Financial is the adverse party, is it a conflict of interest that I have a Capital One Visa card? (Yes, change banks immediately or find a new job.)

–Does anyone have any case law to support our client's position that a 13–year-old plaintiff would be held to the same legal standard as an adult in regard to appreciating the danger of walking onto a street in front of oncoming traffic? (Patron Saint at work again.)

I put the folder away and looked up the weeks 31 through 34; the bottom of the third trimester of pregnancy.

Week Thirty-One:

Mom: *You may feel as if your internal organs are crowded. They are.* Good time to donate a kidney.

Baby: *Try monitoring the baby yourself by using fetal kick counts.*

That sounded like a chocolate bar. I looked up fetal kick counts and found that the baby should move ten times in four hours, significantly less than the ten-second intervals at which my Empathy Belly was kicking me.

Week Thirty-Two:

Mom: *Posture is very important to your comfort.* I'm thinking Xanax would go a long way as well.

Baby: *The baby's irises can now dilate and contract in response to light.* Great, what time does the sun set in my uterus?

Week Thirty-Three:

Mom: *Rib cage and pelvis may be sore.* The bag of horrors continues.

Baby: *Baby is very aware of the surroundings. We tend to think of the uterus as a dark place, but it can be light and dark depending on the mother's environment.*

I stand corrected, maybe the sun does set in my uterus.

Week Thirty-Four:
Mom: *You may start noticing contractions.*
What? I thought contractions started the day of delivery, not two months prior.
Baby: *Baby is urinating a pint a day.*
I'll never look at a pint of beer in the same way.

In May, I met with Janice Robinson of Human Resources to discuss my pregnancy leave. Crunch time. She gave me some forms to take home and fill out, then spent the rest of the meeting trying to pry information from me. Excessive gossiping is an integral part of Janice's position. Essentially, her questions focused on learning information about my mysterious baby-daddy. I gave her nothing.

Janice's other focal point was my wardrobe. Johnson Smith had a very strict and absurd dress code that each employee received on their first day. Thongs were not permitted. Enforcement of this rule made me nervous until I realized Johnson Smith referred to flip-flops as "thongs." The rest of the dress code was not as clear as the "no thongs" rule. On Monday through Thursday, business casual was acceptable. Friday was casual day. Capri pants were considered casual rather than business casual, and were allowable only on Fridays, as were jeans, provided they weren't blue. The dress code specifically states that pink or yellow jeans were acceptable, but not blue jeans.

The problem was that my meeting with Janice was on a Wednesday and I was wearing a pair of Jessica's maternity capri pants. This may have seemed like a flagrant violation, but in my defense, Jessica was approximately five inches taller than me. Thus, her capris fit me like regular pants, which was why I dared to wear them on a Wednesday. Janice did not understand my logic, let alone agree with it.

"I know you're pregnant, and it's tough, but you have to obey the dress code."

I pulled my flip-flopped or "thonged" feet away from Janice's gaze and said, "The pants go down to my ankles."

"The rule in the dress code clearly states that capris are only proper on Fridays. The length of the capris is irrelevant."

"Yes, but by definition, capris are calf-length. These are ankle-length."

"I can tell they're capris, don't wear them again unless it's a Friday."

I was tempted to say something along the lines of "Fuck off," but I didn't want to get fired before my maternity leave.

I took the FMLA packet back to my office and started filling out the forms. Name, address, age, social security number…I was acing this questionnaire so far. Reason for medical leave: giving birth. Doctor's name and signature: I'd fill that in later.

The form had a place to choose eight weeks or twelve weeks maternity leave. What dipshit workaholic would only choose eight? There's gotta be a catch. I Googled it and found the catch. FMLA required that women receive twelve weeks maternity leave after giving birth. A new mother cannot be fired during this time period, but a business does not necessarily have to pay them for the duration. A number of factors dictated the amount of paid leave a business granted to a new mother. At Johnson Smith, women were entitled to take twelve weeks leave, but only eight of them were paid at two-thirds salary. I only had enough in savings to last me three days, but it was still a no-brainer to choose the twelve-week option. I'd figure out how to support myself for the other three-and-a-half weeks when the time came. Hopefully I'd turn pro. Not exactly a cash cow, but I would be paid in "cycling money," which would get me through for three weeks.

The top domestic professional women racers in the United States make salaries of approximately five thousand a year, and not more than forty thousand. Unfortunately, the *domestiques* for these top racers don't necessarily earn more than zero. The term *domestique* is French for "servant." Unlike triathlon or running, cycling is a team sport. The team leader needs people to block the wind, chase down breakaways, get water bottles from the team car, and in the event of a mechanical, such as a flat tire or broken chain, give up their wheel or bike to their team captain.

In women's racing in the U.S., *domestiques* are paid next to nothing, plus some cycling money, which is more valuable than Monopoly money but less valuable than actual currency. *Domestiques* receive a free team bike (worth about five thousand dollars), several uniforms (called "kits"), travel expenses (hotel, gas, food), entry fees, and, if applicable, a split of their captain's winnings (captains get these perks in addition to becoming thousandaires). The prize purses for women's races are often staggeringly less than the men's races. Because *domestiques* get paid in cycling money rather than actual currency, *domestiques* in the women's *peloton* tend to be either extremely poor if they're not college kids supported by their parents or student loans, housewives supported by their husbands or, hopefully, lawyers fraudulently posing as pregnant women.

I would consider myself a success in cycling if I could avoid losing money. Placing in a regional women's bike race nets a whopping fifty to three hundred bucks. After putting these winnings towards my weekend expenses, I've been losing an average of seventy-five dollars per weekend since I started racing. I make much more money as a lawyer than I ever could as a cyclist and my maternity leave is only going to make this worse. My "vacation" of racing the Tour de West and all of the NRC races leading up to the Tour de West will require me to purchase a four hundred dollar plane ticket for myself and two hundred dollar plane ticket for my bike, then pay for entry fees, hotel, car, gas etc. Therefore, four weeks with no income whatsoever will be a hardship without the help of a professional team.

Filling out the FMLA packet was oddly anti-climactic. For six months I had been paranoid that the paperwork was going to reveal my secret. In reality, the paperwork was barely anything. I'd filled out more paperwork for a teeth cleaning. Surely someone had abused this system before.

* * *

Since becoming a full-fledged fat pregnant woman at month six, I had completely bifurcated my life to avoid being caught pregnant by my friends, or not pregnant by my coworkers. This had made training on the open roads of Tampa difficult, so I started riding my bike in St. Petersburg instead. Danny usually accompanied me on these rides, as he did today. As we rode across the Gandy Bridge, I asked Danny how his overdue thirty year checkup went.

Last weekend, Danny had mentioned that he'd set up the appointment to keep his insurance rate low and I'd been scaring the bejesus out of him about the possibility of being anally raped ever since. In truth, I had no idea when men had to get prostate exams nor did I know what they entail. Nevertheless, I spent yesterday at work feeding Danny's fear of the prostate exam by sending him emails regarding prostate exam horror stories, videos of fisting, and the like.

"So," I said.

"So what?" Danny replied.

"How did it go?"

"I don't want to talk about it."

"What happened?"

"I don't want to talk about it," he repeated. Then said, "Let's just ride."

As we started pedaling, I said, "Come on, you have to tell me."

"I can't. You'll laugh."

"I can't promise anything," I said, "but tell me anyway."

"Okay, you can laugh, but you can't tell anyone. And don't judge me."

"Okay, I can promise that," I said.

"Well," Danny started, "The doctor was a young man from the Philippines with small hands."

"This is going to be good," I said.

"Do you want to hear this or not?"

"Yes please."

"He put gloves on and when he stuck his hands up my ass, I just came."

"I'm calling bullshit on that one," I said.

"Seriously, I just came on my gown. I couldn't help it. His hands were so small and delicate."

"Get the fuck outta here," I said.

"I'm not kidding," Danny insisted.

"Okay. Then what happened after you came?"

"A nurse came in and wiped it up. She said it happens all the time."

"No way."

"It does, just like in that movie *Road Trip*. I wasn't even hard. I just came."

My childhood consisted of being continually lied to by my parents to test the boundaries of my gullibility, so I seldom believe anything I hear until I confirm it on Google. Still, Danny seemed pretty sincere and why would anyone make up such a story?

After I finished laughing I said, "Don't worry, I won't tell anyone."

"I'm just kidding," Danny said. "They didn't even do the test."

"What? I thought it was standard. Why didn't you ask for one?"

"I'm not asking a doctor to stick his fingers up my ass."

"Was he at least a small man from the Philippines man?" I asked.

"No. Old guy," Danny said.

"You should really ask for the test, you could have cancer."

"If the doctor was concerned, he'd have done the test. I'm going to rely on his judgment and not request to be violated."

"It's your life," I said as we rode past a patch of Florida swamp land dried up by drought.

After our ride, I drove to the Spanish section of Tampa to go grocery shopping. As the only English-speaking gringo in the store, I felt no fear of recognition. I hate grocery shopping and only subject myself to it a few times a year. When I go to the store, I buy in bulk. Five of all of my toiletries, ten bags of bagels and ten cases of beer. Bagels are six to a bag. I generally repeat my shopping trip every sixty days, when I run out of bagels. I go to the liquor store or drug store in between as needed.

I don't buy anything perishable, as expiration dates make me nervous. I also hate cooking and cleaning dishes. The obvious solution is to eat out for every meal other than my morning bagel, which requires no preparation other than defrosting on my way to work. Generally, I order a large lunch and eat the leftovers for dinner. If I have no leftovers, I order dinner and eat the leftovers for lunch the next day.

Prior to this system, I used to have a burger for lunch and pasta for dinner. I'd probably still have this system today if my friends and family didn't insist otherwise. For lunch, my specialty was buying several pounds of meat, then grilling sixty or so hamburgers on the Foreman Grill, which I would then freeze, along with numerous bags of hamburger buns. Then, every morning before law school I'd grab a frozen patty and bun and put them in Saran Wrap, along with a slice of individually wrapped Kraft cheese, the fake kind that needs no refrigeration. At lunch, I'd eat a burger under an oak tree with my law school friends. One day the topic veered towards the discovery that the burgers I was eating on a daily basis were barely defrosted. After that, my friends averted their eyes during lunch time until I caved into peer pressure and began buying my lunch. My pasta for dinner tradition ended similarly. My strategy for pasta was to make a box of pasta and mix it with a jar of tomato sauce, then eat it for dinner for a week or so out of the big pot I cooked it in. My mom came over once when I was eating out of my vat of cold pasta like a trough, and it made her so ill that I promised never to do it again.

I was on the phone with Danny while I was shopping. He was at my house waiting to give me a massage.

"Sorry I'm late, I'll be right there."

"I would have grabbed bagels for you if you had asked."

"I know, but I needed shampoo too."

"I probably could have swung that."

"Then I'd be making you a list and I didn't want that to be my favor for today. There's a dead roach in my house I need you to pick up."

"Already done. Were you just going to live with that until I came over?"

"You or one of my brothers," I said.

"You're a terrible feminist," Danny pointed out.

"I can't find any bagels. Do Latinos eat bagels?" I asked.

"Not sure," Danny said. "Jewbans do. Just drive home and I'll get you bagels."

"That's okay, I'll get Cuban bread instead. How many loaves of Cuban bread are equal to sixty bagels?"

"Thirty."

"Shut up, I'm not buying thirty loaves of Cuban bread. I'll get two and cut them up. That will get me through the week and you can get me bagels on a day when you're not picking up a roach."

I moved to the shampoo section. "So many choices. Do I want my hair silky and smooth, full of volume, or do I want the color enhanced?"

"All good hair qualities, you should mix them."

"Sure, just get me an Erlenmeyer flask," I said.

"I don't mean create your own silky volume shampoo. I mean get silky and smooth shampoo and extra volume conditioner and alternate days. Then your hair will have both qualities."

"I don't have room in the corner of my shower. Plus, I don't need conditioner yet. For some reason, my shampoo always runs out before my conditioner. The bottles are the same size, I start them at the same time, and use the same amount of each, but the shampoo always disappears more quickly. It's a mystery."

"Good luck getting to the bottom of that one. Go smooth and silky, your color and volume are fine."

"Are you saying my hair isn't silky and smooth?"

"Not when it's humid outside. Then you look like Sideshow Bob."

"Thanks." I said, "It's humid in Florida nine months of the year."

"You look like him in a good way. What else are you getting?"

"Tampons. Do you have any opinions about this product?" I asked.

"Not really. I think I'll sign off now. See you in a few minutes. I'll be in the backyard playing with Sonny."

"Okay, see you in a little bit."

"Holy shit, your dog has a dildo," Danny said, obviously alarmed.

"Long story," I replied. "I'll explain when I get home. Bye."

A Danny-massage is not a relaxing affair. My leg muscles become horribly knotted from riding and Danny digs into them with the pressure of a torturer. As a result, I have created a safe word. If I say, "Ouch," Danny ignores me. If I scream "Mother Fucker!" he backs off.

"So," Danny said, "getting nervous about the pregnancy?"

"Not really. The prospect of losing my job and going to jail is somewhat nerve-racking, but preferable to childbirth."

"What exactly is your plan?"

"I'm just not going to show up for work someday. I'll send an email that I gave birth to an eleven-pound boy."

"Eleven pounds? Isn't that big?"

"Yes, but I want to have the biggest baby."

"You're not even having a baby, let alone the biggest baby. Maybe you shouldn't get competitive about this."

"I'd make him bigger, but I don't want to have the Guinness Book of World Records checking up on the veracity of my story."

"What is the biggest baby?"

"Not sure, but I read an article that said endurance athletes have big babies. My track coach in high school had a ten-pound baby. I want to edge her out."

"How about ten pounds, one ounce."

"I'll go ten pounds, six ounces. Sounds more believable. Mother Fucker!"

"Sorry," Danny said. "You have a knot. It hurts me more than it hurts you when I have to do this to you."

"You are so full of shit. Baby steps on getting that knot out, you're killing me."

"Once again, your dog has a nine-inch cock in his mouth," Danny said, more nonchalantly this time.

I pulled my head out of the massage table, then remembered I'd promised to explain the dildo. "Yeah, it's Julie's. I meant to throw that out while Sonny was sleeping, but I haven't seen it for two weeks and forgot about it."

"I wish I could forget it."

"Don't be so repressed."

CHAPTER SEVEN

The race this weekend was in Webster, Florida, so I was guaranteed not to see anyone with teeth, let alone anyone from my office. The race is called Webster-Roubaix, and is intended to be modeled after Paris-Roubaix, which travels from Paris to Roubaix, in Northern France, during the middle of April each year. The bitch of Paris-Roubaix is that it is two-hundred and sixty kilometers long and fifty of those kilometers are on roads constructed with large cobblestones called pavé. The pavé, which is sprinkled along the course in approximately thirty different sections, is extremely difficult to ride on in dry weather, because it zaps all of the energy from your legs. When it's wet, which is hardly unusual, the pavé becomes as slippery as an ice rink and riders crash on nearly every section. Each year, crowds line the entire course in spite of the fact that it is generally freezing cold and rainy for this Spring Classic.

Florida's Webster-Roubaix bears very little resemblance to Paris-Roubaix, though they are run on the same day. Unlike Northern France, which is practically in Belgium, the weather in Florida is gorgeous, dry and hot in April. Likewise, spectators and cobblestones are nowhere to be found. Instead, the Webster-Roubaix course covers patches of sugar sand, which skinny road tires sink into, making balance difficult and crashes frequent. Essentially, Webster-Roubaix is similar to Paris-Roubaix in that they are both dangerous and deviate from asphalt. My plan for the race was to avoid crashing and work on my technical skills. While the sprint would be more dangerous than usual, I'd at least land on a soft surface. If I avoided crashing on this crazy course, maybe I'd finally conquer my phobia.

The night before the race I went to bed early and fell asleep immediately. I'm a very sound sleeper and generally fall asleep within fifteen seconds of putting my head on the pillow. I'm not sure how long I was sleeping before I heard a loud noise. I was out cold and didn't know what I heard, but the noise was coming from my guest bedroom. Sonny started howling. I looked at the clock; it was three a.m. Almost immediately, I heard another loud noise, like a window breaking and then a thud. Holy shit! Someone was in my house. Sonny kept howling. I became spontaneously religious and prayed that Sonny's howling would scare the burglar away, then grabbed my cell phone and dialed 911.

A lady answered, "911, what's your emergency?"

I whispered very quietly, "Someone's in my house, please come. I'm alone, I'm going to die."

"Ma'am, calm down, where are you?"

"Please trace it. I don't want to talk. I'm a woman and I'm all alone."

"Your phone is registered to an office building."

Shit. Who knew a free cell phone through my father's office would backfire. Sonny stopped howling and came back to bed.

"It's quiet now, is he gone?" the dispatcher asked.

"I don't know. It's quiet because my dog calmed down. Maybe the guy got away. Can you please come anyway, I'm really scared."

"Ma'am, where do you live?"

I whispered my address as Sonny curled into a ball and fell back to sleep. Some guard dog.

"Stay on the phone ma'am. Officers are on the way."

"Okay. Thank you so much. Really, I'm so scared."

All of a sudden, I saw a light in my window. I cupped the phone and began whispering to the dispatcher again. "They're back and they're shining a light in my window. Please come. Please, please, please. Please hurry."

"Ma'am, relax. That's the cop flashing his light into your house, he's walking around your house checking all the doors and windows."

"Oh. Thanks," I said, attempting to regain some composure.

The dispatcher said, "It's okay to hang up the phone and open your door now."

I got up and stood on wobbly legs, very pleased that I didn't piss myself, and opened the door.

Two young cops walked in, a man and a woman. Sonny started howling again.

"These are the good guys, Sonny. Chill out."

The female officer said, "All of the windows and doors in your house are secure. Did an alarm go off?"

"No, I just heard two loud noises."

"In which room?"

"This one." I led the cops to my spare bedroom and turned on the lights. The bed frame was broken and the metal shoe rack that hung on the back of my door was on the ground, with about forty pairs of shoes littered around the room. My new theory, now that I was sure I wasn't burglarized, was that the first sound was my bed breaking and the second, my shoe rack collapsing; possibly because the room shook from the bed breaking.

I could feel my face turning red. "I'm so sorry. I really thought it was an intruder."

"That's okay ma'am," the male officer said. "For some women, shoes are an emergency."

I looked at all the shoes on the floor. Except for my cycling shoes, my mom had purchased all of them and I rarely wore any of them because they were so uncomfortable. I smiled at the cops because I realized I must look like quite the priss, calling the police for an attack on my pristine shoe collection. "Thank you so much for coming. I'm such a dumbass. Sorry."

The lady cop was looking at me like I was a fucking idiot and for a moment, I thought she was going to agree with me. Fortunately, the male cop said, "Don't worry about it ma'am, you did the right thing."

"Thanks again. Good night."

I went right back to sleep and didn't move until my alarm went off the next morning.

* * *

I almost missed the race. First, I was a bit behind schedule because it was hard for me to find a matching pair of shoes in the sea of shoes on the floor of my guest bedroom. Second, my navigation system never heard of Webster, Florida, so I had to find it by stopping at six gas stations and asking for directions.

I arrived approximately forty-five seconds before the race started and was only allowed to start because the announcer knew me and told the people at registration to give me a number and let me pay later. I only had two pins holding my race number to my jersey when the gun went off. The number was flapping around like a sail. I took off hard so that I could avoid being near any people in the first sand section. I gapped the group immediately and by the time I exited the sand, I led by thirty yards. I stood up and accelerated again to put more space between myself and the pack. I periodically looked down beneath my armpit or over my shoulder as I rode and could see that I was continuing to distance myself from the pack. After a minute, my lead had extended to over one hundred yards, so I sat down in my saddle and settled in to a hard, fast pace.

The women in the *peloton* behind me failed to organize a chase. A group of decent cyclists should always be able to overtake an individual cyclist, even if that individual cyclist is stronger, because the group can set a high pace, and rotate so that each rider spends minimal time in the wind while the cyclist they're chasing has no reprieve. For instance, the chasing cyclists can each spend thirty seconds in the wind, then move into the draft to be shielded from the wind as the next cyclist in the group takes a thirty second pull into the wind. To increase the speed of the chase, riders may also create a clockwise or counterclockwise pace line whereby each rider spends only a few seconds in the wind. Both of these chasing techniques are cooperative efforts that are foolproof, provided the chasing riders cooperate. However, the chase often fails when a chaser or two, acting in their self-interest, disrupts this harmony. Once the chasing group starts reeling in the chase, one or two cyclists may try to jump across the shrinking gap to join the breakaway riders, rather than waiting for the entire pack to catch up in one big group. When this happens, the rest of the riders stop sharing the workload and instead accelerate to get within the draft of the person traveling across the gap. At this point, the rider or riders trying to bridge across to the breakaway no longer have any incentive to keep working since they know that, even if they catch the break, they'll do it with the entire *peloton* in their draft. Therefore, the chasing rider "sits-up" and stops working. The result is that the *peloton*, which is now drafting off of the renegade rider, slows down as well. Each time this happens, the chasing group not only slows down, but becomes less likely to resume their harmonious chase because the riders don't trust each other. Consequently, the breakaway rider, in this case me, is able to put more distance between herself and the group of chasers.

The combination of me feeling great and the chase behind me becoming disorganized every time it entered a section of sand allowed me to build my lead. It was clear by the third lap that only a flat tire could prevent me from winning. My luck held and I won the not-so-prestigious Roubaix seventy mile road race solo off the front. I guess I'd have to learn technique and sprinting another day.

I never tell anyone outside of cycling when I win a race because I have the impression my friends and family assume I win every race I enter. I've never told anyone that I win every race. However, I do tell them that I'm a top-level Florida cyclist. That, plus the fact that over the past year I have poured all of my money and time into cycling means I really can't blame everyone for their false assumption. Since no one actually follows cycling, I have never felt obliged to correct this assumption. I do very well, but cycling is not like running, where the strongest person always wins. Cycling has teams, strategy, drafting and scary field sprints, which make it difficult to go undefeated. People know I win prize money, I just neglect to tell them it's not always for first place and that it's very rarely in the three digits. I'd have preferred to have a passion for something profitable, or at a minimum, not a total money pit, but it hasn't worked out that way. At least I'm not into sailing or airplanes.

When I got home from Webster, I took a four hour nap. I'd have slept longer but my mother called to tell me I was late for dinner.

"I'm on my way."

"You sound like you're sleeping."

"I'm at a red light, resting," I said unconvincingly.

"Have you left your house yet?"

"Almost," I said. "I'll be right there."

I wish I could support my cycling habit by napping instead of practicing law, because I'm really good at it. Who knows how long I could have slept if she hadn't wakened me. A weekly schedule of fifty hours of work and 350 miles of riding leaves me with the desire to treat every lull in life as an occasion for some shuteye. I often wish I could challenge the most afflicted narcoleptic to a napping duel, as I'm quite sure I'd prevail.

I was wearing the Empathy Belly when I pulled into my parents' driveway just in case David drove by. Once the coast was clear I ditched the Empathy Belly and ran into the house with Sonny.

I wasn't fully in the door before my mom said, "Jenna, I have a guy for you to meet."

"I'm good," I said.

"You don't have to marry him, just go out with him."

"I'm good," I repeated.

"He's really cute. He's an elementary school counselor and music teacher."

"That's an odd combination."

"He was a music teacher. Then he became a guidance counselor. With cutbacks, they decided to use him for both. He only teaches music a few times a week."

"You're a middle school guidance counselor," I said to her. "How did you meet an elementary school guidance counselor?"

"The elementary school guidance counselors always bring the fifth graders to my school so they can see the middle school they'll be attending the following year. Anyway, he saw your picture in my office and asked for your number. I gave it to him."

"That's creepy. Are you crazy?"

"I'm just helping out," my mom said. "You're not meeting anyone on your own."

"I am too, just not 'the one.'"

"Well maybe Andy is the one. You never know."

"I sincerely doubt Andy the elementary school music teacher and guidance counselor is my soul mate. I am not exactly a music connoisseur or sensitive to the problems of others."

My mom added a few more items to that list and then said, "And he doesn't ride bikes. Opposites attract."

"That's not opposite, that's unrelated. Where does he live?"

"Not sure, but he works in the Pinellas County School system, so probably somewhere in Clearwater or St. Petersburg."

"Strike two. That's an hour away, completely out of my dating jurisdiction. I wouldn't date George Clooney in Pinellas County let alone Mr. Holland's Opus."

"I'm sure Andy will drive."

"Not interested," I said emphatically.

"Jenna," my dad said, "just go for it, what else do you have to do?"

"Work, ride my bike, sleep, hang out with my friends. I do stuff."

"Just go out with him. He's got balls, it takes balls to ask a girl out."

"He asked my mother out," I pointed out.

"He asked you out via Mom," Dad responded.

"Mom, what picture do you have up in your office? Last time I was there you had my high school picture up. He might be a pedophile. He's got the perfect job for it."

"He's not a pedophile, and I update your pictures quarterly. I have the picture of you at John and Julie's wedding up and you look beautiful."

* * *

Andy called me on Tuesday, but I didn't answer the phone. I had become adept at ignoring the phone since my date with Quinton, who still called me every three days to see if I'd changed my mind. Andy left a voice mail.

"Hi, Jenna. This is Andy, I work with your mom. Give me a call when you get a chance." He left his number.

This would never work out because his area code indicated that he lived too far away to be datable.

Still, I called him back. Not because I'm a dutiful daughter, but because I didn't want to hear about it again next Sunday night, and the Sunday after that. We made plans to meet on Thursday for dinner. There was no small talk and I was convinced Andy had no personality based on my thirty second phone conversation. On the plus side, I scheduled dinner for 8:30 p.m. so that I didn't have to cut my bike ride short.

Andy rang the doorbell promptly at 8:30. I had just emerged from the shower. I looked through the peephole. Not an attractive man. He wasn't exactly ugly, but he was a mouth breather and a little on the heavy side. Not fat, but not fit or athletic either. I was sure he'd find a wonderful lady some day, just not me.

I called to him to come in and sit on the couch, because I wasn't ready yet. He obeyed and I started getting ready. Sonny was howling and humping him while I tried to pick out something ugly to wear so that he would be equally uninterested in me. I had already decided not to blow dry my hair, but that was out of laziness. I needed something ugly to wear to match my unkempt hair. As I stared at my closet, a bunch of maternity wear stared back at me. Perfect!

I walked out. Andy was shocked by his first sight of me but trying to act natural. "Hi, Jenna. Ready?"

Gotta love a guy who ignores the elephant in the room. "Sure, I'm starving. Eating for two you know."

No response. Clearly he wasn't going to officially acknowledge my unexpected pregnancy.

We went to a local tapas bar with great sangria. I sat down and ordered a pitcher. Andy stared at me disapprovingly, but refrained from mentioning the pregnancy.

"So," I said, "how's elementary school these days? It's been a while for me."

"I like it. The kids are sweet and I get to teach music and help advise them when they're troubled."

"What sort of problems do they have?"

"Peeing their pants, bullies, dealing with divorce, some of them still breast-feed coming into kindergarten."

"That's funny. I'll totally do that with this kid," I said.

"Really?" he asked nervously. Andy had not lost the deer-in-headlights look since spotting my belly.

"No," I responded. I was afraid the conversation would switch to pregnancy details, so I moved the topic back to his interests. "So," I said, "what kind of music do you teach?"

"A few things. I teach violin and chorus, and I play the piano while they sing."

"Do you know 'Chopsticks'?"

"Yes."

"Me too, but only the du dununu du dununu part. I don't know the dunt dunt dunt, dunununu part."

"I know them both, but there are no words so I don't play that for them."

"Oh yeah. Do you teach marching too?"

"No, that's high school band," Andy explained.

And we were out of conversation. We sat there awkwardly until Andy said. "What do you want to order? We can share a few tapas dishes."

"Okay."

We both looked at the menu and it was the least awkward moment of the night.

While we read the menu, Sarah Smith walked over to our table. Thank God I'd worn the Empathy Belly. When I saw Sarah at the office, we exchanged pleasantries. Outside of work, Sarah and I were evidently best friends. She screeched, "Hi Jenna! What are you doing here, sexy? Is this yo baby daddy?"

"No, this is Andy," I replied calmly.

Sarah hovered over Andy and stuck her huge boobs in his face, then leaned down and kissed him on the lips, ignoring his outstretched hand. "Sorry Charlie, I do hugs and kisses, not handshakes."

"Um, actually, it's Andy," he responded, seemingly unaware of the phrase "sorry Charlie."

"I know," Sarah said as she pulled up a chair to our table.

I guessed she was staying. In an effort to avoid this, I said, "Who are you here with?"

"My friends Sarah and Sarah. We've been friends for thirty years. All three of us are named Sarah. Isn't that crazy?"

"Yes, it's such a rare name," I offered helpfully.

Sarah turned to Andy and said, "This one's a smartass huh," as she grabbed his thigh.

He shot straight up. "Uh. Yeah or no, I don't know, I mean, I just met her."

Sarah moved her other hand to his thigh and said, "You mean, you guys aren't together?"

"No," we said in unison.

"We just met," I added.

The waitress came by and we ordered. Sarah ordered something extra for the table. I was fine with a third wheel, but did it have to be Sarah? I wished I could trade her for one of the other Sarahs. Then again, as friends of Sarah Smith, I was sure they had their own problems.

After the waitress left, Sarah took over the conversation, presumably trying to win Andy over with her charm. She started telling a story about the death of her goldfish, Fatty. Apparently Fatty was fat and was her favorite goldfish. It was really heartbreaking, but I managed to hold it together.

Sarah leaned into Andy to be comforted. Andy looked like he was in hell, which was not far off the mark. A pregnant lady and a sixty-year-old is not an ideal ménage à trois.

The first dish came. Sarah made a production of eating the olives as suggestively as possible, sucking her fingers unnecessarily after every bite. The full court press was on. As Sarah described her tattoos, the ones she had and the ones she planned to get, the rest of the food arrived. This wasn't so bad. I was out of the house in an English-speaking part of town enjoying good food and low-brow entertainment.

My mind started wandering as I ate. I have a friend who has this idea for a sandwich shop where, instead of letting the customer order, the owner makes you a sandwich based on what he thinks you'll like as a result of your appearance. Genius plan. I started to think of what I would make for Andy and Sarah. I would give Sarah a tuna melt. For Andy...

"Earth to Jenna, do you want that last piece of eggplant?"

"Meatball sub."

"What?"

"Nothing. No, you can eat it." I thought I just said meatball sub out loud. Whatever.

The waitress came back over and asked us if we wanted dessert. "Whatcha got?" Sarah asked, as Andy and I said, "No just the check," in unison. The waitress rattled off desserts and Sarah settled on flan. "You guys will help right?"

"No, I hate flan. I'll help with anything else though," I said.

"But I'm craaaaaaving flan." Sarah whined.

After a little persuasion, Andy agreed to help. By virtue of her incessant nagging, Sarah could have convinced Andy to eat a plate of shit.

The flan and the bill came together. Andy offered to pick it up. Normally, I'll make a courtesy offer then allow the guy to pick up the check. However, Andy had had a rough night and rumor had it that teachers earn shit pay. So, I insisted on paying one-third of the check, hoping to incite Sarah to add her card to the table as well.

The subtle hint didn't work. I tried a more direct route. "Sarah, can you pay one third too?"

"That doesn't seem fair, I ate with my friends."

"I'm not suggesting you don't pay one third over there as well," I replied.

Sarah gave me a death glare and put her card on the table. "I'll pay for the flan." She said this as though she was doing us a favor even though she'd ordered it and ate the entire dish.

"You had four drinks too."

Sarah agreed to pay for what she herself ordered. It was obvious by the way she offered that she hoped Andy would tell her not to worry about it. He did not oblige.

Mercifully, the night ended. Andy dropped me off and I was quite confident he would not be calling for a follow-up date. I walked into my house, took off my belly and crashed.

Over the rest of the weekend I started to feel bad about tricking Andy. I thought about calling to apologize, but I really wasn't into him and thought he was probably better off not knowing that I pretended to be pregnant to avoid dating him. By the time work rolled around on Monday, I had forgotten about the entire night. That is, until Sarah came in my office and shut the door.

"Jenna, I hope you don't mind, but Andy and I are together."

"What? When?"

"Promise you won't get mad?"

"I think I can manage that."

"Well, I followed you guys home to your house, which is very cute. I really love the old South Tampa bungalows. Anyway, when he walked you to your door, I got on the hood of his car."

In my mind, I was comparing a hot twenty-year-old woman on a Ferrari, with Sarah on Andy's gray Honda Civic. Not as likely to wind up on a calendar. "So?" I said.

"You know…"

"You had sex on the hood of his car outside of my house?"

"Not exactly. We were in the backseat."

"You're kidding right?" I started to praise God that I opened Sonny's doggy door and let him out back instead of walking him out front. First, I would have been busted without my pregnant belly, but more devastating, I would have witnessed teenage car sex between Sarah and Andy.

"No," Sarah said. "It was very spontaneous and romantic. There was this vibe throughout dinner and I just knew we were meant for each other. Couldn't you tell?"

"Not in the least," I responded before I realized it was a rhetorical question.

"You're not mad are you?" she asked.

"No, just stunned. I didn't pick up on the vibe. Are you guys seeing each other again?"

"We met halfway between our houses last night."

"Did you go on a date?"

"No, more hot car sex."

Eww. Why did I ask? "You didn't grab dinner or a drink or something first?"

"Nope. Anyway, I meant to ask you for his number."

"Why didn't you get it from him?" I asked, in disbelief.

Sarah said, "He wouldn't give it to me. He said he'd call me."

"This sounds weird. Is he married?"

"No, why?"

"Because he met up with you for car sex at a neutral location and won't give you his number."

"That's only because of his job."

"Pardon?" I said.

"He didn't say exactly, but he implied that he's in the CIA or Secret Service or something. Why don't you just give me his number?"

"Tell you what," I said, "I'll give you his top secret work number."

I looked up the number for the elementary school he worked at and gave Sarah the number. This would be interesting. Regardless of whether he was married or just had a car fetish, I was glad to be rid of him and thanked God that I hadn't called him to apologize. What a creep.

* * *

During May, I looked up weeks thirty-five through forty-two to see what sort of acting was in my future. Even though there was nothing else I could do besides wear my Empathy Belly, I figured that I should at least be aware of what women were talking about when they commiserate with me about pregnancy.

Evidently weeks thirty-five through forty-two are hard to predict because women begin giving birth anywhere in this time frame. I planned to take my vacation from July 1 to September 30 and unlike every other pregnant woman, I wouldn't have a kid to fuck up my schedule. Nothing much happens during the last two months except Mom gets fatter, more uncomfortable, sleeps less and pees more. This monotonous state of discomfort remains unchanged until the precursor to the real fun begins. Obviously, the "real fun" is the excruciating labor. The precursors are as follows:

Bloody Show: A mucousy, pink, red, or brown tinged discharge from the vagina. This usually indicates that the cervix is opening. It may or may not signal labor.

I love that they call this a show instead of bloody discharge.

Loss of Mucous Plug: The plug of mucous that fills the cervix to protect against disease and infection. This may start leaking out as the cervix slowly starts opening before labor, or may come out in one big chunk. It can be pink or tinged with blood.

That sounds like a big loogie.

Loose Stools: Loose stools are nature's way of preparing your body for labor. It helps clean your system out and make room for your baby in the vagina. (Remember the vagina and rectum are only a thin piece of skin apart.)

Maybe nature should have put a bigger buffer zone in that region.

I was astounded that people actually believed that I was going through with this insane pregnancy thing. More unbelievable, women used to do this even though there was a good chance it would kill them. Human babies aren't even that cute, especially compared to babies of other species, like puppies and elephants.

Since pre-labor involved a bloody show, losing a mucous plug and loose stools, I was hesitant to research the actual labor. As I started to shut down the page I noticed a link to an article at the bottom of the page. It said, "Orgasms During Childbirth." That's one I hadn't heard before. I had heard childbirth described as excruciatingly painful, and I'd heard of women losing the will to live midway through childbirth, but orgasmic? I clicked on the article.

Some women experience orgasm during childbirth. There are similarities between the process of orgasm and childbirth; both involve involuntary contractions of some of the same muscles. Orgasm releases endorphins, which can mediate the pain of labor, as well as the hormone oxytocin, which is known to play an important role in labor as well as mother-child attachment. Some people have speculated that sexual repression, in particular, the repression of women's sexuality, may be holding more women back, both from having an orgasmic experience with childbirth, and from accepting and sharing the experience when they do have it.

Interesting. I clicked on some testimonials, amazed that my work computer didn't block them as tasteless content. According to several women, birth, like sex, seems to hurt the first time, then it's enjoyable. My mom should like Jason and me more than John. John was twenty-three hours of excruciating pain, while it was possible that Jason and I were happy-ending childbirths. Not to be an asshole, but I prefer to think of my mom as being in excruciating pain rather than orgasmic while giving birth to me. I wonder if you can have multiple intense orgasms for twins or triplets.

The bottom of one of the articles had a link about cesarean sections. I clicked on it. The scar was horizontal through the pubes, which surprised me. I always assumed they just cut the mom right down the center. The cut looked pretty bad, so I would not be having a fake C-section. I began reading the article about cesareans and how they cut through your abdominal muscles when the acronym FLMA stuck out at me. The article said that the Family Medical Leave Act provides women an additional two weeks maternity leave if they undergo a C-section. Hmm, I think my baby just moved into the breach position. A C-section and three and a half months vacation it is.

After reading the pregnancy articles, I had trouble focusing on my work. It was 2:00 p.m. and I was pretty sure I wasn't going to accomplish anything else at work. I decided to go to a "doctor's appointment," so that I could get a nap in before my bike ride.

When I came home from work there was a basset hound in my house. I saw it run outside the doggy door as I came in the front door. Fortunately, basset hounds don't run very fast so I caught her very easily. Her tag said "Molly" and had a phone number. I called the number.

"Hi, is this Molly's parents? I have your dog."

"Oh sorry, where are you?" a woman inquired.

"On San Raphael."

"Do you have the brown dog that howls all day?" the woman asked.

"You mean the really cute one?" I asked rhetorically. "That's me."

"Our dogs play together all the time. I'm the house behind you, you can just send her over through the gate."

"Okay."

I sent Molly home then went back in to see Sonny.

"Busted, Sonny. I didn't know you had a girlfriend. It's like I hardly know you." I kept talking to him in a conversational tone and said, "She's a little big, but very cute." Then, I held my hand up for him to give me a high five even though I never taught him that trick.

Sonny responded by rolling over for a tummy rub.

I obliged and rubbed his belly as I continued to talk to him. "Do you and Molly play with Julie's dildo?"

CHAPTER EIGHT

Work was awkward today because it was the day of my baby shower. I had been to Johnson Smith baby showers before, so I knew what to expect. Namely, that my office would provide a luncheon for me of sandwiches, chips, salad and cake. After lunch, I would open my gifts, a shitload of onesies and a group gift. The group gift would be paid for in increments of twenty dollars by coworkers who were my friends, and increments of five dollars by coworkers who were not my friends but were interested in attending a free lunch with cake. The group gift would be either a stroller, car seat or crib; none of which were on my wish list. I felt bad about accepting these gifts. Then again, I'd spent at least $600 on their baby showers, so it all balanced out. Plus, you can never have too many infant-sized onesies.

I didn't register for baby gifts at any stores, hoping instead to receive cash. No such luck. The room was full of gifts in gender neutral yellow and green pastel wrapping paper because my baby's gender was unknown. I should have registered at the bike shop for a baby trailer and kid's cycling gear. At least I could have exchanged that stuff for something I actually wanted.

During the shower, David did his normal schmoozing. That's what David does. He never socializes to enjoy the company of others; it's always to develop business, even amongst his own employees. I don't think it's ever occurred to David that he is a social liability and should never exit the realm of law. Agoraphobia would actually be a great complement to David's personality. I made a mental note to check David's billing later today to see whether David billed my shower to "business development."

I tried to ignore David, but once we made eye contact I felt compelled to greet him. "Hey David, glad you could make it." I'm such a phony.

"Hi, Jennifer, congratulations!" He's a phony, too. "If you're still happy that is. Are you?"

"No, you want another kid?"

David froze. "No, but there's always adoption."

"Are you kidding? Do you know what you can get for a healthy white baby on the black market?"

"No, what?"

Hmm. Kind of a rhetorical question. "I'd get a good twenty grand, twenty-five if it's blond."

My secretary, Karen, no doubt taking pity on me, interrupted to congratulate me. David walked off. After eating, I took it upon myself to get the show on the road by initiating the gift opening.

My first gift was a "Hooter Hider," to cover my boobs when I breast-feed in public. It was then that I realized these gifts were going to be even worse than I anticipated. Clearly karma was kicking my ass for the gifts I got my friends when they registered for their weddings. For my friends' weddings, I bought them an absurd combination of stupid stuff out of their registry until I reach one hundred dollars. For example, one washcloth, one pillow case, a fork, a wine glass and a napkin ring. I know this is obnoxious, but so is registering for a fork when you're approaching thirty. A wedding is the one opportunity where it's socially acceptable to ask for what you want and I didn't intend to use it for a napkin ring if I ever got married.

On the other hand, at least I could use a napkin ring once or twice in my life, but I was at a loss for an alternate use of a Hooter Hider. I checked in the box for a gift receipt: Babies "R" Us. Shitty.

I opened my next gift. Diapers. I'll hang onto these, I'm sure I'll be incontinent in sixty years and will be too embarrassed to purchase diapers for myself.

Baby bottles. This could work as a water bottle on a bike. I'll see if it fits the water bottle cage.

Swaddlers. Looks like a good rag to clean a bike.

Breast pump. That does not look comfortable.

Baby bathing center. That looked like an improvement to squeezing the kid into a sink.

Neutral-colored pastel onesies, bibs, socks, shirts, pants etc. All could work as bike rags, though the snaps on the onesies could be dangerous to the paint job. I'll have to cut the snaps out.

A box of lip gloss, eye shadow, blush, mascara, moisturizer, and eyeliner? What the fuck! It's from Jackie, the partner I worked for before David. Jackie's dedication to the firm is similar to my own, though she made partner so I suspect she worked hard once upon a time. Jackie spends a lot of her time at work shopping online. It doesn't bother me that she's a material girl or that she procrastinates. I didn't even mind that her hands-off approach to mentoring allowed me to be an attorney for two years and learn absolutely nothing. But, I was a bit offended by her not so subtle hint that I should start wearing makeup to work. I'd wear makeup if there were any eye candy in the office. Couldn't she have just contributed to the group gift? I made a mental note to get her hair dye that was not platinum-blonde for Christmas. Two could play this game.

Stuffed animals. Sonny would love these, though it was too bad none of them had squeakers.

The granddaddy of them all: a stroller that turns into a car seat. This seemed like a big ticket item. Please tell me this was from Target. I checked the gift receipt: Babies "R" Us. Damn.

The firm's maintenance man helped me put the gifts in my car. Once I went down to my car, I didn't have it in me to walk back up to the office, so I went home. I didn't take the crap out of my car when I got home. I didn't know what to do with it, but taking it into my house was out of the question. I could be a good person and donate it to charity, but the stuff was valuable and I was going to need cash on the road. I thought of eBay, but that was time consuming and never gave full value. The other alternative was to return it all and have a gift card to spend at Babies "R" Us in the future. That would tide me over for the next five or six baby showers, probably only a few months given the alarming rate at which my friends procreated. The only problem with this idea was that I have a tendency to lose gift cards very easily. This pisses me off with a twenty dollar Starbucks card, so I didn't really want to test my luck with a six hundred dollar Babies "R" Us card.

I decided to ride my bike into Babies "R" Us and cruise around to see if there was anything good. It's a huge store and I'm immature, so I was sure I could knock out a few hundred bucks easy. I enjoy riding my bike into stores. When a punk kid with a BMX bike walks into a store, he gets kicked out. When a twenty-eight-year-old woman on a $5,000 bike rides her bike up and down the aisles, there's generally no precedent for how to react. By the time an employee thinks to ask me to get off the bike, I'm onto the next aisle.

The first aisle I cruised through was full of "Baby Einstein" gear. None of it looked very challenging. As I looped around to the next aisle, I noticed a sign by the cash register that said Babies "R" Us accepts Toys "R" Us gift certificates and vice versa. This excited me more than it should excite a woman approaching thirty.

When I was in elementary school, I watched a show called *Double Dare* on Nickelodeon. The winners received a shopping spree at Toys "R" Us where they could take home whatever they could fit in their shopping cart in sixty seconds. The kid always just grabbed whatever was closest, often knocking six of the same toy off the shelf and into the cart. I always planned to do a reconnaissance of the store prior to winning *Double Dare* so that I would know where to find the good stuff.

I rode my bike home from Babies "R" Us to get my car. I decided to bring Sonny with me to Toys "R" Us. Sonny gets excited for the leash, but when I pull out the therapy dog cape, he gets out of control; howling and wagging his whole body instead of just his tail. I bought him the cape so he could accompany me places that don't permit dogs. I know it's an abuse of the system, but Sonny likes stores and most shoppers like him regardless of his behavior, which includes dragging me all over the store sniffing and occasionally howling at nothing.

Our first stop was a return to Babies "R" Us. I grabbed a cart, put all of my stuff in it and walked to the returns counter. Sonny jumped up on the counter looking for Milk-Bones. "Down boy, we're not at the vet." The cashier leaned forward to pet Sonny, who wagged his tail like crazy and jumped up to lick her. He is very therapeutic.

I started unloading the cart.

"Reason for your return?" the cashier asked.

"I don't need the stroller and breast pump because I'm not pregnant, and the clothes don't fit me," I said, holding the onsie up to my chest to demonstrate. This answer was sufficient and the cashier started ringing up my returns. I received a $487 gift card to be used at Babies "R" Us or Toys "R" Us.

I drove over to Toys "R" Us. As Sonny and I walked into the store, a remote control car drove right in front of us. Sonny howled and chased it. This was better than fetch, so I decided that I would definitely be buying a remote control car. The problem was, I had no idea where to find remote control cars, or anything else for that matter. I could see the problem on *Double Dare*. I started walking up and down the aisles. Barbies, action figures, dolls, blah. Where were the fun toys? I walked to the outdoor section. Bingo. Trampolines, Slip 'N Slides, electric cars. I could still remember which kid in my neighborhood had each of these toys. I skipped over the Slip 'N Slide, because as I learned from my next door neighbor growing up, you could just unroll a bunch of plastic garbage bags, run a hose on it and call it a Slip 'N Slide. I moved onto the trampoline section and was dismayed to learn that trampolines had evolved to include guard rails. Fucking lawyers; you haven't lived until you've broken your arm being popcorned off a trampoline.

At the checkout, I unloaded my trove: a remote control car for sixty-five dollars, trampoline for one hundred and eighty dollars, and a supersoaker for thirty dollars. I had about two-hundred dollars left. I grabbed the capsules that grow into sponges when placed in water. Now I had about one hundred and ninety-nine left. Bubble gum tape and bubble gum toothpaste for Jason who likes anything that rots his teeth. Down to one hundred and ninety-five dollars. I checked out the battery operated electric Barbie car that I always wanted as a child. It was designed to fit one four-year-old kid in it, so I had to contort myself to sit inside. I pressed the gas pedal and moved forward at a half mile an hour. Must be a low battery. Sonny started howling at me so I began to try to force my way out of the car. It was quite a struggle. As I freed myself, I accidentally hit the gas pedal with my hand. It took off. I guess the battery worked so long as a 110-pound adult wasn't weighing it down. I looked at the box; eighty-pound weight limit. That was a no go. I went down the "entertainment" aisle and got iPod Karaoke Theater. The next aisle had bathtub crayons. That's gotta be four hundred and eighty seven dollars. It was actually four hundred and eighty-nine. I paid the difference and arranged for the trampoline to be delivered later that night.

When I arrived home, my mom was sitting in her car in my driveway. I had to get rid of her before the trampoline arrived. She had been begging me to reupholster my couch and buy new clothes for work for six months. She would freak if she knew I'd purchased child's toys instead and I couldn't exactly explain the circumstances.

My Mom was listening to an audio book in my driveway. I walked up and said, "Hi Mom, what are you doing here?"

"We had a half-day at school. What are you doing here? Why aren't you at work?"

"Had a doctor's appointment," I said.

"Me too," Mom said as she got out of her car. "What did you go to the doctor for?" she asked.

Hmm. Probably shouldn't say fake obstetrician appointment. "Dermatologist." I said. "He said I shouldn't be in the sun so much."

"I'm sure he did with your tan lines. Will you listen to him?" my mom asked.

"I wear a ton of sunscreen."

"You're still really dark," Mom said. "Other than where you're white as a ghost, that is. Anyway, I was down here for the appointment and I'm having dinner near here tonight with Dad. I figured I would hang out here until dinner time rather than driving back home. I was just about to call you to make sure it was okay."

"Great. Want to go get a movie?"

"We could," she said. "But since you're here we should really clean out your closets. You have so much stuff you don't wear and you really should give it to charity."

Fuck. This idea sucked on so many levels. First, it was time-consuming and boring. Second, every time I throw something in the charity pile, my mom tells me how much she spent on it in relation to how few times I've worn it, laying on the guilt pretty thick. Then, she tries to take the stuff I wear all the time and get rid of it, saying it's old and worn. Finally, and most importantly, I have a closet full of Jessica's maternity wear, which would probably raise an eyebrow. "Come on Mom, not now. I'll do it later."

"You always say that and you never do it. Let's just do it while I'm here, it will go twice as fast and I'll be able to sleep at night because I know it will be done. People need the clothes you're not wearing."

I swallowed hard. "Let's go shopping instead."

Mom's eyes lit up. The only thing she likes more than reorganizing and cleaning out a closet is shopping. Having her daughter willingly shop with her has been a dream of hers since my birth. I haven't shopped with her since we looked for my homecoming dress in tenth grade. Then, I'd looked around and found three that I liked, none of which were my size. Mom found sixteen dresses, all on sale and all in my size. She's quite gifted. I tried on all sixteen and bought four so I could avoid the same shopping trip for my junior and senior homecoming dances and senior prom. Getting the dress wasn't the end of it though. I spent the next four hours visiting every store in the mall with Mom. Every rack had at least seven items that Mom was iffy about and my opinion was the swing vote. Like Pavlov's dog, it did not take me very long to realize that every time I said I liked something, the next step was that Mom would try it on. So, I stopped approving everything. After a few rejections, she started ignoring my opinion and resumed trying on everything in sight while I sat on the chairs with the husbands.

My offer worked. I averted the disaster of cleaning out my closet and embarked on the disaster of shopping with my mom. On the plus side, the mall was only open for another five hours and Mom would probably have to leave earlier than that to meet Dad for dinner. This trip would be four hours, tops. I left a note for the trampoline delivery boy.

We went to Westshore Mall. I tried pushing for the outlet malls because they are located forty-five minutes away, thus reducing the chance I would run into someone from work un-pregnant. Mom didn't want to drive that far, so, I shopped in a state of alertness, ready to duck behind Mom if I saw anyone from work.

I tried to be a good little shopper; acting interested in which Ann Taylor shirt and cardigan go best with the pants from Ann Taylor Loft, but I was busy stressing over how many more stores Ann Taylor could possibly have to screw up my day. Nine stores later, we were in Cache when I gave up, sat on the comfortable chair and tried to sleep.

I heard "Jenna," and opened my eyes. Sarah-Mother-Fucking-Smith. "You're not pregnant," she said.

I couldn't tell if she was asking me or telling me that I wasn't pregnant. My heart was pounding. I thought of bribing her, but decided to start with denial. "No, you must have me confused with someone else."

"Oh, sorry. You look just like this woman at my office, except she's pregnant. You look identical." She started sizing me up, not sure whether to believe the impossible. "You're her long lost twin if you're not Jenna."

As I stammered, Mom came up behind me and said, "Jenna, let's go honey."

"Did she call you, Jenna?"

"No, Hannah. Bye." I could tell by Sarah's face that this conversation was not over.

"Where now?" I asked Mom.

"Brookstone, Limited, Bandolino, lots of stuff."

We got back to my house at eight p.m. Because it was dark, Mom pulled out of my driveway without noticing the huge box on my doorstep. I dragged the box into the house without even opening it. Assembling a trampoline would definitely be a Danny assignment. Fifteen minutes later, I was in bed asleep. Is it possible that shopping is more tiring than riding 100 miles on a bicycle?

CHAPTER NINE

The good news, I was into June already, so I only had a little over a month to go. The bad news, it was the first Monday of June. On the first Monday of each month, the attorneys and paralegals of the subrogation department have an obligatory hour-long meeting beginning at 8:00 a.m. Each month, a different associate leads the meeting, discussing a different topic of subrogation law.

David brings a laugh track to these meetings. There is no other way to explain the outbreak of laughter after each statement he makes. A lot of his lines are predictable. For instance, this month we have a new associate in our office, which means he's going to use his "fight song" joke. Other obligatory jokes are the "naming the wrong presenter" joke and the "Geico" joke, none of which I get. In addition to his jokes,

David likes to ask everyone if we did anything interesting over the weekend. He uses this question as a segue to inform us what he and his family did over the weekend. At the end of each meeting, David asks if any of us have any interesting cases. He uses this question as a segue to inform all of us about his interesting cases. These jokes and discussions are to a subrogation meeting as the YMCA and Electric Slide are to a wedding; you hope it's not coming, but you know it is.

The meeting started a little late because Sam, June's subrogation speaker, brought donuts to the meeting. Sam is easily the biggest kiss-ass of the department, not only because he weighs 500 pounds, but also because his perfect day would be to hang out and discuss subrogation waivers with David. He is so big, the carpet beneath the chair in his office has disintegrated and all that's left is concrete and a few strings of carpet attached to the wheels of his chair. I'd feel bad for him if he wasn't so annoying.

While I was trying to discreetly stab a donut to determine if it was filled with white cream or lemon cream before committing, David began his set. "While you are all eating, I'd like to introduce our newest associate, Scott, to any of you that haven't met him yet. Scott went to FSU, booooooo, go Gators!" David paused so that everyone could laugh and shout out their favorite college sports team. They didn't disappoint.

Next, David turned to Scott and said, "Are you ready to sing the Johnson Smith fight song?" Once again, hilarity ensued until David said, "Just kidding, we don't have a fight song." Since this exchange with the new associate happens at least every other month as a result of the turnover at our firm, I quickly calculated that in my three-plus years at the firm, I had probably heard the fight song joke at least ten to twenty times, including the time it was directed at me at my first subrogation meeting.

I sat down with my chocolate-covered white cream donut as David said, "So Jenna, are you ready to give the presentation?" This is the part of the meeting where I'm supposed to freak out until David reassures me that it's actually Sam's month to present.

I gave David a blank stare, which he mistook for fear, then said, "Just kidding, it's Sam's week."

"Oh," I said, "is that why he brought donuts and a PowerPoint presentation?"

David glared at me. I interpreted it as a laugh-or-lose-your-job-glare, so I compromised and smiled. I felt like a complete sell-out.

Once David confirmed that he was hilarious, he moved on. "Did anyone do anything fun this weekend? I took Joseph to his painting competition. Scott, you're new, but Joseph is my thirteen-year-old son. He is an extremely talented artist, also a swimmer and the most popular kid in his school. Anyway, he won first prize and one hundred dollars for his painting of Mesa Verde, which is where our family went on vacation last year. Have you ever been to Mesa Verde, Scott?"

Not this again. David gave us a thirty minute play-by-play of his trip to Mesa Verde when he returned from vacation last August. Fortunately, this time we only had to hear a ten-minute version for Scott's benefit. I zoned out as the Mesa Verde discussion merged back into the Joseph the artist discussion. "...Joseph put the one hundred dollars in his savings account, where he puts his allowance each week. He's really great with money. Joseph actually has everything going for him. My daughter is a pretty good kid, but she's not a popular, athletic, overachiever like Joseph. Joseph has it all."

David said this as though Joseph, never Joe or Joey, was a broker on Wall Street with a sports car and six-figure salary instead of an eight-year-old boy with an allowance and $100 in art money. I'd never met either kid, but based on David's disapproval of his daughter, I figured we'd get along splendidly. As excited as I was about missing three subrogation meetings for my pregnancy, I feared I would miss the meeting where David explained to us that his daughter dropped out of college, got tattoos and piercings and eloped with a Goy. Surely it would happen one of these days.

Mercifully, he stopped talking, looked at Sam and said, "Are you ready?"

Sam pretended to be scared and said, "Man, I'm glad I prepared for this all weekend. I'm ready to go."

Sam's presentation was about subrogation waivers. There are very few subrogation-specific areas of law, so we generally discuss subrogation waivers every three months or so. The PowerPoint presentation was a new development, which pissed me off. Why the hell was Sam raising the bar on a task that was already excruciating, not to mention entirely non-billable?

I zoned out. I always sit so I'm facing the window view of downtown Tampa and today I was treated to watching window washers in the next building. "Jenna, we have a case like that right?"

Oh shit. No clue what he's talking about. Pull something out of your ass Jenna. "Yeah, the watchamacallit case."

David said, "McDowell case."

"Yes. The McDowell case," I repeated.

"Does the waiver apply in that matter?"

"Yes. I plan to recommend closing it."

"Really? I don't know, I think it's the perfect case. Even if it's not, we should keep it open so that we can settle it after we set a precedent."

We have this discussion monthly. David has a fantasy about taking a case about subrogation waivers to the Supreme Court. All he has to do is find the perfect factual case to make subrogation history. David finds it immaterial that all of his arguments have already been unsuccessfully litigated.

"Your case is perfect. It's against Geico." David laughed at his joke, setting off laughter throughout the room. Our firm represents Auto-Owners and Liberty Mutual. I'm not quite sure why these companies are so superior to Geico in the mind of David Greene, but he picks on Geico constantly. I guarantee he would sing a different tune if I disguised my voice and called David posing as the Geico subrogation director. There is no doubt that he would suck up and vie for my business.

At 9:56 Sam was still speaking. This was dangerous because David needs a certain amount of time to talk during each meeting. If the presenter uses up the balance of the hour after David's opening act, we get stuck with a meeting that lasts six or seven minutes longer than necessary. I erred on the side of caution for my last presentation two months ago by preparing only eight minutes of material. Even after David added his "war stories" to my presentation, we were out at 9:48 a.m., a wild success in my opinion. At this rate, Sam's presentation was going to spill over the one hour time allotted to subrogation meetings.

Sam finished speaking at 10:02 a.m. What an asshole. David said, "Thank you Sam. That was a great presentation. Before we go, does anyone have any cases they'd like to discuss with the group?"

Sam raised his hand. No way. Your monologue is over.

"Yes, Sam," David said.

"I have a two million dollar case set for mediation this week, so keep your fingers crossed."

"That's great, Sam," David said, as his eyes turned into dollar signs. "Anyone else?"

No one else raised their hand. I started to stand as David said, "Just so you guys know, I was recently honored by Who's Who of American Subrogation Attorneys and it was reported in *Subrogator* Magazine." It must have killed David to sit on that information for the entire meeting. A few people started clapping and giving their congratulations. Apparently, David thought this was a good note on which to end the meeting. He stood up, and we all followed suit. It was 10:04 a.m.

As I walked towards my desk, I felt a shadow. I turned my head and saw Sarah. I kept walking, but Sarah caught up to me and said, "I'm onto you."

I played stupid. "What do you mean?"

"You're not pregnant. You have the exact same zit on your chin and un-tweezed eyebrows as you did yesterday at the mall."

"Thanks for noticing." Surely I have a beauty mark she could have focused on.

"I also noticed the scar on your mouth when you smile."

I do not recall smiling then and I sure as shit was not smiling now, but she had me. "Please don't tell anyone."

"Why are you faking a pregnancy? Do you feel left out because everyone else your age is pregnant? You're not too old yet, you can still have kids."

"I'm twenty-eight," I said incredulously.

"I know," Sarah said, looking at me with pity. "There are even women in their thirties having kids."

"There's women in their sixties that have kids, you should keep using birth control."

"Ha ha. You can't stay pregnant forever, sooner or later you're going to have to face the fact that you don't have a kid and won't have one in July."

"Let's analyze me later. Are you going to tell David?"

"No, don't worry," Sarah said.

Sarah has worked for David for over twenty years. She doubles as his paralegal and fluffer; there is nothing she wouldn't do for him. On the other hand, I am a total condescending bitch to her, so I was a bit skeptical that she would keep my confidence from David. There would be a catch.

"You know," she said, "Andy and I broke up."

It was three weeks since they'd met and one week since she'd told me they were in love. Still, I wasn't the least bit surprised. She stared at me, begging me to ask her what happened. I was actually curious, as it was bound to be a great story, but I hated to behave in accordance with Sarah's wishes. Nevertheless, I was a sport and asked her what happened, partly because I was trying to get on her good side and partly because I knew Sarah would tell me the story whether I asked her or not.

"He was just hot and cold, you know. Like he would tell me he was crazy about me, then he wouldn't call for days, then he would text me and tell me he loved me and I was the best thing that ever happened to him. It was so frustrating. Then I met Josh. I'm with Josh now. Andy blew it."

"Good for you." Please don't tell me about Josh, please don't tell me about Josh, please don't tell me about Josh.

"You know Josh don't you?"

"No, I don't think I do."

"He works for E-Copy."

E-Copy is the in-house copy and shipping center for Johnson Smith. I know what most of them look like, but don't know their names.

"He's the young hot guy with the surfer hair and glasses."

"The guy with the long black hair split down the center?" I said in disbelief.

"Yes!" Sarah said, "I call him my baby boy. I love hot young men."

I couldn't decide if I was more shocked by the relationship, or Sarah's description of Josh. First, Josh was probably thirty-five years old, which was young compared to her sixty years, but hardly a baby. Second, he was not hot, though it was possible that he could be decent looking if he cut his hair and didn't behave like a mass murderer. He speaks in a monotone voice and walks quickly with his hands in his pockets while staring at the ground. I've always gone out of my way to be nice to Josh because I'm quite sure he will walk into the office and open fire one day. By building a rapport with the freak, I hope to be spared on the day he blows.

"Good for you, Sarah," I said.

"I just wanted you to know that if you were interested in Andy, he's available now."

"I'm good," I said.

"In that case, I have a different guy for you."

Yikes. "That's okay," I said.

"It would actually help me out a lot. See, my son still lives with me and this girl broke his heart and he hasn't done anything but pine over her for weeks. He's always there when Josh is over and it's annoying. It would help me and him if you went out with him."

This was worse than anything I could have imagined. I was ready to shell out money, clean her house and do all of her paralegal work, but dating her son was out of the question. "Sorry Sarah, I don't think that will work out. Isn't your son forty-something?"

"Yes, forty-two."

"I'm twenty-eight. That's a pretty big gap."

"No it's not. I'm sixty and I'm dating a thirty-six-year-old."

Probably not the time to tell her how much that grosses me out. Was it really necessary for me to explain to this lady that a forty-two-year-old guy that lives with his mom is undatable and that, P.S., I would never date anyone with Sarah Smith blood coursing through his veins. I tried to be tactful and said, "Hmm. Sarah, I just don't know if this is a good idea. I mean, maybe it's too soon after having his heart broken."

"It's the perfect time. I actually think you and Tony would really get along. He was a cyclist when he was younger and he's been getting back into it recently."

"I don't think it will work out Sarah," I said again, more desperately this time.

"Jenna," Sarah said glaring at me, "I would meet Tony if I were you."

The threat was clear so I said, "Okay." As the word came out of my mouth I was already thinking of how to get out of the situation.

My office phone rang, and I could tell by the caller I.D. that it was my dad, but I answered the phone in my work voice. "Hello, Jenna Rosen."

"It's me," Dad said, "I thought you had caller I.D."

"Yes, let me just pull that file up." I covered the mouthpiece and told Sarah I had to take the call.

Once she left, I said, "Hi Dad. Sorry, I was trying to get someone out of my office."

"Want to have lunch?"

"Yeah. It's not too hot on my deck in the shade, let's do lunch there at noon. Can you pick up sandwiches?"

"Sure."

Just before I left for lunch, I received a junk mail email from a person trying to recover her sunglasses, which were stolen right off her desk. I added the email to the stolen goods file even though it wasn't that spectacular. Other thefts at Johnson Smith included:

–I had a large umbrella next to my desk this morning with George Washington University on it and it is missing. I normally wouldn't care, but it has sentimental value (Interesting side note, it was raining the day this email was sent).

–Please let me know if you received a check in the amount of $245,000 from Casualty Company Southeast made payable to Johnson Smith. (Oopsy Daisy).

–Missing green and blue Asian-style mug with hatch-mark relief. It has been missing for over a week. This is my favorite mug and is very special to me. I appreciate your assistance in having it returned. (I'll send you back one piece of the mug at a time until all of my demands are met).

–The candy bars in the kitchen cost $1.00 each. My kid needs the money for his fundraiser and I don't appreciate the person who ate the chocolate, filled the wrapper with paper towel, and put it back in the box to be sold. (She attached a picture. The person did a decent job covering up the heist).

I was out cold on my hammock when my Dad arrived, a few minutes late for lunch. Dad finished tax season a month and a half ago, and he was just now getting to his "Jenna" list, which he brought to lunch today. Dad's lists are notorious, specifically, his grocery, movie, restaurant and tax lists.

When I was little, Dad bitched to my Mom about not having Fiber One when he specifically put it on the grocery list. Instead of going back to the store, Mom went on strike and told Dad to go himself and get whatever food his heart desired. The first time he ventured into the store, it took him seven hours. After that, he decided the problem with the grocery store was that it was not organized in the order in which the Rosen household ran out of food. He decided to create a list, in aisle order, of all of the products my family buys. He had his secretary type the list and ever since, one of her duties has been to update the list as new and exciting food products are introduced into the marketplace. This was a pain in the ass when I was a kid because if I wanted crackers, I couldn't just write crackers on the list. I had to find it, highlight it, and specify which kind, how many ounces, and request either regular, low fat or fat-free. I haven't seen the list in eight years but Mom tells me it's up to four pages now.

Dad's movie list is equally anal. Every Friday, the newspaper publishes a blurb about each movie currently playing and lists its average review from various critics. Dad reads these blurbs, then cuts out the movies he wants to watch. Next, he glues the blurbs onto his master list, which he photocopies in triplicate. He keeps one copy at his office, one at home and one in his fireproof safe. Every time Dad watches a movie, he crosses it off all three lists. He watches these movies in order and will not deviate. He is currently up to 1986.

His restaurant list is another meticulous compilation based on reviews in the Friday paper. I've always looked forward to trying one of the restaurants described on that list, but for the last seven years that I've gone out to dinner with my parents, Dad has never been in the mood for anything except a grouper reuben and sangria from BallyHoo's Restaurant.

The final list, the tax season list, is actually a compilation of notes, email printouts, articles and records from the end of January to the end of April. This annual list begins when Dad becomes too busy during tax season to attend to all but the most pressing matters. If I don't include a red flag in the subject line of an email between January and April, it goes into the "Jenna" tax season folder along with other "Jenna" documents. In May or June, he gets around to opening the folder to go over each item. Of course, the folder is a time capsule by this time.

"Did you get the exterminator's phone number?" Dad asked.

"Yeah, I got it from Mom and he's come twice since that email was sent."

"Did you find Webster, Florida?"

"Yes. That was from my phone. I was on the road texting you on my way to a bike race I couldn't find."

"You think I'm helping you find a bike race so you can break your teeth again?"

"You'll be happy to know I found the race and won."

"What did you win?"

"A hundred and twenty bucks."

"How much did it cost to fix your nose and replace the teeth you lost?"

"Out of pocket, five thousand dollars. What's next on your list?"

"I saw this in *Parade* magazine, it's an article on pet insurance. I thought you might want to look into it."

"I saw that too. I'm good for now. Next."

"Here, sign this so that you're renewed with Triple A."

As I signed, Dad said, "Here's an email from you in February asking me to go to lunch with you. That's safe to throw out." He flipped to the next paper in the folder and said, "Yes you can borrow the kayak two months ago. Did you go?"

"Yes, at low tide. I pretty much walked the kayak through the mangroves. What's next?"

"Here's an article you sent me on Nalgene bottles causing cancer, you should have sent that one to me with a red flag for urgency."

"You've been using them for years, what's a few more months? Besides, the reverse study has already come out. Nalgene is safe again. Next."

"What the hell is that?" Dad said.

I looked down at Sonny and said, "A penis."

"Was the teacher Mom set you up with that bad?"

"Yes, actually, but I didn't touch, let alone cut off his penis. That's Sonny's dildo and you don't want to know where it came from. I actually haven't seen it in a while, he must have unburied it especially for you."

"Great," Dad said, returning to his list rather than addressing the dildo in his granddog's mouth. He said, "This one says you want to borrow my car in March. Oops, sorry."

"That's okay, I borrowed Jason's."

"How did he get to school?" Dad asked.

"He probably skipped school," I said nonchalantly.

"Don't take his car so that he can't go to school."

"He wasn't going to go anyway. I kept him from getting into trouble elsewhere."

"Does he really not go to school?" Dad asked, suddenly serious.

"Of course not. He doesn't smoke, drink, stay up late or have sex either."

"That kid scares me. Do you still need the plumber's number?"

"No, Danny helped me," I replied.

"Do you still need a warranty for your washer?"

"No, I just paid to fix it."

"Why don't you keep your records?" he asked, a little exasperated.

"Because you keep them for me."

"I'm going to stop doing that and give you all of your files."

He tells me this every year. I'm terrified that he'll follow through at some point, so I quickly changed the topic and asked, "So, what movie are you up to?"

"*Ghost*. Have you seen it? It has Patrick Swayze and Demi Moore in it."

"Yeah, it was my favorite movie in fourth grade. It's good, you'll like it."

"Man, I could sit out here on your deck all day," Dad said.

"You're sixty, you own the company and you're a month and a half out of tax season and still catching up. I say go for it, you can't buy a minute."

"I think I will. I'm going to sleep in the hammock for a bit. Can you call and wake me at one-thirty? I have a meeting at two."

"No problem," I said.

I went out to go back to the office and realized Dad had parked behind me. I let him sleep and just drove over my lawn to get out. I returned to work and started to get out of my car, but I felt like something was off. Son-of-a-bitch! I forgot to put my belly back on. I drove back home.

It was only one-twenty when I got home, so I decided to let Dad sleep for ten more minutes. I grabbed the belly from under the bed along with the maternity clothes I had worn to work that morning, changed and rushed back to the office. I was somewhat efficient for the rest of the afternoon to compensate for the time spent at the subrogation meeting and my long lunch. I was finalizing a letter to a client at three-thirty when I got a call from Dad.

"Thanks for waking me," he said.

"Oh shit! Sorry."

"Lucky for you, Sonny woke me up right on time when a squirrel had the audacity to be in a tree."

"I told him to do that at one-thirty before I left. That's why I didn't call," I said.

"Hey," Dad said. "I meant to ask you, when did you get the trampoline?"

"A few days ago."

"Why?" he said in his most judgmental voice.

"They're fun and you never got me one when I was a kid."

"That's because they ruin your lawn and attract kids to come by and break their arms. Your insurance is going to cancel. How much did you spend on that thing?"

"Less than on my new remote control car."

"You need therapy, Jenna, before you regress completely."

"Thanks. Bye, Dad." That went better than expected.

I called Danny and told him about my forced date with Sarah's son Tony.

"Ha. You really are lucky in love."

"I know, I have a gift."

"This is the beginning of the end," said Danny. "It all comes crashing down from here."

"Have some faith. I'll figure something out. In the meantime, I want to get out of here. Are you doing the St. Pete ride today?" I asked.

"Yes. I'm meeting Travis and Jesus at my house at four."

"Great. Swing by my house at four-thirty and I'll ride over with you guys. I'm going to finish up a few things here and take off."

I left work early to go to the 6:00 p.m. group ride in St. Petersburg. As I entered the elevator to go to the parking lot, I came face to face with Ryan Smith from Italian Fest. I thought of jumping out of the elevator, but that would be too obvious. Instead, I faced the other direction. He didn't seem to notice me let alone recognize me. My face was completely flushed and my hair was damp by the time we parted ways on the first floor.

I stopped shaking by the time I got to my car and was calm again when I pulled into my driveway at four-thirty. Prior to my pregnancy, I had to leave my office at five p.m. and kill myself to get to the start of the ride on time. But because of my "obstetrician appointment," I'd left the office at four, enabling me to cruise over to St. Pete at a leisurely pace.

I met Danny and two of our friends, Jesus and Travis, at my house and we rode our bikes over to St. Petersburg. Jesus and Travis are both married, but constantly flirting with me. It's playful, though I have a feeling that, were I inclined, it would turn from playful to serious pretty quickly.

"Hi, Mami."

Jesus is Cuban. He came to America twenty years ago and speaks English well, but with a strong accent. He calls me, and every other woman under the age of sixty, Mami and asks them to call him Papi. This seems to be a common request among Latino males, so even though I don't understand why the Spanish name for "dad" has a sexual connotation, I've come to terms with the fact that it just does. I really hope female Latinos call their real fathers something else.

"I told you, call me Papi,"

"I think Papi is a step down from Jesus." I always pronounce the J when addressing Jesus.

"Why won't you call me Papi? Don't you like Cubans?"

"Sure, they're great sandwiches," I replied.

"No, the people!"

Travis chimed in and said, "She likes the dark meat."

"No, no, no," Jesus said, as oblivious to sounding racist as my grandmother. "You don't date black people do you?"

"To tell you the truth, I'm not even comfortable with you guys using our water fountains," I said to Travis.

Travis did a double take when I said that, then laughed and said, "You're lucky you're hot."

"I'm just kidding." I said, hopefully unnecessarily. To be on the safe side, I offered him a sip from my water bottle.

Instead of telling me not to worry about it or just taking a sip, Travis dumped it all over his neck and head to cool off, then gave the empty bottle back to me while cracking up.

This blatant but harmless flirting is common in cycling, which is a predominantly male sport in spite of the shaved legs and Lycra shorts. Objectively, I'm attractive. However, the only reason I attract so much attention in cycling is because I'm one of a small handful of female cyclists in the Tampa Bay area who can actually hang with the fast guys. All of us get hit on, both playfully and seriously. Occasionally, I forget that I'm the only game in town and let the compliments go to my head. When this happens, Danny likes to remind me that cycling is not exactly beach volleyball.

At the Tampa side of the Gandy Bridge, we met seven other cyclists and continued heading to St. Petersburg. The eleven of us continued at a conversational pace, though we took a time-out from talking to sprint to the top of the hill on the bridge. Technically, the "hill" is an incline on the Gandy Bridge that allows boats to pass under. However, in flat Florida, any encounter with any increasing gradient instigates a "king of the mountains'" competition. I beat everyone but Jesus to the top of the hill. I'm a good climber, but so is Jesus and he can wipe the floor with me on the sprint at the top. Fidel Castro had personally assigned an eleven-year-old Jesus to be a cyclist based on his superior muscle-tone and lung capacity. Even though he's at least forty now, if not older, he's been unchallenged as the best rider in Tampa since he defected here from Cuba in his late teens. Those commies know how to pick an athlete.

We coasted down the hill and resumed talking. It was nice to head to St. Pete at a leisurely pace. If I didn't have my fake doctor's appointment, I'd be pedaling into the headwind as hard as possible in order to get to the start of the ride on time. Like clockwork, as I marveled at my luck, my tire went flat. Travis, Jesus and Danny stopped and waited for me as I started changing my flat.

Technically, I know how to change the tube out of a flat cycling tire. However, it takes me forty-five minutes to complete the task instead of the usual three. Normally, Danny will change my flats for me, but he evidently didn't want to look like my bitch in front of Travis and Jesus, because he just sat there and watched me fumble with it. After several minutes of watching me try to remove the tire from the rim, Danny said, "For God's sake, this is like watching a monkey fuck a football! Give me that wheel." A few minutes later, we were off and running with plenty of time to ride easy and conserve our energy until the start of the St. Pete Olympics.

The St. Pete cyclists take their rides very seriously. Very few of them attend official races. There's no need to when they treat their Tuesday, Thursday and Saturday group rides as fierce competitions. Once, I cut in front of a rider we call "MMA" to avoid being hit by a car. MMA, who easily avoided crashing, responded by calling me a "stupid fucking cunt." MMA got his nickname because it stands for mixed martial arts and he starts a fight two to three times on every ride, sometimes with cyclists, sometimes with motorists. He's the only person I've ever seen fight in cycling shoes. It's not an advantage, but he held his own. Even though I'm a girl, I would not put it past him to punch me in the face. Thus, while I don't take his tirades personally, I try to avoid being within three bike lengths of MMA at all times.

At five forty-five, we rode into the parking lot, where a good crowd had assembled. MMA was joined by "Muscles," who made a beeline toward me. I rode directly into the ladies' room to avoid him since a year of rejecting his advances has done nothing to curtail his enthusiasm for asking me out and turning everything I say into a sexual charged double entendre that makes absolutely no sense. "Muscles" a.k.a. "Steroids" a.k.a. "Festina," is on steroids and proud of it. He has only one cycling kit, a Festina jersey and shorts modeled after the 1998 Festina cycling team. In 1998, one of Festina's team cars was caught at a border crossing with over 400 pills in it just three days before the start of the Tour de France. The Festina team was not allowed to start the 1998 Tour. Three years later, the team disbanded. Nevertheless, Muscles is a loyal fan, wearing the kit daily and rarely washing it. After each ride, he changes out of his Festina outfit and into his personalized T-shirt, the front and back of which are adorned with photographs of himself posing in various body building stances wearing nothing but a banana hammock. Once the coast was clear, I came out of the bathroom, refilled my water bottles and rode to where the riders were congregating.

Danny and I named Muscles and MMA, as we name everyone on the ride. Mostly because we're assholes and the names are apt, but also because we don't know their real names. I started riding with the St. Pete training ride with Danny about a year ago and being from Tampa, neither of us knew anyone on the ride. After many Tuesday, Thursday and Saturday encounters, we gradually met everyone on the ride in brief conversations during the warm-ups and cool-downs. Soon enough, we knew what everyone did for a living and all of their best jokes, but still not their names. Since it's awkward to ask someone their name after you've known them for a year, neither of us ever bothered. Plus, we really don't need their names. If we want to talk to someone, we'll ride up next to them and start talking. The only reason we need their names is to talk about them behind their backs to each other.

In addition to Muscles and MMA, there's "Old School," whose bike and kits are all from the 1960s; "Ivan Drago," who looks like Rocky's nemesis from Rocky IV; "Sunscreen," who puts zinc oxide on his entire body so that he looks painted white; "OCD," whose bike, and every component on it, are meticulously cleaned before every ride; "B.O." who stinks so much that you can't ride within three bike lengths of him without gagging; "Ned Flanders," who looks like Ned Flanders from *The Simpsons*; "Slobber," who spits at you as he talks; "Sprinkler," who sprays a constant stream of sweat as he rides, regardless of the temperature; "Bra," who is a guy, but wears a skin-tight triathlon midriff bearing shirt; "Sandspur," who freaks out when anyone cuts through the grass to refill their water because he insists we'll get sandspurs in our tires and get a flat; "Tighty Whity," who wears underwear under his cycling shorts; and "Junk Miles," one of many cycling personal trainers on the ride. I met Junk Miles when he told me that my training plan of riding from Tampa to St. Petersburg and back three times a week is nothing but junk miles, and that I'd be much faster if I paid him to coach me.

My plan for the ride was the same as it has been for the past few months: to grow some balls and learn how to mix it up in the sprint. I was a month away from my professional cycling debut and if I wasn't in a breakaway off the front at the time of the sprint, I regularly floated to the back of the *peloton* to avoid the crash that seemed sure to happen every time the pack of riders accelerated to between thirty-five to forty miles per hour within inches of each other. Sometimes the crash happened, but usually I just placed last in a clean sprint, not only behind the good sprinters, but behind the pack fodder that barely managed to stay in the *peloton* during the ride.

The first sprint was just after a drawbridge. Jesus attacked up the hill as I knew he would, and I immediately jumped on his wheel. He jacked the pace up to thirty miles per hour on the incline and sped up to forty-five miles per hour on the descent. I stayed on his wheel up to the finish line and glanced behind me. No one else was in our draft; they were charging for us fifty yards back. Jesus sat up just before the sign that is the finish line and I sprinted past him with a smile on my face, letting him know that I understand that he's the real sprint winner.

Cycling has unwritten etiquette for group rides and races. It is not cool to sit on someone's wheel for a mile, let them do all the work distancing the pack, then outsprint them when they're tired. It is okay if the person is on the front burying themselves with the understanding that they're leading out the sprint for the entire pack; in that case everyone can sprint. However, if it's just you and another guy on a group ride, and the other guy did all the work, it is poor etiquette to sprint against him. However, if the same situation presents itself in a race, you can sprint against the other person who was dumb enough to lead out the last mile for you.

The two sprints on the way back to St. Pete did not go as well. Not surprisingly, my sprinting skills did not miraculously develop overnight, and I had a hard time staying towards the front of the pack as it wound its way on flat fast roads around tight corners to the second and third sprint points. I started the sprint in the pack, but drifted far to the left so I'd have an out in the event of a crash. The problem was that the outskirts of the *peloton* were windier than within the pack, where there's a draft on all sides. I came in a solid last place.

Aside from my horrendous sprint, I rode superbly. My training was really beginning to pay off and I could tell I was stronger than I had ever been. However, no matter how strong I was, a professional team wouldn't want me if they saw my name at the bottom of the standings every single time a race ended in a sprint finish, which was at least eighty percent of the time.

On the way home, I asked Travis, Jesus and Danny if there was an easy trick to learn to sprint.

Jesus said, "Let's take her out to a field and play bumper bikes with her. Once she learns to fall she'll be fine."

"I don't want to learn to fall, I want to learn to sprint. Falls are going to happen and they're going to suck no matter how much I train myself to enjoy crashing. I'd like to sprint well without worrying about crashing and I'd like to pick it up immediately, like when the Karate Kid learned karate by painting a fence and Rocky Balboa learned to box by catching a greasy fast chicken. Can't I just do something slightly challenging and unrelated to cycling to learn to sprint, like watching television on my head or eating spaghetti through a straw?"

Danny gave me a deadpan look and said, "I think being the bitch in a gang bang is good for sprinting in cycling. Wanna give it a shot?"

"Sure Danny. You're last," I replied.

"Fine with me," he said, "as long as I'm in the rotation."

"Shut up, there will be no gang banging. I'm serious."

"You'll figure it out," Danny said."Just relax."

Eighty-six miles and five hours after leaving my house, I arrived home. John, Julie and Jason were in the backyard jumping on the trampoline with the dogs, our new favorite activity. They put all of their dogs on the trampoline and bounced them in the air. John and Julie have four dogs: a rat-poo, which is a rat terrier mixed with a toy poodle, a yorkie poo, a poogle and my favorite, a shih-tzu poo. Their names are Blinky, Pinky, Inky and Clyde. Combined, their four dogs still weigh less than Sonny's sixty pounds. That's why it's all the more embarrassing when their dogs enjoy playing on the trampoline and mine cries and jumps off in terror.

"Hey, Jenna." John said, "I still can't believe you bought a trampoline. I'm really enjoying your regression."

"Thanks. I agree it was a brilliant purchase. You guys want to grab dinner?"

"Sure," Julie said.

"Great," I said. "Let's go to St. Pete, there's a great place for crab legs." I wanted to go to St. Pete to avoid another pregnancy incident like the ones I'd had with Sarah and Ryan. John and Jason are obsessed with crab legs, so the Crab Shack seemed like the best carrot to get them across the bridge to St. Petersburg.

* * *

The Crab Shack was located a mile past the end of the Gandy Bridge connecting Tampa and St. Petersburg. In the mile between the bridge and the restaurant, cars that looked like they were tailgating lined the highway along both sides of the road. Technically, these people were on "the beach." However, if they drove twenty more minutes, they would be treated to a real beach instead of the Redneck Riviera, which was essentially three inches of sand on either side of a six lane highway.

While we were on a bench at the restaurant waiting to be seated, a man in baggy jeans, white T-shirt, diamond earrings, chain necklace and a sleeve of tattoos sat next to me. I immediately pulled my purse closer and away from the thug. Jason, on the other hand, walked up to him and said, "Hey man, where'd you get that fade done up at?" My head almost fell off my neck as I turned around.

The thug said, "Huh?"

Jason repeated himself, "Fuck'n, where'd you get that fade done up at n'shit?"

"Fade Masters," tattoo man grunted.

"That's where I go," Jason said. "Who do you see?"

It turned out that Jason and the thug both got their haircuts, or "fades," done up on Nebraska Avenue by Big Tony. I think Jason might have the most street cred of his entire confirmation class at synagogue.

In hindsight, all-you-can-eat crab legs for $9.99 was not a good idea. The inevitable gastrointestinal distress followed like clockwork. I was unable to move further than seven inches from my toilet the next morning when Sarah called.

"Where are you?" she asked.

"Home shitting mud. You?"

"What?" Sarah said.

"I won't be in today. What do you need?" I asked.

"I just wanted to tell you that I told Tony you'd meet him tonight."

"Sarah, I can't meet him tonight, I'm ill."

"Fine, tomorrow night?"

"I can't, I'm going away for a week for work and I need to get packed, set up dog care and a bunch of other things. Can I meet him when I get back next week?"

"Okay, but you have to go out with him. You'll thank me, trust me."

"Yes, Sarah, I'm excited to meet Tony. I can't wait until next week."

That bought me a week, but I didn't see any way out of the Tony date.

CHAPTER TEN

I actually did have depositions scheduled throughout the week. Not only that, in Alabama. I thought about using the "I'm giving birth in two weeks" excuse to get out of them, but I preferred to get out of town and avoid my date with Sarah's spawn. The trip also provided an opportunity to stay in a beautiful beach community just outside of Mobile.

The depositions were for the Champions Bar case, which involved nine parties: three defendants and six plaintiffs. Due to scheduling conflicts, the depositions had been scheduled over eight months ago, with the middle of June being the first week available for all of the lawyers involved. Consequently, I had completely forgotten about the depositions until my secretary asked me if I preferred a flight Sunday night or early Monday morning.

As I do whenever I travel, I checked the cycling schedule to see if I could combine my trip with a race. The two races I found were a regional race in Cuba, Alabama, which is a real place, and a professional race in Bristol, Tennessee. The race in Cuba was scheduled for the weekend after the depositions, so there was no scheduling conflict. Nevertheless, it wasn't my preference because according to the Alabama race results for the season, Southern Belles didn't race. In the past four Alabama women's races, only four women had competed in the CAT 1, 2, 3 combined categories. The Bristol race was a four-day professional women's stage race run from Thursday through Sunday. The down side of Bristol was that it was ten hours away and conflicted with the depositions; on the up side it would give me a preview of my professional career and conflicted with the depositions. If I could find a way to skip some of the depositions, Bristol was my plan. I had my secretary schedule my trip from Sunday evening through the following Monday. Oddly, she didn't ask why I wanted to stay in the shit-kicking buckle of the Bible Belt for an additional three days.

The only question remaining before take-off was whether to pack and pay for my good bike to travel, or to take my travel bike. Bringing my good road bike and time trial bike to Alabama would cost $100 for the bikes each way. They would also be a pain in the ass to disassemble and reassemble before each flight. Finally, the bike box in which my road bike would travel was huge and I'd have to rent a van to haul it around. My travel bike, called a Bike Friday, was the alternative. I'd purchased it so I wouldn't have to pack my bike, or worse, miss a day of riding, during work-related trips. The Bike Friday had twenty-inch wheels, handlebars that part in half and other unique features that enabled it to fit into a normal suitcase and travel for free. It was also foldable and easy to assemble.

I had never ridden the travel bike other than for solitary riding while traveling for work. While it was a decent road bike, the frame wasn't nearly as light, nor the components as responsive as those on my carbon road bike. After much debate, I decided that I would race the Bike Friday since it was cheaper and more convenient. Additionally, if I competed in the local Cuba race, I'd still be able to wipe the floor with a foldable bike. If I raced with the pros, I would surely be noticed on the miniature foldable bike.

The next question was whether to wear or check the Empathy Belly. I preferred to check it, but I wore it because I was paranoid that I'd run into a colleague at the airport un-pregnant, a real concern considering the frequency with which lawyers in our firm traveled throughout the Southeast. This would be my first trip traveling with the Belly. The novelty of the Belly wore off about twelve minutes after I put it on. It was tight, heavy, hot, and kicked me at regular intervals. On the plus side, there wasn't a kid in it.

I checked the travel bike and suitcase and carried on my laptop bag, backpack and purse. To make walking slightly more awkward, I had a helmet hanging off my laptop bag, a Nalgene water bottle attached to my purse and one cycling shoe velcroed to each strap of my backpack. I felt absurd, but no one at the airport seemed to notice. Chivalry was officially dead; not a single person attempted to help the single pregnant woman with three bags.

Unfortunately, the only person to notice my condition was the woman in the seat next to me. She was a mother of three and could not wait to commiserate about pregnancy, but assure me of the rewards of motherhood. This arrangement was not going to work. First, the woman was a liar. Her children were seated across the aisle and, objectively, they were nothing special. Second, I was very committed to sleeping during the flight. I generally fell asleep before takeoff, woke up during the landing and took a cat nap while the plane was taxiing.

The plane started to roll towards the runway and she was still talking. I unhooked my helmet and put it on my head for takeoff, assuming that this was a level of crazy that would distance the woman. Not so. Next, I started rhythmically banging my head against the window. That did the trick. Convinced I was insane, she abruptly stopped talking. Nap time.

* * *

Like the rest of the Panhandle, Mobile was a catcher's mitt for hurricanes and rednecks. It was surprising that the Champions Bar case was not a hurricane case, but rather a neon sign case. A neon sign company had improperly fabricated the Champions Bar sign, causing it to catch fire and burn down an entire strip mall. Each tenant in the mall, including Champions Bar, suffered damage and was represented by a different attorney. The defendants were the sign fabricator, the electrician who installed the sign, and the owner of Champions Bar. I represented the subrogation interests of the Champions Bar's insurance company. Consequently, Champions Bar was both suing and being sued in the same case. Champions Bar had defense counsel in addition to me as plaintiff's counsel. There were nine attorneys on the case. We were all in town to depose four experts and take the depositions of the employees and corporate representatives of the sign and electrical company.

On the boredom scale, deposing an expert in the fabrication of neon signs fell somewhere between a full Catholic wedding Mass and reading the tax code. At the end of the day, I learned about transformers, ceramic bushings versus plastic bushings, conduits, the importance of caulking around conduits, and that the conference room of Banker, Bolt & White LLP has 486 ceiling tiles. I was the only attorney not to ask the deponent a question. In my opinion, the dead horse was sufficiently beaten by the time it was my turn.

Lunch was in the presence of Mobile's legal boys' club. The topics of conversation ranged from hunt'n to fish'n, occasionally deviating into red state politics. The day was shaping up to be the longest period I'd gone without speaking since I was a year old.

When the workday came to an end, I went for a long bike ride that passed through a state park, a 300-year-old graveyard, mansions, trailer parks, beaches, and farms before arriving in downtown Mobile. Mobile is very proud of its confederate heroes and has statues of them throughout the city. At least Germany has the good sense not to honor Heinrich Himmler as part of its "heritage." There was also a pre-revolutionary fort in the city called Fort Conde. I rode my bike into the fort and looped around before being kicked out.

On my way back from Mobile, I could feel my period starting. I pulled into a grocery store to pick up tampons, but couldn't find any. There were pads, but no tampons. There was a gray-haired employee at the end of the isle and I asked her if they had any tampons in the back.

"You mean Satan's little cotton fingers? No! This is a good Christian grocer and we don't sell that fornicatin' stuff."

"No," I said, thinking she'd misunderstood. "Tampons." I had no idea what she was talking about and my best guess was that in hick-speak, tampon sounded a lot like vibrator.

"I'll tell you one final time," she said, "we don't carry Satan's little cotton fingers. Now grab a pad and move along."

I left and went to the next store I saw. Once again, pads but no tampons. I grabbed one pad out of the bathroom dispenser and attached it onto the thick pad already sewn into my cycling shorts and rode thirty miles home feeling like I was wearing a diaper.

Fortunately, the CVS in Daphne carried Satan's little cotton fingers. I Googled the phrase when I returned to my hotel. I clicked on the first link and it provided the following information:

"Toxic Shock Syndrome is God's way of punishing unsaved harlots who choose Satan's cotton fingers over a Godly pad."–Pastor Deacon Fred

The next link I clicked on had helpful testimonials:

I was arrested last month for setting fire to the tampon display in my local Eckerd Drugs in Griffin, Georgia. I spent three days in jail and received a $45,000 fine but it was all worth it. The number of women whose vaginas will not be abused by Satan's little finger makes it all worth it.–Mary Beth Salliston

The entire girls swim team at Rossington High School owes you our lives. We don't attend as many meets as we did but at least we aren't going to Hell now.–Ruth Whitley

Since I stopped using SATAN'S DIRTY FINGER my marriage has gotten even better. Before I gave them up, my husband was jealous of the tampons and made me feel like a whore. Now I am a whore for Jesus! God Bless YOU!–Lilly Penergrass

I read about the horrors of tampons and emailed the links to all of my friends before falling asleep.

On Tuesday, work was more of the same. I decided to ditch work and race my bike at the professional race in Bristol, Tennessee. I figured I could update the client about the depositions after reading the transcripts. I registered for the race Tuesday evening for a steep $155 fee, and began the trek north. I broke the trip into two days because it wasn't possible for me to drive ten hours straight without napping into a guardrail or median. I finished the trip at 2:00 a.m. the day of the race.

The reward at the end of the long night of driving was that the official race hotel was an 8 Repus. It's actually called Super 8, but since it was the exact opposite of "super," cyclists began calling it an 8 Repus long ago. My late arrival was a blessing in disguise because even though

I'm borderline narcoleptic, extreme exhaustion helps when trying to fall asleep on sheets with a higher cigarette-burn count than thread count. Normally, I opted to camp rather than stay in a crappy hotel, but I didn't feel like packing a tent and sleeping bag in addition to my other luggage for this trip. On the plus side, the Empathy Belly was in the trunk and wasn't coming out for four days.

Bristol was a four-day race comprising five stages: a prologue, two road races, a time trial and a criterium. A prologue is a short time trial. A time trial is a race against the clock. A race against the clock means drafting is not allowed. Thus, instead of being in the *peloton*, riders take off at thirty-second intervals and the rider that completes the course with the lowest time wins. A time trial is generally between ten and thirty miles, whereas a prologue is usually two to four miles. The Bristol prologue was two and a half miles, the time trial was ten miles, the road stages were seventy-two and seventy-eight miles and the criterium was sixty minutes plus five laps. By comparison, the men's road races were 112 and 118 miles, and criterium was ninety minutes plus five laps. Clearly, this race was not being promoted by a feminist.

A cycling stage race honors the winner of each stage as well as the winner of the overall race, also known as the general classification. The winner of the general classification is the cyclist who completes all of the stages with the lowest cumulative time. The Bristol Stage Race awarded cash prizes to the top ten finishers of each stage and the top fifteen finishers of the overall race.

Because I was on my foldable Bike Friday, I was thankful for the injustice of riding less than the men. I was especially thankful the prologue was only two and a half miles and that the ten mile time trial was mostly uphill. While the foldable bike was clearly a disadvantage during the road races and criterium, the disadvantage was not nearly as pronounced as in the time trials. Because drafting was legal in the road race and criterium, my inferior bike was shielded from the wind by the *peloton*. However, in a time trial, it is the cyclist against the wind and aerodynamics are paramount. When racing a prologue or time trial at home, I ride on my time trial bike with aero bars, use a disc wheel and wear a pointy helmet and skin suit, all of which are especially suited to aerodynamics. I was without my aero-gear for this prologue and time trial. The only reason the missing gear didn't kill me was because there was only so much time I was capable of losing during a two and a half mile prologue or traveling uphill, where aerodynamics are not as important since the speed into the wind is not as fast.

Afterward, on my ten-hour drive back to Mobile, I had plenty of time to reflect upon the race. The prologue wasn't so bad. I placed eighth, fifteen seconds behind the winner and a minute ahead of last place. Likewise, my sixth place finish in the uphill time trial was decent. I believed both finishes would have been even better if I were on the proper bike with the proper equipment. The road races and criterium were a different story entirely. As it turned out, my fear of sprinting in a pack of riders extended to a fear of descending down a steep mountain with a pack of riders.

The mountains in Bristol were not steep enough or long enough to spread the field. Each mountain descent contained a pack of at least forty women. During each descent, I fell behind and had to work furiously to catch up to the *peloton* when I hit the flat section, wasting energy. This was a problem in a four-day race with hills and small mountains; it would be devastating in a three-week race in higher mountains like the Tour de West. I found it somewhat amusing that by living in flat Florida, I'd managed to race for over a year without noticing my phobia of descending with company. On a positive note, my fearful and inept descending was nowhere near the level of my fearful and inept sprinting. Other than the women who got dropped from the draft and didn't finish the road races and criterium, I came in last place on each stage, tucked safely six feet behind and to the left of the pack.

In cycling, each rider finishes with her front wheel practically glued to the rear wheel ahead of her. Thus, everyone who finishes together in the *peloton* is awarded the same time; though first, second and third place often have bonus seconds subtracted from their overall time as a reward. Consequently, even though I finished last on the sprint finishes of the road race and criterium, technically a few feet from the bunch, I was awarded the same time as the rest of the *peloton*. By placing eighth and sixth in the prologue and time trial, respectively, and not losing time in the road race and criterium, my overall placing in the race was fifth. Awards were provided to riders placed ten deep for each stage, and fifteen deep overall. As a result, I was the recipient of fifty, seventy-five and one hundred twenty dollars for each placing. I deducted this windfall from the gas money I spent on driving 1,200 miles, staying four days in a hotel, and paying a $155 entry fee. In spite of this success,

I drove back to Mobile without any leads for a professional team. On top of all of this, I could feel a cold coming on.

* * *

On my return flight, I was selected for enhanced scrutiny at security. I suppose I looked slightly more like a terrorist than the eighty-year-old woman drooling on her colostomy bag in the wheelchair next to me, but it was a tough call. I carried the same stuff I'd brought with me, only this time I had my Empathy Belly slung across my back. I wanted to take advantage of not having it on my stomach, which makes my back ache, at least until I arrived back home in Tampa.

I took off my shoes and put them in a tray with my purse. I took my laptop out of my bag and placed it in another tray. The helmet and bike shoes took up a third tray and my Empathy Belly a fourth. I set my two bags in fifth and sixth position in the caravan, then moved into the enhanced security area, put my feet on the big footprints, and waited to be felt up by security. The wait was long because I had to wait for a woman. By the time the female frisker showed up, my Empathy Belly was going through the machine. It was being strictly scrutinized by three attendants. "What is this?" they yelled to me.

"It's an Empathy Belly," I said, then added, "I teach sex education. This is a pregnancy simulator to teach safe sex."

"Abstinence is the only safe sex," replied the screener, perhaps exceeding her job mandate.

Shit, I forgot I was in Ala-fucking-bama, to quote *My Cousin Vinny*. What to do? Do I point out that the pill, patch, Depo-Provera, condoms, diaphragms, intrauterine devices, spermicide, sponge, cervical cap, oral sex, tying tubes, hysterectomy and vasectomy were also perfectly acceptable methods of avoiding pregnancy, not to mention that pulling out and the rhythm method would get you by in a pinch. My sixth sense told me this should not be my final answer.

"Yes ma'am," I said, "that's what I teach. Abstinence."

"That's great. God's work is what that is. Problem is, in looking at that there screen, you appear to have more than three ounces of liquids in that there belly, so you can't bring it on the plane."

Technically, there were eleven pounds of water in the belly and six pounds of water in the bladder pouch.

"I'm giving a seminar, I have to have this belly with me."

"Oh, bless your heart. Tell you what, you can check the belly in the belly of the plane."

The woman cracked up at the dual use of the word "belly."

"Thanks," I said. "My plane leaves in twenty minutes, how do you get it on there?

"Follow me."

Ten minutes and fifty dollars later, I checked my third "bag." I practically flew towards my gate since I was now traveling light; with only two bags, a purse, an oversized maternity outfit and dangling bike equipment. I arrived at the gate with ten minutes to spare. Now my only concern was whether the belly would make it through the plane change at Atlanta and whether I would make it to baggage claim to pick it up without running into anyone from my office in an un-knocked-up state. In spite of these fears, I slept soundly through the flight.

When I woke up, a cold had settled in with a vengeance. I needed to get home, rest and get an antibiotic. As the plane taxied, I opened the overhead compartment to get a jump start on getting off the plane. The flight attendant told me to sit down and I passed out.

My first thought when I awoke was that the airlines were getting heavy handed about the "stay seated" rule. As it turned out, my seat mate was a shot-putter for the University of Tampa track team, and his eight-pound shot put hit me in the face as I opened the overhead compartment. That was gonna leave a mark.

My eye was swollen and the airline's legal team was surrounding me. "Where's my luggage?" I asked.

"Right here, we got everything for you and will help you take it to your car."

I did a quick inventory and noticed everything was there except the belly. I asked about the belly, but the airline personnel said they saw nothing like it. Normally, I would stick around and raise hell until my property was found or replaced. However, I couldn't hang out at Tampa Airport without risking running into at least a handful of attorneys from my firm. The only alternative was to blow another $500 on a new Empathy Belly, which would have to be over-nighted at the cost of an additional arm and leg. I chose this option, planning to bill it to the airlines.

The next morning, after receiving my new pregnancy belly, I put in an appearance at work even though I was exhausted and sick. Right after I came in, David swung by my office. He sipped his coffee and asked about my trip. The tone of his voice suggested I'd been in Hawaii instead of taking depositions in Mobile, Alabama.

"Good," I said, hoping that would suffice.

Hardly. David liked to talk about the depositions of experts. He'd had several neon sign fires in the past and was eager to ask questions involving the words "fabrication," "Hayco bushings," "transformers" and "conduit." I'd spent five days repressing memories of these topics and one day nursing a head injury, so I didn't even attempt to engage him.

"I'm going to go over my notes and draft an update to the client, you're going to have to be in suspense until then."

"Okay. You'll never guess what happened to me this weekend."

I could feel a horrible story coming on, but asked what happened anyway.

"I went to the beach with my wife. She was facing the ocean and I was facing away from the ocean reading my newspaper. I was under the umbrella, listening to my iPod."

Interesting. I'd never gone to the beach to face the parking lot and tune out the sights and sounds of the ocean. More interesting was that David had an iPod. I couldn't imagine what he listened to.

"Anyway, my wife nudges me, so I lower my paper and look toward the showers. There was a topless woman in one of those up-the-butt-line-things taking a shower. She must have thought she was in Europe. Can you believe my wife pointed that out? I'm the luckiest guy in the world."

"What's an up-the-butt-line-thing? You mean a thong?" I asked.

"Yes, a thong. Anyway, I kept lowering my paper to check it out. It was the longest shower I've ever seen. I was in heaven."

David made the motion of a man reading a paper, lowering it, and raising an eyebrow at something he likes. He repeated this motion ten times. As he explained, "It was so funny, I just kept lowering the paper."

"Sounds like a good time."

"It was. What happened to your face?"

I was starting to think I didn't have a huge black and blue mark, raised like an egg, covering the left side of my face and that I didn't sound completely sick and congested. He noticed one out of two. "A shot put hit me in the face on the return flight."

"I used to shot put," David said. "Have you ever done it?"

Not exactly the sympathy I was looking for, but I answered. "Yes, I threw it like a baseball and destroyed my shoulder. It was a great time."

"You can't throw it like a baseball." David set his coffee down and showed me the proper way to throw a shot put. He used my Johnson Smith paperweight as the shot put and threw it straight up into a ceiling tile. The ceiling tile bumped up a little bit, but did not break. The best part was that his follow-through moved him just far enough forward to be hit in the head with the paperweight on its way down.

"Are you okay?" I said.

"Of course. If that ceiling tile weren't there, it would have gone at least seventy feet."

"Isn't the shot put record like seventy-five feet?" I asked.

"Yes. I'm almost as good as the Olympians and I barely train and have a full time job as a named partner at a large prestigious law firm. If I wasn't here, I'd probably be the record holder. Have you ever practiced shot-putting?"

"No, but maybe I'll practice this weekend," I said as convincingly as I could.

"Can you shot put pregnant?" David asked.

"Probably not too well. I'll have to wait until after the kid pops out to learn that skill."

"When is that?"

"A week or so."

"Man, getting down to the wire. Have you had any hemorrhoids? My wife had them all the time."

I thought hemorrhoids were something in your ass and didn't know what they had to do with pregnancy, but since they sounded gross, I assumed it was par for the course with pregnancy and said, "Yes."

"They're just excruciating huh? My wife was in such pain."

Gross and painful, not surprising. "Yeah, they're no fun."

"Are you effacing yet?" David asked next.

Hmm. No idea what that was. At least I'd heard of hemorrhoids from commercials. Effacing? What the fuck. "Yeah, a little." I said.

"Just a little? Wow, my wife was fully effaced and two centimeters dilated for an entire month before delivering."

Of course he was asking me how big my vagina is, he's my boss, why wouldn't he. "I'll see you later."

David left and I called Danny as I looked up hemorrhoids and effacing.

"Hey," I said, "have you ever had a hemorrhoid?"

"Yeah why?"

"David thinks I should have hemorrhoids at this stage of my pregnancy. I was looking it up."

"You're lucky you don't. It was so painful. It hurt to shit, so I avoided shitting. But eventually, you just have to go. Seriously, I thought about naming that shit when it finally came out of me."

"Lovely. Here's the more formal definition. 'Swelling and inflammation of veins in the rectum and anus caused by increased straining during bowel movements by constipation or diarrhea.'"

"Is this why you called?" Danny asked.

"Yes. Oooh, fun fact. Based on their very low incidence in the developing world, where people squat for bodily functions, hemorrhoids have been attributed to the use of the unnatural 'sitting' toilet.' Maybe Jason is right to shit in the backyard."

"Bye, Jenna."

"No wait, David also asked me if I was effacing."

"What's that?"

"Looking it up now, but based on my context clues, I think he was asking me if I was dilated yet. He wants to know how big I am down there."

"You should abandon the pregnancy story and just sue him for sexual harassment."

"Maybe. I could probably get a class action suit going with the other women here."

"Good luck. I'll see you later."

I closed out the hemorrhoid and effacement research and began my treatise to the client regarding the previous week's depositions, of which I had actually attended only three. Four minutes later, I thought about giving birth prematurely just to avoid this assignment.

CHAPTER ELEVEN

The cold that started coming on while I was away got worse. I left work early, went to the doctor and got my Z-Pak, the antibiotic that always makes me feel perfect within four days. Doctors caution against using antibiotics, claiming the body builds up a resistance, causing them to become less effective when you really need them. I don't know the exact definition of "really" sick other than potentially terminal. However, I do know I'm always ready to stop coughing and sneezing out green mucous, mouth breathing and feeling fatigued. As a result, I eagerly signed up to punch one of my antibiotics tickets.

Mom called me on my way home from the doctor. "Hi Mom."

"You sound terrible," she informed me.

"Yeah, I just left the doctor. I'm on my way to get antibiotics from the pharmacy."

"Did you get yogurt?"

"No, I hate yogurt."

"Antibiotics give you a yeast infection if you don't eat yogurt."

"Says who?"

"Science," my mom replied as though she had actually answered the question.

"I'm only going to be on them a few days, I've never had a yeast infection, and I hate yogurt. I'm good."

"If I get you yogurt will you eat it?"

"No, but feel free to pick me up some dinner."

"Yeah, right."

"I'm sick," I said.

"Did you ride your bike today?" she asked.

"Yes, but I only spun around an hour easy."

"Then just make an easy dinner."

"Bye, Mom."

"Bye, Jenna. Feel better."

A few days later, Danny came by my house to give me a massage. I asked if he'd ever heard about the connection between yeast infections and yogurt.

"Absolutely. It's true," he said.

"How the hell does that work?" I asked.

"You just rub the yogurt on your hoo hoo and voila, yeast infection free."

"You're so full of shit. You eat the yogurt as a preventative, you don't wipe it on your crotch as a cure."

"I took a shot," he said. "You gotta take a shot."

"You almost got me," I said sarcastically.

I didn't want to say anything to Danny, but ironically, the discussion of yeast infections made my vagina itch. Must be the power of suggestion. I tried to focus on something else, but it was difficult unless Danny was doing one of his torture pressure points. When that happened, the pain shifted to that area for a bit, then back to my itchy crotch. It was the first time in my life I was anxious for a massage to end.

When he'd finished, I got dressed and Danny came out to remove the sheets and fold up the table. While I was writing him a check, he said, "What's that?"

"What?"

"That stain on the sheet?"

"What stain?" I said.

"Right there, where your crotch was until just recently?"

Holy shit. There was a small off-white clump resembling cottage cheese on Danny's blue sheet, exactly where my crotch had been during the massage. How the hell was I supposed to get out of this one? I considered telling him the massage turned me on rather than have him think I excrete yeast, but I decided to go with denial. "I don't see anything."

"Right fucking there." He pointed, but didn't touch it.

I played stupid. "Whatever, there's nothing there, just put the sheets away." A few seconds later I decided I needed a backup plan. I said, "If there was something there, don't tell anyone, please."

"Of course I won't tell anyone. Don't worry about it. There's actually a medical term for it we learned in massage school."

"Yeast infection?" I said.

"No. That's a layman's term," Danny replied.

"What's the scientific term?" I asked.

Danny looked serious for a moment and his voice took on a professorial tone as he said, "Rank pussy." He then cracked up.

"Very funny," I deadpanned, cracking a smile in spite of my bright red face.

After Danny left I thought about taking my pregnancy leave immediately in order to avoid facing him again for at least three months.

* * *

Sure enough, my cold was gone by Friday. I had one race weekend and one week of work left prior to my maternity leave. Great news, blunted only by the fact that it was "T" day: the day I had to meet Tony Smith. Over the past few weeks, Sarah had called me daily to arrange "the date." She had been dropping very strong hints that my secret would not be safe if I reneged on my promise to date her son. With no illness, work trips or races, I ran out of excuses to avoid seeing Tony. I thought about being pregnant for the date since, in my experience, it's quite the turnoff. However, such a stunt could piss Sarah off enough to squeal to David. I was stuck hoping Tony was one of the few men not transfixed by my beauty and charming habit of being overly judgmental and self-centered.

Exactly on time, my door bell rang. I opened the door and there stood Quinton. He was grinning broadly with a look of amazement. Clearly he thought the stars had aligned. Reflexively, I slammed the door shut. All of a sudden I was eager for Tony to show up and shoo Quinton away.

"Jenna?"

I opened the door again. "Sorry, Quinton, I was surprised. I'm expecting someone else."

"Wow, this is fate. I swear to God that until I got to your address, I didn't realize it was you."

"What in the hell are you talking about?" I said, dreading the answer.

"I'm Sarah's son."

Until this moment, I thought that I had experienced all of Quinton's bad traits during our one and only date. Not so. His catastrophic lineage had gone unmentioned over dinner at IHOP. I recovered and said, "You're a schizophrenic and go by Tony and Quinton?"

"No, Quinton is my real name. My mom started calling me Quintony and Macaroni and other nicknames when I was growing up. Eventually she shortened it to Tony around the house."

"Makes sense. Well, I'll let your mom know that we already have dated and that it didn't work out."

"Come on, Jenna, give me another shot. You have nothing else to do tonight."

"I can improvise," I said.

"Come on, I owe you after the last time. Let's go to Ruth's Chris or Berns, and get a good steak."

"That's okay," I said. "You don't have to do that."

"No really, my treat. I'd like to start from square one with you."

"That's going to be hard, but I guess we can grab dinner."

"Thanks," Quinton/Tony said, then added, "You know what though? I'm not really in the mood for steak. I'm really in the mood for a burrito. Want to go to Moe's?"

"That's quite the bait and switch." I felt rude saying it, but he was the one who threw out the expensive steak dinner idea. I never would have suggested it. I pondered whether Moe's was even a step up from the International House of Pancakes.

"Fine," said Quinton, "we can go to Ruth's Chris, Little Miss High Maintenance."

"Oh my God." I said, by this time exasperated. "I don't care where we go, let's just get it over with."

"That's the spirit," Quinton said, in all seriousness.

I both dreaded and anticipated the night immediately. After all, what I saw on the first date was Quinton's A-game. I couldn't wait to see how he acted when he wasn't trying to impress me.

The date was like *Groundhog Day*. It was as absurd as our first date, the only difference being that this time I expected drunken insanity. Moe's didn't have a full bar and only sold Corona, so it took a little longer for Quinton to get drunk, but the end result was the same. He didn't ask me about the pregnancy, leading me to believe that he didn't know about it or the fact that our date was a result of blackmail.

This time, however, I was also drunk by the time we swung by the Tiny Tap. I ordered a Pabst Blue Ribbon on tap, sat back, and enjoyed the mayhem. At one point Quinton stood on the bar and pissed into the trash can at the end of the bar. His buddy followed suit. All this time I had thought "pissing contest" was an expression.

I presumed, as we left the Tiny Tap, Quinton again with a roader, that we were on our way to pick up ice cream and apple pie again, which I planned to put in the freezer before tucking in Quinton on my doorstep. As I dreaded this task, a cop pulled Quinton over.

"What should I do, Jenna?"

"Get out your license and registration."

"I mean legal advice. I can't get another DUI."

"Another one? Seems like you may know more than me about the subject."

"You've never handled a DUI?" Quinton asked.

"No. I'm not a criminal attorney."

"Didn't they teach you about DUIs in law school?"

"Nope," I said nonchalantly. "That's one of the misunderstandings about law school. We don't learn jack shit about avoiding a traffic ticket or DUI. I can teach you about the rule against perpetuities though."

"What the hell is that?" Quinton asked.

"Basically it means that no interest is good unless it vests, if at all, not later than twenty-one years after some life in being at the creation of the interest. It limits a testator's power to earmark gifts for remote descendants." As I was explaining this, Quinton tanked his roader beer in order, as he explained it, to "avoid having an open container in the car in case the cop inspected it." He really was dumber than I imagined.

Quinton was busy chewing an entire pack of watermelon Bubble Yum gum to disguise his breath when the officer said, "License and registration please."

He opened his wallet as he hit the skip button on his CD player. Evidently he wanted to hear one more good song before heading to the slammer.

Quinton handed the cop a toll booth receipt along with a credit card.

"Are you paying attention to me, sir?" the cop asked.

"Yes sir, I um, it was an unconscious move. I'm a channel surfer."

"License and registration," the cop repeated as he handed the receipt and credit card back to Quinton.

Quinton started fishing around for his actual license and registration as the officer said, "Do you know why I pulled you over, sir?"

"Did I cross the center line?" Quinton asked, unsure of himself.

"Yes, and the line on the right side. Weaving if you will." The cop turned to me and said, "Ma'am, has he been drinking tonight?"

As I debated the extent to which I would throw Quinton under the bus, he said, "Nope. I'll take a Breathalyzer test to prove it."

Quinton blew into the portable device like an innocent man, clearly under the impression that Bubble Yum disguises intoxication. After blowing a .29, far above the legal limit but far below the .36 I predicted, Quinton began a series of field sobriety exercises to prove his innocence. His balance and hand-eye coordination were actually good. His lack of focus, no doubt due to his extreme ADHD, was the reason for his miserable performance. He couldn't seem to remember the easiest instructions regarding walking heel-to-toe or doing the one leg stand.

The cop pulled out the cuffs and started reading Quinton his rights. Quinton asked me to call Sarah, but fortunately he couldn't remember her number. I called my brother John to pick me up, then went home and got a good night's sleep.

Sarah was crazed the next day at work. This was her "little Tony's" third strike. He would be in jail for at least a month, have his driver's license suspended and it would cost a lot of money. She demanded to know how I, Jenna Rosen, insurance lawyer extraordinaire, or at least mediocre, let him get arrested?

"You did it on purpose. You never wanted to go out with him. He told me you're the one who broke his heart all those months ago. I'm half-tempted to tell David about your little fake pregnancy."

My heart stopped and bullshit started flowing out of my mouth. "No, Sarah. I don't hate Quinton, or Tony, or whatever else you call him. In fact, we had a great time. We'd probably be going out again tonight if he wasn't, you know, in the clink."

"Really?"

I gulped hard. "Yes."

"He'll be out in a month or so, you know," Sarah advised.

"Great. We can just pick up then. In the meantime, you're not going to tell David about the pregnancy are you?"

"Of course not. You'll need to keep this good job to support my baby when he moves in with you."

Yeah. That's going to happen.

* * *

My final races before maternity leave were in Clermont. Clermont boasts Sugarloaf Mountain, the highest hill in Florida. Not only is Sugarloaf the highest, but also the steepest. The center has a twenty percent incline. Granted, it's only about a kilometer long, and the steep section is only 100 meters, but it's tough. There are a number of professional triathletes who train in Clermont during the winter. Additionally, a number of teams trained there prior to the Atlanta Olympics. The family that lives at the summit of Sugarloaf is well aware that the property sits on the highest peak in Florida. They put a six gallon supply of fresh ice water outside their house each day of the year, and often bring food out, as well. One weekend a year, they allow their front yard to be the finish line of this race.

I love Sugarloaf Race Weekend. I had won last year and was very motivated to do so again. There were three good climbers at the race, the best a talented forty-five-pound sixteen-year-old girl. Being a lightweight is an advantage in the mountains, where the person with the strongest power to weight ratio tends to win. This applies to hills as well, though obviously bigger riders have an easier time powering over a hill than a mountain. Oddly, Brenda was there. Though she was a decent hill climber, she normally robbed me of the opportunity to kick her ass in the hills by not showing up.

The women's race started at nine a.m. and finished at high noon. Racing a bike at midday during the Florida summer is like being in a sauna on the surface of the sun. Thirty minutes into the race, my drinking water was hot enough for a tea bag, but I kept drinking it. Disgusting, but necessary. In the draft, I was hit from sweat from the two riders ahead of me and it was delightfully refreshing. For laps one and two, I opened a huge gap on the entire field at the steepest section of the hill. However, after the hill, Brenda and two of her teammates shared the work to reel me back in. On the third and fourth laps, I conserved energy, confident that I could beat everyone up the hill for the finish without having to break away from the pack beforehand.

With a mile to go, a woman from Tallahassee attacked. She was extremely strong, but I didn't think that at five-ten and 150 pounds, she could make it through the steep section without being caught. Accordingly, I gambled and let her go and stayed in the pack until the base of the climb, when I attacked. Two-thirds up the hill, I knew I'd won. I kept pedaling, but easier now. Fifty yards before the finish line, I glanced back and saw the closest person to me was six bike lengths away. I relaxed, took my hands off the bars, and began to coast toward the finish. With thirty meters to go, I saw something out of the corner of my eye. It was the sixteen-year-old. She drew even, then shot by me before I could put my hands back on the handlebars. That little kid had been sitting on my wheel since I'd attacked at the base of the climb and I never noticed because I couldn't hear her over my own breathing or see her because she was tiny and in my blind spot. I accelerated and closed the gap immediately, but I ran out of road and she won by the width of a tire. I finished second as a result of user error and hated myself. I'd never take my hands off the bars and celebrate a finish again until after I crossed the line. Hell, I would never even slow down from now on until I crossed the line. "Jenna Rosen, you're a stupid fucking dumbass," I said to myself over and over, even as I was enthusiastically congratulating the junior on her first win.

Brenda finished fourth, but was smiling so much you'd have thought she'd won. She was clearly delighted that a high school kid beat me even though the high school kid was a very good racer.

I talked to Danny on the way, updating him about Quinton's relation to the maniac paralegal I always talked about.

"Holy shit! Quinton's mom is the Sarah Smith you talk about? I've fucked her."

"What?"

"A long time ago, before she was Sarah Smith actually. I forget what her married name was at the time. Anyway, I was drunk at Quinton's house after a party he had and she started hitting on me."

"I'm going to throw up."

"Why? She was a hot forty-year-old at the time and I was fifteen years old or maybe even younger. I raced in the junior category at the time. Anyway, she was a MILF, what can I say?"

"I think it's a MIDF once you actually hit it."

"What's that?"

"Mom I Did Fuck. Seriously, you're grossing me out. I have to go."

The race pissed me off so much that I couldn't eat or talk at dinner. I'm pretty sure my foul mood could have continued for days if my mom hadn't healed it with the most memorable line ever uttered in the Rosen household.

"Hey, Jenna and Julie, do you guys squirt?" She said this in the most innocent and inquisitive voice.

Julie almost choked on her rice as John asked, "Did you just ask my wife and sister if they squirt?"

"Yeah," Mom said. "There are no secrets with family."

"Yeah, there are," John, Jason and I said in unison.

"What brought this to mind?" I asked.

"My middle school kids were talking about it in the cafeteria. I never heard of it before."

"Do you know what it is now? Have you seen it?" I asked.

"Where would I see it?" she answered.

"You really need to learn to Google anything you're curious about. I'll show you, it's kind of funny."

"I have no idea what we're talking about," Dad said.

"I'll show you, too," I said. John and Julie were dreading the awkwardness as much as I was looking forward to shocking the hell out of my parents.

I went to my parents' computer, pulled up the Google bar, and typed in the "W" to start the phrase "women squirting." "Women titties," "women fucking," "women eating women," and "women: lesbians until graduation or 'LUGs' for short" appeared in the tool bar. Clearly, Jason had occasionally been using this computer. I typed in "women squirting," and in no time up popped countless links to just that.

Unfortunately, the first video clip didn't start with just squirting. I backspaced and clicked on the next link. Same problem. I didn't mind watching the spectacle of squirting with the family, but a sex scene was awkward. I looked away until I heard Mom shout, "Ewwwwww." I turned back towards the computer and saw a girl, spread eagle, squirting like a geyser into the air.

"Get the fuck outta here!" Dad shouted. "What the fuck was that? Play that again."

I was laughing uncontrollably as I hit replay.

"Geri," said Dad. "I can't believe you just asked Jenna and Julie if they squirt."

"Thank you," John said from the corner of the room, where he was sitting and passing on porn for the first time in his life.

"I didn't think that's what it would look like," said Mom, to redeem herself. "Looks like a lot of clean-up is involved."

"It looks like trick photography is involved," Dad responded. "What is it?"

I Googled the phrase to get a more clinical, less visual, explanation.

Female ejaculation refers to the expulsion of noticeable amounts of clear fluid by females from the paraurethral ducts and/or urethra during orgasm. The exact source of the fluid is debated, although some researches believe it originates from the Skene's gland. There is no solid information about the source of the fluid, but chemical analysis performed on the fluid has revealed that while it sometimes contains at least traces of urine, it regularly contains chemical markers unique to the prostate (whether male or female).

"Didn't your parents tell you about the Skene's gland and female ejaculation during the birds and the bees chat?" I asked my parents.

"Hardly," Dad responded.

Everyone was in a good mood as I was leaving my parents' house, so I thought it was an opportune time to tell my parents about their upcoming dog sitting assignment. Usually I just dropped off Sonny when I was away for the weekend. I had never dropped him off for more than three days, so this was going to be a tough sell. "By the way guys, I'm going to be traveling for work for about three months starting next week, so I'm going to need you to watch Sonny."

"Three months?" asked Mom in a high pitched voice with a stunned look on her face. "How can your office make you travel for three months? What if you had a kid?"

I smiled at the irony and said, "But I don't."

"But if you did." Mom said, "what would you do with Sonny if we weren't here?"

"But you are."

"But if we weren't? What are you doing for three months?" Mom asked me.

"We're opening an office in Charlotte soon. I volunteered to help develop the subrogation department because I wanted to chill out up north for a while."

Dad chimed in and said, "That means you just volunteered us to watch your dog for three months, Jenna."

"Sorry, Dad, I thought it was a good way to get ahead at the office." If there's one thing for which my parents are suckers, it's aiding in my future success. They immediately softened.

"Where are you staying up there?" asked Dad.

"A hotel."

"Will you be home at all during that time?" asked Mom.

"Not sure. Maybe."

"Geri, she'll be gone as long as she's gone. It's about time she took her career seriously."

"I was just asking," Mom said. "I don't care. Good for you, Jenna."

"Thanks. Sorry, I know he howls a lot, but you'll grow to love him."

"It's not that we don't love him. It's just that he's crazy and loud and humps our guests," said Dad.

"Sorry, bad parenting. He's so cute though."

I felt bad about neglecting Sonny for three months and sticking him with my parents, but it would be too hard to travel with him. Plus,

I couldn't leave him in the car in July while I raced or trained for four to six hours a day. I also felt bad about lying to my parents, but it had to be done.

* * *

On Monday, I knew I couldn't handle the excitement of leaving over a period of an entire week, so I planned to leave a day early. I decided have a C-section around lunch time Thursday and not see anyone again for three months. From what I could tell, this was normal procedure. Human resources would distribute the obligatory email "Jenna Rosen gave birth to John Doe this afternoon at 3:47 p.m. Mom and baby are doing fine." Everyone would hit "reply all" and send their congratulations and hopefully that would be the end of it until my return in October, at which point I'd explain that I had to leave the kid at the fire station because it had no work ethic and was constantly crying, shitting and sleeping.

Tuesday was a big day of ignoring my work and planning my departure. I cancelled my cable, Netflix and newspaper. Danny agreed to grab my mail whenever he rode his bike by my house and said he'd send my bills my way, wherever I was.

After printing out directions to all the races I planned to attend, I ran out of procrastination methods and started searching for an online crossword puzzle that wasn't banned by WEBSENSE. I found a first grade level puzzle and another that was extremely difficult. I got seven words on the difficult crossword, but then aced the other to boost my confidence back up.

I closed the crossword page and stared off into space. I had reached a level of boredom where I actually considered answering my overdue discovery requests. Instead, I got up and strolled into Kimberly's office. Kimberly was in the middle of a heated email discussion with David and Ralph, an attorney in our Alabama office. Apparently, Ralph, on the brink of making partner, offered to assist David and Kimberly with their upcoming trial in Mobile. David's response was, "TABLE'S FULL!"

Ralph, who was born and bred in Mobile typed, "Fine, let the New York Jew and woman from Chicago go to trial against the attorney whose great-grandfather fought alongside the judge's great-grandfather during the Civil War."

David was unfazed. He typed, "I went to law school in Georgia and I can put on a drawl and mix it up with any southerner."

This was partially true. While David did attend law school at the University of Georgia, his fake accent was atrocious and he could not "mix it up" in any social situation, let alone amongst men reminiscing about their granddaddys' roles in the "war against northern aggression."

Ralph responded, "Suit yourself."

Kimberly typed to Ralph, "You can have my spot at the table."

Ralph responded, "Thanks. I'm good."

They stopped typing and I took a seat across from Kimberly in her office. We shot the shit for over an hour, then I returned to my desk, talked to a few friends on the phone and called it a day.

On Wednesday, I couldn't face a full day at the office even though I knew I wouldn't do anything. So, I rode the sixty mile group ride in the hills of San Antonio before strolling into work at 11:30 a.m. No one even questioned me; it was as though it was expected that I would come and go at my leisure at this late stage of pregnancy.

Thursday! I woke up at three in the morning after having a dream that I became a professional bicycle racer, and to celebrate, had a party where I served chips and dip on my law diploma. The dream was so exciting I couldn't get back to sleep. Instead, I began packing so that when I left the office to give birth, I could drive north immediately. Sonny stayed glued to my side, as he does whenever I pack. He associates my suitcases with abandonment. When I left for work, I assured him that I'd be back, but he refused to budge, even when I fed him and opened his doggy door. I slithered out the door so he couldn't follow me and I heard him crying and howling until I pulled out of the driveway. Poor little guy. I wish he understood English so I could tell him he would just be at Camp Rosen for a little bit.

After checking email, cycling news, and my bank statement, I lifted my ban on avoiding work to respond to a scathing letter from an opposing counsel. The tone of my letter was calm and rational, addressing each of his points in an easygoing manner that accentuated the fact that the tone of his letter was that of a raving lunatic. Once that was finished, the plan was to surf the Internet for the remaining seven hours of the day.

By 10:00 a.m., I was already thinking of leaving early. However, David swung by my office and asked me to go to lunch with Kimberly and him. I said yes, because I didn't want to subject Kimberly to a solo hour with David. I really am a good person.

By lunch, I was so excited about my impending departure that I didn't mind eating at Jackson's. Jackson's was on Harbour Island, directly on the water. It was a large place with several bars and great indoor and outdoor seating. The restaurant was able to thrive in spite of charging exorbitantly high prices for less than mediocre food because it was right on the water and had a spectacular view. Of course, David was the only person who went there and insisted on sitting indoors. Today, this didn't bother me. My escape was near so I was on cloud nine as I walked towards my twelve dollar greasy club sandwich with David Greene.

We sat down and David ordered his first of many Diet Cokes. He's a chain Diet Coke drinker and has an irrational fear that the waiter is conspiring to bring him Coke instead of Diet Coke, or for dessert, regular instead of decaf. This fear can only be placated by David grilling the waiter every time he comes to the table with a refill. "Are you sure?" "Who puts the taps on?" "How do you know that glass is mine?" "Did you make the coffee?" "Did you see who put it in the pot with the orange handle?"

We sat in a window seat and David kept staring at the table on the other side of the window, just outside. It was awkward; Kimberly and I pretended not to notice. Eventually, I said, "You know David, that's not a one-way mirror, she can see you staring at her." David responded, "She? I was trying to figure out if that was a girl or a boy from the second we sat down."

I looked over. She was thin, had short hair, a sleeve of tattoos on both arms and was wearing a wife-beater tank top, cargo pants and boots. Thankfully, she was texting on her phone and not paying attention to us.

I said, "It's a girl David, please don't ask her to confirm." This was a real concern of mine.

David replied, "I won't."

He said this as though blatantly staring at her for the past ten minutes and talking loudly enough so that she could possibly hear him through the glass wasn't just as rude as inquiring directly about her gender. Fortunately she was looking at the water and not at us.

David couldn't let it go. He said, "Do you think she's, you know, well, you know, bi?"

"Bisexual?" I asked.

"Yeah," David said.

"You mean if I had to speculate as to her sexual orientation just by looking at her and assigning a stereotype?" I asked.

"Yes," David replied without hesitation or an inkling that he had veered far from political correctness. He was staring at me, waiting for an answer.

"Then I'd guess lesbian."

"That's what I meant," David said. "I just, you know, wanted to be politically correct."

I smiled at the irony and his ignorance. "I don't think bisexual is P.C. for lesbian, David."

"Sure it is," he replied, like I was an idiot for not knowing the proper nomenclature initiated by my own generation. Jesus. I was excited about racing my bike for three months, but getting away from David for three months would be almost as exhilarating.

Kimberly was in the same situation, sans the impending three month vacation. She was noticeably more somber with this the awkward conversation. Next, we talked about David's children, subrogation and my pregnancy. On any other day, these topics would result in a Jenna-shaped hole through the wall, but today, I contributed. I complimented David on his ability to produce such a great artist and dancer, engaged in a discussion about subrogation waivers and held in my lunch as David explained the many positions to have sex with a pregnant woman. The hour seemed to fly by as if it were only two, instead of the usual four-to-one-hour ratio I experienced in David's presence. I wasn't even upset when David failed to pick up the check despite earning nine times my salary, inviting me to lunch, selecting the restaurant, picking the seats and dictating the conversation.

After lunch, we headed back to the parking garage. Jackson's was attached to a hotel and there was a big circular driveway in front of the hotel you have to walk past to get to the garage. We walked under the awning parallel to the valet stand in order to stay out of the sun. As I calculated that I only had to drive back downtown with David, about four minutes, before taking off for three months, I heard, "Watch out!" I turned and saw an SUV traveling in the wrong direction, headed directly for me.

The crash happened instantaneously, but in slow motion. The car was braking, but not fast enough. I had no time to turn to get out of the way. To protect my cycling legs I pointed my stomach toward the SUV, so the Empathy Belly would take the brunt of the impact. I was knocked flat, three feet behind where I was standing. My back hurt from the fall, but otherwise I was unharmed.

Kimberly and David ran over with a look of sympathy mixed with disgust. I was confused by their reaction until I remembered that I had just thrust my fetus into an oncoming vehicle. I looked down at my stomach. It was leaking. Two lead balls, added to tack fourteen pounds onto the already ridiculously heavy belly, were rolling slowly next to me.

"Call an ambulance!" David screamed.

"I'm okay," I said and stood up, trying to figure out how to flee the scene.

"Your water broke," said David

My "water" was all over my stomach rather than flowing from my nether region. Kimberly, who instantly deduced that I was not with child, hovered over me and began stammering to try and cover for me.

I stood up, turned away from David and said, "David, I'd really be more comfortable with Kimberly and the doctors."

"I'll turn away," David replied, "but I don't feel comfortable leaving until the ambulance arrives." As he said this, he checked his watch. David never took more than one hour for lunch and he didn't want my near-death experience to interfere with his billable hours.

The innards of the Empathy Bbelly continued to ooze out as we waited. David was turned the other way tapping on his BlackBerry. As the ambulance approached, sirens blaring, a crowd began congregating. I practically sprinted into the ambulance to get away from them.

For a minute, I was afraid that David might insist on accompanying me to the hospital, but he was already walking off towards his car. I don't know why I was even worried, as there was no way David was going to go to the hospital with me instead of billing clients.

On the way to the hospital, which was a mile away on Davis Island, an EMT looked at me for the first time and said, "You're not pregnant."

Obviously he graduated at the top of his class. "Yeah," I said. "This is a big misunderstanding. If I could just hop out."

The EMT ignored me and started inspecting my head. By the time he determined there'd been no head trauma, we were at Tampa General and I was being unloaded. The EMT called for a psych consult and I knew I had to get out of there before I was admitted. If I were admitted, my carefully executed plan would be in shambles, I'd have exorbitant medical bills and be wearing a straightjacket. I was already dreading the bills and paperwork related to my one-mile ambulance drive.

I decided to fake a seizure. I have a friend named Roy who is an epileptic and I'd seen him seize a number of times. I started shaking, then fell off the stretcher onto the floor. As the orderly pushing the stretcher took off to get help, I ran in the other direction.

I exited Tampa General and ran towards the bathroom at the nearby tennis courts. I often stopped there when I had to pee while riding on Davis Island. In the bathroom, I called Danny on my cell phone and asked him to pick me up. The phone had some Empathy Belly water on it, but it still worked.

As I sat there, Sarah called and said, "I just heard what happened."

My pulse sky rocketed and I said, "Are you going to tell David? I don't think he noticed that I wasn't pregnant."

Sarah said, "No, I'm not going to tell him. Jenna, I don't know why you faked a pregnancy, but everyone thinks you just went into labor. Use this time off as a maternity leave and get the mental help you need. Who knows, in a few months when you're sane and Tony is out of jail, maybe we'll hear wedding bells. Then you can have a real baby and you won't have to pretend."

She was so far off the mark I had to suppress a big laugh. "Thanks, Sarah. Give my best to Tony and I'll let you know when I've worked through my issues." We hung up, and I felt relief wash over me.

Ten minutes later, there was a knock on the ladies room door, "Jenna, are you in there?"

"Who is it?" I asked.

"Danny."

"What's the safe word?"

"Mother fucker," Danny replied.

I opened the door, ran out and got into Danny's car and told him the story as we drove to my house. He said, "So let me get this straight.

You were hit by a car, David thinks you killed your kid, Sarah thinks you're going to a mental institution before marrying Quinton, your parents think you're on a work trip and you think you're just going to go race your bike for three months and get away with it?"

"Don't forget that I just skipped out on what is probably going to be a fourteen-hundred dollar ambulance and morphine bill."

"Oh, yeah. You're golden. I'm thinking of letting you out right here to walk. I think this is called aiding and abetting."

"Just take me home. I won't involve you," I said.

"Please. Like I'd leave you on the side of the road."

"Don't worry, I'm Ferris Bueller."

"That doesn't make any sense. Are you okay to drive? Did you just say you're on morphine?" Danny asked.

"No, the guy tried to give me morphine but couldn't find a vein. I think he was new. It took him a while to figure out I wasn't pregnant, too. Anyway, I wouldn't be surprised if he billed me for it. He took it out of the case and tried to inject it."

"So why the hell are you claiming to be Ferris Bueller?"

"I'm invincible like Ferris Bueller. No matter how fucked up this situation gets, it keeps working out for me. I'm embarking on a pro cycling career, subsidized by my office. My parents are watching Sonny, Quinton is in jail, and Sarah is my biggest advocate. I'm starting to think the world actually does revolve around me."

As we neared my home, Danny said, "I never thought of you as a 'the glass is half full' kind of girl, but your assessment of this situation is overly optimistic. This is the calm before the storm. Enjoy it, Ferris."

"Thanks for everything, Danny."

I got in my car and headed north to Pennsylvania.

CHAPTER TWELVE

My car was filled to the brim with two bikes, helmets, shoes, pump, spare wheels, tent, sleeping bag, books, a laptop and a laundry basket full of clothes, both cycling and regular, for any type of weather. With one of the rear seats removed from my Honda Element, there was plenty of room for everything without having to pack strategically. As I do for every race, I placed my bikes in the car then dumped my cycling clothing in between so the bikes wouldn't chip the paint off one another during transit.

The first race destination was the Pennsylvania mountains near Altoona. The plan until the August thirtieth start date of the Tour de West was to become stronger, faster and braver on the bike. To pump myself, I decided to travel all the way to Pennsylvania listening to nothing but the theme songs to *Chariots of Fire*, *Rocky*, *Rudy*, and *Hoosiers*. If I could accomplish that, I could accomplish anything.

I planned to attend six professional stage races and eight professional one-day races prior to the Tour de West. During these races, I had to be "discovered" to secure a spot in the Tour de West. In addition to riding strong, I had to learn to race confidently. No team would want a rider that raced squirrelly, which is to say, all over the road and unpredictably. Granted, my Bike Tourette Syndrome had improved since my crash, but I was still far from easy going yet. During the first leg of my journey north, I visualized sprinting and descending like a daredevil. By the time I rested at a camp ground near Atlanta, I was confident in my ability to race under any conditions.

The next morning, I drove two hours north to test my newfound ability in the mountains of Dahlonega, Georgia. Riding on a new road is always exciting. I'm told golfers have the same sensation whenever they tee off on a new course. That it was seventy degrees and sunny in the mountains at the base of the Appalachian Trail was a bonus. I rode eighty miles over four mountains and felt great. I flew up and down each mountain. Then again, there was no one around to freak me out on the downhill. While the pack generally thins out during a climb, particularly a steep or long one, there is still a group of five to twenty riders at each summit depending on how fast the pace is pushed on the way up. These lead riders descend in one long line, following the wheel of the person in front of them. Essentially, you're trusting that the person ahead of you is taking a good line, and keeping an eye out for traffic and other road hazards. During my inspirational pep talk to myself on yesterday's seven hour drive, I became more and more comfortable with the idea of trusting someone else. After all, I'd only been racing seriously for a year and a half, so it made sense to put my faith in seasoned professionals rather than myself. I was convinced of this wisdom as I rounded a corner at forty-five miles per hour and passed a bicycle hanging from a tree; no sign of the rider. Best not to think about that.

After the ride, I showered at a campground: fifty cents for three minutes. The three spiders in the shower didn't chip in. I hit the road and was soon in South Carolina. After leaving the long state of Florida, the states ticked by relatively quickly. A few miles into South Carolina, I saw the first South of the Border billboard since I was a kid.

When John and I were young and Jason was a baby, we took many vacations by car to visit family up north. Our parents made up a game for us. The first one to spot one of the South of the Border billboards and yell "Beaver!" got a point. The first person to see the giant sombrero that dominated the South of the Border amusement park got ten points for saying, "Big Beaver!" The beaver game, as we called it, was tough because Howard Johnson's billboards looked remarkably similar to a South of the Border billboard from afar. If you called beaver for a Howard Johnson billboard, you lost a point. I always won the beaver game. I thought it was my superior intellect, but in hindsight it was most likely because John didn't give a shit and wasn't playing.

Danny called to shoot the shit as I passed the second South of the Border billboard. I said, "Beaver!" and explained the rules to Danny. He started laughing hysterically.

"What?"

"You seriously don't get it?" he asked.

"It's a stupid game my parents made up, there's nothing to get."

"Beaver. South of the border. You don't think there's perhaps a double entendre here?"

"Holy shit! What kind of parents do I have? Who plays the beaver game with their young kids?"

"Sounds like a good way to pass the time with annoying kids in the car. They must have really loved that you actually kept score."

"Now that you mention it, I think they did get a kick out of it. Beaver! It's a fun game. I'm winning."

"Good for you."

"Hey, I'm going to concentrate on the beaver game. Can I call you in North Carolina, Virginia or Maryland when there's nothing to do?"

"Sure. I'd rather play beaver than talk to me too," Danny said.

"That's the spirit."

I called it a night at Shenandoah National Park. It was slightly out of my way, but had a good campground, and more importantly, would provide me with a beautiful but challenging bike ride the following morning.

The next day I rode decently through Shenandoah National Park though my legs were a little dead from sitting in a car for two days. My descending seemed to improve, literally overnight. I passed a few cars on the way down each of the mountains. This feat should be an automatic since road bikes travel between forty-five and sixty-five miles per hour down a mountain and cars drive a more conservative thirty-five to fifty-five miles per hour. But, this was the first time I managed to overtake a car. After four hours of riding, I showered with one spider and a dead roach for a dollar-fifty before commencing the final leg of my journey.

Just after dark, I pulled into a campground near Altoona. I went into the bathroom to brush my teeth and pulled the curtain back to check out the insect population and the cost per minute of water. New highs on both fronts: four spiders and a shitload of mosquitoes at a rate of one dollar for every two minutes. These accommodations were particularly frustrating because I have family in Altoona whose lavatory is both free, and bug free, with whom I could stay. Unfortunately, as far as my family was concerned, I was working in Charlotte, North Carolina, not riding my bike near Aunt Lauren.

At that moment, my cell phone rang and I saw it was my Mom's number.

"Hey."

"Hi Jenna, it's Mom and Dad. We're on our walk and wanted to see how your first day of work went up there."

Mom and Dad walked together for an hour every night and called me during walk-time to catch up. They put the phone on speaker which was fine for Mom, but Dad, who has been hard of hearing since his stint in the artillery unit of the army, needs constant translations. "It was okay," I said.

"What's the office like?"

I'd never really been a liar, especially to my parents. Granted, the fake pregnancy was quite a whopper, but as far as small details, I had always been pretty truthful. Inventing a day of work would involve some details, but I tried to stay vague. "It was good."

"What did she say?" I heard Dad ask in the background.

"She said 'it was good.' How are the people?"

"Good."

"What did she say, Geri?"

"'Good,' she repeated. "Is your office nice?"

"Yes."

"Huh?" Dad said.

"She said 'yes' Michael. Jenna, what's wrong with you? Usually we can't get a word in edgewise."

"Sorry. I pretty much just met with the new partners today. There's nothing to tell."

"Is David there?"

"No, he's there with you in Tampa," I said, praying my parents didn't run into David over the next few months where they'd be sure to talk about my pregnancy, the trip to the hospital or my business assignment in North Carolina. "Basically I just met everyone and set up my office."

"What exactly are you doing there?"

"Good question," I said, then paused to let the bullshit accumulate for a moment. "Basically, we have a lot of cases throughout the southeast. So when we opened our Alabama office, we moved all of our Alabama cases there and someone went there to help with the transition. I'm doing that for the Charlotte office. That way, we have lawyers licensed in North Carolina to handle these cases."

"What?" asked Dad.

"She's helping to transition the Florida cases to North Carolina."

"That makes sense."

"Where are you staying Jenna?" Mom asked.

"Holiday Inn."

"Did you bring your bike?"

"Of course. It's pretty here."

"Please be careful. You don't know where you are, you don't know the roads, you're by yourself,"

"I'm being careful," I said, cutting her off before she went into all the ways I could die riding a bike in North Carolina by myself.

"Any cute guys there?" she asked.

"Not yet."

"What?" Dad asked.

"She hasn't met any guys yet."

I used this language barrier as an excuse to get off the phone. "Can I talk to you later when we're not playing Pete and Repeat?"

Dad helped my cause by saying, "I missed that last part, say it one more time."

"She said you're annoying her by not hearing her and she'll talk to us later."

"Bye. Love you Mom, tell Dad I love him after I hang up, I can't listen to him say 'what' again."

"Huh?"

I hung up before the translation and started setting up my tent for the third night in a row.

The entry fee for the Tour of Pennsylvania was two hundred per person or nine hundred per team. A team consisted of nine riders, so racing for a team was a helluva bargain and yet another incentive to turn pro. I paid the entry fee, picked up my race packet and took off on an easy two hour ride to spin out my legs and view the course for the following morning's prologue, which was three miles long, ending on the track at Penn State.

I rode my time trial bike to reacquaint myself with the position before tomorrow's pain. On a road bike, a rider's body has flexibility; they can sit up or lean down and move their hands about the drops, tops and hoods, the three different spots of a road bike's handlebars. On a time trial bike, a rider bends in half, putting all of the weight of their upper body on their crotch and taint instead of their taint and ass. While neither position is particularly comfortable, the latter combo is far superior.

There were at least one hundred male and female cyclists scattered throughout the prologue course checking out the route when I showed up. I tried to avoid wearing a completely dopey grin as I passed by the professional cyclists that I recognized from Velonews and Cyclingnews, but I was very excited and probably not hiding it well. My excitement evaporated when I saw Brenda coming my way in a kit I didn't recognize. I asked around and found out that Brenda was on a composite team sponsored by a chain bicycle store out of California, Sunshine Cycling, that was looking to be competitive at the Tour de West.

After the ride, I took my laptop to a Starbucks to see when and how Brenda's new team formed. As it turned out, three days ago, the first time in two years that I was not sitting at the desk in my office checking cycling news on an hourly basis, Sunshine Cycling posted an article regarding the creation of a women's team to race the remainder of the National Race Calendar (NRC) schedule, starting with the Tour of Pennsylvania and ending with the Tour de West. The sponsorship no doubt came about because of Sunshine Cycling's desire to advertise its

158 California bike shops by having nine women wear their logo each day of the Tour de West.

It was not uncommon for teams of CAT 1 riders to form prior to a big event. The typical women's stage race permits approximately 120 women to participate. Because there are only about seven professional women's teams in the United States, there are vacancies prior to most races. Individual CAT 1 racers such as myself often seek out other individual CAT 1 racers to create a composite team for these stage races because even when entering as a team is not required, which is often the case, it is cheaper to enter a stage race as a team rather than individually. These CAT 1 racers hail from all over the United States, so finding a matching kit is tough. Cycling shops, bike companies or local businesses often offer to "sponsor" women by letting them wear a kit with their logo on it in a race. It's free advertising for the business and the women all match as required.

I'd thought about joining a composite team for the Tour of Pennsylvania, but opted instead to wear an unmarked white jersey and shorts so that if I did well, any interested professional teams would know I was an available racer. It hadn't occurred to me to keep an eye out for composite teams for the Tour de West because it was previously reported that there would be no vacancies since the professional teams from Europe, Australia and Canada would flock to the Tour de West and fill the field, along with the continental professional teams in the United States. I continued to read and learned that Sunshine Cycling was granted a wildcard entry because it was such a huge supporter of cycling throughout the west coast. The article also stated that the team was accepting race resumes until fifteen days prior to the Tour de West. Obviously, it would be easier to join a team that was forming rather than a team that had already formed and raced together for over half a season. I decided to draft a race resume immediately.

I started forming my academic resume when I was in fifth grade and turned down the role of "lead" safety patrol in order to be in charge of the bookstore, where I could get some real transactional experience, such as selling pencils and erasers. From there, my academic resume continued to improve over the next twenty years. By contrast, my cycling race resume was short and unimpressive. While all of my victories were hard fought, they all had taken place in Florida towns with names like Immokalee and Vernon. Adding insult to injury, the races I'd won often had names like the "See You Later Alligator Criterium" or the "Race O' Rama Cyclorama." I might as well be walking into a law office with a G.E.D. and three art credits from a community college because my race resume would get me nowhere unless I beefed it up quickly. In the meantime, I had to become friendly with the riders and the coach, called a *director sportif*, of Sunshine Cycling.

While I'm not shy, meeting professional cyclists without appearing to be a pathetic jock sniffer would be a difficult task. Cyclists don't get money and fame like other American athletes, but they tend to have a cult following of cycling enthusiasts who want to meet them at races, become Facebook friends and stay in touch. So, I did not relish being the lawyer on vacation trying to interject myself into the ranks of the professional women's *peloton*. My task would be doubly hard because, even if I managed to have an opportunity to engage the *director sportif* and athletes of Sunshine Cycling in conversation, I would have to do it out of Brenda's earshot. Team Sunshine Cycling would not be interested if they knew I had bad blood with someone on the team, regardless of how petty.

Aside from the three-mile prologue, the Tour of Pennsylvania comprised a seventy-six mile hilly road race that would likely end in a sprint; a sixteen-mile time trial, two mountainous road races that were seventy-four and seventy-one miles respectively, and a circuit race in downtown Philadelphia. A circuit race is generally two to three miles; longer than a criterium and shorter than a road race. This circuit race course would go through Center City Philadelphia, starting at the Art Museum steps Sylvester Stallone climbed in *Rocky*, turning through Rittenhouse Square, passing the Liberty Bell, then ending on the cobblestone streets in front of Independence Hall.

My best finish during the Tour of Pennsylvania was fifth on the second mountain stage, a road race that ended at a mountain summit. That day, I hung with fourteen other riders up the first mountain and the main pack never caught us. On the last climb, the group split up. I hung onto the front group but got dusted in the sprint finish. I finished three seconds in arrears of my four breakaway companions. Fifth place on a professional road stage was good for anyone, but it was downright impressive for an unattached rider competing in only her second professional stage race. My hopes for finding a professional team soared.

Unfortunately, the rest of my Tour de Pennsylvania results were between mediocre and shitty. Out of ninety-two women, I placed a fairly anonymous eighteenth in the prologue and twelfth in the time trial. This was something I would have to work on. In the circuit race, I maintained the caboose position throughout. What was worse, I was often a detached caboose, shotgunning off the back of the field. My modus operandi for these races was to slow down into each turn, slipping out of the draft of the pack; then knock myself out on each straightaway to catch up just in time to slow down going into the next corner. Another area that needed improvement. I did well during the hilly road race, riding towards the front of the pack and escaping in a few breakaways, but the *peloton* eventually reeled in the breakaways and the race came down to a sprint finish. In character, I choked and racked up another last place finish.

The only real shock was that I did horribly on the first mountain stage. As a cruel joke, the Tour of Pennsylvania started its first mountain stage at the top of the mountain rather than the bottom. Consequently, ninety-two female cyclists, who were fresh aside from their effort on the previous day's three-mile prologue, raced each other to the bottom of the mountain. I started out conservatively then slowed down after someone ate it into the metal railing lining the road. As with every crash I had witnessed, I smelled burnt rubber, heard metal cracking, then saw the actual crash; the exact opposite order of how one would imagine the senses perceive a crash. After witnessing the crash, I panicked and slowed to a snail's pace for the remainder of the descent. I was over a minute behind the *peloton* at the bottom of the mountain and the gap only grew from there. The *peloton* worked together against the wind while I sat in the wind all by my lonesome. I tried to think of the *Rocky* theme song to pump me up, but *Against the Wind* was stuck in my head instead. I passed a handful of racers along the course, but all of them wound up being time cut because they did not finish within four percent of the winner's time. If a rider is time cut, they cannot start the next day's stage. Of the finishers, I was last. Of my three last place finishes, this was the most disappointing because I had visions of winning that mountain stage.

Fortunately, a cyclist only has to list her good results on a race resume. A fifth place on Stage 4 of the Tour de Pennsylvania looked a lot more impressive when not surrounded by numbers in the high double digits. I beat all of team Sunshine Cycling on Stage 4, so it was possible that I was better at riding up mountains than anyone on their short list for the Tour de West roster. Brenda, master of sitting comfortably in a pack, then sprinting through a small dangerous hole of riders, placed seventh on the circuit race and ninth on the hilly road race that came down to a sprint. She did poorly on the prologue, time trial and mountain stages, but that was to be expected since she's a pure sprinter.

CHAPTER THIRTEEN

Over the first few weeks away, I became quite adept at lying to my parents. While my situation necessitated lying, I really ran with it. I justified this because I was on vacation and the key to a good vacation was pleasure. I would hate for my traveling, racing, drinking and napping to be interrupted by a nagging parental concern about my professional and social life. Since I had to lie anyway, I decided to tell my parents everything they wanted to hear, then sit back and bask in their approval. So now they were very happy with my commitment to work, handsome new boyfriend Adam and all around cheery disposition, though the cheery disposition is actually genuine now that I'm living the dream.

The last time my mom called, I wound up telling her that the four secretaries at my new office were named Geri, Lauren, Tara and Stacy, which are the names of my mom and her three sisters. A bizarre lie, I know, but Mom is very entertained by coincidences. When her gas tank fills and lands on the dollar, like thirty-eight dollars exactly, she is sure to share the news. Knowing this, and wanting to give her some sort of story on our daily phone conversations, the needless lie came out. I told her that my boyfriend, Adam, and I spent a few hours each week volunteering with underprivileged children. She seemed to appreciate that her commitment to charity had finally rubbed off. At first, I felt guilty each time I hung up after lying. However, she seemed so pleased that I actually felt like a good person each time I lied to her.

Yesterday, Mom called and asked if I got her package. She used to send me packages when I was in college or went to camp, so I wasn't surprised that a package was en route. "No, I haven't gotten anything yet," I said. "Where did you send it?"

"To the Holiday Inn near your Charlotte office."

"Hmm. I haven't received anything. What is it?"

"It's a surprise."

"Is it clothes?" I asked.

"No."

"Jewelry?"

"No, you have to wait," she said.

This was going to kill me. I had to know what was in that package. I'm still disturbed that I don't know what was in the package in the movie *Castaway* with Tom Hanks and that had nothing to do with me. "Come on Mom."

"You'll see."

"How's Sonny?" I asked.

"He's horrible."

"What happened to him?"

"Nothing, it's what's happened to me, Dad and the neighborhood. He howls all day, takes up our entire bed at night, digs through our garbage, tracks mud in the house and buries his Milk-Bones in my house plants."

"Ah, that's so cute. I really miss him."

"It's not cute, he's nuts," Mom said.

"You know you love him."

"We do, when he's at your house. Dad and I are thinking about visiting you up there, what do you think?"

"That's okay," I said, wincing at the thought of them showing up at the Charlotte office of Johnson Smith. "I'm really busy with work and volunteering and stuff. I'll hardly see you. Plus, I'm afraid you won't be able to resist decorating my hotel room and that's really not necessary."

"We'll see. If you're busy, Dad and I will just visit you briefly. Then we'll hike in the Smoky Mountains."

"We can talk about it later, I have to go. Love you." I said this quickly, and hung up. This could get dicey. I called the Holiday Inn to have them forward my package to the race hotel of the Tour of Vermont, my next stage race.

Before the Vermont Stage Race, I had several professional one-day races on Saturdays and Sundays in upstate New York, Massachusetts and New Hampshire. These races were populated by professional women and local CAT 1 racers. The format for each was a road race on Saturday, then a criterium on Sunday. Each race had its own winner; times were not accumulated over the weekend to arrive at an overall winner.

I placed in the top five for the road races in New York, Massachusetts and New Hampshire, but came in last in all three criteriums. Still, my race resume was beginning to shape up. But I had yet to make headway with any of the professional teams, including Sunshine Cycling.

The New Hampshire criterium was the final race before the Tour of Vermont. During the criterium, where I finished last, there was some drama when Brenda cursed at a local girl who cut her off. The girl went to a race official in tears after the race and complained about the foul language. The official disqualified Brenda, who then began her own hysterics, yelling up a storm.

I was enjoying the scene, but decided to seize the opportunity to make an ally on Sunshine Cycling.

"Hey, Brenda," I said, "what happened?"

"None of your business," she snarled.

Her tongue and teeth were stained with red Gatorade, and her hair had been flattened by her helmet. I suppressed a laugh and decided to prey on her legendary stinginess. "I heard them disqualify you. Want some help?" I asked.

"What could you do?" she asked me as bitchily as possible.

"Defend you. I specialize in cycling litigation."

"I thought you practiced segregation," she said.

"I handle desegregation, subrogation and cycling litigation."

"Why would you help me?" she asked.

"Because you're always so sweet to me," I said.

She looked at me skeptically, so I added, "There's only a fifteen-minute protest period after the race and you're running out of time. You came in third so you're about to be relegated and lose three hundred and fifty bucks. On top of that, once the decision is final, USA Cycling can fine you for cursing."

"Okay."

"Okay, what?" I said.

"Work your lawyer magic," she said.

If there's one thing I've learned being a lawyer, it's that people think you know everything. I've been asked to help sell a house, handle a child custody case, start up a business, apply for a patent, defend a vehicular manslaughter case, and my personal favorite, sue a grocery store for a loaf of bread with mulch in it. While all of these are lawyerly tasks, I hadn't a clue how to do any of them. To avoid revealing this secret, I generally Googled the area of law, read quickly, then made something up. My advice sometimes sounded crazy, but as long as I gave it with confidence, I was rarely questioned.

I decided to put my confidence routine to the test with the USA Cycling official. I handed him my business card and told him that the disqualification was questionable pursuant to the USA Cycling handbook. I cited to provision 8(a) of chapter 7 to make it sound more official.

"The decision is already made," he said.

"I'll file suit on Brenda's behalf, which you'll have to defend for at least nuisance value. That will run you about ten grand. You'll probably lose though. I've already spoken to several girls who said that the other girl cursed Brenda out and not the reverse. Brenda is trying to qualify for Sunshine Cycling to race the Tour de West. If you strip this result without sufficient proof, you've ruined her career and damages will be substantial." I smiled as I said this, thinking of the ridiculousness of a large trial, with witnesses, over the loss of $350 in a New Hampshire criterium.

The official disappeared for a minute then came back and reinstated Brenda's third place finish.

"So," Brenda said, "what do you want?"

"Thirty-three and one-third percent will make us square."

"Yeah, right. That took you two minutes."

"Plus three years of law school and four years of experience," I said.

"I'm not giving you a hundred dollars."

"I know. You're giving me one hundred and sixteen dollars and sixty-six cents."

"You're out of your mind," she spat at me.

"Okay, tell you what," I said. "Just introduce me to your *director sportif*."

"Why?" she said, calmer now.

"Because I haven't been cycling for the past twenty years like some people and I could use a little help making contacts."

"Win a few races, you'll get to know people," Brenda said. Her tone had reverted to pure bitchy.

"Great, in the meantime give me the one hundred sixteen dollars and sixty-six cents," I said.

"Fine. I'll introduce you. Follow me," she said.

"Can you build me up a bit? Sound enthusiastic? Pretend you don't hate me?"

"Hi, Erica. This is Jenna Rosen, a lawyer from Tampa." Brenda stomped off after that grand introduction.

Erica was about fifty and fit, but with the obvious sun damage of a lifelong cyclist. "Hi Erica," I said, thrusting my hand out. "I'm actually a cyclist, as well. I came in eighth place on Stage Four of the Tour of Pennsylvania and I've had a few other top five finishes over the past few weeks."

"I saw that," she replied with an Australian accent. "Nice to meet you, I'm Erica Murphy, team director," she said as she held out her hand.

"So, does Sunshine Cycling need any more racers from the Sunshine State?" I asked.

"We're still playing around with our roster until the Tour de West. Send me your race resume," Erica replied.

"Will do, but I'm relatively new to racing, so keep an eye out for me at the Tour of Vermont, too."

"Okay, I will," she said. "Nice to meet you."

After Erica left, I walked back toward Brenda, who was filling her water bottle nearby. "Hey Brenda," I called.

Brenda walked back toward me. "What now?"

"Don't talk shit about me now. If I race well and don't get the spot, I'll take that hundred and sixteen bucks plus interest."

"You can't do that," she said without much confidence.

"I'll sue you for it. Breach of contract. I'll spend every last dime of mine getting back your money, plus interest and punitive damages for intentional infliction of emotional distress. I'll also sue you for slander because whatever you say to Erica probably won't be true. I'll get her on the stand, too. You'll be out thousands."

"Don't threaten me," she said.

"I'm not threatening you. My hope is that you talk me up and I get on Sunshine Cycling for the Tour de West. Then we can be teammates, who knows, maybe even friends," I said, flashing my most charming grin.

Brenda walked away again, but I could tell she believed me. I grinned. If I could turn a one hundred and sixteen dollar unpaid legal fee that we never agreed on and some run-of-the-mill shit-talking into a windfall, I'd already be rich and retired.

As I was walking back to my car, a teammate of Brenda's approached me. She was five-ten with long thick black hair that must have weighed a ton when she started sweating on the bike. I could tell by looking at her that she was a sprinter, as no climbers could be as tall and built like her. She'd overheard our conversation and said, "She's been talking shit about you all week, so Erica already knows who you are."

I had noticed this teammate over the past few weeks, along with the rest of Sunshine Cycling, because I'd been trying to get "in" with them since the Tour of Pennsylvania. When we were face to face, I realized that I had seen her before, beating Brenda in several sprints over the past few weeks. That, plus the fact that she was confiding in me, led me to believe she and Brenda were not friends. "What did she say about me?" I asked.

"I don't know," she said, "I generally tune her out."

"Does Erica tune her out as well?"

"Pretty much. I'm Alyssa, I'll re-introduce you to Erica after tomorrow's race if you want."

"Great, thanks." Then I added, "I'm Jenna Rosen."

"Yeah, I know. Brenda seems to hate you as much as me, so I've been meaning to introduce myself to you."

"Why does she hate you?" I asked.

"Because we're both sprinters and I'm competition. Same reason she hates you I presume?"

"No, she hates me because I killed her cat," I replied.

"What?" Alyssa said, horrified.

"Just kidding," I said. "You're right. She hates me because I'm the first person to beat her in Florida in a decade."

Alyssa smiled and said, "Well don't worry. I have your back if she starts talking shit to Erica."

"Great, see you in Vermont." I said.

* * *

I hadn't been to Vermont since I went with my family as a child. Vermont held a special place in my heart because it was the first time in my life that I really enjoyed nature. Until I reached the age of twelve, Rosen family vacations resembled the Bataan Death March. Each year my parents picked a destination where we would hike for two weeks straight then drive home.

It makes me cringe to think of it now, but I vividly remember that my favorite part about the Smoky Mountains in 1988 was the three hours I spent in the eyesore that is Gatlinburg. Bill Bryson is one of my favorite authors specifically because he dedicated several pages of two separate books describing the extent to which Gatlinburg sucks. It's clear that someone went out of their way to locate the most beautiful place in Tennessee, and then mowed it down to put up fluorescent lights and hock crap. However, for me at the age of nine, Gatlinburg was a diamond in the rough, especially after two weeks of hiking up and down mountains for no apparent reason. I was equally nonplussed as a youngster by the beauty of Colorado, California, Montana, Oregon and Canada.

I don't know what happened the year I went to Vermont. As with the other places we hiked in the past, Vermont was lush and green, with beautiful lakes, waterfalls and mountains. The only difference was that I finally "got" hiking. Instead of dragging my feet and asking "how much further" at four-minute intervals, I ran to the top of each mountain. Once there, I explored until I found the perfect spot to enjoy the view until the rest of the family caught up.

Vermont hadn't lost any of its beauty since my last trip. I stopped at several lookouts to admire the views as I drove to the race start. One of the lookouts had a historical sign reciting the history of the Native American tribes that had at one time fought each other to lay claim to the area around Mount Mansfield. I could only assume that all of these tribes were pleased that the white man settled the issue once and for all *and* provided them the opportunity to become civilized in Oklahoma.

The landscape and weather in Vermont were made more beautiful by the fact that I kicked some ass there. Not that I won any stages, but I was consistently good in the mountains, placing third, fifth and fourth on the mountain stages. I completed a solid prologue and time trial, placing fifth and fourth, respectively.

Even more impressive, I came in fourth in a fast, technical criterium, albeit through a stroke of luck. As always, I spent the entire criterium shotgunning off the back of the field. With fourteen minutes plus five laps to go, I got a flat. In a criterium, if a rider has a mechanical such as a flat tire or broken chain, they get a free lap as long as the mechanical occurs during the timed section of the race. Once the race goes to laps, you're out of luck. After putting my spare wheel on the bike, I was released into the charging *peloton* as it swarmed towards the wheel pit. There was a sharp turn ten feet after the wheel pit and I knew the *peloton* would be entering the turn at approximately twenty-eight miles an hour. In anticipation, I accelerated as fast as I could to make sure that the *peloton* didn't sweep past me before I could get into the draft.

I entered the turn in ninth position. As I rounded the turn, I feathered my brakes like a total pussy, then accelerated so that I didn't lose the draft of the person in front of me. This took a superhuman effort because whoever was driving the pace into the wind was really drilling it. The lead cyclist pulled over and flicked her arm so the person behind her would know that it was her turn to take a strong pull into the wind. As the new leader began pulling, the woman who had just finished reentered the draft directly behind me. As an unknown rider wearing a generic white kit, I thought it was odd that this obviously seasoned professional chose to sit on my wheel. Because you can easily get gapped from the pack if the person in front of you gets gapped from the pack, riders are particular about whose wheel they choose to draft off of. I turned around to see who she was and noticed that I was the last wheel available. The other eighty-five women were about ten feet behind, well out of our draft.

My incompetent cornering had caused the girl behind me to open a gap, which no one closed, resulting in a break in the field. I knew that if the main field caught us and it came down to a mass sprint, I would come in last as always. So, I put all my energy into driving the breakaway to succeed without caring that such efforts would cause my sprint to suffer. It was a nine woman breakaway, so I was guaranteed ninth place as long as the pack, still only ten feet behind, didn't catch us. I wasn't going to get greedy and try and save my energy for the win. We held off the main pack and, in the less intimidating sprint of only nine women, I placed fourth.

In addition to a top five finish in every stage, I placed fourth overall in the Tour of Vermont stage race, a little under two minutes behind the winner.

After the race, Erica approached me and offered to let me ride for Sunshine Cycling in the Tour of Colorado. The understanding was that if I didn't blow it, I would be on the roster for the Tour de West. She gave me a Sunshine Cycling kit for the Tour of Colorado and told me to meet the team there next week. I had no idea whose place I would be taking and I didn't really care.

I was on cloud nine.

After the race, I checked back at the race hotel one final time to see if my package from North Carolina had arrived. After five no-show days, I wasn't really expecting to see it. But it was there and I ripped it open hurriedly. A box full of jump ropes, sidewalk chalk, bubbles and little bouncy balls. What the fuck? As I walked towards the car, I called my mom.

She answered the phone, "Hi, Jenna, I was just about to call you. Where are you?"

"My package finally came. What is all that shit?" I asked.

"It's for the kids you volunteer with."

Wow. She really is just an adorably nice lady. "Thanks Mom, they'll love it."

"Where are you?" Mom asked again.

"At the hotel."

"Where?"

"The lobby," I said as I threw her package of kids' toys into the backseat of my car and started driving in the general direction of Colorado.

"I didn't want to ruin the surprise, but we're here too," she said.

"Here where?" I asked nervously.

"At your hotel. We asked for your room at the front desk, but they said you weren't a guest. We tried looking it up under the name of your firm, but that didn't work either. So, we went for a hike and came back. We're right by the desk. I can't believe we don't see you. The lobby is so small."

I moved from cloud nine to a lower cloud. "I'm actually at a different hotel," I said.

"Then how did you just get the package?" Mom asked.

"Well," I said, "it's a long story, but I'm out of town for a few days."

"What? Where? Why didn't you tell us?"

"I was going to tell you," I said as I pulled over to the side of the road and banged my head against the steering wheel.

"What's that noise?" asked Mom.

"My head exploding. Can I call you right back?" I hung up without waiting for her reply and shouted "Fuck!" at the top of my lungs. It didn't help. I pulled back onto the road and decided to brainstorm while driving. Within seconds, my phone started ringing. It was Mom again.

"Jenna, what happened?"

"Not sure, we must have been disconnected." I said.

"So, where are you?"

"Taking a deposition," I replied.

"On a Sunday?" Mom asked.

Shit. Without work I'd lost all concept of time. Every day is Saturday. "I'm taking the depositions this week, I just had to drive out here today."

"Where is here?"

God, I need this interrogation to end. "I am. . ." Where should I be? Where should I be? Somewhere they won't want to visit. "I am. . ."

"Jenna, use your words. Where are you?"

"Arkansas."

"Where in Arkansas?"

I knew the name of exactly one city in Arkansas. "Little Rock," I said. "It's for one of my cases in Tampa."

"Well, we'll be here until the middle of next week, so at least we'll still get to see you for a little while."

"You'll still be there next week?" I said in disbelief. "Great, can't wait to see you. Let me call you back in just a bit."

I hung up and called Danny.

"Hey, Jenna. How did the last stage go?" he asked.

I had spoken to Danny after most of the stages of the Vermont race, so he knew I'd been doing well. "Fourth in today's crit and fourth overall," I said. "Plus, I get to ride with Sunshine Cycling in Colorado and, if I do well, I'm on the team for the Tour de West as well. In other news, the shit hit the fan." I spent the next few minutes updating him on my parents' arrival.

"Well I have more bad news for you," said Danny. "I got your mail today and you're getting letters from Tampa General Hospital. You have an ambulance bill."

"Well I was really hit by a car. It should be paid by my insurance company and they can get their money back from the insurance company of the douche bag that hit me. Forward the bill to me and I'll take care of it," I said.

"Sure. What are you going to do about your parents?"

"I don't know. I'm thinking of just telling them the truth. What's done is done. They'll be pissed, but in an effort to avoid getting me arrested, they'll be forced to cover for me. It will save me from inventing stories about Arkansas all of next week and from inventing stories about North Carolina for the next two months. Plus, it will help me in case they run into David."

"Damn," Danny said, "can you conference me in on that call?"

"No, but I'll fill you in. I think I'll call them now and get it over with during drive time."

I dialed my mom and when she answered I gave her the news quickly, like tearing off a Band-Aid. "I'm in Vermont. I just finished a cycling race."

"But, you have work in Arkansas tomorrow," Mom said. "How are you going to get there from Vermont?"

"Mom, I have some news for you. I'm not working in North Carolina or Arkansas. I'm racing my bike."

"Did you quit your job?" Mom asked, confused.

"Not exactly," I said.

"Leave of absence?" she offered as her next guess. Worry was now palpable in her voice.

"You can do that?" I replied, thinking that probably would have been easier.

"Yes," she said, "it's just not paid."

"Well, it's not a leave of absence. I'm actually on maternity leave."

"Jenna, you're not making sense. I'm going to put you on speaker phone. Dad's driving me crazy trying to hear what's going on."

"Please don't put Dad on," I pleaded. "You can tell him later."

"Why don't you want me on the phone?" Dad asked.

"Wow, you heard that?"

"Yes. I finally got hearing aids. That's part of the surprise. What were you just telling Mom?"

"Nothing. Just that I'm in Vermont and driving to Colorado. I faked a pregnancy so I could get maternity leave and race my bike."

On the other end of the line there was dead quiet.

"Hello?" I said.

"We're here," Dad said. "In North Carolina to visit you that is. How long have you been lying to us?"

"Well, including the actual gestation period, almost a year, but mostly just over the past month and a half."

"Have you been volunteering?" Mom asked.

"Christ, Geri, who gives a shit," Dad said, almost shouting now. "She's going to get fired, disbarred and possibly arrested. Not to mention killed on that goddamn bike if she's not kidnapped and raped before then, traveling by herself all over the country. Where are you staying, Jenna?"

"Campgrounds," I said sheepishly.

He exploded. "A woman, by herself, sleeping in a canvas tent with a zipper? I'm nervous when you're in your house in South Tampa with the alarm system. Are you out of your mind?"

"Just calm down there, Mr. Positive. I'm not going to get fired, disbarred, arrested, maimed, raped or killed. I'm going to race in Colorado and at the Tour de West, then go back to work."

The "you'll get raped and killed" argument had worked on me every time as a kid. I was terrified to go outside of my house alone well into my second year of college, when my *goyum* friends finally convinced me that sometimes, when you go outside by yourself, you don't die. My parents first used the "you'll get raped at gunpoint" scare tactic when I started running track in sixth grade. I went outside to run alone through our deed-restricted neighborhood and my parents freaked out and made John run alongside me. John was not into running five miles a day, so after one run, he rode a bike instead.

As it turned out, biking five miles a day wasn't for John either, so he started driving. Through all of the years of this routine, I was never approached by rapists, though I was always on the lookout. My parents told me to be especially afraid of roofers, construction workers and landscapers, but people in general were suspect. To my parents, an old woman gardening in her yard could be a rapist in disguise, waiting to pounce. Thus warned, I grew up sprinting past neighbors and blue-collar workers as fast as I could, just in case my bodyguard wasn't paying attention.

"Don't you think someone will ask about the baby?" Mom asked.

"Adoption," I said.

"Jenna, this isn't funny." Mom said.

"I'm not trying to be funny. That's seriously my plan."

"What about medical records?" Dad asked, ever practical.

"No one asked for any, I looked pregnant. But, there's a doctor I ride with who will sign anything for me if I have a problem."

"Who?"

"Dr. White."

"The proctologist?" Dad asked.

"Yeah, I know, wrong hole, but you'd be surprised how close those holes actually are."

"Do not ask Dr. White for anything," my dad said, "you'll get his license revoked as well."

"No one's license is getting revoked," I assured him.

"That'll be the least of your problems if you get caught. This is fraud, Jenna, you could go to jail."

"I'll be fine," I said, though he did have a point.

"You don't seem the least bit scared," Dad continued. "You know you can't train on that bike in jail, maybe that will scare you."

That fear had definitely crossed my mind, but I didn't let on and said, "Chill out. No one is going to suspect I lied about being pregnant." I said this with a confidence I didn't feel.

"Jenna," Mom chimed in, "if you hate your job so much why don't you just do something different?"

"I don't hate it. Well actually I do, but that's not the point. The point is I want to be a professional bike racer. I'm not going to like any other job, so I may as well keep the one I'm at."

"If this was John I'd understand. Being a funeral director must be miserable. But you have a good job, working from eight to five in air conditioning and making good money. Why are you jeopardizing that?" Mom asked.

"Because sitting in an office nine hours a day sucks."

"What do you want to do?" Dad asked.

Wow, I was pretty sure I just covered that. "What I'm doing now." I said. "Racing my bike. I also like taking naps and drinking beer, but not too much right now because of training."

"Great, how much money are you making doing that?" Dad asked.

"So far I'm breaking even on the cycling and napping and losing a bit on the beer. It's not a very marketable trifecta."

"This isn't a joke. What does breaking even mean?"

"I'm recouping the money I spend on gas, hotels and entry fees by winning some money in races."

"So you're saying that you're at a zero dollar income," Dad said. His voice was more "angry dad" than "accountant dad" as he broke down my finances.

"No, I'm at two-thirds salary since I'm on maternity leave."

"Don't be a smart-ass. I mean you're at a zero dollar income from cycling. That's a great career move."

Mom interrupted. "Jenna, if you want to get paid to do nothing why don't you just marry rich?"

"First, I'm not 'doing nothing.' I'm racing in professional cycling races. Second, I'm not opposed to marrying rich if I meet the right guy, but I've been in a bit of a dating rut for my entire life. So, until I find Mr. Right, I'd like to make it on my own."

Dad cut in again. "You're in a dating rut because all you do is ride that stupid bike. And, by the way, taking a fraudulent maternity leave isn't 'making it' on your own."

"Not in the traditional sense," I said, "but you have to admit it shows ambition and ingenuity."

Dad disagreed. "It exhibits stupidity, Jenna, that's what it exhibits. What if the race is televised and someone sees you?"

"Now that's stupidity," I ventured. "This is cycling. Even on the rare occasion it is televised, no one watches. Relax. I'm having fun and holding my own. I may have secured a contract today."

"Great, what's that worth?" Dad asked, not relenting in the least.

"So far I got a free kit, valued at one hundred dollars."

"What's that?"

"A uniform."

Mom tried to defuse the situation. "Jenna, come home and we'll talk about this some more."

I replied, "I'm not coming back to Tampa until my maternity leave is over and I've raced the Tour de West."

"Yes, you are," insisted Dad.

Mom, who was clearly starting to take pity on me, cut in. "Michael, maybe this is good for her. I mean, in spite of everything, she's been volunteering and has a steady boyfriend. That's progress."

"Not exactly," I offered.

"You lied about volunteering?"

"And a few other minor details," I said.

"Is Adam real?"

"Nope, but I'm sure I'll meet a real Adam someday," I said, not necessarily believing or caring if I would.

"I suppose the four secretaries with the same names as my sisters and me was a lie too."

"Sorry," I said feeling genuinely bad that I'd betrayed my mother.

"Jenna, Dad's right. You're coming home and we'll talk about this then."

"I'm not coming home," I said holding my ground.

"Yes, you are," Mom demanded though she must have realized she had no real power to compel my cooperation.

"I've avoided pointing this out until now, but I'm twenty-eight. You can't make me do anything."

"Maybe not legally," Dad said, "but your roommate is at our house and if you're not back in Tampa in four days, we're taking him to a nice family on a farm far away."

"You're going to kill my dog?" I said incredulously.

"I don't know Jenna. We're going to do something to stop you. This is crazy." Dad was sounding increasingly desperate.

"Why can't you just ride your bike around the neighborhood like normal people?" Mom chimed in, appealing in vain to my sense of normalcy.

"I don't know. I'm obsessed with being ranked and beating people. Must be some sort of pattern of achievement and reward I became accustomed to as a child."

"Don't blame this on us," Mom said, anger starting to replace the frustration in her voice.

"Blame?" I said. "I'm crediting you."

"Jenna," Dad said, "we love you the way you are and want you to be happy but—"

"Great," I interrupted, "so you'll keep watching Sonny while I race?"

"Fuck no," said Dad, unable to be persuaded by his little girl for once. "You're throwing away your career and risking your life. If we watch Sonny while you do that, we'd be helping you destroy yourself. So, Sonny has to go. It's the only way we can talk sense into you."

"Are you serious?" I asked.

"We won't kill him, but we won't keep him. We'll find a good home. If you want to race, it's going to cost you your dog. Sorry, but it's the only leverage we have. If we could ground you or put you in timeout we would."

"I'll think about it," I said without conviction.

* * *

What I meant by "I'll think about it," was that I'd think of a way to race my bike and keep my dog. I wasn't that worried, because I knew there was no way that someone would actually take Sonny home and keep him for more than twenty-four hours. Regardless, I needed a plan. I called Julie.

"Hey, Jenna, what's up?"

"Nothing much."

"Aren't you with your parents in North Carolina?" Julie asked.

"Not exactly." I gave her the short version of the events that led to my call. "Now, they're holding Sonny hostage until I agree to stop racing."

"Back the truck up, what happened?" Julie asked. I was relieved that she sounded entertained rather than angry.

I realized the story was so bizarre it couldn't be absorbed in one quick telling. I told her again. "Well," she said, "you're in luck, because John and I are watching Sonny while your parents are in North Carolina. Don't worry, we'll hang onto him as long as you need."

I thanked her profusely and filled her in on my trip thus far. When I got off the phone, I called Danny and told him that I broke the news to my parents.

"Were they pissed?" Danny asked.

"Does the pope shit in the woods?" I responded. "They're holding my dog hostage and threatening to kill him." I filled Danny in on the rest of the story.

"Once they lose the Sonny leverage, they're going to write you out of their will," he said. "It's all they have left."

"They're pretty healthy. If they write me out, I'll have a good twenty or thirty years to get back in their good graces. What are you up to?"

"Nothing," Danny said. "Business is slow and I have no Jenna-Related Activities to keep me busy."

"Don't worry, I'll think of some JRAs for you. If the dog wasn't with John and Julie I was going to have you break into my parents' house for him."

"From pumping your bike tires to breaking and entering? That's quite a promotion."

"What can I say, you're that good," I said.

As soon as I got off the phone with Danny, my phone rang again. The caller ID told me it was Quinton. How could a day start so well and end so badly? I let his call go to voice mail, then checked the messages. "Hey, beautiful. I'm out of jail. Just seeing what you're up to tonight. Give me a call."

I deleted Prince Charming's message and called his mom, Sarah.

She answered the phone, obviously drunk. "Hi, Jenna, sexy mama. What's up?"

"Nothing much, what are you doing?" I asked.

"Tony's out of jail. We're partying!"

"Yeah, about that," I said, "I'm going to need a bit more time in the loony bin to fully regain my mental health. Can you cover for me in the meantime? I don't want Quinton to think I'm crazy, or not interested in him."

"Sure thing. I'll cover for you babe," Sarah said.

This conversation allowed me to successfully table the Quinton issue, but it seemed unavoidable that it was going to bite me in the ass eventually. I would have to choose between marrying Quinton or having Sarah reveal my secret. I decided to worry about that later, after the Tour de West. Once I got back to Tampa I would have to focus all of my energies on making Quinton as uninterested in me as I was in him.

* * *

Lance Armstrong once compared cycling to a combination of NASCAR, chess and marathon running. Cycling is indeed like NASCAR but with two wheels and no motor. Both involve strategy, drafting, crashes, flat tires, teammates making sacrifices for the good of their captain and a lot of petrol. While riding a bike as transportation is good for the environment, competitive cycling is a huge waste of natural resources. Cyclists fly and drive to races all over the country every weekend. For a local cycling event, race officials, cops and a wheel truck follow races throughout the day. The vehicles accompanying the race increase along with the level of racing, so that all professional road races are led by a caravan of cars that sponsor the event. At the Tour de France, the caravan is over a mile long. In addition, the race officials' car and team cars form a two mile line after the cyclists pass, brought up by the "broom wagon," the last car to pass, following the last rider. Plus, each professional team has a gas-guzzling RV that travels with the riders for team meetings before and after the race. Finally, several helicopters hover over the hundred mile race course to provide aerial views of the race unfolding. The idea that cycling is a "green" sport is patently ridiculous.

Equally ridiculous is comparing cycling to chess and marathons. While there is a mental element to cycling, as in chess, it's not rocket science. Further, to the extent cycling is like chess, it's like playing chess with a phone-a-friend to Bobby Fischer. Cyclists wear earpieces and microphones, like the Secret Service, to talk to their teammates and *director sportif*. When an opportunity for thinking arises, a cyclist can punt their concern to their team. As a result, a stupid or uneducated person will fare much better in cycling than in chess. Recently, there's been a movement to ban race radios to make the races more exciting. Some pro tour races have even already started the ban. The riders and *director sportifs* are strongly resisting this, even boycotting races, arguing first, that it's dangerous because race radios alert racers to perils in the road thereby preventing crashes. Second, it's unfair, as a cyclist who punctures needs a radio to request a speedy wheel change. And third, it's unnecessary, as race radios do not make the sport dull. Surprisingly, no one is arguing the obvious: that cycling is a team sport and as such, the racers deserve a coach. I'm sure basketball would be more exciting if a coach couldn't call a time-out when their players are choking; football more entertaining if the coach couldn't call a play; baseball if the runner had to figure out for himself whether it was safe to run to home plate. Why even have a coach if he or she is not allowed to coach on game day?

As for a marathon: you can suck and still race a marathon. It may take you seven hours, but you can finish. If you suck in a cycling race, you're off the back of the pack in five seconds and a race official pulls you from the course. There are no medals for participation or pats on the back for trying, only humiliation. While both marathons and cycling involve speed and endurance, a marathon lasts from two hours to seven hours, depending on your speed. A cycling road race is almost always over one hundred miles for men and seventy miles for women and takes between three and five hours. A stage race lasts one to three weeks of this schedule. With all due respect to marathoning, cycling is in a league of its own, though I think Kenyans could cross over quite smoothly.

The Tour of Colorado was my first race with teammates and a team strategy. Granted, the team was newly formed and didn't have the camaraderie of a full season together, but they were still pretty close. Most of the women knew one another before the formation of Sunshine Cycling, some even raced together on composite teams occasionally throughout the years. All of the women were excited to be a part of the inaugural Tour de West. Their attitude toward me was very welcoming, but I could tell that my presence was slightly unnerving to some. I think I served as a reminder that their spot on the roster could be replaced at any moment.

Because our team was considerably weaker than the established professional teams, our tactics were somewhat lax. The plan was for everybody to do her best, but for nobody to waste energy doing the work of the big teams such as setting the tempo, chasing breakaways, or making any other sacrifices involving time in the wind other than to get water bottles from the team car.

Florida is humid and at sea level. Colorado is dry and at altitude. The Tour of Colorado was my first time at altitude since first grade. I didn't recall any ill effects from altitude as a six-year-old, but this time I was out of luck. In addition to a headache and nausea, I felt like I was breathing through a straw for the first three days of the race. My health improved for days four, five and six, but I was still unable to do anything impressive. My position on the team was definitely in jeopardy with the Tour de West a week away.

After the last stage of the Tour of Colorado, I met with Erica. As I suspected, the news wasn't good. Apparently, while I showed a lot of promise for such a new rider, Sunshine Cycling preferred to go with someone more experienced and consistent for the big race.

"Who are you taking?" I asked.

"Janice Barnes."

I knew of Janice, though I had never met her. She rode with Sunshine Cycling in Pennsylvania and Vermont, but rode as an individual in Colorado. I finished ahead of her in every stage of the Tour of Vermont and beat her handily in the Tour of Pennsylvania on all of the stages except the three where I placed dead last. Her results were decent, but not exceptional. Not that I'd been exceptional, but she was no doubt getting the nod because she'd been around for ten years and was much more experienced and consistent than I. I had nothing against Janice, but the bitch was in my way and I'd come too far and risked too much not to go down swinging. "Come on," I said, "I'm better than Janice. I just had some altitude sickness. By next week, my time in the altitude will have made me stronger."

"I'm sorry, Jenna. I told Janice after the Tour of Vermont that I'd take her unless you did something special in Colorado. I can't justify taking someone with two months of professional experience over someone with ten years, even if you do have more potential."

"I come with a free massage therapist," I said, improvising.

"What do you mean?"

"My friend offered to act as massage therapist for the entire team for three weeks," I lied.

"Are you sure? We don't have the budget to pay a massage therapist," Erica said.

"Yes I'm sure. He's really excited."

"Well, if this is true then I'll tell Janice you come with a perk. You're in."

"Thanks Erica," I said, then ran out before she changed her mind.

On the drive back to my campsite, I called Danny.

"Well?" he said.

"Well I sucked in Colorado, but I'm on the team for the Tour de West. I'm going to the Tour de West!"

"Congratulations! That's great! Anything you need?"

"Funny you should ask. I have a little JRA for you."

"Name it," Danny said.

"You have to come west and be the massage therapist for the team."

"Sure, sounds fun. I love working stage races. What are they offering?"

"Well, nothing. You were kind of my bargaining chip to get into the race. Erica rejected me, then I told her I came with a free massage therapist, and voila, I was back on the roster. I'm really sorry. I'll pay your transportation and for every massage."

"I would give you massages for free since this is huge, but seven other girls on a daily basis is crazy."

"Actually, it's eight other girls. It's a full nine riders at the Tour de West."

"Okay, so I have to cancel my clients for a month, fly to California, follow a race in a car for six hours each day then do nine massages each evening...for free."

"I thought you liked being the team massage therapist at pro races," I said plaintively.

"I do, when I get paid," Danny responded.

"Don't worry, I'll pay you. Unfortunately, I'm entering the four weeks of maternity leave where I don't earn any money, but I'll pay you back. I promise. Name your price."

Danny started calculating the tab out loud. "Let's see, nine massages a day for twenty three days at seventy per massage, plus a four hundred dollar plane ticket. That's going to cost you about fifteen grand."

"Yeah, right. What do you usually charge?"

"A thousand bucks a week plus travel costs. It would be about thirty-five hundred or so."

"I'll do you one better. I'll give you five grand," I said. "Thanks so much. Really, this is a dream come true and I couldn't do it without you." That rate was actually more than fair, which absolved my guilt. He rarely made half that over three weeks in Tampa and he loves working stage races.

"No problem. It'll be fun."

"Thanks again."

My celebration over this little coup was interrupted by a call from John. "Come get this dog before I kill it," he threatened.

Oh no, Sonny again. The potential hostage was putting my entire plan in jeopardy.

"What's wrong?"

"He's howling, digging, and humping, and Mom and Dad are putting a ton of pressure on us to give him back to them. If we leave the doggy door open at night, he goes outside and howls. If we shut the doggy door, our dogs pee in the house."

"Then potty train your dogs," I suggested.

"They are potty trained, when the doggy door is open. Don't you have another friend who can watch him for the next month?"

"I'll get back to you, but hold onto him until I get back to you," I said frantically searching my mind for a solution. "I'll figure something out."

I hung up and called Danny again, completely abandoning my plan to not take advantage of him. "Hey, Jenna again. How would you like to drive to California?"

"Drive? You're joking. Why would I do that?"

"Well, the Sonny issue has resurfaced." I explained the problem. "I was hoping you could drive him here."

"That's like a sixty hour drive," Danny pointed out.

"Try going via Vermont to Colorado."

"What are you going to do with Sonny while you race?"

"He can sit in the car with Erica," I said, trying to convince myself that that would be okay.

"Does Erica know that?"

"Not yet. We'll figure that out later. I'll put him in a muzzle and a straightjacket for three weeks if I have to. It's better than 'the farm' and I'm not missing this race."

"Okay, I'll call you back in a little bit. I need to grab a dog and drive across the country right now."

I was now sure that Danny was in love with me. "Thanks! I'll rent you a car. Then you can return it here, use my car during the race, and we can drive back together."

"You mean I drive back while you sleep in the passenger's seat?"

"Pretty much," I replied, acknowledging how well Danny knew me by now. It's times like these that I am frustrated at myself for not being interested in Danny.

"I'll see you soon," Danny said.

"Call me from the road if you get bored."

"Oh, you'll get a call," Danny said, "You better start saving material to entertain me with during this drive."

"Will do, but don't be afraid to grab a few CDs, maybe an audio book or two."

CHAPTER FOURTEEN

I called both of my parents on the drive from Colorado to California. Dad first.

"Hey Dad, still mad at me?"

"I'm not mad," he said flatly. "I'm concerned and I'm not going to stop being concerned until you're in Tampa and the statute of limitations runs on your fraudulent insurance claim." He was getting mad now.

"It's not that bad. I'm on a team now and I'm staying with them instead of by myself. I'm being careful on the bike and no one at my office has a clue. I won't be arrested." I don't think he wanted to hear about my issue with Sarah and her crazy son that I might have to marry in order to keep my secret.

"Will you just do me a favor?" he asked.

"Depends. I'm going to race," I said.

"Wear a motorcycle helmet."

"I'll wear a cycling helmet," I responded, marveling at his request.

"A motorcycle helmet protects your face. I'd rather you were in one of those."

"A motorcycle helmet weighs four pounds and has no ventilation. My cycling helmet is just over a half of a pound and has twenty vents. My neck won't be able to support a motorcycle helmet for one hundred and fifty hours of riding and even if it could, I'd pass out from heat. There's no way."

"What about a mouth guard?" he suggested.

"Nope. Won't be able to breathe."

"I have a client who designs helmets for sports. He made a wrestling helmet for some guy so he could wrestle with a broken jaw. Same for basketball. What if I have him make you one?"

"I don't think that'll work. I need to wear my sunglasses. If I don't, I could get a bug in my eye and crash. If you want to make a cycling helmet and face mask that is lightweight, ventilated, and allows me to breathe and wear glasses go for it, but I doubt it will be wearable. Even if it is, it won't be ready within four days. What else is new?" I asked, trying to change the topic.

"Nothing much," Dad said. "We can take Sonny back if you want. We won't give him away. Though I'd rather John and Julie keep him so that I can continue to sleep at night. It's impossible with that dog, he hogs the entire bed and cries all night if you don't let him on the bed."

Shit, I thought. That would have been good to know yesterday before Sonny was half way through Texas. "Yeah, he's a good little snuggler," I said. "Thanks, but don't worry, a friend is watching him. I love you Dad."

"I love you, too, Jenna."

I called Mom next. "Hi Mom."

"Hey, did you make up with Dad yet?" she said in a concerned voice, clearly forgetting that we had a rift as well.

"Yes, I'm working on you now," I offered.

"Really? Are you sure you're not lying about that?" Mom said sarcastically.

I chuckled. "Sorry. I was just trying to get you to stop worrying. I didn't mean to be a liar."

"You have a ways to go before I stop worrying."

"Relax. I'll be fine."

"It makes me more nervous when you say that." Mom says that every time I tell her to "relax."

"Sorry," I said. "I'll be fine though. I love you."

"I love you, too. Be careful," she said.

I got off the phone just as Danny was buzzing in. "Hey. What's up?"

"Hey, yourself. How are you doing?" Danny asked.

"Good," I said without much conviction. "Are you still in Texas?"

"Yeah. It's a long-ass state. How are your parents?"

"Putty in my hands, just like everyone," I replied.

"You really do have a gift."

"How's Sonny?" I asked.

"Lazy. He hasn't had his eyes open the entire trip except for the ten minutes he licked his ass."

"That's not good," I said. "He'll be ready to play when you're ready to sleep."

"Looking forward to it. I think I'm going to pull off the road and sleep now. I should get to California in two days or so."

"Bye Danny. See you then if I don't talk to you before."

* * *

I arrived in San Diego three days before the Tour de West. I was looking forward to staying in a hotel instead of camping, but it was not to be. Team Sunshine Cycling was on a tight budget and would rely on host housing throughout the entire Tour. Essentially, every day of the race would take us to a new city and in each of these cities, we would stay at the house of a stranger who had graciously offered their home to a team of nine women, as well as their eighteen bikes, coach, massage therapist, and mechanic.

Our first host house, where we would stay until Sunday's prologue, was a mansion owned by a couple named Grant. The Grants had offered the third floor of their house to us because it was empty except for when their sixteen grandchildren visited throughout the year. After hauling my suitcase and cycling gear to the third floor, I walked into a room that looked like an army barracks at Neverland Ranch. A row of sixteen twin-sized beds lined the room, eight on each side. A miniature railroad track weaved between and under each of the beds and a train circled the track continually. In between the train track and tiny beds, the room was littered with stuffed animals, rocking horses, toy cars, Barbies, costume jewelry, Legos, a fake kitchen set, toy guns and a bunch of other toys that I didn't recognize but wished I had seen on my trip to Toys "R" Us.

Alyssa was unpacking her bag in the furthest corner of the room when I walked in. I walked towards her, dropped my suitcase next to hers and said, "Do you even fit on one of those beds?"

Alyssa had obviously not yet realized that at five-ten, she would be sleeping in the fetal position until we moved into the next house. "Shit," she said. "This is the nicest house I've ever been in and now I'm dreading the next four days."

"Yeah," I agreed, "it's not like we can complain either."

"Do you have any water?" Alyssa asked. "There's no bathroom up here and I don't feel like going downstairs and back up again."

"No," I said, "but let me check the fridge." I stopped unpacking and walked over towards the fake kiddy refrigerator a few feet from my bag and opened it, pretending to look for water. A bunch of maggots and fruit flies greeted me. "Shit!" I said, "One of the grandkids put real food in there. Who knows how long that's been rotting."

We laughed, then quickly chose the two furthest beds from the vermin in the refrigerator. "So when did you start cycling?" I asked to strike up a conversation while we were unpacking.

"When I was a kid. My dad actually raced professionally throughout Europe, so I got into it at a young age."

"Let me guess," I said. "You're a former Junior National Champion, lost interest in the sport when you went to college and recently got back into it."

"Close," she answered. She was lying on the bed talking to me, her feet dangling off the end. "I was a National Junior Champion three times and World Junior Champion once. I got burned out in high school and took it up again five years ago."

Cycling is not a sport kids pick up in the neighborhood or at a local little league. Unless your parents buy you a three thousand dollar bike and drive you to races all over the state, you can't be a kid cyclist. There are very few child cyclists, and even fewer female child cyclists. Of the fourteen cyclists I know that race in the Junior category, five have been National Junior Champions and two have been World Champions. Generally, these kids develop monster egos at age nine, then have an identity crisis in their late teens when they start racing with adults and get their asses handed to them. Alyssa didn't seem to be an exception.

"Why did you get back into it?" I asked.

"To get in shape. Because it's something I'm good at. I like it now that there isn't a ton of pressure. I teach middle school and race in the summer when I'm off."

"Maybe I'll do that," I said. "I hate my job and could use summers off."

"I heard you're a lawyer. You'd be crazy to give that up to be a teacher. The pay is shit and the students and parents are pretty shitty too."

"So I've heard," I said, as I sat down on my bed which was inches from Alyssa's. "But you're only around once and you can't buy a minute. I want my summers off to race."

"You seem to have a pretty good vacation policy," Alyssa observed.

"I'm on a leave of absence." I changed the topic and asked, "Did you ride yet today?"

"No, want to go for a spin?"

"Sure," I said. "Let's check out the prologue course."

We rode two easy hours, including three reviews of the course, then returned to the mansion. I was practically giddy to have Alyssa as a friend. We really hit it off in the short time we spent together and I was so thankful to have a friend. I was really worried it was going to be Brenda and the team against me. Now I wouldn't be isolated and Alyssa seemed pretty awesome.

Danny and Sonny were at the Grants when we returned. Sonny went ape shit when he saw me. I tried to pet him, but he kept barking with excitement and running around in circles. Danny grabbed a ball out of the car and threw it to him. Sonny disappeared and I used that minute of quiet and calm to say hi to Danny and thank him again. He looked exhausted after the ride but said he was psyched to be here.

I introduced Danny to Alyssa and then directed Danny to our quarters. He looked like he really needed to crash. At the foot of the stairs I pointed up and said, "Third floor." I should have taken him up myself, but there was no way I was climbing those stairs until I had to. It sounds insane considering I was about to race almost two thousand miles, but climbing stairs was a huge waste of energy I planned to avoid as much as possible over the next four days. Besides, I wanted to hang out with Sonny since I hadn't seen him in almost two months. I told Danny to come back down and hang out when he was unpacked and rested.

Sonny was happy to be out of the car. I continued to play fetch with him for about ten more minutes in the Grants' backyard. Then he got tired and decided to sniff every blade of grass and pee on every other blade of grass. While he was occupied, I climbed into the Grants' hammock. My phone rang. It was my office. I let it go to voice mail, then checked the message. It was David. He called to ask me about a case and left his number for me two times. Each time spelling each number out slowly.

I couldn't believe it. First, it was so nice of him to check on me two months after my fetus and I were hit by a car. Second, I had been out of the office so long that I didn't even remember the name of the case he was talking about let alone the facts. There was no way I could discuss it intelligently. Finally, what a dumbass. The number he gave me was the number for the entire office, including mine, and he'd given it to me twice. I decided to call him back later, after I was sure he'd left the office, and leave him a message telling him I didn't recall the file but would look into it next month when I returned from maternity leave.

* * *

The days before the Tour de West passed very slowly. We were in top shape and eager to start racing, but none of us wanted to waste any energy. Those of us who arrived in San Diego early just sat around all day other than the occasional training ride or to get food.

On Friday, Erica arrived. Prior to her arrival, I had been taking Sonny up to the third floor each evening, where he would hog three-fourths of my twin bed. I was scared shitless that Erica would put the kibosh on Sonny. I didn't want to board him in a kennel for the next three weeks, then drive back from Seattle to San Diego after the race to get him. Fortunately, Erica turned out to be a dog lover and really liked Sonny. We didn't even discuss the matter.

The prologue of the Tour de West began at high noon on Sunday. It was the biggest women's cycling event that had ever taken place. The entire 1.8 mile course was lined with fans, mostly locals, who wanted to see what cycling was all about. I'm sure they walked away disappointed, as watching one woman after another pass you at thirty second intervals 117 times in a row is not very entertaining.

The course was rolling and there was a tailwind, so the times were very fast. I placed fourteenth with a time of just under four minutes; putting me twenty seconds out of first place and thirty seconds out of last place. Such time gaps were negligible with 1,853 miles left to go.

The next day, Stage 1, was the first serious stage. Just before the start I was in the staging area twenty feet from the start line trying to stay as calm as possible so as to not burn up nervous energy. I looked around and noted that I was in a sea of women who were virtually indistinguishable as they were all young and tan, with skinny arms, bulging quads and hamstrings, and glasses and helmets disguising a good portion of their features. It was hard not to be intimidated.

Once we were permitted to move forward to the start line, there was a mad dash to get as close to the front as possible. We were packed in so tight that I could barely see anything aside from the girl directly in front of me and the ones on either side of me. I had lost my teammates in the shuffle forward and did not have enough room to even twist my body to find them. The noise from the racers and the crowd only added to the confusion. I decided to just relax and concentrate on hearing the start gun. Minutes later, it went off and I heard the sound of over one hundred women clipping into their pedals at the same time. I got chills.

I got over that sentimentality quickly. The pace was fast from the gun, particularly for the first hour as riders tried to escape from the pack. Every time someone darted out, the pace increased to catch them. Once the catch was made, someone else sprinted ahead. Finally, four women got away that the big teams did not seem inclined to chase. The pace slowed and steadied until thirty miles before the finish, when the big teams organized and chased the break. All four women in the break were exhausted from working in the wind all day. The catch was made a mile before the finish in Long Beach, one hundred and twelve miles from San Diego, and ended in a field sprint.

The final sprint was slightly downhill and since it involved one hundred and seventeen women full of caffeine and adrenaline there was, not surprisingly, a crash. It was on the left side of the pack and I easily avoided it because I was far out of the mix as usual. There's a rule in stage races that if there's a crash within three kilometers of the finish, anyone who gets caught out by the crash is given the same time as the *peloton*. So, I didn't worry about losing time even though I was at a full stop behind the crash as the winner, a woman from Germany, crossed the line with her arms in the air.

After the race, Alyssa and I grabbed burritos from Chipotle. I ate half and drank two Nalgene bottles of water. I couldn't stuff anything else in my mouth. I wrapped the other half of the burrito to eat after the massage. I had to eat at least five thousand calories a day to compensate for the calories burned during the race, a difficult task because I needed to eat food high in energy and nutrients, not just ice cream and brownies. It was also difficult because I was riding my bike through midday, so lunch generally consisted of a Clif Bar every hour for four to seven hours. Even though the bars are okay, it's not the most enjoyable way to consume 1,000 to 1,500 calories.

When we got back, Alyssa went to meet Danny for her massage, while I sat outside on the porch sipping water and rubbing Sonny's belly. Brenda came out and with her usual tact said, "You and that dyke are really getting along, huh?"

"Who?" I said.

"Alyssa."

"She's gay?" I said in disbelief.

"You're kidding right?" asked Brenda incredulously. "How could you not know?"

"Because she looks completely feminine."

"Ever heard the term 'lipstick lesbian'?"

I had, but I thought they just looked feminine compared to the muscle-bound lesbians with spiked hair. I didn't know they were actually feminine looking, let alone pretty. Besides, I had always assumed that any lesbian involved in sports was leaning towards the butch persuasion.

In addition to being shocked by Alyssa's sexuality, I was embarrassed that Brenda, who was clearly homophobic, had better gaydar than me. "Yes I've heard of lipstick lesbians," I replied. "I just didn't know Alyssa was one."

"You would have found out soon enough. She'll probably hit on you," Brenda said. "Fucking carpet muncher."

"I doubt she'll hit on me," I said. "I've told her enough dating horror stories for her to pick up on the fact that I'm straight."

Brenda left and few minutes later, Alyssa was standing across from me on the porch. She said, "Your turn."

"Thanks," I said. "Hey, great race today," I added, realizing I'd never said that at Chipotle.

"I came in twenty-somethingth place," Alyssa said, puzzled.

"Well, it was nearly one hundred places better than me," I said smiling and trying to think of something else to say, completely forgetting that it was my turn for a massage. It dawned on me while I was smiling at Alyssa and trying to think of something clever to say that I was flirting. I stared at Alyssa. Objectively, she was hot, even with her hair all greasy after her massage. But she was hot yesterday and I wasn't flirting with her then. Hell, I'd been around hot women all my life and hadn't flirted with them.

Was I a lesbian? I had considered the possibility before, such as when I obsessed over various actresses, but I'd always dismissed the idea as crazy. I'd heard that everyone had that "what if" scenario in their head when looking at a gorgeous actress. Plus, I'd never been attracted to any of the lesbians I've met. Never mind that all of my friends are straight and, to my knowledge, I'd never actually met any lesbians other than some professors in college and the fat woman with the crew cut that worked at Blockbuster. I always assumed that as long as I was never attracted to a lesbian and didn't have a desire to chop all of my hair off, bind my boobs and wear men's clothing, that I was heterosexual. Now I was confused. Alyssa wasn't an unattainable actress or a butch woman I wasn't attracted to. She was, however, the first lesbian I'd ever met that I didn't evaluate and say, phew, I'm not attracted to her so I'm not gay. Instead, she was a hot and interesting woman whom I didn't realize I was attracted to until the second Brenda mentioned she was gay and therefore an option. If Alyssa looked feminine and was gay, I could be, too.

I turned the thought over in my head. I was twenty-eight and had never had a relationship longer than a month, and most hadn't lasted more than one date. Plus, I was a total tomboy, hated shopping and had an appreciation for sensible footwear. In fact, I avoided sensible footwear because I didn't want to look like a lesbian. Oh my God, I was one of those self-hating lesbians! What was wrong with me? I looked at Alyssa, who was now next to me on the porch swing relaxing, and pondered whether to say something. As I was trying to decide what to say, Danny came out and said, "You're up Jenna."

I got up and followed him towards the room. He stayed outside, while I stripped and got on the table. I yelled to him that I was covered and it was okay for him to come in and the second the door shut I said, "Did you know Alyssa is a lesbian?"

"No. That's pretty hot," Danny replied.

"You know, I would have bet my life you'd say that and you didn't disappoint."

"I'm predictable," he admitted.

"Do you think I'm a lesbian?" I asked.

Danny paused. My head was face down on the massage table so I couldn't see his reaction. A few seconds passed, then Danny said, "Did I miss something? Did you have another bad date in the last few hours that finally converted you?"

"No. I'm just feeling suddenly gay," I replied. "Alyssa's a feminine lesbian, maybe I am, too."

"You're not feminine or a lesbian," Danny said, ever helpful.

"I am too feminine."

"No, you're not. You look feminine, but the second you open that mouth of yours the femininity goes out the window."

"You're right. Plus I probably only look feminine because my feminine mom shops for me. But that's beside the point. Forget shopping, sports, and femininity. Am I gay?"

"The answer is no," Danny said with conviction.

"How do you know? I loved Elizabeth Shue and Michelle Pfeiffer as a child and I still do, though my current obsessions are with Juliette Binoche and Salma Hayek."

"So what. You love George Clooney, too."

"So do you," I offered.

"True," he said, "but that doesn't make me gay. And you're not gay either, regardless of what actresses you like, because you date and fuck men."

"Not often," I said, "and that's beside the point. Hear me out. It's not that I've never thought of this before. But I've never been attracted to any of the lesbians that I've met."

"How many lesbians have you met?"

"Maybe three that I know of, but Alyssa's a prime example of me being oblivious to lesbians. All of the attractive women I know are either straight, or I assumed they were straight, so I never thought of them in that way. It's like when you meet an attractive man with a ring on his finger, you just don't flirt. Anyway, Alyssa is the first lesbian I've met in the flesh who's hot and I'm attracted to, so that must mean something." I noticed that my run-on sentence was getting ridiculous and shut up. Danny was so silent that if he wasn't rubbing my calf, I would have thought he left the room. I was glad my head was in the massage table and I couldn't see his face.

"So, you're saying you've been dating men for the last twenty years because you thought all lesbians in the entire world were ugly?" Danny said this in a very rude and sarcastic tone.

"I don't know, maybe. It's like art. If I go to the Louvre, I browse and appreciate, but I can't buy anything so I don't really look. However, if I'm at a store where I can buy a piece of art and take it home, I'm more interested."

"You don't like art or shopping."

"It was an analogy, and I've shopped for stuff for my house and gone to the Louvre."

"So you like Target better than the Louvre, great example." Danny scoffed.

"I want to go on a date with Alyssa to make sure I'm not gay."

"You just sounded like you want to be gay. Which is it?" Danny spat at me.

"No I don't want to be gay," I said. "Who wants to be gay?"

"Well you seemed pretty enthusiastic a second ago," he pointed out.

Danny and I had argued before, but playfully, over irrelevant things like tire pressure. He was argumentative now, not playful.

"Mother Fucker!" I said as Danny pressed into my hamstring.

"Sorry."

"I'm not enthusiastic," I said. "I'm freaking out a little and it's making me sound excited."

"Why are you freaking out? What do you have against being gay?"

"Nothing," I said. "I just don't want to be gay."

"Why? You've always been a supporter of them getting married. I thought you liked gay people. You love that one token gay guy of yours from law school."

"I support gay marriage because I'm not a bigoted asshole, not because I want to be gay. It's like the bar. The Florida bar is a really hard test and I would never say that someone who fails it is stupid. However, if I failed it, I'd feel like a fucking idiot."

"You lost me," Danny said. He was calmer now, but sounded a little exasperated.

"I empathize with the oppressed and wish them the best, but that doesn't mean I want to be in their shoes."

"Relax, you're not gay. You hang out with guys all the time and most women annoy you."

"Same for you and you're still sexually attracted to women."

"I can't believe we're having this conversation. You're not gay. There's no way you're gay and didn't notice it until you were twenty-eight."

"That happens to lots of women, older than me even, and who have been married with kids. Meredith Baxter, Kelly McGillis, that woman from *Sex in the City*, um, Wanda Sykes. There's gotta be more."

"I have no idea who you're talking about."

"You really should read *People* magazine, Danny. *Family Ties, Top Gun*, woman from *Sex in the City*, funny comedienne. Famous women, Danny."

"Are you attracted to any of them?"

"In hindsight, I may have liked *Top Gun* and *Cocktail* more for Kelly McGillis and Elizabeth Shue than for Tom Cruise. Jodie Foster's hot too. These are all movie stars though."

"So if you'd run into one of them on the street twenty years ago you could have avoided this late realization?"

"No, they're all movie stars. They don't count. Alyssa counts."

Danny just stared at me.

I continued, "This isn't the first time I've thought about it. But when I read about a prominent politician throwing away his life to fuck a strange dude in a bathroom stall I thought, 'Well the urge isn't overwhelming me that much, I must not be gay.' That's probably not a normal thought."

I turned over from my stomach to my back at this point and saw Danny's face. His jaw was clenched and his face was red. He resumed his rude tone and said, "You're not exactly repressed. If you thought you were interested in women, you'd have dated a woman already."

"Not necessarily. I have no idea how to meet lesbians. I don't even think I know any. What am I going to do, go to a gay bar or online and say I might be gay, let me experiment on you and we'll see?"

"That doesn't sound so crazy," Danny said.

"I just told you I don't want to be gay. Why would I go out of my way to go down that road? Right now, I can do it conveniently with little risk. I know Alyssa, she's right here, I'm attracted to her and no one in Tampa will know about the experiment."

"You're not gay," Danny said again, more forcefully, clearly hoping repetition would make it more convincing. "You just think you are because you don't think you've met the right man yet. The problem is you've just been dating assholes."

I pretended not to notice that he said "You don't think you've met the right man" instead of "You haven't met the right man," presumably referring to himself as the right man. I responded, "That's possible, but lesbianism is also a possibility."

Danny didn't say anything.

When the massage ended, Alyssa was asleep. It was only 8:30, but 112 miles in the saddle will knock you out. I guess my interrogation would have to wait for another day.

CHAPTER FIFTEEN

I tried talking to Alyssa during Stage 2 of the race, but it was impossible. Once again, the first hour was intense until a non-threatening trio escaped off the front. The pace settled down, but the course wasn't flat enough to make conversation. While we didn't cross mountains, the road was constantly undulating.

The chase to reel in the three breakaway riders began in earnest with thirty miles remaining and the catch was made two miles before the finish. At that point, each team began setting up their sprinters. The sprinters for team Sunshine Cycling were Brenda and Alyssa. Alyssa had better top speed than Brenda, but was not quite as crafty when maneuvering through the pack. Then again, Brenda was five foot three and Alyssa five foot ten. Alyssa placed ninth and Brenda sixteenth on

Stage 2. After I did my work moving Brenda and Alyssa to the front of the pack, I got out of the way and placed my customary last position in the field sprint.

I immediately washed my hands and began downing a Clif Bar on the way to our new host house. My normally obsessive hygiene had reached a new level since I began racing full-time. Travel and extreme exercise were recipes for illness. As a result, my bathroom ritual now resembled Howard Hughes scrubbing in to perform surgery.

The new host house had three guest showers, so it did not take long for all of us to clean up. Once we got settled, Alyssa and I took my car to grab some food. On the way, I made a subtle segue into discussing Alyssa's homosexuality by saying, "I hear you're a lesbian."

"Problem?" Alyssa asked.

"Not at all. This is awkward, but I have a shitload of questions for you."

"Why?" Alyssa asked.

"Because I've never met a cute lesbian before and I want to make sure I'm not one."

"How do you know you haven't met a cute lesbian?" Alyssa asked. "You've been out and about for over twenty-five years, chances are you've encountered one."

This was not going well. She was right of course. "I could be wrong. Obviously my gaydar sucks since I had no clue about you. I just mean that I've thought I might be gay before, but I just ignored it. Now, after having met you, I'm rethinking that logic."

"Thanks, I think," Alyssa said. Fortunately, she seemed more amused than offended. "So, what do you want to know?" she asked, humoring me.

"Have you ever been with a guy?"

"Yes. When I was eighteen. I wanted to see what all this heterosexual sex was about. A lot of lesbians are not gold star."

"Gold star?" I asked.

"Lesbians that have never had sex with a man," Alyssa explained.

"Oh, good to know. If you lost your heterosexual virginity at eighteen, how old were you when you first slept with a girl?" I asked.

She thought for a second and said, "Fifteen I think. Maybe sixteen."

"Shit," I said, "you lost your virginity twice before I lost mine. How old was the girl?"

"She was twenty-six. We dated for a few years."

I couldn't help myself and started to laugh.

"What's so funny?" Alyssa asked, seeming slightly annoyed for the first time.

"I'm trying to picture myself dating a fifteen-year-old two years ago, when I was twenty-six. It seems absurd. Where does a fifteen-year-old even meet a twenty-six-year-old lesbian?"

"You've been racing a while. Haven't you noticed any lesbians in their mid-twenties around here?"

"Good point," I said. "But isn't that pedophilia?"

Alyssa rolled her eyes a bit and said, "Technically, I guess. But trust me no one was twisting my arm. I was a grown up fifteen-year-old. All I did was race. I didn't even know any other fifteen-year-olds. I was home schooled on the road for most of the year."

"That sounds way better than high school," I said. "When did you come out?"

"I don't know that I was ever 'in,'" Alyssa responded. We were in the parking lot of a sandwich place I spotted from the road, but neither of us had gotten out of the car yet. Alyssa continued, "When I was fourteen, my parents sent me to a camp at Wesleyan University for a liberal summer program. We got to pick a different seminar every day and one day there was a seminar on homosexuality. I didn't really think I was gay, but I went anyway because this hot girl Jessica was going."

I started laughing again. I really liked being with Alyssa and was relieved that she was answering my questions with amusement rather than offense. I exited the car and changed the topic to the race. My mental list of questions had run out and I was afraid to start asking them off the cuff, especially while hungry. The filter between my brain and mouth is not my strong suit and I needed time to think about my next move. In the meantime, the more I talked to Alyssa the more it became obvious that I was gay and had a crush on her.

That night, my mind raced instead of going to sleep. I had no control over the random thoughts that popped into my head. I thought of all the guys I dumped for "acting gay," such as dressing well, manscaping their body hair, wearing jewelry, gelling their hair or going to tanning salons. A bit hypocritical in hindsight. In addition to evaluating my sexuality, I focused on Alyssa. I really liked her. How crazy would it be after dating a hundred different men if I found the right woman for me on the first shot?

* * *

Despite my lack of sleep, I felt great during Stage 3. Nevertheless, a problem emerged. As in the previous stages, a small group of women broke away during the first hour or so of the race. Today, it was a break of seven, and my teammate Lynn was one of the lucky riders. I thought about escaping in one of these breaks, but wanted to see how I would do on the time trials and mountain stages before wasting my energy in the wind on a long breakaway that would most likely be caught before the finish. I planned to sit in the pack for the first week of the race, expending as little energy as possible, considering that we were riding over one hundred miles per day.

The drama on Stage 3 began when Lynn's breakaway reached one minute ahead of the main field. Erica and Danny drove the team car past the *peloton* to follow the breakaway riders in case Lynn needed water or a new wheel if she got flat tire. For the next five hours, my earpiece channeled the sound of Erica encouraging Lynn to work hard in the break and not give up. In the background, I could hear Sonny howling his ass off and Danny yelling at him. Two hours into the race, Brenda rode beside me to tell me that she could no longer listen to race radio because "that goddamn dog is so annoying."

I knew the breakaway didn't have staying power, but hoped I was wrong. If the break succeeded and Lynn won the race, team spirit would be high and Sonny's issue would move to the back burner. It was not to be. After sixty miles, the *peloton* began working together to catch the break. The catch took place three miles from the finish and the race ended in yet another field sprint. Erica grabbed me as I crossed the line and insisted, "Do something about that psychotic dog!" I guess everyone's love for animals has a limit.

I walked over to Danny and asked, "Why was he barking?"

"I don't know. He doesn't like cyclists. We rode ten to fifteen feet behind Lynn and he looked out the window and barked at her the entire time. Once the *peloton* made the catch and we got back into the caravan, he fell asleep."

"That's not good. The race is going to break up after San Francisco and hopefully, I'll be in the lead group with my team car not too far behind."

"Good, it's only right that you should have to listen to that mutt."

"I heard him on the radio," I said.

"You need to be right there to truly appreciate how annoying it is."

"I'll buy him a muzzle and some toys," I said, without any confidence that it would work.

The problem with Sonny went beyond the barking. He was also having a severe humping issue. Around new people, he got excited and humped anything in site. Each night, that meant one of my teammates or that night's hosts were sexually assaulted by Sonny. Even the "dog people" were getting annoyed by Sonny's amorous tendencies. Because I didn't have Sonny's elephant, there was nothing to give him to replace the human legs he coveted. I offered mine repeatedly, but he was only interested in new conquests. I decided to buy him a girlfriend.

I went to the pet store and bought Sonny a large tyrannosaurus rex stuffed animal and brought it to the Gomezes', our hosts for the evening. After forty-five minutes of watching Sonny hump T-Rex and thrash him around the room, my teammates were finally beginning to forgive Sonny for the previous four days of humping and the six hours of howling during Stage 3. Sonny ruined this temporary truce when he ripped open the T-Rex, which was stuffed with thousands of small beads. The beads spilled out all over the floor and into Brenda's suitcase. The next day, throughout Stage 4, she complained she had beads stuck in the lining of her chamois, the pad sewn into a cyclist's shorts to cushion the butt, and that the beads were causing chafing. I gave Sonny some extra treats for this.

After Stage 4, Alyssa and I grabbed lunch. I felt badly that Danny was giving massages and couldn't come, but I was happy for alone-time with Alyssa. As I was thinking of poor Danny, Alyssa said, "That guy Danny is really nice."

"Yeah," I said, "it's an illness."

"I love that he's into alternative medicine in addition to massage," she said.

"What are you talking about?" I asked. "Danny isn't a quack."

"I didn't call him a quack. I think he's a genius. I've always had this problem with my back and during my massage, he felt my aura and figured out the problem."

Yikes, I thought. Alyssa sounded like a freak. I'd dumped people for less. "So, what's the problem?" I asked with a bit of a smirk on my face.

"Danny said that the heat and pressure from my back revealed that my pain is from a former life. He said I was once a conquistador and that I died in battle when I was struck in the back with an ax."

"Really?" I said. "That's weird because I've always had this horrible ache in my hand and I think it's from my former life, when I was an Aztec and I nicked myself throwing an ax through someone's back."

"I sense skepticism," Alyssa responded, ever astute.

"You sense correctly. Even if this were true and Danny wasn't completely fucking with you, which he was, how does that help you?"

"What do you mean?"

"It seems you're now resigned to a painful back because of your past life."

"Not at all. Now that Danny knows what it is, he's treating it," Alyssa said.

"How, pray tell? Did he kill a chicken, pour the blood down your back then bury the carcass under your bed?"

"Ha, ha," Alyssa said without a hint of humor. "Actually, he used kinesio tape and massage."

"Interesting," I said. "Taming the spirit of the conquistador is accomplished the same way as curing sore muscles."

"Doubt all you want, but I'm a believer."

This was the point in any relationship where I would kick someone to the curb. However, I found it entertaining coming from Alyssa. Unlike men, it seemed cute and acceptable for a woman to act completely illogical.

When we got in the car to drive back to the house, I asked Alyssa if I could kiss her. We were sitting in the parking lot of a strip mall.

"What?" she said, no doubt stunned by the sudden change in topic.

"Oh, sorry. I kind of just assumed you were into me because you're a lesbian and we're hanging out and we had that talk yesterday. Are you at all interested in me?"

"I don't know. Maybe." She seemed honestly caught off-guard, which was not a good sign. I thought it was obvious I was into her. "Are you just experimenting with me?" she asked.

"Yes and no. I think I really want to kiss you. I'm sure of it. But I also might freak out and throw up. So, yes, I'd say this is an experiment." I said this with a smile and hoped like hell she wasn't offended and would kiss me.

"A little more sweet talk like that and I'll be ready to kiss you," Alyssa said sarcastically.

"Great," I said, but couldn't lean into the kiss. It was easily the most awkward moment of my life and I'd had quite a record of awkward moments. Finally, after staring and giggling for a few minutes, I leaned in.

The kiss was nice. Softer than with a man, because her face didn't have scruff or facial hair. I enjoyed the softness and thought of the irony that I always preferred men with a little bit of beard growth. Not the feel of it, just the look sometimes. She touched my face and hair and I did the same to hers. I couldn't help myself. I had never enjoyed kissing before. Whenever I kissed a guy I got bored quickly. It was like an amusing ritual that I didn't like or dislike. With Alyssa it was different. At first, I could only think, Holy shit I'm kissing a chick, but that faded quickly, and I got into it. I couldn't get enough of touching her hair, face and neck. I was turned on and savoring the taste, wanting more.

"So?" she said, and snapped me out of my reverie and back to the reality that I was kissing a woman.

"You taste like a Spanish conquistador," I replied with a smile, reverting to sarcasm, my default response in any situation.

"Shut up!" she said.

"I'm just kidding," I said smiling. "Thank you. I enjoyed that."

"Great, you should get your gay card in two to three weeks," Alyssa advised.

We drove back to the Gomezes' and when I walked in, I felt like everyone knew of my newfound lesbian leanings. It was the same feeling I had the first time I hung out with my parents after losing my virginity. But, no one seemed to notice.

An hour later, it was time for my massage. I got on the table, facing up, and told Danny to come in. "Nice job telling Alyssa she's a conquistador reincarnated," I said to him.

"You like that?" he asked, smirking.

"Yes. Very funny." I said, laughing again at his story.

"I gotta find some way to keep myself entertained during nine hours of massages daily."

"Sounds like you're doing just fine. Any other good massage stories?" I asked.

"That girl Krista on your team has a really bad obsessive-compulsive disorder and she freaks out if I don't do the same number of strokes on the left side of her body as the right. She keeps track for me. She might be the craziest cyclist I've ever massaged and people that race their bikes a hundred miles a day are a crazy crowd."

"Yes," I agreed. "She's cool, but that might be the most bizarre thing I've heard this week. Right up there with me being gay."

Danny froze mid-stroke and stopped the massage. He looked disappointed for a second, but quickly masked his expression and said, "You still think you're a lesbian now that you and Alyssa won't work out?"

"Why do you say that?" I said.

"Because she's a fucking idiot and believes she's a reincarnated conquistador."

"I'm not rejecting her for that," I countered. "I think it's cute that she believes in that crap."

"Hi, I'm Danny, nice to meet you. What's your name?"

"It's still Jenna. I'm just practicing acceptance of people's flaws."

"You've got to be kidding me," Danny said.

"I kissed her," I said.

Danny offered no visible reaction other than clenching his jaw. He simply said, "And?"

"I liked it."

"So that's it? You're gay now?" Danny asked.

"I'm pretty sure I have at least one more hurdle to overcome before I make that statement, but I must say that I'm feeling gayer all the time. Don't tell anyone though."

"So now you're gay and closeted. Awesome."

Closeted. I cringed on the inside, but didn't say anything.

Danny broke the silence. "Don't worry, I won't say anything to anyone."

* * *

Stages 5 and 6 continued to advance us north via the most indirect route possible to stretch the five hundred miles from San

Diego to San Francisco to eight hundred race miles. On Stage 6, our teammate Valerie crashed and broke her collarbone, so our team shrank to eight. I felt bad for Valerie, she was really nice, and like me, this was her first big season of racing. I tried not to think of how quickly it could be me with the broken collarbone because I was the happiest I'd ever been. Alyssa and I talked on the bike and ate together on these days. I was definitely developing a huge crush on her, the crush that all of my friends had in high school but I'd never experienced. Nevertheless, we had yet to make out again since "the kiss." At first this made me happy, as I was afraid that date number two would include sex and that made me nervous. However, as each day passed, I became more used to the idea of sex with Alyssa and the anticipation was beginning to weigh on me. It was also weighing on me that Alyssa wasn't pushing the issue, but I tried not to dwell on it since communal living and five to seven hours a day of racing were not exactly conducive to romance.

Stage 7 was the San Francisco time trial. The course was twenty-five miles through the city, ending atop the hill near Coit Tower. It was the day my race would start in earnest since there would not be a sprint finish. The time differences would blow apart on Stage 7 and grow from there, as most of the stages between today's time trial and the time trial on Stage 14 would be mountainous. The mountain stages would start in Muir Woods, then move inland through the mountains surrounding the wineries near Napa and Sonoma. The first of two rest days was scheduled after Stage 9, a godsend considering the next week of racing.

As excited and confused as I was regarding all things related to Alyssa, my concerns melted away and my mind refocused on cycling the evening before the time trial. At the start line the following morning, I was extremely nervous. The time gaps for the overall classification had not shifted since the prologue even though we had ridden over sixty hours since then. For each of the six stages, the racers finished together and thus, there were still only fifty seconds separating the overall contenders. If I wanted a shot at a high overall placing, I had to have the ride of my life at the San Francisco time trial.

A good placing at the time trial would also go a long way toward improving my stature on the team. In addition to being the new girl with the loud dog, I had the distinction of placing last in each of the sprints on stages one through six. Both Brenda and Alyssa had two top-ten finishes and four top-twenty finishes, making them the most valuable team members thus far even though, because of the prologue, I was placed fourteen seconds ahead of Brenda and eleven seconds ahead of Alyssa on the general classification, and likely to kick both of their asses once the race entered the mountains. I wanted to do well to prove that I deserved that last spot on the team.

Two sayings about San Francisco are, "If you get tired of walking around San Francisco, lean on it," and Mark Twain's, "The coldest winter I ever had was a summer in San Francisco." Sadly, these sayings are not exaggerations. The high for the day would be 40 degrees and we'd be cresting nine hills with grades of up to twenty-five percent. The time trial course toured the city, winding through Haight-Ashbury, the Castro, Fisherman's Wharf and Lombard Street ("the crookedest street in the world"), before finishing atop the hill next to Coit Tower, the hardest of the nine ridiculously steep hills on the course. Crowds lined the route, most of which I managed to tune out through intense concentration. I was surprised to learn afterward that I passed a quarter-mile stretch of streakers without noticing. I finished a solid eighth, which moved me into twelfth overall on the general classification. The nearest team member to me was Lynn, who now sat two minutes behind me in forty-ninth place. Alyssa and Brenda, who had no illusions of placing high in the overall race, rode the time trial just hard enough to avoid being eliminated by the time cut.

On Stage 8 the next day, we crossed the Golden Gate Bridge and ascended into Muir Woods. I knew that if I did well on this mountain stage, there was a good chance I could do well overall. On the first climb, I hung with an elite group of eight climbing specialists. Some other riders caught up to us as we descended into Sausalito, and the group swelled to fifty as we wound around San Pablo Bay. Finally, the group shrank to approximately twenty riders over the mountains surrounding Napa Valley. The day ended in Sacramento. I placed fifth for the stage. That was the good news. The bad news was that the muzzle I'd bought for Sonny didn't work as planned.

Erica and Danny had driven just behind me throughout Stage 8. While Sonny's muzzle cured his barking problem, it created a new problem. In an effort to get the muzzle off, Sonny clawed at himself and created a pool of blood in the back of Erica's car. Erica felt bad for him and took the muzzle off, where upon he resumed barking at the breakaway and smeared his blood throughout the car. I was thirty feet away, riding into the wind with an earpiece, and I could hear him loud and clear. I was quite sure that without today's result, Erica would have dismissed Sonny, and possibly me, without a qualm. However, I was now sitting seventh overall, first place on the team, and third among the Americans in the race. While Erica had hoped that her Bad News Bears team would do decently here and there, she hadn't expected one of her riders to exit the first week in the top ten. Though Erica seemed happy, I got the impression that Sonny's continued presence as team mascot was contingent upon me not having any crappy performances. I would try to oblige, but I also needed to fix the situation.

While I was getting my massage after the day's stage, I brainstormed with Danny about taming Sonny. He suggested tranquilizers, but that involved a veterinarian and I was a little hesitant to drug my dog unconscious.

Then I remembered and shouted, "A dildo!"

"What?"

"He loved Julie's dildo. I'll get him a new one."

"I am not sitting next to that dog while he chomps on a dildo," Danny said.

"Why not? At least he'll be quiet and not bloody," I replied.

"Where are you going to get a dildo?"

"I don't know. I was going to make it a JRA."

Danny laughed and said, "There's a better chance of you shoving a dildo up my ass than me getting one for you."

"Alrighty, I guess I'll just Google the nearest sex shop."

The team car and my car were gone. Instead of waiting, I called a cab and pondered the pros and cons of inviting a girl I shared one kiss with to go to a sex shop with me to get my dog a dildo. I ended up extending the invitation after explaining the dildo story and Alyssa, laughingly, accepted. She grabbed a jacket and followed me. Even though it was still summer, it was only thirty-five degrees while we waited for the cab to take us to Papi Cock. I blew into my hands and felt my phone ringing in my pocket. Quinton. I let it go to voice mail. A few minutes later, I checked his message only to realize I had five new voice mails. Good to know Tampa hadn't forgotten about me. I dialed my code and listened to the first message.

"Hi, Jenna, it's Mom. Oh, shit. I forget why I called you. I'll think of it and call you back. Love you." Delete.

Message number two: "Hi, Jenna. Mom, again. I remembered. My school is having a shoe drive and I was wondering if you had any shoes you don't wear that I could go pick up. Give me a call later. Love you." Delete.

Message number three: "Hi, Jenna. It's Mom. I left a message for you to call me, but Dad and I are going to bed, so don't call me until tomorrow. Bye, love you." Delete.

Message number four: "Hi, Jenna. Did you get my messages yesterday? Call me back." Delete.

Message number five: "Hi, Jenna. It's Quinton. I saw your name in the results on Cyclingnews. That's awesome that you're better and racing. I think I'm going to come out and see you at some point in Oregon. Maybe go from there to Seattle with you. Good luck."

Replay. It was not a dream. The message played the second time exactly as it had the first. Time to panic.

"What's wrong?" Alyssa asked.

"Nothing, just a message from that psychotic guy I dated that I told you about."

"Which one? There seems to be so many."

"Quinton slash Tony," I answered.

"What did he want?"

"To come out and spend time with me. God, I hope he gets arrested again soon."

The cab, a white Oldsmobile, arrived. The driver was a lanky man with a ratty ponytail. From the backseat, I could tell that his ponytail was actually meticulously placed to cover his bald spot.

"Where do you want to go?" he asked.

"Eighth Avenue and Drew Street," I replied.

"What's the place called?"

I hesitated then said, "Papi Cock."

"You know," the cabbie said with a new expression, one that I recognized from many horrible dates. "I'm not really a cab driver. I'm actually head switchboard operator for the cab company. Not only does it pay more, but it has a lot of perks. Cab drivers tip me to send them to good calls and the Russian mob pays me to send certain drivers to certain locations."

Clearly, he was thinking threesome. You couldn't really blame him. It was probably not often that he picked up two attractive girls to go to a porn shop at 9:30 p.m. on a Tuesday. He must have thought we were a wild couple of kids. I cringed at the thought of the cabbie's sexual fantasies, but remained polite. My mom raised me to be ridiculously friendly to people with crappy jobs so they don't think I'm above them. So, I gave the guy a pass for trying to impress me with unimpressive lies and just said, "Can you put up the window? I'm cold."

"Don't be silly, it's delightful out, you can have my jacket."

Obviously the driver hadn't noticed me opening the cab door with my foot, closing it with my elbow and covering my hands with my sleeves so as to not touch anything in the car. "That's okay," I said, as he threw a jacket at me. The jacket was black with a deteriorating white lining and smelled like bologna. I wiggled in my seat to get it off me without touching it. Alyssa laughed.

"So, do you have any children?" the cabbie asked us.

"No," we replied in unison.

"I do. Three in fact. They were just the most beautiful three kids ever made."

"That's nice," I said, trying to abort the conversation.

"All three died at childbirth, so I never got to be a dad. I've always wanted to be a dad," he said to me with a hopeful look.

I hadn't wanted to engage, but now I had to talk to the poor guy. "I'm sorry. How did they die?"

"Something called SIDS. You ever heard of it?"

"Yes I have. Three cases of SIDS is pretty suspicious. Did they do autopsies?"

"Why would they, we already knew they died of SIDS."

"Right," I said. Hard to argue with that logic. Alyssa and I avoided looking at each other so we wouldn't laugh. We arrived and told the cabbie, "Wait right here, we'll be right out."

I grabbed the first dildo I saw and walked over to the checkout. I thought of browsing with Alyssa, but we'd only shared one kiss and so I didn't want to be presumptuous. Besides, the meter was still running. Alyssa was walking around and I peered out of the corner of my eye to make sure she wasn't looking at whips. She was looking at restraints.

Try as I may, when I see restraints I think of John, Julie and my mom. A year ago, my mom was in John and Julie's bedroom trying to leash up their dogs but couldn't figure out how to hook the dogs to the black leather leash attached to the bed posts. Awkwardness ensued.

After the clerk rung me up, I walked over to Alyssa and said, "You ready?"

"Sure."

I wasn't sure if Alyssa thought this was a sexual mission and I didn't want her to think I wasn't down with that, so I said, "We can shop around some other time if you want. Sorry, meter's running."

Alyssa either didn't know what I was talking about, or pretended not to, because she did not respond or react to this comment in any way. I followed her out the door, feeling a little embarrassed for having said anything at all about the sex shop.

As we got back in the cab, a strong cologne odor wafted toward us. Clearly the cabbie was going to start giving us his A game.

"Where do you want to go now?" he asked.

"Back to the house where you picked us up," Alyssa replied.

"I know a great bar with a live guitarist we could go to instead," he offered opportunistically.

I thought about hopping out of the car and running, but I didn't want to tire myself out for tomorrow's race. Plus it wouldn't be very impressive to leave Alyssa in the car with this guy. "We're good," I said. "Let's just go back to the house on Jasmine Street."

"Sure thing," said the cabbie disappointedly. "I have to get up early anyway. I have a project I'm working on with the government. Have to be down in San Francisco tomorrow to meet with some federal agents. This cab job is just my cover."

"Is head switchboard operator part of your cover too?" I asked without a hint of sarcasm.

The cabbie obviously didn't recall his previous lie. "What are you talking about?"

Before I could respond, he said "Hang on," and he answered his cell phone. The conversation ate up a good minute and a half of drive time before he hung up and said, "My daughter. She only calls me for money."

"The one with SIDS?" I asked dryly.

"She had it, but she got better," the cabbie replied.

"Good for her," I said, hopping out of the car the second we pulled up in front of the house. The ride cost twenty-two dollars. I gave him a twenty and a ten and asked for three dollars back. "I don't have any change," he said. "But I'll drive you up to the store to get it free of charge."

There was no way I was getting back in that cab, so I said, "Just keep it," and we walked away, mission accomplished.

The next day, the dildo brought brief comic relief to the team. Unfortunately, Sonny wasn't interested in this dildo. Instead, he barked throughout the entire stage again. This wasn't just annoying, it made my emergency dildo purchase look a bit ridiculous. I was sure my teammates now thought of me as a sick fuck for trying to force sex toys on my unwilling dog.

I placed fourth in the stage and entered the first rest day in sixth place overall. Going into this race, I thought I was capable of placing in the top twenty. My new goal was a top ten, or even top five overall.

I called Julie after the stage and begged her to search my backyard for her former dildo.

"I think he buried it," she said.

"I'm not asking you to dig up the backyard, but if you could look around, I would appreciate it."

"Why don't you just buy him a new one?"

"Tried that. He's pretty monogamous with the one you gave him."

"I'll see what I can do," she said.

A rest day in cycling is a bit of a misnomer because it is merely a rest from racing. Taking a day off the bike is unheard of because it causes the legs to stiffen up. Riders generally spin for two to three hours on each of the two rest days. Team Sunshine Cycling met for coffee at ten in the morning then went for a thirty mile ride. After the ride, we sat around the Jensens', our host family for two full evenings in a row, and ignored each other while we each typed on our laptops.

I was sitting next to Alyssa and sent her an Evite card entitled "Girls Night Out." I filled in, "a sit-down restaurant" for the place and "in two hours" for the time.

She responded immediately, "YES, very funny. Where do you want to go?"

I typed, "I don't even know how to get out of this neighborhood." then added, "We'll find something."

"Sounds good."

I spent the hours in between the ride and my date stressing about Quinton. I couldn't tell Sarah to take care of it because then Sarah would know I was racing instead of in the nut house. Ignoring Quinton wasn't an option either because he was such a loose cannon that anything could happen, the least of which would be my office finding out about my fake pregnancy. I finally decided that I had to call him back and attempt to control him.

"Hi, Quinton, it's Jenna."

"Hey, Jenna. That's awesome that you're out there racing. I can't wait to come and see you."

"About that. It would really make me nervous if you came out. Can I just see you when I get back to Tampa?"

"I already got a week off work," he whined, "and okayed the trip with my probation officer."

"Well, maybe you could go somewhere else," I offered helpfully.

"No way. I want to see you and help you in any way I can. Don't worry, I won't make you nervous. You won't even know I'm there."

"I'm sure you'll blend in fabulously, but I'm doing better than I ever imagined and I think it's because I'm so focused. I really don't want any distractions."

"We'll see."

"Hey, Quinton, what did your mom tell you about my absence?"

"I forget. Something about visiting Betty Ford's house. She said I should go there too, but I'm more of a Saab guy myself."

"I think its Gerald Ford's wife, not Henry Ford." The guy was hopeless.

"Hey, I gotta go. I'm at Tiny Tap and there's a competition about to start. Whoever can remove twist-off beer caps with the most body parts wins. I can do hand, butt, forearm, forehead, toes, underarm pit, neck, calf and probably other stuff. I gotta go win me a beer. Love you, babe."

I hung up without saying goodbye, trying to fathom how our relationship had elevated to the love and pet name stage after only two lousy dates.

* * *

Alyssa and I found a reasonably-priced Italian restaurant and decided to go there and carb-up. Instead of discussing cars and jobs, we gossiped and talked about cycling. She also told me that if I was gay, I had to have a root. It was the best date I'd ever been on.

"What's a root?" I asked.

"From the movie *But I'm a Cheerleader*. You need a list of gay books and movies before you date anyone else. You should know what a root is."

I looked at her like she was crazy when she mentioned dating other people. I'd finally met "the one."

After dinner, we got back in the car, and instead of driving off, I kissed Alyssa. It wasn't the ideal location, but we couldn't exactly hook up on the Jensens' couch in front of Team Sunshine Cycling. Over the past week, all I'd thought about was kissing and touching Alyssa. I felt like it was now or never so when she accepted my kiss, I stopped holding back. After kissing her, running my fingers through her hair and moving my hand up and down her breasts and stomach, I moved to the back of the car. I felt a little hypocritical since I had just made fun of Sarah for having teenage car sex a few months ago, but these were extenuating circumstances and I could not wait any longer. We only had a week and a half left until the end of the race. I'd go back to Florida and Alyssa would go back to Georgia.

Alyssa followed me to the back of the car and we continued. I barely noticed the discomfort of the car, as I was busy enjoying the new experience and marveling that I liked the exact opposite of what I always thought I liked: Alyssa had white skin with freckles instead of a tan; a soft but flat stomach instead of a six-pack; her breasts were fuller than mine and felt different and lovely on top of me instead of a hard chest; her face was full and soft instead of having a prominent jaw-line. I couldn't open her bra, even after I focused, because the clasp is reversed when it's on a person you're facing instead of on your own back. Eventually I just moved it up out of the way. This bit of awkwardness was topped only when Alyssa tried to reposition herself and fell off the car seat onto the floor of my car. My car had a large space where I removed one of my rear seats to make room for my cycling crap. Alyssa landed hard on the base of my bike pump, which caused it to flip upright and hit her in the face. But she laughed and the moment didn't make us skip a beat.

I felt like a teenager because I had no idea what I was doing. I told Alyssa I was better at blow jobs and she told me to shut up. I took her advice and didn't say anything else the entire evening. At first it was an effort. I was so turned on and nervous, I had to stop myself from making stupid jokes. Fortunately, I became speechless as I became more and more aroused. Until Alyssa pulled my pants down, I feared I would come in my pants from the very little bit of pressure my jeans put on my clit. I avoided that, only to climax when I straddled Alyssa, her stomach touching me as she sucked my nipples was too much. I was embarrassed by how quickly I came, but Alyssa didn't seem to mind. I began concentrating on getting Alyssa off and came again while going down on her. Thank God I wasn't a guy. I'd have to work on my stamina.

When we got back to the Jensens', everyone was asleep. We tiptoed in and went our separate ways.

The next day, I told Danny that I was officially gay.

"So you're cool with never seeing a cock again?" he said as only Danny can.

"Yes siree," I answered. "If I could whistle, I'd be whistling now."

"Really? You can't whistle?" Danny asked, not engaging in the other discussion even though it was obvious from his face that it was where his focus was.

"Yes. Don't know how." I said, perfectly content to end the discussion there.

A few minutes passed, then Danny decided not to let it go and said, "You've been dating guys your whole life. You don't think you'll miss it?"

"I was hoping to fuck Alyssa and think, phew, I'm straight. That didn't happen."

"You don't think you're at least bi?" he asked as neutrally as he could, though it was obvious he had a vested interest in my response.

"I may be too into Alyssa to make that decision objectively right now, but I'm pretty sure. I hope I'm gay."

"I thought you just said you would have been relieved if you hated sex with a girl."

"Yeah, it would be easier to be straight than gay and not have to tell everyone I've known since birth that, oopsy daisy, I like pussy. But, I'd rather be gay than bi. Bisexual has such an 'I fuck-anything' connotation."

Danny scoffed and said, "Your dating criteria is so strict you should open up the field to both sexes, and animals. You'd have more success."

"Well hopefully this works out. I'm sick of dating and I think I really like Alyssa. Plus this would be such a convenient relationship. We could drive to races together and hang out."

"She lives in Georgia," Danny said.

"Maybe I'll move there."

"This would be a good time to tell you the oldest lesbian joke in the book," Danny said.

"What's that?"

"What does a lesbian bring to a second date?"

"What?" I asked.

"A U-Haul."

"Ha ha," I said dryly, a little annoyed that Danny was being such a dick. "It's good training up there, it wouldn't just be for Alyssa."

"How do you feel about taking the Georgia bar?"

My stomach heaved. "Fine, maybe I won't move there, but I'll still see her often enough. We both go to pro races nine months of the year."

"No you don't. You race during your three week vacation time. Except when you have maternity leave."

"Well, I want to start racing full time. I'll figure something out."

"I'm sure you will," he said. Danny had always admired my ability to get whatever I wanted, but this time he sounded bitter.

CHAPTER SIXTEEN

On Stages 11, 12 and 13, we continued north on some of the steepest roads I'd ever encountered. By design, Route 101 along the coast never had an incline of more than eleven percent because the road had to be accessible to logging trucks. As you ride it, you can still see the forest being carted away on large trucks. Unlike Route 101, the mountains around wine country have grades of up to twenty-four percent, which is essentially a wall. Though I failed to win a stage, I placed in the top five consistently during these stages, as well as the stage that took us through Redwood National Park. Throughout it all, Sonny sat ten feet behind me in the car, howling incessantly. Erica had nixed the muzzle, deciding she preferred noise to bloodstains. While she was clearly annoyed with him, she listened to him without complaint because I was now in fourth place, inching nearer to the podium every day.

During these stages, I hung out with Alyssa a lot. When I wasn't with Alyssa, I was analyzing every homo and hetero thought I'd had since birth. What was my "root"? When I was a kid, kindergarten age, I begged my mom for a pixie haircut. She finally relented and when I went to camp shortly thereafter, everyone called me a boy and was mean to me. I didn't tell my parents about it, or that I cried every night, but I started trying to act girly after that experience. I never had short hair again. Wow, that's a sad story.

I remembered telling my parents that boys were gross and I'd never like them. As I grew up, my parents' friends would ask me in that tone of voice adults use to tease children and think it's funny, "Do you have a boyfriend yet?" Right up until fifth grade I said, "No. Boys are gross." That was around the time my parents seemed concerned instead of amused. I could sense they thought I was abnormal, so the next day I got myself my first boyfriend. A boyfriend didn't actually mean anything in fifth grade except proving normalcy, as all we really did was hold hands. In middle school, I realized that everyone else was French kissing, so I had my first French kiss even though I wasn't overwhelmed with desire to kiss my sixth grade boyfriend of the week. In high school, it was not a challenge for me to be a tease and stay a virgin. However, in college I felt odd being a virgin so I lost my virginity. I didn't have a root that made me gay, I had a lot of anti-roots that kept me straight. Though I was the happiest I'd ever been, racing and hanging out with Alyssa, I spent a lot of my days focusing on how stupid I was that it took me twenty-eight years to figure out the reason I'd never had a successful relationship with a guy.

* * *

In Eureka, California, just south of the Oregon border, we stayed in a host house with five guest bedrooms, enough for each of us to have a bed if we shared two to a bed. As luck would have it, Alyssa and I were assigned a queen-sized bed in one of these rooms.

After the race, the team went out for dinner. I spent the entire meal eagerly anticipating my evening with Alyssa, the first since our car date. But when we got back to the room, Alyssa, to my considerable disappointment, turned on the television to watch *The Bachelor*. We watched together and when it was over, she said good night and went to bed. I sat there, wanting to touch every part of Alyssa all night in lieu of sleep and she had her back to me. I thought about initiating conversation, but didn't know what to say. I was mystified and confused.

I walked over to Danny's room.

"Hey there vagina town," he said. "I didn't think I'd see you again tonight."

"Hilarious," I said, chuckling a little in spite of my mood.

"So how was it?" Danny pleaded, "You can tell me details. I won't get grossed out."

"There are no details, we watched *The Bachelor* and she went to bed."

"What did she say?"

"Just that she was tired and going to bed. She didn't say it apologetically either. It's like she didn't even notice that we were alone together for the first and probably last time during this race."

"So, she's tired," Danny offered.

"Of course she's tired. We're all tired. What does that have to do with anything? There must be something else. She had enough energy to watch that show and trust me, that's taxing."

"What else could it be?" Danny asked.

"I don't know," I said. "You massage her, did you notice anything?"

"Like a white spot of yeast infection discharge on my massage table sheet?" Danny responded innocently.

I cringed but smiled a little. It was pretty funny. "No." I said. "I mean does she have any weird chafe marks or saddle sores she might not want me to see?"

"Nope," he replied, "not that I saw."

"I'm pissed," I said.

"Pissed or frustrated?" Danny asked.

"Both, but mostly pissed at this point. I shaved my legs even though I didn't have to for a few more days. I bought and applied really expensive good smelling lotion instead of just letting my dry skin flake off, and wore my best black lacy bra and underwear instead of sitting around in my comfortable pajamas."

"So, are you still wearing all that?" Danny asked suggestively.

"I'm not saying that to be titillating. I'm venting. That underwear has never gone to the wash unnoticed or unappreciated. This would never happen with a guy."

"No it wouldn't. So are you reevaluating the whole lesbian thing?" Danny asked, clearly focusing on keeping his face and voice as neutral as possible.

"Not sure, but I'm reevaluating the whole Alyssa thing."

"Really?" Danny asked.

"No. I wish. I'm still obsessed with her. I just don't get it. She seemed completely uninterested in me."

"How is it that you're interested in someone who watches *The Bachelor*?" Danny asked.

"I don't know. That and the reincarnated conquistador thing really should have cured me of my crush."

"Just get some sleep," Danny suggested, trying to sound supportive though I think he was enjoying my misery. "You have some big stages coming up."

I went back to the room and lay next to Alyssa, wanting to press my body against hers as she slept. I wanted unlimited access to her body and I wanted it immediately. Instead of sleeping, I stared at the ceiling and thought of every excuse in the book for her to deny me. The obvious fear was that it was because I sucked in bed. However, I knew she came last time and she should cut me some slack since it was my first crack at it and we were in a car. She could also just be uninterested in me, but I pushed that thought away because I thought I might cry like a little girl. I thought up other excuses, ones that didn't involve me. Maybe she was tired. After all, she was a sprinter not a mountain climber, so these climbing days were harder for her even though she was going slower than me. Or, I thought, she could be jealous because I was doing so well. Or, maybe she doesn't feel comfortable having sex in a stranger's house. Or she could be having her period. After creating all of these excuses, I finally fell asleep knowing that something wasn't right. Where there's a will, there's a way. I slept lightly, afraid I might accidentally snuggle with her in my sleep.

The following day was another steep mountain stage. Though I'd slept poorly, I had a good day and placed fifth. Consequently, I entered the second and final time trial, a twenty-five mile course through Eugene, Oregon, in fourth place overall. It was beyond my wildest dreams, but instead of being content, I wanted to move up, onto the podium.

Eugene is home to the University of Oregon and the time trial course was lined with students drinking beer and cheering us on, cameras ready to catch any crashes for YouTube. Unfortunately for the students, crashes were rare in the solitary time trial. I placed fifth, my highest placing against the clock thus far. I attributed my improvement to better recuperation after the long mountain stages than the time trial specialists that had beaten me earlier, before we had more than a thousand miles in our legs. The time trial result moved me up to third place overall. I was ecstatic at the prospect of entering the second rest day in a podium position, with only six days left of racing.

That evening, I couldn't take it anymore. I waited until Alyssa was alone on the couch she would be sleeping on and asked her what was wrong.

"Nothing," she said. "What do you mean?"

"Well, we missed an excellent opportunity for sex last night and you've seemed distant since then. Is it something I said or did?" I asked.

"No," she said.

"Nothing?" I asked again, and again.

"Well," she said, her resolve softening. "I'll tell you if you promise not to tell anyone."

"Okay," I said, more than curious.

"I have herpes," she said.

"What?" I couldn't disguise the disgusted look on my face.

"I've never given it to anyone to my knowledge so I'm sure there's nothing to worry about. I've never even had it really, I just know I'm a carrier."

I knew this game. She was telling me she had herpes so she could get rid of me without hurting me. In high school, it was my strategy for getting rid of guys guilt free, though I never made up an STD. I didn't want that answer from Alyssa, I wanted the real reason she'd lost interest in me. I wanted to know so that I could fix it and make her like me again. "Well, it was sweet of you not to infect me last night, but you could have already infected me last week so I don't buy it."

"I'm sure I didn't. It's never flared up."

"So, you don't think it's contagious, but even if it is, you may have already infected me. I don't think that's the problem. What's the real reason you didn't sleep with me last night?" I asked, even though I knew how annoying it was to be in her situation.

She stared at me uncomfortably, "I'm sorry, I don't know what's wrong. I just, I don't know, I hit a wall with you."

"What the hell are you talking about?" I asked. My heart was beating quickly and my mouth tasted like bile.

"Nothing, I still really like you and want to hang out, but I hit a wall and I need to figure stuff out."

I stared at Alyssa. She was barefoot and wearing jeans and somehow made it look sophisticated. This made me realize that I was sitting cross-legged like an elementary school student next to her. I unfolded my legs and crossed them, then leaned back into the couch. Alyssa was looking down and fidgeting with the remote but not touching any buttons. I had no fucking idea what she was talking about. And I was livid that she'd either exposed me to herpes or didn't have herpes and just brought it up to get rid of me. With that, I walked away.

I sat outside the massage room, waiting to be the next customer. When I got in, I told Danny what Alyssa said.

"Don't worry about herpes," he said, "It's a cold sore, you'll live. It will be good for you, you'll be ugly briefly and see how the other half lives. What the hell is a wall?" Danny asked.

"A crappy metaphor for I'm not into you," I replied.

"Did she give any other reasons besides the wall?" Danny asked.

"Other than herpes? No." I said.

"Are you sure you didn't do something to her? Say something mean?"

I thought about it and said, "Normally that would be a valid concern, but no Danny, I don't think so. I've never been so nice. For God's sake, I watched *The Bachelor* with her. If I did anything to her it was being too pathetic."

"That could be it, no one likes a pathetic person."

"Could be, but she likes the show, along with most of America, so she probably doesn't realize how much I sold out by watching it."

"It's been a long two weeks," Danny said, "Maybe she's just tired. After tomorrow's rest day, she'll come to her senses."

"We'll see," I said, but I seriously doubted it.

* * *

The next day, the second rest day, Alyssa was gone when I woke up. A few hours later, she and two other teammates came into the house. They had taken my car to get coffee and hadn't even invited me. They did the same thing a week ago, but I didn't care then. Now, hate and jealousy rose up into my throat as we prepared to go for a two hour team ride to spin the legs out.

As we took off, I positioned myself next to Alyssa. The entire team was riding two abreast. Each pair would spend five minutes or so in the wind, then peel off and move to the back of the line. I rode next to Alyssa for fifteen minutes, wanting to say something, but not knowing what. Finally, it was our time to pull into the wind.

The pace for the previous fifteen minutes had been twenty-two miles per hour. When Alyssa and I took over, I half-wheeled her. Half-wheeling is when you're riding next to someone at a conversational pace and you lift the pace by a half a wheel length or so, upping the ante slightly. The message is, "My easy conversational pace is faster than your easy conversational pace." Alyssa responded by meeting my half wheel and raising me a half wheel a few seconds later. Neither of us got out of the saddle or made an obvious effort while raising the pace; the idea was to make the lift appear unconscious, that it's so easy you don't even notice you're doing it. I reciprocated, bringing the pace to twenty-four miles per hour.

Twenty-four miles per hour is still a conversational pace, but not effortless. Alyssa half-wheeled me again and I reciprocated until we were up to twenty-six miles per hour, doable, but no longer conversational. I can hold twenty-six for a while, but hadn't planned to do so today because I just wanted to spin out my legs easy. Alyssa upped the pace yet again and so did I. Then we did it again. We were now traveling thirty miles per hour, a pace neither of us could sustain very long. It was now a matter of who blinked. I would sooner slit my throat than ease up and lose, but it was becoming harder to appear at ease and I was supposed to be resting my legs. My breathing was getting louder by the second. I covered this by casually taking a sip of water, so Alyssa could see out of the corner of her eye that I was not in difficulty. That seemed to do the trick and she slowed down.

I won the meaningless half-wheel contest and felt good, briefly. I pretended not to notice that Alyssa failed to keep pace, and kept riding at thirty miles per hour for a few more seconds. Then I turned my head and pretended to notice, for the first time, that Alyssa was having difficulty with our little jaunty pace. When I looked back, she was already thirty yards behind me. Our teammates were nowhere to be seen. Obviously, they were content not to burn out their legs on their rest day, as even sitting in the draft at thirty miles per hour is an effort.

I turned around and rode back to the host house by myself. After a few turns, I realized I was lost. I sat at a red light, panicking that I'd spend the entire rest day lost, in the sun with no food or water. As I straddled my bike on the side of the road, a pickup truck pulled alongside me and turned on his windshield wipers, knocking wiper fluid into my face. He cracked up and peeled out. Asshole.

Two hours later, I finally found the host house. I grabbed Sonny, and went outside. The euphoria of my triumph at the "half-wheel" game was long gone. I sat outside and felt sorry for myself in the shade. Danny came out back and asked, "Did you eat lunch?"

"No," I said. "I'm not hungry."

"You need to eat," he said.

"I will."

"You need to snap out of this before you ruin your race. She's not worth it. You're acting like a girl."

"I am a girl."

"You're acting like the type of girl you don't like."

"Yeah, I am pathetic," I replied. "I just can't stop thinking about her. I'm confused. I just want to know what happened."

"Does it really matter? How many people have you dumped who had no clue why you dumped them?"

"All of them," I said. "That doesn't mean there wasn't a reason. There's a reason and I want to know what it is. She put opera on in the car when we drove back from hooking up and I changed the channel. Maybe she thinks I'm not cultured."

"You're not cultured," Danny said helpfully.

"So, should I be dumped for that? Fuck culture. Who wants to hang out with someone cultured?"

"It's possible that Alyssa does," Danny replied. "Who cares what it is? It could be anything. Maybe it's because you curse every other word, or because you're a total slob."

"I am not," I insisted, though I knew he was right.

"Your car looks like you took a garbage can and dumped half of it in the front seat and half of it in the back."

"True, but eight women are using that car right now. I doubt she realizes the car always looks like that. Plus, I'm not a total slob. My clothes are clean, I'm clean, my bike's clean. Maybe it's because I'm a music idiot."

"This is a fun game," Danny said. "I'm learning all of your insecurities. Why do you think it's because you're a music idiot?"

"Because she had a lady singing on her voice mail and it sounded so unpolished, I thought she sang into her voice mail because it sounded a little like her. She looked at me like I was an idiot and said, that's so and so. Some lady I never heard of. From the context, I take it that it was someone famous, but I don't know because I'm a loser and listen to Neil Diamond and Barry Manilow."

Danny laughed hysterically and said, "Don't forget Air Supply."

"That's not the worst of it. I tried to cover my mistake by saying, 'I know that, I thought maybe it was you singing her song into your recorder.'"

"I think we're getting closer to the problem, but does it really matter? What will you do when if you find out?"

"Depends," I replied. "If it's a valid reason, I'll change. I'm all about self-improvement."

"Right. You'll change. You'll be a neat, cultured music snob, then you and Alyssa will live happily ever after."

"Maybe," I said. "Part of me wants that. The other part of me just wants her to like me again so that I can then crush her soul."

"That sounds healthy," Danny said.

"That's the way it is. I don't even know if I'm thinking about her because I like her, or if I'm thinking of her because I'm competitive and don't want to be rejected. Either way, I want her back."

"You have to stop taking this personally," Danny said as if getting dumped isn't personal. "You'll ruin your life like that guy who didn't realize you dumped him for confusing the words advice and advise, in an email to you."

"But I didn't do anything stupid like that," I said.

"That music thing was pretty dumb if it's really someone famous. But forget it, you read that sex advice columnist, Dan Savage, right?"

"Yes," I said.

"Well, one time some guy wrote in and said he was weirded out because he caught his girlfriend having sex with her brother. Her excuse was that they started doing it as kids and never stopped as they entered adulthood. The guy wanted to know if he was being a jerk for judging her for fucking her brother when she was great in every other way. Dan's advice was, dump the mother fucker. He then explained that the guy shouldn't worry about it because there's some other man out there who is going to think that's the hottest thing in the world. Let her find *that* guy."

"I'm confused," I said. "Am I the judgmental boyfriend or the brother-fucker in your scenario?"

"Neither. The point is, whatever Alyssa doesn't like in you, someone else will love. Meet that person."

"I've met plenty of men that love my flaws and I'm sure there will be women, too. I don't want them, and actually, I usually can't stand them. I want Alyssa for some reason."

"Then you'll get her back." Danny said, "You always get what you want. And, once you get her, you'll realize you're straight and not interested in her."

I knew Danny was trying to help, but I was in no mood to hear how I always get what I want. I was also sick of him telling me I was straight. It was like Danny had no concept that I was going through a tough time because I was gay and heartbroken. I lashed out. "Do you know how I know I'm not straight? The thing that seals the deal?"

"How?" he asked.

"Because of you. You're jealous of Alyssa and you've never been jealous of anyone before. And you're jealous because you're in love with me and always have been and now you know it's not going to work because you know I'm gay even though you're trying to convince me otherwise."

I stopped when I saw Danny's face. It was bright red, including his ears, but he was just standing there taking it. I had never been mean to Danny before because I valued his friendship so much and didn't want to lose it. But I was so mad and hurt about Alyssa, and so mad that Danny had been such a dick about it, that I couldn't help myself from turning into a raging bitch. After looking at Danny for a few moments, wishing the words never came out of my mouth, even though I knew they were true, I said, "I'm sorry."

Danny responded by saying, "You need to eat." Then he walked away.

"I will," I said to myself, knowing that I had even less of an appetite than before. I'd heard of people losing their appetites when they get dumped. Break-uporexia I believe it's called. This was the first time I ever suffered from it and the timing could not have been worse.

* * *

The next morning, Danny was gone. I asked around, but no one knew anything. I didn't have time to look, as Stage 15 was about to begin. Stage 15 was the stage after the rest day and turned into the bad day I had been dreading the entire race. In cycling, there are inevitably days when you just don't have the legs. The odd thing is that sometimes you can start a cycling race and not feel strong, then after a few hard efforts, your legs and lungs are better than ever. Unfortunately, the reverse is also true. Sometimes you start a race feeling great, then all of the sudden each pedal stroke is an effort and you lose the will to live. I drank a can of Mountain Dew, praying that the caffeine and sugar would give me energy rather than make me vomit. Neither happened.

The stage finished with two mountains. The second mountain started as soon as the first finished. However, neither were very steep or long. They were actually just steep enough to dislodge the sprinters, though this was mostly because the sprinters weren't interested in overall time and thus content not to kill themselves up the climb. Normally, I'd be able to hang on this terrain without any problem. However, as the road tilted upwards, vicious attacks ensued. After three accelerations, my legs revolted. They kept turning, but decidedly slower. This was particularly bad, because the third acceleration took place with sixteen miles remaining of the ninety-eight mile stage. Normally, I would take these gradual climbs in my big chain ring, using intermediate gears that I could push fast enough to accelerate, but that were big enough to keep a high speed. Instead, I switched into my "granny gear," the easiest of my small chain ring and cassette. I generally only use my small chain ring for easy rides where I'm spinning out my legs, or when I'm climbing a steep hill or mountain. The granny gear is reserved for insanely steep hills or mountains. However, on this day, I remained in granny gear and struggled to turn the pedals the entire time. I cursed Alyssa. It was possible I would have sucked on this stage no matter what. But my hard rest day workout and failure to eat could not have helped.

I wound up finishing with the *gruppetto* or *autobus;* the group of sprinters and domestiques unconcerned about their overall time. The *gruppetto's* only concern is to beat the time cut so she can target a different, flatter stage in the future. The time cut varies on each stage, but is generally twenty percent of the winner's time on a mountain stage and five percent of the winner's time on flat stages. Staying with the *gruppetto* was actually a challenge for me, but Alyssa was in there, so I killed myself to stay in the pack, well aware that I was riding on pure hate.

I would have liked more than anything to have finished ahead of Alyssa, but I stayed just behind her so she couldn't see me, as I looked like pure hell. In an effort to get as much energy as I could, as soon as possible, I ate and drank everything I could get my hands on during the climbs. In addition to the Mountain Dews, I had two bottles of water, a Snickers bar, two cookies and three sugary gel packs. My stomach hurt and became so distended that I couldn't stand to have the elastic of my cycling shorts around my waist. I moved the waistband down to my pelvic bone, causing me to flash my ass crack for the final ten miles of the stage. I had never suffered so much on a bike.

I finished inside the time cut, but lost eight minutes on the stage. Overnight, I dropped from third place overall to an anonymous eighteenth. I'd lost the race, Alyssa and Danny within twenty-four hours. I didn't even have the energy to change out of my sweaty cycling gear. I just sat at the finish line, staring off into space.

An hour later, I slid into the Greenburgs', our hosts for the evening. I wanted to go unnoticed, but everyone was right by the door when I walked in. My teammates tried to comfort me and their support made me tear up. Even Brenda seemed sad for me. Erica looked both sympathetic and upset. She took a chance on me and I let her down. I was holding back the tears successfully until Alyssa came up to me and apologized. I left to sob in peace, with no idea where I was going in this big house.

My race was ruined and everything else seemed insignificant. Of the six stages left, only two were mountainous, so I would have very little opportunity to improve my overall position. A podium spot or top-five finish was now out of the question and a top-ten was a long shot. I wanted to call Danny, but I was such a bitch the day before that I didn't know what to say. I thought about calling my parents, but even if they weren't anti-cycling, they were very anti-feeling-sorry-for-yourself, and would tell me to cheer up since I wasn't starving, deformed or suffering from cancer. The last thing I wanted to do when I was throwing myself a pity party was to think of the triviality of my situation. Granted, it wasn't the end of the world, but I had trained five hours a day and risked disbarment, jail and poverty to compete. I felt entitled to do well.

The next day, my legs recovered as if nothing had happened. I placed third on the stage and leapfrogged some people, moving into eleventh place. Once again, Sonny howled at me throughout the entire stage. Despite my good finish, Erica was suddenly more annoyed than usual by Sonny. If I was going to suck in this race, I at least had to do so with a well-behaved dog. Just as I was thinking of a solution to the psychotic dog situation, Julie called to tell me that one of her dogs dug up "the" dildo in my backyard. I told her to overnight it to tomorrow's host house in Astoria, Oregon.

I took the rediscovered dildo, Sonny's favorite, as a good omen; clearly my luck was changing. I called Danny, said I was sorry, and asked him to meet me for dinner if he wasn't halfway to Tampa already. He told me he was sorry, too, and that he was still local at a local bar drinking Jameson.

We met for dinner and it was as though nothing had happened. Both of us wanted things back the way they were, so we talked about everything except Danny being in love with me and me being gay. After we ordered, I announced, "I'm better. No more wallowing about a broken heart or damaged ego or whatever the hell it was. No more racing conservatively. I have nothing to lose. I'm testing out that dildo tomorrow."

"Pardon?" Danny said.

"Julie sent me the original dildo that Sonny loved. Tomorrow, I'm going off the front from the gun, so we'll see early on whether Sonny wants to bark at me or chomp on his favorite cock while I'm racing."

"The stage is one hundred and four miles long, I wouldn't take off from mile one," Danny advised.

"Why not? It's the perfect day for it. It's a flat course the day before the last tough mountain stage. The leaders will want to rest, so they'll probably let me go since I'm over eight minutes behind and no longer a threat."

"Then go for it," Danny said. "You've worked hard, you can still get back into the top ten, maybe even the top five, if you have a good day tomorrow and the *peloton* gives you a little latitude."

The next day started cold and rainy, and the forecast was for more of the same throughout the day. This was good news. If the pack went slow because of the weather, it would be a long, cold ride, which I hate. I'd rather ride hard so that I can keep warm and get through it quicker. Plus, when it rains, water and mud sprays off the wheel of the rider in front of you directly into your face. I had no desire to be cold and have mud flung in my face for five hours. I wanted to gut it out in the rain all day.

When the gun went off, a group of three attacked off the front immediately. I jumped away from the pack to join them. The pack chased this group down pretty quickly. Another group of four then went away. I waited until this group got 200 meters away, then jumped away from the pack again, closing in on the group of four almost immediately. Instead of catching the foursome and joining in their rotation, I flew past them. One of them gave chase, which ruined their cooperation. The pack behind quickly caught the three that didn't chase me, then reeled in the fourth rider shortly thereafter.

The race was being controlled by the eight teammates of the woman in first place, as well as one or two of the teammates of the women in second and third place. The leader's team seemed content to let me go since I was over six minutes behind and would be dangling in the wind all by myself for one hundred miles. This was not an uncommon cycling strategy, as the eight teammates of the leader could easily share in setting the tempo throughout the day to keep me within striking distance, and let the sprinters' teams chase me down in the last hour since they always want their shot at glory. It's relatively easy for a group of fresh riders to pull back a tired rider over the last twenty miles of a race. After ten miles, I had a two-minute lead.

Even in the atrocious weather, it felt good to be on the open road by myself after so many days in the *peloton*. There was a slight tailwind, which helped move me along quickly at only seventy percent effort. As a bonus, the dildo worked. Sonny completely ignored me on my bicycle ten feet in front of him in favor of chowing down. I could hear Danny and Erica on the race radio laughing at Sonny and encouraging me to keep it up.

At the sixty-five mile mark, my lead over the *peloton* had stretched to eight minutes. This was the first time I really thought I could win the stage and get some of my time back that I'd lost the day before. Over the race radio, Danny encouraged me with his best Phil Liggett and Paul Sherwen impersonations. Liggett and Sherwen have been cycling commentators since the invention of the wheel. Both are British and perform live commentary for every televised cycling event in English-speaking countries, including America. Partly because they're British and partly because they're stuck commentating about people on bicycles for five hours straight, they tend to use bizarre words and phrases, which have become legendary among cyclists.

In a bad British accent, Danny said, "Well, Rosen sure has packed herself a suitcase full of courage today. She is either superhuman or a fool. We shall see."

All of my teammates got the joke, as the "suitcase of courage" is a very familiar reference. The other girls started chiming in on race radio as well. Lynn said, "Rosen is pushing a monster gear, her legs must be screaming."

"Monster gear nothing," Erica said. "Rosen is just dancing on the pedals in a most immodest way. She seems to have sprouted wings."

"She sure does look resplendent in that Sunshine Cycling kit," someone said.

One of the riders announced there was a crash and Erica broke character to respond. "Is everyone okay?"

It obviously wasn't serious because Lynn kept up with the impersonation and said, "Nothing but a touch of wheels." This was one of my favorite lines. Liggett or Sherwen say it every time there's a crash that does not subsequently involve a rider being airlifted. "Just a little touch of the wheels and they're off again." It doesn't matter that the rider left half of his kit and one-third of his skin on the road and that he's dripping blood.

Alyssa had joined in the commentary and involuntarily, I thought, does this mean Alyssa and I are on speaking terms? Then I banished the thought and the jokey commentary in my ear so I could keep my focus on the task at hand. I was regaining huge amounts of time and could wind up back in the top five or ten, depending on when the *peloton* started to chase me, and how hard. I knew the chase would start soon, because if I kept my pace and they kept theirs, I'd be in first place at the end of the day; something the leader's team would never let happen.

At the ninety-mile mark, it was clear I would win the stage though my lead had shrunk from eight minutes to four. I became giddy at this realization and started pedaling with renewed energy. With three miles to go, I passed over a drawbridge. Even though I knew I would win today's stage, I was still killing myself to make up the time I had lost in the overall classification. The last five-hundred meters were lined with cheering locals oblivious to the weather, probably because they lived in it daily, even during "dry season." Instead of lifting my arms in celebration for the last two hundred meters as is customary, I continued to ride hard, trying to gain back as many seconds as possible. Finally, I crossed the line, pulled my jersey down proudly, put my hands up in the air and rode over to the team car to give Danny, Erica and Sonny a big wet hug. I tried to act modest. After all I was only able to escape because I was no longer a serious contender. However, I had just won my first professional stage after being in the lead for one hundred and four miles and I couldn't get the dopey grin off my face.

According to race radio, the *peloton* was three minutes behind, but based on their speed, they would cross the line two and a half minutes behind me. This would put me in sixth place, not too far behind the third place I was in before my legs crapped out on me. However, I now had a stage win, and with a little luck on the last mountain stage, I could climb back into the top five or even onto the podium.

I changed into dry clothes and peed into a cup for the doping controls. Doping controls are required for the winner of each stage. I was flattered to finally be good enough to be tested for doping.

I went to the podium area and waited for the second and third place riders to join me. But something was holding up the *peloton*. Erica told me that the drawbridge was raised and appeared to be broken, trapping the *peloton* on the other side. Man, was I glad not to be sitting on the other side of that bridge in wet clothes. The minutes ticked by and still the bridge was not fixed.

It took over nine minutes to fix the bridge so the *peloton* didn't finish until more than thirteen minutes after I crossed the finish line. Race officials seemed confused about how to score the day's stage. The obvious and fair resolution was to score me four minutes and thirty-four seconds ahead of the *peloton*; the gap that existed when I crossed the line, but cycling has a long history of inequities.

In the 1922 Tour de France, there was a rule that each rider had to fix their own mechanicals without outside assistance. Eugene Christophe, the first cyclist to wear the yellow jersey in 1919, was leading the race again in 1922 when his fork broke in the Pyrenees. He hauled the bike to the nearest blacksmith and forged the fork together while a race official looked on. Though Christophe completed the repair himself, he was still penalized for allowing a small boy to help him fan the fire. His penalty was tacked onto the time he had already lost repairing the fork. To add insult to injury, Christophe's repair failed and he was forced to abandon the race when his fork broke on the descent of the famed Galibier Mountain in the Alps.

Fast-forward almost one hundred years and cycling was still being altered by happenstance. In the 2006 edition of the Paris-Roubaix road race, the race leader crossed a railroad track thirty seconds ahead of the three men chasing him. As the second, third and fourth place riders approached the railroad crossing, the warning arms were lowered, though the train was far away. The three riders crossed the track. Objectively, there was no danger, but the riders were disqualified for breaking the rule against proceeding through a closed railroad crossing. Ironically, the fifth through seventh place riders, who stopped because there was a train in the way, went through the warning arms as well, albeit after the train had passed. This second group of violators was not disqualified even though they'd broken the same rule. Such is cycling on the open road.

On the podium, I was given champagne and flowers. I set the flowers down and sprayed the champagne in celebration, then drank some straight from the bottle. The bottle was neither expensive nor refrigerated, but Dom Perignon could not have tasted better.

After the award presentation, I went to find out if my overall placing had been determined yet. To my surprise, the race organizers had me in first place overall. The drawbridge delay would not be discounted. I knew this was horribly unfair, and would cause all of the racers and spectators to hate me. I tried to protest, but the European coach of the rightful overall winner was already fighting that battle for me. He was engaged in a hysterical argument with the race officials and I didn't want to interrupt. The coach wasn't speaking English, but it was clear he thought the ruling was a bit unfair.

As the argument wound down, it was my turn to be the martyr, a role I was unfamiliar playing. They told me to come with them to the podium again, this time to get my yellow leader's jersey. I made the case, but it fell on deaf ears. Their minds were made up. Still, I opted to forego the ceremonial presentation of the yellow jersey. There was plenty of precedent for this, especially when the first place rider crashes and the second place rider comes into the leader's jersey without "earning" it. To my knowledge, eleventh place has never inherited the jersey from first place as a result of a broken bridge, but I felt the protocol should be the same.

I was proud that I'd won the stage, but the officials' decision ruined my celebratory mood. I was somber during my massage.

"Sometimes," Danny said, "it's tough having the world revolve around you, isn't it?"

"I never thought I would say this, but yes it is. This sucks. If I win, it's because it was handed to me on a silver platter. If I lose, it's a huge choke. Plus, what if the newspaper reports this and it gets back to my office?"

"Now you're just talking crazy," Danny said. "You think the *Tampa Bay Times* is going to report on Stage Seventeen of women's cycling in the state of Washington?"

"True, but it still sucks. I need to figure out a way to put myself back where I should be. Maybe I'll just stop before crossing the line and wait about nine minutes before finishing."

"You can't. They'll enforce the time cut and you'll get disqualified."

"I'm surprised they didn't disqualify everyone except me today, since they're such sticklers for the rules."

"They never enforce the time cut against the majority of the *peloton*," Danny said.

"Maybe I'll just give back a little bit of time each day until I reach nine minutes and thirty-four seconds, the undeserved amount of my lead."

"You're a winner. Just deal with it." Danny said.

"I'm a sixth placer and a stage winner. How the hell did the drawbridge break anyway?"

"No one said, but I'm sure the city is looking into it. They're very embarrassed."

"They should be. They pissed off Jenna Rosen."

"You're not the victim here. That lady who used to be in first place is the victim."

"I am still a victim even if I'm not the victim. Everyone is going to hate me. I'll be the cyclist with the asterisk by her name."

"Yes, starting today, when people think of Roger Maris, they'll think of Jenna Rosen."

"Mother fucker."

"I'm just kidding, Jenna. You know that." Danny continued to bore down into a knot on my back as he said this.

"No, ouch. That hurts. Safe word. Stop, Mother Fucker, you're killing me."

"Oh. Sorry, got the knot out though."

"At least tradition dictates that I don't wear the yellow jersey tomorrow. I'm pretty sure no one knows who I am without it identifying me."

"Sure they do," Danny said. "They refer to you as the strong girl who can't sprint or descend in a pack."

"Mother fucker."

"I'm barely touching you."

"That time I was calling you a mother fucker."

When I got back to my room, I had a message from Quinton. "Congrats, Jenna, you can take it from here." That dumbass thinks this is good news, I thought as I hit delete.

Once the lights were out, I slipped into my yellow jersey. Even though I didn't earn it and wouldn't race in it tomorrow, I couldn't resist wearing it at least once while I had it. Instead of sleeping, I petted Sonny and felt sorry for myself all night, something that was happening with disturbing frequency of late.

CHAPTER SEVENTEEN

At the start of Stage 18 the next day, I tried to apologize to the rider who'd been leading the overall race, and tell her that I would sit up before crossing the line and let her take back the lead. However, I couldn't spot her because she was no longer wearing the distinctive yellow jersey and the pack was too big to weave in and out of everyone trying to spot her. I decided to just sit up at the end of the stage and she'd figure out that I was doing the right thing.

Before the stage, we learned that investigators had determined that the drawbridge had been intentionally sabotaged and that police had a few leads on the perpetrators. It was probably the same stupid group of kids that thought it was funny to throw glass and tacks onto the road during the race. I really hoped they'd catch the douche bags.

The stage was mountainous. As a result, riders were scattered along the course and I finished with a group of three riders. In this stage, bonus seconds were awarded to the top three finishers. There was also prize money on offer, so I decided to sprint for the finish and give my time back on one of the flat stages where I had no shot of winning. I finished second, earned $460 and had ten bonus seconds subtracted from my time. This result would have advanced me into fourth place if I weren't already in first place by dumb luck. As I've done with all of my winnings, I gave it to Danny so I could put a dent in the money I owed him.

There were two more flat stages prior to the final stage, which was also flat. I calculated that I could give back four minutes and sixteen seconds on each stage without being time cut, and thus claim my rightful place; fourth. I was going to finish last on both of the sprint stages anyway, so I liked the idea of making it look intentional rather than the result of incompetent sprinting.

I gave back four minutes and sixteen seconds on Stage 19 and planned to do the same on Stage 20. As I was getting ready for Stage 20, I had a call but the caller had an unfamiliar area code. All of my friends ignore calls from numbers they don't recognize, but I'm too curious to let it go. In fact, if I miss a call from an unknown number, I call back to find out who called. I answered and, to my surprise, it was Quinton.

"Hey Jenna," he said. "I need some legal help."

"Not now, I'm at the start line and I really have to go. Call your mom, she's 'like' an attorney." I hung up and rolled to the start.

Just prior to firing the start gun, the race commentator announced that the police had apprehended the person who rigged the drawbridge, and that someone by the name of Quinton Smith was in custody.

My blood went cold. I looked down at my power meter and noticed that my heart rate spiked above threshold even though I wasn't exercising.

Today's race would take at least five hours, enough time for the police to realize that Quinton Smith, of Tampa, Florida, had placed two calls to the cell phone registered to the race leader, Jenna Rosen of Tampa, Florida; one from his cell phone and one from jail.

After stressing the entire race, I stopped my bike just before the finish line to wait for four minutes before crossing to restore the race to its proper balance. As I waited, a race official approached me and told me that my boyfriend was in custody and it was too late to try and right a wrong. He was about fifty years old, balding, and wearing the light blue polo shirt of USA Cycling. His tone was flat and neutral, merely explaining the situation, but I took it as harsh since he was essentially telling me my race was over.

"This is a huge misunderstanding," I pleaded. "Quinton is not my boyfriend and I had no idea that he was even in this time zone let alone rigging a drawbridge."

The race official looked skeptical. "Come with me, the police need to talk with you."

"I'll be happy to clear up this situation in two more minutes," I said, still determined to yield back the time the drawbridge malfunction had bestowed upon me.

"You're wasting your time," the official responded. "I'm sure we'll be disqualifying you once the truth comes out."

"We have just under two minutes if you'd like me to explain it now," I offered.

"Save it," was the curt reply.

"Okay, I probably couldn't tell the whole story in under two minutes anyway."

After standing there awkwardly for a minute, the official said, "Can I lift your bike?"

"Sure," I said, stepping off the bike. "Just don't let the front wheel cross the finish line." Picking up another's bike is to cyclists what sniffing each other's ass is to dogs.

"Damn, that's light," the official said, suddenly friendly and smiling instead of all business.

We talked about bikes until the balance of my four minutes and sixteen seconds were up, where upon I walked two feet forward, crossed the line and said, "Nice talking with you. I have to go for questioning now."

"Good luck," he said, having been softened by my charm.

"Thanks. Hopefully, I'll see you tomorrow."

I went into the police station and explained my story, leaving in the part about Quinton being psychotic but taking out the part about my fraudulent receipt of insurance benefits for a childless maternity leave. The cops were quite entertained by my story, but said they would have to look into it and get back to me.

"Please, tell the race officials that I didn't do it so I can race tomorrow," I said to the cops.

"I don't know for sure that you weren't an accomplice," said the cop, who was short, mustached, and overweight. "You just say you didn't do it."

"Okay, then please tell them you can't prove I had anything to do with it. That way they'll let me race tomorrow. After that, I'm not worried. I know the truth will come out."

"I'm a police officer ma'am, not a referee. You talk to the race officials."

* * *

Danny picked me up from the station and the first thing I said was, "Did you know Quinton was here?"

"No. I'm assuming you didn't either," he replied.

"Negatory," I said. "What an idiot."

"How did he know that you would be in a breakaway?" Danny asked. "Otherwise rigging the bridge wouldn't have made sense."

"Who knows," I said, "he's obviously more psychotic than I gave him credit for. He must have been spying on us at dinner when I was talking about having nothing to lose and going for it from the gun on that stage."

"Maybe our salt shakers had microphones," Danny suggested, only half in jest.

"I know it sounds paranoid, but he's obviously insane and he figured it out spite of being a fucking idiot."

"I have no doubt that he is spying on you," Danny said.

"This is awful. I'm the Tonya Harding of cycling. It's only a matter of time before I'm fighting Paula Jones in *Celebrity Boxing*."

"It's not that bad," said Danny, always looking for the silver lining. "At least he didn't break the kneecaps of the three women ahead of you."

"There is that."

"Relax," said Danny. "This is cycling. It will get cleared up before anyone hears about it."

"This is no longer cycling. It's drama."

"True, but I'm sure you'll be fine. If the news had spread, your parents would have heard it and called you."

"My parents don't watch the news. They'll call when it's in the paper tomorrow."

"It's not going to be in the paper."

"It's my parents," I said as I answered my phone.

"Did you make Danny break a bridge so that you could win a race?" asked Mom.

"Of course not, Mom, and for the record, I don't 'make' Danny do anything. He's an adult."

"Barbara just called me and told me she saw you on the news and that you had some guy break a drawbridge so you could win a race."

"Well, that's not what happened. First, the guy wasn't Danny, it was some psycho I went on one date with. Second, I didn't ask him to do it; he's like John Hinckley, Jr."

"Were you arrested?" Mom asked.

"No, just questioned."

"Jesus, Jenna." Dad chimed in.

"Hey, sorry. I gotta go. The other line is ringing."

"Hi, Jenna, it's Kimberly."

"Hey, how are things at the office?" I responded dryly.

"Dude, you are all over the news. Someone at work is going to see this."

"Thanks, my other line is ringing. I have to go." I turned my phone off.

"Well, bridge rigging has officially hit the news," I said to Danny. "It's only a matter of time before a reporter discovers that I'm on maternity leave and starts wondering where my kid went."

"Yeah, you are definitely not Ferris Bueller. Remember the good 'ol days, yesterday that is, when you were only worried about your broken heart, losing a race and being hated for getting an unfair advantage? Now you're practically a felon."

As we pulled up to the host family's house, we could see at least twenty news vans. Twenty more than would normally cover a women's cycling race.

"Where's big sunglasses when you need them?" I asked.

I got out and waved like I was on the red carpet and the questions started coming.

"Jenna, is Quinton your boyfriend?" "Did you tell Quinton to rig the bridge?" "Where's your baby?" "There's no record of you giving birth, why is that?" "Why did you give up the race lead?" "Are you disqualified?"

"Listen," I said, trying to be heard above the din. "This is all a big misunderstanding, I didn't do anything unsportsmanlike. I'll explain the rest later. I need to get some sleep. I have a race tomorrow."

I thought about telling the entire story, but I didn't want to admit to the pregnancy part on the remote chance I could still get out of this without losing my job, getting disbarred and being arrested for fraud.

As I walked into the host house for the evening, the woman of the house glared at me disapprovingly, before smiling for the cameras. Clearly she considered this her fifteen minutes of fame. Once I was inside, the swarm of reporters was replaced by my teammates, who had a cold beer for me. I'd told each of them the story of my date with Quinton, just because it was funny. They put two and two together and knew I was innocent. I chugged the beer, thanked them, and went to the basement, my sleeping quarters for the evening. Alyssa was there.

She was reading a magazine with Sonny curled up next to her.

Lucky me, we were roommates again. "Stop trying to steal my dog," I said.

"From the lady who tried to steal the race."

"Come on," I said. "You know I didn't do that."

"Figured," Alyssa responded. "Was it the alcoholic that took you to IHOP?"

"Yes. I didn't even know there was a bridge on the course," I said as I grabbed Sonny.

"I believe you," Alyssa said, "but are you ever fucked."

"Put your wall back up," I said, "before you ruin my day even more by making me stare at the ceiling wondering if you're telling me this because you feel sorry for me or because you might like me."

Alyssa leaned in and kissed me. I was startled and confused but instead of asking questions, I decided to get laid now and ask later.

Afterwards, I said, "Alyssa, how do you sprint?"

She laughed and said, "Now that's some hot pillow talk."

"Sorry. It's just that if I'm allowed to race tomorrow, all eyes will be on me, the girl who threw her life away to race her bike. And because it ends in a tight circuit, I'll place last in the field sprint after struggling off the back of the pack on every corner."

"You'll be fine," Alyssa assured me.

"No, I'll suck, as always. My first goal is to not come in last place. My second goal is to place in the top three. If I do that, I'll get bonus seconds and place third overall."

"Yeah, but that's not going to happen," Alyssa said, a bit too frankly. "You won't even be in the draft, let alone the front of the pack, let alone the lead."

"I know," I said, now hoping to place in the top three just to rub it in Alyssa's face. I asked again, "Come on Alyssa, how do you sprint?"

"By not being a pussy," she responded.

"Great, thanks. How do you not be a pussy?"

"Just stop thinking," she said. "If I see an opening, I go through it. When you see an opening, you tap your brakes. Stop doing that."

"Okay, don't tap my brakes while sprinting," I repeated. "That makes sense. What else?"

"You're the smart lawyer, you'll figure it out someday," she said.

"I won't, I'm like a gifted idiot. Besides, I don't want to figure it out someday, I want to figure it out tomorrow."

"Just stay on my wheel tomorrow and you'll be fine," she said.

"I've been trying to stay on your wheel for three weeks. It hasn't worked."

"That's because you're a pussy. Remember rule number one, don't be a pussy."

"Right. I'm pretty sure I'll be a world class sprinter tomorrow. Thanks."

"No problem," Alyssa said, as she fell asleep.

I spent the night cuddling between Sonny and Alyssa, trying to visualize sprinting instead of focusing on reading Alyssa's mind, or fearing my future disqualification, disbarment and incarceration.

* * *

The next day, *The Olympian*, the local newspaper in Olympia, Washington, cleared up any doubts I had about the whole truth and nothing but the truth coming out. A blurb on the bottom of the front page read, "Tour de West Wraps Up Today: Complete Coverage in Section B3, Including a Report on Race Saboteur, Jenna Rosen." I turned to the article.

Jenna Rosen, the Tampa lawyer-turned-cyclist, overcame a seven minute time deficit in the Tour de West several days ago by embarking on a daring solo breakaway against the entire field of cyclists in the 104-mile Stage 17. The main pack of riders, the peloton, *was on pace to cross the finish line in Tillamook, Oregon, approximately two to four minutes after Rosen, but were delayed nine minutes by a broken drawbridge.*

An investigation by police and race officials quickly revealed the bridge was intentionally sabotaged by Rosen's boyfriend, Quinton Smith of Tampa, who is now in custody. Reached by phone last night, Quinton's mother, Sarah Smith, also of Tampa, said, "If Quinton did it, it's because she [Rosen] told him to. He would do anything for her." Rosen's boss, David Greene of the Tampa law firm of Johnson Smith Jones Greene Taylor LLP, was also reached for comment: "I don't know anything about Jenna and her boyfriend rigging a bridge, but he may be the father of her kid."

No details about Rosen's alleged child were immediately available, though it has been confirmed that Rosen is currently on maternity leave from her law office. However, there appears to be no evidence that she ever gave birth.

Rosen is currently in fourth place overall in the Tour de West after voluntarily gifting back the time she gained as a result of the bridge incident. She has not yet commented on the situation.

Today's final stage starts at ten-thirty a.m. in Olympia and travels 60 miles into Seattle, where riders will complete fifteen laps of a technical two-mile course around Seattle.

I read the article twice and immediately decided it would not make my scrap book. I checked voice mails and found my mailbox completely full. I had no interest in listening to any of the messages and tried instead to distract myself with *Parade* magazine. I made it to "Ask Marilyn" when two race officials approached the host house and asked to speak with me. One was the older official from the day before and the other was young and fit, clearly a racer. They were both wearing the light blue polo T-shirts from USA Cycling. I brought my food with me and stepped outside. I wanted to eat as much as I could before the ninety-mile race.

The race officials informed me that I had been disqualified and that I would not be permitted to start the last stage.

"For what?" I replied.

"You're kidding, right?" the young official responded.

"No, I'm dead serious," I said. "I didn't rig a bridge or tell anyone else to. Besides, after it was rigged, I tried to avoid taking the Yellow Jersey and protested taking the lead. Then, I gave back the time I didn't rightfully gain."

"We've confirmed that you weren't involved in the bridge incident. That's not why we're disqualifying you. You took a maternity leave to race but have no baby. That's extremely suspect."

"That has nothing to do with this race," I insisted passionately.

"It just doesn't seem right to let you race."

"I didn't kill a baby, and I'm in fourth place. I'm not exactly deciding the outcome but I'm close enough to make it a heartbreaker. If it turns out later that I'm a baby killer and bridge rigger, you can disqualify me and take back my prize money. If you disqualify me now and I turn out to be innocent, I have no recourse."

"Are you a baby killer?"

"No. I know Casey Anthony gave Florida moms a bad name, but I'm not a baby killer and I'm not even a mother. I'm a frustrated lawyer who needed to find a way to race her bike."

"How are you on maternity leave?" They still hadn't put two and two together, yet.

"I faked a pregnancy so that I could compete in this race."

"That's fraud, which is unsportsmanlike. You're not racing," the official said firmly.

"That's a very broad reading of the 'unsportsmanlike' clause," I argued, referring to the cycling rule book that I'd never actually read. "Don't you think my time in jail will be punishment enough for my unsportsmanlike conduct?"

"That's completely unrelated to this."

"My point exactly," I said.

"You're not racing."

Hmm. Do I go with guilt and gentle persuasion, or threats? I started with the former.

"Come on, my boss is a total douche bag and I work for insurance companies, it's not like I made a mom and pop shop fund this trip. I really love cycling and my one wish before I become disbarred, arrested, and destitute is to finish this race."

"I'm sorry. The decision is final," the shorter official said.

I had no choice but to escalate to threats. "I'll sue."

"Sue who?"

"You, USA Cycling, the race promoters."

"For what?"

I looked him in the eye and started spouting off nonsense, mostly in Latin, "*Forum non convenienes, demurer, ipso facto, mandamus, certiorari, quantum meruit, in limine, lis pendens, res ipsa loquitur, and sua sponte.*"

"What the hell is that?"

"You'll find out," I said in my most threatening voice.

The officials looked at each other in confusion, then responded in unison, "Fine, you can race."

"Great, see you out there," I said.

I finished eating and got ready. We had a team meeting before the race. I was only four seconds out of third place, so standing on the overall podium was technically possible if anyone in positions one through three crashed out, or if I placed in the top three today and picked up bonus seconds. I didn't want option one and option two was highly unlikely unless I was in a breakaway, which never happens on the last stage, since all the big teams want to win and won't let anyone get away. Because of my abysmal sprinting, the team agreed it would work for Brenda and Alyssa today unless I got into a break, in which case the team would block for me by setting a tempo slower than my speed, but fast enough so that no one would try to attack.

* * *

As I approached the start, I heard someone call out, "Pearl." No one calls me by my middle name except my dad and it sounded a lot like him. I turned around to see my parents standing there.

"Did you come to see me race?" I asked in disbelief.

"No, we came to bail you out of jail." Their expressions definitely looked more like concerned parents instead of proud supporters. I gave them both a hug.

"You may still have your chance, but I have to go now," I said.

"Here, Jenna, wear this," said Dad.

"What the hell is that?" I asked.

"It's a specially designed cycling mask. It's fiberglass and fits the contours of your face and under your helmet. There's a space for sunglasses, too."

"How did you get the contours of my face?" I asked as I held the mask up to my face, amazed at how well it fit.

"Your undertaker brother made a mold with the same material he uses to reconstruct accident victim's faces," Mom said proudly.

I smirked that they were proud of their kid molding dead people's faces but concerned about their athlete. Then I looked at the mask which was beyond goofy. "What's with the big nose and mouth?" I asked.

"It's a built-in airbag and trip wire system," explained Dad proudly. "If you face-plant, the second the long nose touches the pavement the mini airbag goes off and your face is saved."

"You're kidding, right?"

"No, I also have this Hannibal Lecter model you could wear if you prefer," said Dad, holding up an equally ridiculous looking contraption.

"I'm not wearing a mask," I insisted.

"Please," Dad implored, sounding both concerned and non-negotiable. "I even have a cutout for your peripheral vision."

"Is that what that is?" I asked. "I thought it was a hole for what's left of my dignity to seep out during the race."

"Wear the mask for your father, Jenna." Mom said sternly. "He's been buying off Tampa judges for the last twenty-four hours and I think he has more work ahead to keep you out of jail back there."

"Sweet," I said, "I can't believe I've been worrying. I forgot how corrupt Tampa is."

"The mask," Dad said.

"Fine, I'll wear the mask. It will be a good disguise from the media."

"One more thing, Jenna," said Dad. "Can you race on the sidewalk? The street makes us very nervous."

I couldn't tell if he was making a joke or really thought this was a safe alternative. "That's not going to happen," I said. "But don't worry, the course is cut off to traffic."

The mask fit right under my helmet and was lightweight and ventilated. I rode to the start, excited by the prospect of racing my bike after the last twenty-four hours of hell. Obviously, my number one goal for the race was to place on the podium on today's stage, securing a third place overall finish. A not-too-distant secondary goal was to not place last. My third goal was to avoid testing out the airbag-facemask in front of my parents.

After taking it easy for the first sixty miles, mimicking the ceremonial ride into Paris of the Tour de France, the race started in earnest as we entered the city limits of Seattle. The course through Seattle was a two-mile circuit but had tight corners like a criterium. I instantly moved into last place, barely hanging on, as soon as the circuit began. The race became strung out in a line almost a quarter-mile long, consisting of the ninety-two women that were still in the race after three long weeks and 1,855 miles. Every few minutes, the race slowed down a fraction when one breakaway was caught and the next attempted to get away. Normally, I'd use these moments to take my hand off the bars and get a drink, or just to breathe, but today I kept going. I made up twenty spots in two city blocks before the pace stepped up again. I didn't want to lose the position, so I forced myself to move my hands. Normally, I ride with my hands hovering over the brakes and tap them frequently. In an effort to avoid touching them, I removed my fingers from their vicinity. It was scary, but I held my place through the corner, then another corner. The next time the pace slowed, I accelerated another fifteen spots, putting me within the first one-third of the pack. For the first time in a professional race, I could actually see the front of the *peloton* in a criterium.

With one two-mile lap remaining, I was still positioned in the front third. Now the jockeying for position began in earnest. A rider came up on my left as we entered a right hand turn and tried to pinch me into the corner. Instead of touching my brakes, I stuck my elbow out and held her at elbow length; a perfectly legal move in cycling I had always been afraid to try at high speed because if it doesn't work, you're pinched in the corner. It worked. On the next turn, I intentionally took the inside line with my elbow out to deter anyone from getting near me. I made up three spots in the corner instead of losing ten.

Instead of concentrating on my fear, I fixated on the lyrics to that song "Move Bitch", by Ludacris. I was practically singing aloud. *Move Bitch, Get Out the Way, Get Out the Way Bitch, Get Out the Way*. It worked beautifully. All I knew was the chorus, but that's the inspiring part. By the time we rounded the last corner, I sat in sixth position. Entering the final straightaway, I saw Brenda jump on my right. Instead of checking behind me to see if anyone was on her wheel, which there surely was,

I pounced, knowing that Brenda always found a way through the pack. I positioned my bike one inch behind Brenda's rear wheel and after sitting in her draft for three seconds, accelerated up the left hand side of the pack through a very narrow opening, crossing the finish line third on the stage, thus securing third place overall for the Tour de West.

I screamed and raised my arms in triumph. I made such a spectacle of myself that the winner of the stage turned around to inform me that she and second place both beat me by over a wheel's length, a sizable margin in cycling.

"Good for you," I said as I continued with my victory lap, hands in the air, screaming, "Yo, Adriane! I did it!" I had no idea why I was imitating *Rocky*, and neither did the winner, but there I was. The winner looked very confused. I started to explain, since she was from one of the European teams, but instead yelled directly to her, "Yo, Adriane! I did it!" Whereupon she punched me square in the face. I didn't feel a thing other than the heat from the two small airbags in the mask. I laughed. Nothing could keep me down. The whole team, including Brenda and Alyssa, plus Erica and Danny, were all hugging me.

* * *

I stood on the third step of the podium for the award ceremony. It took all of my self-control not to cry like Miss America as I held up my flowers. Despite all of the adversity, I'd done it. I'd gotten out of my office, raced as a pro, learned how to sprint and kicked ass at the biggest women's cycling race in history. From the podium, I could see my parents cheering for me. As I walked over to them after the ceremony, I passed Alyssa. "Good job," she said. She was smiling with no indication that she was pissed at being beaten by the climber.

"That was pretty impressive," Dad said. "And I mean both getting third place and not dying."

"It really was," Mom said, as they both hugged me.

"Now, back to reality," Dad said, content that the reverie had gone on long enough. "You're fucked."

"Thanks for the buzz kill Dad. Let's talk about it later. I want to enjoy this moment a bit longer."

Mom hugged me again, this time knocking into my ribs. "Oh my God, you're so thin," she said.

I turned away so she couldn't see my hollowed out cheekbones. "That's what happens when you race your bike over a hundred miles a day for three weeks. Don't worry, I'll gain it back." I said this with the utmost sincerity so she wouldn't try to commit me to an eating disorder clinic. As a Jewish mother and guidance counselor, she had a tendency to be hyper suspicious of anorexia.

"How long are you going to be out west?" I asked my parents, mostly to change the topic.

"As long as our baby needs us," my mom said, half seriously.

"Great, hang around for the next sixty years or so because I am a fuck-up."

"No arguments here," Dad said, with a smile. "How long are you staying out here?"

"I'm planning to start driving back with Danny and Sonny tomorrow."

"Do you want to get dinner tonight?" Dad asked.

"Yes, but much later. I need to collect my prize money now," then added, "for third today and third overall."

My parents responded with a deer-in-headlights look. They knew by my tone that congratulations were in order, but they had no idea what I was talking about. I could see the wheels spinning and knew they were thinking, How did she get third place twice" I let it go. "I also need to go back to the host house and pack up. I'll call you later."

When I got back to the house, Alyssa was packing. She was wearing a Sunshine Cycling shirt, jeans and flip flops, the exact outfit I was wearing, but somehow it looked dressier on her. "Congratulations, speedy," she said.

"Thanks. So, what are you going to do now?"

"Fly back to Georgia," she replied.

"Want a ride? You can go with Danny and me."

"That's okay," she said, closing the hard case containing her bicycle. She hugged me and gave me a kiss on the cheek, then began walking away.

I stared at her, debating whether to let it go or confront her. I took a deep breath so that I could get a last whiff of her lotion or shampoo or whatever made her smell so good, and decided to let her go. But once she got near the door, I panicked. I barely knew her but I was interested in her, a rarity for me. "What the hell is with your wall?" I blurted out. "I am killing myself trying to figure you out."

"I don't know. The wall comes and goes. I'm fickle, what can I say."

"What are you looking for?" I asked incredulously. "I'm hot, smart, a cyclist, funny, well-employed, or at least I was well-employed, I treat you well and I cut my nails off."

Alyssa continued her flippancy. "You're right. I'm sorry. I don't really know what I'm looking for."

I knew I should let it go, but I couldn't. I was starting to seriously dislike her but was worried I'd never meet another girl that was hot and into women even if they existed somewhere in the universe in droves. Or, even if I did, that I wouldn't know since I had such terrible gaydar. I needed to go all out even if she was borderline bipolar. "You were looking for that last week and yesterday," I said. "Why not today?"

"I don't know," Alyssa said, her tone suddenly serious. "Haven't you ever just changed your mind?"

"Yes, but always for a reason," I said. "What about now? It's been a few minutes, are you into me now?"

Alyssa laughed. "I like you a lot Jenna. I need to figure things out. I'll call you."

Alyssa started to walk off. As I stared at her perfect ass in her jeans I lost any shred of my remaining dignity and asked, "Well you need a ride to the airport, don't you?" As the words came out of my mouth my self-loathing spiked, but I thought that if we could just hang out a little more, she'd like me again. Then I could figure whether I really wanted to be with her or not.

"That's okay, thanks," Alyssa said.

I sat there staring at the door. My trance was interrupted by Danny, who walked up to me, saw my expression and asked seriously, "What just happened?"

"I just got nicely dumped again. No biggie."

"When did you get back together?" Danny asked.

"Last night. You just missed me making a complete ass of myself, begging her to like me. I don't recognize myself. I've always hated people that breakup and get back together. One shot, that's it. I'm pathetically obsessed with a person I've known for less than a month and she's a total head case. I want her to like me even though I kind of hate her and want nothing but the worst for her. What's my problem?"

"Yeah, I've been meaning to tell you you're losing it. Were you crying on the podium?" Danny asked.

"A drop or so. What's happening to me?"

"You've had three weeks of highs and lows and passion and lots of other crap. You'll be your normal jaded self once you return to your life of sitting in your office watching life pass you by."

"Glad to hear there's a light at the end of the tunnel. Actually, as pathetic as that life was, at least I wasn't chasing pathetically after people who weren't the least bit into me. Maybe I should just go sit in an office until I die so I can die with dignity."

"First, being a lawyer isn't pathetic and second, aren't you forgetting that you'll probably never practice law again?"

"Whatever. I can't say I'll miss it. I'll just miss the paycheck."

"So what's your plan?" Danny asked.

"I guess we'll pack up and leave tomorrow," I responded.

"No," Danny said, "for your life."

"Other than race my bike and get back together with a psycho who doesn't like me, I don't know. I'm only twenty-eight. I didn't think this crisis would happen to me for at least another ten years."

"What can I say?" Danny said. "You're a prodigy."

"Thanks. I'm going out with my parents for dinner tonight. Want to come?"

"That's okay, they're going to give you some tough love and I don't think I can watch my cynical lawyer friend cry twice in one day."

"I think I'll hold it together," I said. "See you tomorrow. I'll complain the whole way home and bitch about everyone, just like old times."

"That sounds great," Danny said sarcastically. "In the meantime, relax. Seriously, you always come out smelling like a rose and this will be no different."

"Thanks," I said, grateful for Danny's undying faith in my cynicism and resiliency. "And thanks for coming and everything else. I couldn't have done it without you."

"I wouldn't have missed it. You really were terrific," he said.

* * *

My parents took me to a restaurant with a white tablecloth, the first one of its kind I'd been to in over three months other than my date with Alyssa. We talked about everything except jail, disbarment, unemployment, and cycling. We became quite drunk and closed the place down at one a.m. When Dad kissed me goodbye, he told me to call him as soon as I returned to Tampa. I left knowing that my next meeting with him would not be quite as pleasant.

* * *

The next day, Danny and I began our long drive back. We made it halfway through Texas on the first day. I probably drove twenty minutes to Danny's ten hours. I was half-asleep when Danny turned up the radio.

"I didn't know you liked Billy Joel," I said.

"I like this song, it reminds me of you," he responded.

"She's Always a Woman To Me" was on the radio. "That's mean," I pointed out.

"Why?"

"Are you saying you still think I'm a woman even though I'm a lesbian?"

"No, it's always reminded me of you," Danny responded.

"That's still mean. I'm not a fan of this comparison."

"Why? The girl in the song sounds awesome."

I listened to the lyrics, thinking I might be overreacting.

A minute later I said, "Nope, not a fan of this comparison. I don't steal, cut, give up and unfortunately, I rarely change my mind, even when I should. Should I go on?"

"No offense," he said. "I meant it in a good way. It's like how you're mean to everyone but me."

"You're digging a hole, dude. I'm gregarious and charming to everyone, including you."

"You better hope this song is you," Danny said. "Unfortunately, I think you can be convicted, regardless of your degree."

I tried not to think about that and started belting out the lyrics instead.

CHAPTER EIGHTEEN

Danny and I arrived home the following Wednesday after the long cross-country trip. The following morning, I went to work as if nothing had happened. I got to the office early and turned on my light. Everything was exactly as I had left it. I turned on my computer to start reading the 100 emails a day that had accumulated over the past ninety days or so. But, my password didn't work. Not a good sign.

I walked over to Kimberly's office.

Kimberly stared up at me and laughed. "Wow, you have some balls showing up here. Big brass ones."

"No news is good news, right?" I replied.

"I doubt that's the case in this scenario," she said. "How was your trip?"

"Great," I replied. "What have you been up to?"

"Hey Jenna, can we do lunch sometime, away from the office? I'd love to catch up but you're a bit of a pariah right now and I don't want to be guilty by association."

"No problem. I should go start packing my office anyway."

I walked back to my office and realized there was little in there I wanted. I was quite sure I was about to be disbarred and that I would never work in a professional environment again. Nevertheless, I took all of my diplomas and certificates with me on my way out. I could have that party I dreamed of and serve chips and dip on them.

On my way to the parking garage, I passed one of the partners and a few secretaries. They nodded politely. I was suddenly nervous that the news of my return would spread before I made it to my car. I picked up the pace. I could see the hiring partner, Jerry Jacobson, out of the corner of my eye, so I picked up the pace even more. Once I got to my car I threw my diplomas in the back and started backing up. I heard a knock on my window.

"Got a second Jenna?" Jerry said. He was leaning in my window and chomping on gum that I could tell was peppermint. He was a large man, both tall and wide, with white hair and a full white beard and he looked uncomfortable trying to lean in my window.

"Sure," I replied innocently. "What's going on?"

"You're fired," he said.

"Anything else?" I replied, as though he asked me to pick up eggs and I thought he might want milk or bananas as well.

"You should probably know that it's been recommended that you be disbarred, and that there's a warrant out for your arrest."

"Anything else?" I said again.

He held out his fingers and counted. "Fired, disbarment, warrant. That's pretty much it."

"Thanks, Jerry."

I pulled out of the parking lot and did the mature thing; I called Dad. I gave him a quick recap.

"Are you nuts going in there? Of course you're fired. I didn't realize you were back in town. I told you to call me. You need to go with your lawyer to the police station right now. I'll meet you there."

I had no idea I even had a lawyer, let alone know who he was. Still, I didn't ask questions and just started driving. I walked into the station, but didn't know what to do. I went up to the front desk with my hands up. "I'm surrendering. Do I need to sign in or something?"

The desk deputy asked my name. I figured the next step would be my arrest or fingerprinting, but instead, I went into a room where my dad sat with three other people: my attorney, Buddy Melendez; the state prosecutor, and Hymie Goldstein, a family friend. I had met Hymie a handful of times in my life. He was a five foot two Jewish television salesman who somehow became the godfather of Tampa. His involvement led me to believe I would be the recipient of a sweet under-the-table deal.

The meeting started and I sat there with my heart racing, ready to piss my pants. However, no one addressed me. The good-ole-boy network just discussed the terms of my future without acknowledging my existence. For once, I did not play the feminist card. There were a lot of references to "what we had discussed," so it was clear to me this was not the first meeting about the fate of Jenna Rosen. Every few minutes, Hymie farted. He was an old man, and all of us pretended not to notice, but after a few minutes, I was less concerned with my future and more concerned with not offending Hymie by laughing while he tried to help me. I looked around the room and could tell everyone else was trying not to laugh, as well.

After an hour of holding in my laughter, the prosecutor stepped out of the room. While my dad and Buddy talked, Hymie approached me. He gave me a hug, and farted. This time I couldn't help it. The laughter I'd been holding in exploded, the type of laughter where your body shakes, but no noise comes out. I hoped Hymie didn't notice. I was on the verge of collapse when Hymie opened his hand and said, "Look, it's a fart bag."

He held out a tiny tube in the palm of his hand and squeezed it. I looked at him incredulously. "You've been fake farting every five minutes for the last hour?"

"Yes, I've been doing it all week, no one ever says anything. I love watching people pretend not to notice. Here take one," he said and handed me a small box. "I just bought a thousand of these things. They're going to be huge."

How in the world had this guy achieved widespread respect and financial success, I wondered. "Sounds like a great investment. So, what else is new?"

"Nothing much. I heard you had a great race. I wish I'd seen you out there."

"Thanks," I said. Everyone says that and doesn't mean it, but I believed Hymie because I knew he was enough of a sports fanatic that he would actually watch cycling, and probably bet on it, regardless of whether he understood the rules.

Dad and Buddy stopped talking and turned to me. "Here's the deal," said Buddy. "The insurance company agreed not to press charges as long as you pay restitution. That is, return all of the insurance proceeds you received over the past three months, plus interest. You also have to pay a five hundred dollar fine and complete one hundred hours of community service hours. Once that's all done, the case will be dismissed. No jail, no probation."

"How much money is all of that?" I asked.

"Twenty grand or so," the lawyer said. "It probably didn't seem like much when you got it, but you earned a lot on maternity leave."

My eyes widened in shock. It was then that I noticed Buddy's tailor-made three-piece suit. I knew I could tack another five grand in attorney fees. Twenty-five thousand bucks. Fuck. Still, I knew it was a sweet deal for felony fraud.

I said goodbye to Hymie and Buddy, then Dad and I went to lunch.

"I'll pick up lunch if you loan me twenty-five grand," I said to Dad. It was a bad joke, especially since it was a given that he would pick up the twenty-five thousand dollar tab. After all, I'm Daddy's little JAP, and I'm broke and facing jail.

"You think this is funny?" Dad replied, clenching his jaw just enough to realize that I pissed him off in addition to disappointing him.

"No. I'm really sorry." And I was. I was sorry and felt guilty about both the $25,000 hit my dad was going to take for me, and the knowledge that I wouldn't change a single thing now that I knew I'd be getting off scot-free. Dad had worked hard for his money and it would be a great learning experience for me to go to jail and come out twenty-five thousand dollars in debt. That would be the sort of learning experience that would leave me with some regrets.

I looked at the menu, hating myself a little for the first time in my life. I had never been ashamed of my self-centered narcissism, choosing instead to focus on what a strong and independent woman I was. I took pride in outsmarting my office and the system to chase the dream. Looking back, I could see I was only bold enough to go for it because I had a larger safety net than anyone deserved.

As I had every time I'd doubted myself over the past three weeks, I thought, Maybe this is why Alyssa doesn't like me. I'm almost thirty years old, I should tell my Dad "Thanks, but no thanks" and deal with the consequences of my actions. Then again, there was no way I was turning down twenty-five thousand dollars and a get-out-of-jail-free card. There was also no way my dad would let me go to jail, so the offer would just sound insincere.

"Cheer up," Dad said. "This is good news for you."

"I'm sorry," I said. Then said it again.

Then I started crying. At first it was just a lump in my throat and teary eyes. Then, I couldn't stop. I even felt guilty for crying because I knew it would make my Dad take pity on me and I didn't want him to feel sorry for me on top of having to pay a twenty-five thousand dumbass-kid tax. I wanted to tell him that I'd handle the situation on my own, and I actually wanted to handle it on my own, but really, I was screwed without him. Over the past few days, I had hoped that a rich cycling sponsor who admired the balls it took for me to risk everything and go for it would bail me out of the whole situation and pay whatever was owed. It should have been a no-brainer that family is more reliable than cycling, but I put so much more into cycling than family, it shocked me. I felt my shirt get wet and realized I was crying and snotting all over myself.

Dad moved his chair over and hugged me. We sat there like that for a while, ignoring our food.

* * *

Unfortunately, Hymie Goldstein didn't have any pull with the Florida Bar or the office of Johnson Smith. I didn't contest my disbarment in order to avoid a public proceeding regarding my "crime of moral turpitude." Likewise, I let the Johnson Smith lawyer gig go without a fight.

With no job prospects on the horizon that didn't involve wearing a name tag, I rented out my adorable house in South Tampa and Sonny and I moved back in with my parents. My fall from grace was complete. I lived there for three days before my luck ran out and I ran into my new neighbor, David Greene. He drove by as I was walking Sonny and stopped to talk.

"Hi, David. Sorry about the whole fake-baby-slash-fraudulently-sneaking-away-from-my-job thing."

"No problem. Guess what?" David said without giving me a chance to guess. "I settled that Heathcliff case of yours for eight hundred and fifty thousand dollars."

"Wasn't that worth five million?" I asked, trying to make David take the smug look off his face.

"That was what the insurance company paid, but our recoverable damages were much less. It took some finesse to settle. Our client and the insured didn't even want to be in the same room as each other, but I got everyone to come to dinner and we settled the case without the court, mediators or arbitrators. Everyone involved was just in awe that I brokered a settlement."

Holy shit, I thought. I faked a pregnancy, in part to avoid him, and all he wanted to talk about was my former case list. It hardly seemed possible but David Greene was even more self-centered than me. "Steak and wine probably works better than all that stuff anyway," I said.

"Wine nothing. I told the waiter, if it ain't on fire, we don't want it."

This didn't make much sense, but I assumed David, who didn't drink other than wine for Shabbat, thought that alcohol was only real if you could set it on fire.

"What were you drinking?" I asked, knowing it was either water or Diet Coke.

"Water. It was a work function and I was driving."

"Good for you, David."

"You know," David said, "if you want I can pull some strings and get you a job. You're no longer an attorney, but I could use another paralegal. You could work with Sarah."

I pictured myself doing the same crappy work, but for less money in a cubicle next to Sarah Smith instead of in my office, and laughed out loud for the first time since Hymie fake-farted a week ago.

"I'm good," I said, "thanks."

"Suit yourself," David said and drove off.

* * *

I resumed training with Danny.

"So," he said, "how's living with the parents?"

"Jason, too," I said. "Actually, it's delightful. I get free room and board, food, utilities, and cable with the good channels. My parents work all day and Jason usually goes to school. My only job is emptying the dishwasher and setting the table. I can't believe I ever moved out."

"You've been there a week, let me know how you feel in a month."

"I made it eighteen years straight before, and that's when there were rules. I think I'm staying until they kick me out."

"That's going to hurt your social life."

"What social life? I don't think I'm ever going to have a date again. I have no idea where to meet lesbians. I went to a gay bar and there were about ninety gay men and only four women, all of them post-menopausal and partnered."

"So, you're fully committed to this lesbian thing?"

"Yup. No doubt in my mind. Sorry."

"What do I care?" Danny said. "Either way, you won't be fucking me. Just choose what makes you happy."

"When have I ever done anything that doesn't make me happy?" I asked rhetorically.

"Good point," said Danny. "I think you should at least try guys again. I don't think you ever dated our best representatives."

"Like Alyssa was such a great representative of women," I pointed out.

"Actually," Danny said, "she's contrary, has a low libido, and gives you mixed signals. I think she's par for the course."

"Whatever. I'd like to meet a lesbian I'm attracted to other than Alyssa."

"Have you talked to her at all?" Danny asked.

"No, just email. Every time I send her an email I check my inbox for a response at thirty second intervals until she replies. Often days later. Then I get as giddy as a schoolgirl, email her back and start the process over again. I really hate myself when I do that."

"You should. That's pathetic," Danny said. "Do your parents know you're a lesbian?"

I shook my head and said, "No, I'm not trying to kill them."

"Why?" he said. "What would they do if they knew?"

"Nothing. They'd tell me they still love me and that they just want me to be happy, but they'd be disappointed. They want the best for me and to them, that's normalcy. Besides, they're still reeling from my disbarment, unemployment, near incarceration and the fact that I'm approaching thirty and living in their house. I feel like I should pop out a grandkid just to make them happy. I think I'll hold off telling them I'm a lesbian."

"I think they'd handle it just fine," Danny said.

"I know. I'll tell them I'm gay when I want to introduce them to a girlfriend," I said. "I'm not going to mention it in the abstract. Actually, at this point, I don't think they'd care if I dated a woman so long as she's rich. After the twenty-five grand in legal fees my Dad just shelled out, he'd hand me off to a donkey if it would get me off his payroll."

"Speaking of that, do you plan on getting a job any time soon?"

"I'm thinking about being a teacher."

Danny started laughing. "Why the hell would you want to teach?"

"I don't *want* to teach. I want insurance and my summers off to race. I think teaching is my only option."

"What would you teach?" Danny asked.

"Hopefully, high school," I said. "Those younger kids are like petri dishes full of germs and I can't train if I'm sick all the time."

"What about teaching college?"

"Ha ha," I responded in monotone. "I doubt many universities want a disbarred lawyer without a PhD."

"True. So if you have your summer off, do you have any leads for teams next season?"

"Quite a few actually," I said, "but the most I'll get is an annual salary of fifteen thousand with mediocre insurance, plus a bike, kit, and travel. I need a job so I can get my own place."

"I thought you wanted to stay with your parents forever," Danny reminded me.

"I do, but it's embarrassing, for them and for me. Plus, you're right, if I ever date anyone, living with the parents will be a problem. I need to get out."

"Sounds like a plan. Will the school system hire you?"

"They should. I have a degree, a pulse and no criminal record as long as I finish my goddamn community service. Speaking of which, want to go pick up garbage with me for eight hours tomorrow? It will be fun."

"I'll pass. Go easy on the goddamns. I don't think you can curse in front of the kids. Can you handle that?"

"Fuck if I know."

EPILOGUE

I lucked out and got a job as a substitute teacher at a school near me. If I performed well, I would get a job as a full-time teacher there whenever a position opened, and I could avoid faxing my resume all over town. My first teaching gig was a fourth grade math class. They were learning the metric system. Evidently schools were still telling kids that America was converting to the metric system. I told them to memorize it for the test then forget it, unless they wanted to race their bikes in Europe, in which case learning kilograms and kilometers could be helpful. The kids seemed to like that. This job could work out for me, I thought.

At lunch hour, I went to the teacher's lounge. An athletic-looking woman in Adidas shorts, a tank top and a cute pixie haircut was seated at a table. The P.E. teacher, obviously. She had to be gay. I sat down next to her. Maybe this wouldn't be so hard after all.

I introduced myself and after we talked for a bit, she got up to leave. I wasn't overwhelmed by her, but she was cute enough. I figured that even if I didn't date her, I could probably meet other lesbians through her so I asked her if she wanted to get a drink sometime. "Jesus Christ, I'm not fucking gay," she responded. That attracted a bit of attention. I waved at everyone and continued eating my sandwich. My face felt hot and I knew it looked like I just got a horrible sunburn.

When I finally had the nerve to look up again, a sexy woman in black slacks and a crisp white blouse was in front of my table. "I'm the resident lesbian around here," she whispered, almost touching my ear. She was about five-nine, had a great rack, short blond curly hair and a beautiful ass. The term "brick house" came to mind.

"What do you teach?" I asked, already liking her so much more than the P.E. teacher.

"I'm the vice principal."

"Nice. I need a job," I said, then added, "I'm Jenna."

"Monroe."

"Were your parents fans of Marilyn, James, or the Doctrine?"

"Marilyn," she said, smiling.

We talked for a bit. Like Andy, the high school teacher my mom had set me up with a year earlier, Monroe was a non-cyclist, a teacher, and lived in St. Petersburg instead of Tampa. Unlike how I felt about Andy, I didn't give a shit. Within ten minutes Alyssa was a distant memory. The bell rang, and as I was getting up Monroe said, "Hey, I have to go, but do you want to grab a drink some time?"

"I sure would," I responded.

* * *

Two years later, Danny, Monroe and I were riding towards St. Petersburg after work. Monroe didn't wear her cycling gloves in spite of the heat because she wanted to show off her new ring. Danny didn't notice, though he did notice that I'd cleaned her drivetrain. Cyclists are selectively observant. Finally, Monroe couldn't take it anymore and flashed her bling in Danny's face.

"Is that an engagement ring?" he asked.

"Yes," we said in unison.

"How do you decide who proposes?"

"You're so original. My parents asked me the same question," I replied, then added, "The only thing more disturbing to my parents than the fact that I'm a lesbian is the idea that I'm the butch one in the relationship, which they deduced by the fact that I proposed."

"Your parents aren't really upset are they?" Danny asked.

"Not really. They love Monroe and are really supportive. But I'm sure that deep down, they hope we both meet great guys someday and laugh about this engagement on a double date."

"So how did you decide who proposed, seriously?" Danny asked.

"It was easy," I said. "Only one of us gives a shit about the ring. Monroe wanted one, so she got one. Me, on the other hand, who doesn't care for rings, is the one that shelled out a ton of money."

"You are getting a ring," Monroe chimed in from behind. She was drafting, but listening to the conversation.

"Can I get an engagement bike instead?" I asked.

"No," she responded.

"Did you get on one knee?" Danny asked.

"Not exactly," I replied.

Monroe started laughing.

"What's so funny?" Danny asked.

"Tell him." Monroe said.

"I don't know if he can handle it."

"I can handle anything," Danny pointed out.

"Okay," I said. "Yesterday, in bed, I went down on Monroe and gave her an earth-shattering orgasm."

"Wow," Danny said, "maybe I can't handle this."

"It gets hotter," Monroe announced.

"After I got her off, I leaned over into my dresser and got out a Tiffany box. She freaked out, crying with excitement, and opened it and told me how much she loved it without even looking at it. Of course, yesterday was April Fool's Day, so instead of an engagement ring, the box had my high school ring in it."

Danny started laughing. "You gave her your class ring in a Tiffany box? That's a dick move."

"Exactly," Monroe agreed. "I told you it wasn't funny."

"Danny did just laugh," I pointed out. "Anyway, once she realized it was a class ring, she got pissed. I told her to relax and that it was just a joke and she told me it wasn't funny. I told her that it was in fact hilarious, and that all of our friends would think it's funny. She told me not to tell a soul, let alone her friends, because they'd think I was a huge asshole."

"That's a distinct possibility," Danny said.

"So, at this point, I'm trying to get her to go down on me, because the real ring, the diamond ring, is in my pussy."

"Jesus," Danny said, pretending to nearly crash into the curb.

I continued, "So the ring is down there, but she's so pissed at me, she won't go down there, so the joke is lasting way longer than I meant for it to last."

"You put a Tiffany ring in your pussy?" Danny asked incredulously.

"Not really in it," I responded. "More on top, resting on the clit. Actually, it was barely resting there and the weight of it made it keep sliding. So I kept putting it back on my clit. Monroe thought I was getting myself off while she was pouting about my prank, so she got even more pissed."

Danny started cracking up.

"So, she tells me to knock it off. But I couldn't, because the ring kept slipping out and I wanted it there to surprise her when she finally went down on me. However, she wasn't getting over it really well. I kept having to put it back and she kept telling me she was upset and to just wait a minute and stop touching myself. At this point, Monroe's practically crying and I'm absolutely giggling, which is pissing her off even more."

Monroe moved up from behind our draft to finish the story. "So, I pulled back the covers, and see this jewelry and I immediately think it's a clit ring, so I scream 'What the fuck.' Fortunately, Jenna took the ring out at that point and gave it to me."

"That is the most fucked up and romantic engagement story I've ever heard," Danny said admiringly.

"You haven't heard the good part yet," Monroe pointed out.

"There's more?" Danny asked.

"A little bit," I said. "Monroe didn't like the ring I picked out, so she exchanged it. The pussy ring is back at Tiffany."

Bella Books, Inc.

Women. Books. Even Better Together.

P.O. Box 10543

Tallahassee, FL 32302

Phone: 800-729-4992

www.bellabooks.com